THE DRAMA TEACHER

THE DRAMA TEACHER

A Novel

KOREN ZAILCKAS

CROWN
NEW YORK

This is a work of fiction. Names, characters, places, and incidents either are the product of the author's imagination or are used fictitiously. Any resemblance to actual persons, living or dead, events, or locales is entirely coincidental.

Published in the United States by Crown, an imprint of the Crown Publishing Group, a division of Penguin Random House LLC, New York.
crownpublishing.com

CROWN and the Crown colophon are registered trademarks of Penguin Random House LLC.

Library of Congress Cataloging-in-Publication data is available upon request.

ISBN 978-0-553-44809-2
Ebook ISBN 978-0-553-44810-8

PRINTED IN THE UNITED STATES OF AMERICA

Jacket design by Alex Merto
Jacket photographs: Innis McAllister/Millennium Images, UK

10 9 8 7 6 5 4 3 2 1

First Edition

For teachers, who are a kind of home,

and the following, who have been mine: Donald Darr, David Gates, William Glavin, Carl Haarmann, Mary Karr, Donna Lanza, Judith Mandelbaum-Schmidt, Charlie Miller, and Amber Smith

It's good to possess a sense of truth but you
also need to have a sense of lies.

—Konstantin Stanislavski, *An Actor's Work*

GRACIE MUELLER

I guess you are kind of curious as to who
I am, but I am one of those who do not have
a regular name. My name depends on you.

—Richard Brautigan, *In Watermelon Sugar*

CHAPTER ONE

The desk clerk walked behind me with purpose, adjusting the name tag on his lapel.

Poor casting, I thought when I saw his reflection in a mirrored alcove. His expression seemed to be aiming for stern, but his pimpled chin gave him a look of teen angst. If I'd seen him looking as cheesed-off anywhere but there—at The Odell Resort and Spa, described by *Forbes* as "a modern château nestled at the foot of the Catskill Mountains"—I would have guessed he'd failed maths or been friend-zoned by a girl.

"Hi there. *Ma'am?*" He was so square, you could wage a game of chess on him, and I reckoned he had the sort of bohemian parents that were a regional trend. Some failing authority figure had left him with no other course of rebellion. When sex, drugs, and a vegetarian diet are the norm, only steady employment has shock value.

"Looking for something?"

"Mum-*eee.*" Kitty pulled the belt of my white cotton robe. My hair was swept over my left breast, where the hotel's logo should have been.

"Darling, please don't tug."

The robe, a gift from my first husband, Oz, was my last bastion of luxury. A few years earlier, it had been my Christmas present. It was the last thing Oz gave me before he was indicted for fraud.

Fitz, who was five going on thirty, echoed: "*Kitty*. Mum said don't tug."

I had planned that afternoon for Fitz in particular. He'd had his first ever swim in Cannes, surrounded by superyachts, but he'd grown sadly accustomed to the Catskill Community Pool, where the deck chairs are spattered with bird shite.

"You're so very kind," I told the clerk. "We're meeting friends."

In general, I could count on my accent to give me an air of refinement.

Back in my native Britain, people heard *culture clash* when I spoke. The British associated my cut-glass accent with *grasping* or some variant: *putting on airs*. I'd grown up striving for the upper classes' attention to *h*'s and *t*'s, but fell into the dirty habit of elongating my vowels so that I might fit in with my working-class mates.

But in the States, there was only one type of English accent. Upstate New Yorkers assumed I was educated and worldly, cleverer than they were. Shopkeepers praised my pronunciations ("vitamins" or "oregano") as though I were a rare, exotic vocalist. The other mums at Fitz's play-school treated us as though we ate cucumber sandwiches for tea and hoarded money offshore.

But this young man seemed impervious to my BBC English. "I can look up your friend's room number at the front desk."

I pored over my mobile's blank screen, pretending I'd received a new message. "Oh. It appears our friends have been waiting by the pool for thirty minutes. Shall we go meet them, Kit? Fitz?"

Just then, my phone legitimately vibrated. It was my current "husband," Randy, calling from Florida.

I gestured to the clerk: *One minute, sorry.*

"Hiya, Randy, you all right?'

"—cie. Hi. Can you hear—e?" His voice was breaking up. Either a result of the looming mountains or the resort's thick walls.

I slowed the children near an ebony sideboard and watched them shuffle travel brochures at twice the speed it took me to return them to their proper piles.

"I hear you. But it's not a brilliant time. We're late meeting friends."

"Where?" he asked, a question that was shorthand for: *How much will it cost?*

I turned my back to Fitz. "The YMCA," I said softly.

"How's it going with your Social Security number?"

The question always hit me like a punch to the solar plexus.

"Look, Mummy! A choo-choo!" Kitty said. Leaflets for a railway museum rained like war propaganda across the lobby's pristine floor.

"Going well." I laid a hand on Fitz's elbow—stopping him seconds before he wiped his nose on a silk sofa arm.

"So you got it?" Randy asked.

"Getting it."

"I just don't understand why it's taking so long. Or why you didn't request a social when you applied for your visa."

"It was an oversight."

Two years ago, I'd applied for the green card that would have entitled me to a social, but the letter that arrived from the Department of Homeland Security informed me that the documentation I'd submitted was incorrect. Rather than going back to Britain, I'd faked an immigration interview at Twenty-Six Federal Plaza on a day when I knew Randy had a real-estate closing. I took a bus to Manhattan, treated myself to a steak at Mark Joseph, and returned to Catskill, six hours later, with a story that held him over until a forgery-mill website delivered my novelty resident card. I'd waited until the morning after his bachelor party to show it to him, rightfully suspecting he'd be too hungover to notice the smeary blotches under the laminate.

The phony green card wasn't even the biggest lie I had brought into our marriage. On paper, at least, I was still married to Oz, because filing for divorce would have created a paper trail, and police wanted me for my role in his bogus property deals.

Randy, still on the phone, shifted into estate agent mode:

"Gracie, you need your own credit line. Now. That way, if we need to borrow money, no one will know we missed a few mortgage payments."

"A *few*? You said last month was the first time."

He lowered his voice. "Gotta go. A lead just walked in."

I hung up, herded the children through the sliding-glass doors, and slammed headfirst into the day's crippling humidity. It was 2010, the hottest summer on record in New York. The gray sky, unexpectedly bright, seared my eyes. Waves of hot exhaust rippled across the parking lot.

Fitz urged Kitty to hold on to his back and run in tandem. "Come on! Be my jet pack!"

"Careful," I warned, as the game almost always ended in skinned knees.

"We *are* being careful," Fitz said with a look that accused me of needless drama.

The pool gate squealed on its hinges, and a few women rubbernecked at the sound.

I had never put much stock in vanity, but I wondered what those freshly waxed and mud-bathed ladies saw when they looked at me.

Had they met me at Guildhall, my dramatic arts college, they would have seen a loosely defiant young woman with a burst nest of ginger curls and an attitude that said drinking cider on wet lawns was just as educational as reciting Shakespeare. I sang in a twee pop band and rolled immaculate joints. My fashion choices were daring and my mates even more so: hot pants and kimono, with a crusty, bisexual chap from the Royal College on my arm. I wouldn't say strangers instantly noticed when my younger self walked into a room, but I had a certain heady trifecta: ambition, charisma, and a fair bit of luck.

By my early thirties, Fitz was in a fashionable sling across my chest and dreams of acting in the West End were a distant memory. But even then, I'd retained an air of sophisticated rebellion. I wore Peter Pan collars with black leather miniskirts. I peppered my speech with French and obscenities. I could act at ease in fifteen-bedroom country houses and even help Oz woo investors for Turkish condominiums he didn't own.

Then, of course, there was the indictment and the separation, and my mid-thirties found me in America, "married" to Randy, a top-earning Realtor. Too old to play the ingénue, I took on the role of the pampered housewife instead. Randy supported me by flipping houses, leasing out his income properties and closing on two or three real estate deals every week. And I lived a life of relative leisure, organizing menus and playdates, collecting Le Creuset cookware and Jo Malone perfumes, getting pregnant with Kitty. Then, just when I didn't lack for anything, the real estate market collapsed, and life demanded austerity measures.

If anyone noticed me that day at The Odell, it was apt to be in pity, not awe. Having quit the salon, my hair was reaching red-gray. Without a gym membership, my body was slackening at the midriff and hips, widening and collapsing like a carnival tent after the fun's over and the punters have gone home.

I panned the poolside, taking in our chaise options. There were no friends expecting us, of course. I'd planned on letting Fitz down gently, with a little white lie about how something came up: car troubles, stomach illness, someone had drunk a bad juice box or stuck their finger too far up their nose. "Caleb's mum texted."

That said, I had neglected to pack a lunch, so it was well worth making myself friendly.

Near the shallow end, there was a pensioner who looked promisingly lonely. She was sipping cucumber water in an Indian-style *dupatta*, wearing her wealth like the face-lift scars around her ears. I paused in front of her and pretended a deep yawn, which she mirrored with subconscious empathy. But then she glanced at Kit and Fitz with a look of child-hatred, so I carried on down the line of chairs, searching.

We walked by a toddler who was clutching a tennis ball as she trailed her Caribbean nanny. "Do you want to be in the shade?" the woman asked, loudly dragging a chair.

We passed a trophy wife who was describing her lunch to another: "I had the noodle bowl, and it was ah-mazing. Instead of pork, I had them throw in an egg and a whole bunch of veggies."

There, I thought.

On the far side of the kiddie pool, a pair of yummy mummies discussed their children's class assignments for the coming school year while a third woman, on the periphery, pretended not to eavesdrop.

"Who does Izzy have again?" one woman asked. "Ah well. All the third-grade teachers are a win-win. I heard Layla's in that class too. And Willow. Oh, and Ollie Guerra. His parents just bought the Dylan house."

When the onlooker's phone chimed, she quit spying and rifled through her hideous charity tote bag, which was printed with the slogan KINDNESS IS ALWAYS IN FASHION.

I nudged the children closer and sat as near to her as possible without seeming too keen. Leaving an empty sun lounger between us, I watched her divide her attention between her mobile and the supervision of an Asian girl in pink goggles that matched her pineapple-print suit. She was wearing the sort of expensive-looking Panama hat that Manhattanites wore when they came up for the weekend. But I caught a whiff of something gauche and suburban as well: her overbaked tan looked sprayed on, whereas the city mothers kept their skin liberal-pasty.

She was proud, not scolding, when she unknotted a bit of hair from her child's earlobe: "Those earrings are probably not good pool earrings. Because they're Grandma's pearls. Do you know what I mean?"

I set to work, delicately removing Kitty's dress. No sudden movements. Nothing attention-seeking. Just enough motion to make the woman gradually aware of me.

Goggles in hand, Fitz galloped toward the pool.

"Walk, please," I called. Then, to Kitty: "I'd like you to wear this hat so your lovely face doesn't burn."

"I don't *want* a hat!"

In my peripheral vision, my mark pecked away at her phone with a manicured index finger.

I sighed a little louder than necessary. "Last time we were here, you sizzled, Sausage. I felt like the worst mummy of all time."

The woman glanced up, making me wonder which part of what I'd said had captured her interest. A sense of superiority, maybe. Women are moths to the flame of others' failures.

"Your mommy's right," she told Kitty. "Last year, at Long Beach Island, I sent my Gabby to the beach in pigtails and forgot to sunscreen the part. Her scalp blistered. She looked like she'd had hair-transplant surgery."

"Is it all right to shift over?" I asked, already moving my bag to the empty chaise between us.

"Sure," she said in a falsetto I liked. It had a girlish lack of authority.

"Cheers. The glare is blinding."

Up close, I studied her designer swimming costume. It had a plunging neckline and complicated cutouts on either side of her pencil-line waist. She was reed-thin, with arms that weighed more in fuzz than actual meat. I wondered if she was body dysmorphia-ed—a dinghy who thought herself a barge.

I took off my dress without making my usual efforts to hold in my stomach. Mine weren't abdominals, they were abominables.

"Summer always makes me nostalgic for the twenties," I said.

"You couldn't pay me to be twenty again." She began to frown, then glossed it over with the poor impression of a smile.

"I meant the 1920s. I would have worn those required leg coverings quite happily."

She began to protest—"Oh please"—but lost conviction.

I slapped an invisible mosquito. "So many mozzies." Accent as understated as a football chant.

She smiled and named a brand of natural repellent made from clove and catnip.

"Back in Britain, natural insecticides include a gin and tonic before dinner."

"Right. You're English." A look of micro-rage flickered over her face. "I should have picked up on your accent. Haa-aah. I must be dazed from my massage."

Her daughter scurried over, dripping water and pleading: "*Now* can we have ice cream?"

"We'll order lunch first. OK?" She shrugged as if discounting herself.

Privately, I wondered whether it was more difficult to say no to an adopted child. Her girl was Chinese. She looked Jewish or Italian.

"How did you manage a massage with that adorable little one?" I asked.

"It's a weekly tradition. I come up from Woodstock with my girlfriend Abigail—"

"Oh, you know Abigail Brown?"

"No, Abigail Wheeler. Do you know her?"

I shook my head. I didn't know a soul in Woodstock. I just wanted to suggest we traveled in the same circles.

"Abigail and I buy season passes every year. She watches the girls by the pool while I have a massage or a facial. Then I return the favor and watch her little girl, Chloe. It keeps us sane."

"She's at the spa now?"

"She was earlier. She had to leave early today."

"What a brilliant system. I think the last massage I had was prenatal." I gestured toward the kiddie pool, where Fitz was half-submerged and Kitty, holding the metal railing, was making kicking splashes. "She's mine. Kitty. She's two. And Fitz, over there, is five."

"Those are names you don't hear often."

"Kitty's short for Katherine."

"Kitty. That's cute." She made an awkward purring sound, then reached for her dinging phone.

"I'm Gracie. Mueller. By the way."

But I had electronic competition. She was preoccupied with something: an app, or a text or a gif of a cat playing snooker.

"Tracey Bueller? Nice to meet you." After one last scrolling motion, she reached out and shook my fingertips. A platinum timepiece hung heavily on her bony wrist. Her knuckles looked almost as unwieldy as her enormous diamond ring.

I felt my lips part. A second passed. Then two. And instead of clearly repeating myself (*Gracie*) or making a joke about how screaming children cause hearing loss, I nodded and smiled. It was more sensible to use a fake name, given what we were up to.

"Melanie," she said, still fixated on her phone. And with those three syllables, the misunderstanding was fixed. The noon sun emerged from its cloud, and the moment for correction was gone.

CHAPTER TWO

For twenty minutes, I listened to the incessant dinging of Melanie's phone, each new message delivering her a fresh hit of dopamine. Finally, I said, "This sun is brutal. Do you fancy a drink?"

I didn't actually have the cash to follow through, but I remembered the way my father claimed psychological ownership of every hotel, restaurant, and party we ever crashed. Placing himself in the dead-center of the room, he'd introduce people and dispense food to "his" guests. At his most audacious, he thanked people for coming.

"You're going to the café?" she asked.

I nodded.

"We'll come with. I'd love a lemonade. Or better still, a cocktail. Gabby?!" She called out. "Gabby, are you ready for lunch?!"

Her daughter arrived, faintly chattering in the shade of a passing cloud. "Yeah. I'm hungry. Can I have a *penny-knee*?" she asked.

"What about a rice bowl? Or that apple and celeriac salad? Would you be OK with that instead?" Saying *no*, even hinting at it, seemed to make my new friend anxious.

"I want a penny-knee!"

"A panini. What the hay." Melanie reached into her purse and emerged with a Ferragamo wallet the size of a Ken Follett novel. I noticed its varied credit cards in shades of gold and black. "Spinach and feta?"

"*Just* cheese," the child said. "*Regular* cheese."

"We've been working on healthy food choices," my friend confided in a stage whisper, as though the little girl wasn't watching us with dark, velvety eyes.

"That sounds like a lovely lunch," I said, letting my voice carry slightly on the last word. Moments later, Kitty, who had an appetite like a mud dredge, was pulling the skirt of my swimsuit, demanding food as well.

I hoisted her to my hip and sniffed. "Oh dear," I said, peering down the back of the swimming costume she called her "babysuit." "Good luck this didn't happen in the pool."

"She's had an accident?" Melanie whispered, mortified on Kitty's behalf. "Can I do something to help?"

"Oh no. We'll only be a minute. You go on without us."

"Do you want me to order for you? The kitchen can be kind of slow."

"I don't want you to trouble yourself."

"It's no trouble. Do your kids like paninis?"

I nodded. Kitty, who thought the word "sandwich" was synonymous with Skippy peanut butter, gave me a sideways look, worried about what I'd agreed to.

"And what about you?"

"You're so kind. I'd love the noodle bowl. But instead of pork, I typically have them throw in an egg and a load of veggies."

I was holding Fitz's hand and shielding Kitty's clean backside with my robe when a hotel employee with long, al dente, blond hair cut us off at the pass.

"Oh, look at you!" she said to Kitty, in the manner of people who have no talent for speaking to children. "Are you having fun swimming?"

Kitty stared blankly.

I tried to maneuver past, but the woman stepped as well, nearly knocking me into a potted fern.

"Excuse us. We just need to tend to a little accident."

"Sure. I just need to stamp your guest passes."

"Marvelous. We'll only need a minute to get situated." Reiterating: "My daughter needs the toilet."

"It's just that my manager said—"

"Sorry, may I ask your name?" Big smile like I'd reached the end of my tether.

"Amanda."

"Amanda, I'm Tracey Bueller."

Fitz raised his eyebrows, but I gave him a warning look: *Don't interrupt.*

"Tracey?" she confirmed, reaching for the walkie-talkie on her hip.

"That's right. Tracey Bueller. We're guests of Abigail Wheeler. She had to leave early today. One of her children was suffering from swimmer's ear."

Melanie wasn't at the pool when we returned. And Kitty had the thousand-yard stare of someone who desperately needed a nap. So I sank back into our lounger, cuddled her against my chest, and inhaled the greasy, SPF smell of her.

Fitz chest-flopped off the pool stairs in his water wings. His face, usually so watchful, was transformed into a look of pure abandon. He dove down to fetch a submarine a smaller child had dropped to the bottom, then emerged with seal-slick hair, his eyes bloodshot with chlorine.

Inhaling, I filled my diaphragm. The mountain breeze was so much crisper than the air in the Catskill house, which had the odor of a well-matured Stilton. We'd owned it three years, and it got moldier every summer.

Melanie's afternoon reading material was stacked on the table between our chairs. There was a damp copy of the latest divorcée-makes-good memoir. Beneath it: *The Celestine Prophecy*, indicating spiritual aspirations. I also found a women's glossy advertising "60 SEX TIPS" (Melanie must be eager to please), and *Martha Stewart Living* (she had a strong sense of domestic superiority).

The subscription labels read: MELANIE ASHWORTH.

I removed my phone from Kitty's sleeping grasp and entered Melanie's name into a search bar.

Lucky for me, Mel was an Internet oversharer. The privacy settings on her social media accounts were turned to "exhibitionist," so everyone and their grandmother could admire the escarole salad she'd had for dinner and read about how her husband always put her daughter's clothes on backward, "LOL." I found a photo of her modeling a diamond bracelet, whilst her husband kissed her collarbone. The caption was even more revolting than the necking: "Christmas present from Victor, who managed to profit in the worst economic crisis in seventy years! #blessed #thankyou #blingedout."

I typed "Victor Ashworth" into a search bar and found her #hubby's résumé. He worked for a New Jersey company called AKA Financial Guaranty Corporation, which focused on something called "municipal-bond insurance." Before that, he'd worked at AKA Management LLC. Before that, AKA Capital Holdings.

When Melanie returned, her walk was half-shuffle in her gold glitter moccasins.

"That took foreeeever," she said loudly, within earshot of the hotel employee who was carrying our tray of food. "Oh no, you've been waiting so long she conked out."

We both looked down at Kitty. Her thumb was half in her mouth.

"So sweet," Melanie cooed. She brought a hand to her heart. The gesture was well timed, but not entirely sincere.

I hoisted my bag onto the chaise and rifled inside for my wallet. "What did it come to?"

Those dark eyes went blank with bewilderment. I could feel her weighing the real price of the transaction, wondering whether the exchange of bills would compromise the growing friendliness between us.

We endured a minute of polite debate—each of us "insisting" and clutching our thoraxes in ways that implied earnestness—but Melanie stood firm. She handed me a margarita, dripping condensation, and said joining her in an afternoon drink was reimbursement enough.

I put my wallet away and doubled my bluff. "Well then, you must let me treat Gabriella to that ice cream later."

The cloud that had positioned itself over the sun was dragging others into its orbit. The sky matched the concrete surrounding the pool.

"Are you enjoying that?" I asked, pointing to her dejected copy of *The Celestine Prophecy*.

Melanie flicked her hair, self-conscious. "I just started it. It's hard to find time to read with kids."

I said something supportive about how I hadn't read anything longer than *Good Night, Gorilla* in years. Meanwhile, I averted my eyes from the phone by her side, which was undoubtedly the most time-consuming charge in her care.

I considered telling her to stick with it. Maybe plagiarizing one of the online reviews I'd read while she was gone. But I wasn't certain I could carry off those new age platitudes. *Know your weaknesses*, my uni teachers always said.

She held up both hands, mock defensive. "I know what you're going to say. It's *life-changing.* I *know.* I'm *reading* it. When I can . . . When there's time."

"Good heavens. What makes you think I'd say that?"

Melanie rubbed an invisible spot of suncream on her arm. "It's one of those books everyone up here always asks if you've read."

"Typical," I said. "Like *The Clan of the Cave Bear.* Or *Zen and the Art of Motorcycle Maintenance.*"

Melanie paused, then gave me a look: *You get it.*

"So, you're from Woodstock too?" she asked.

"Catskill. So how does it strike you, really—the regional reading list?"

Melanie shifted in her seat, looking like someone who'd sooner die than give the "wrong" opinion. "I just don't like the way all these books are like . . ."

I could feel her waffling.

"A secret handshake?" I ventured.

"Or like a test you have to pass. Unless you get the references, no one's going to get to know *you*."

"One thinks *Woodstock*, like people must be very inclusive—"

"Yes!" she said. "Sooo Kumbaya."

"Very 'feel the vibe, roll a spliff.' "

"Haa-aah. But no. It's not like New Jersey. When Victor and I moved to Summit, the whole neighborhood came to introduce themselves. We had more houseplants and cookies than we knew what to do with. It's so different here. I don't know even one of my neighbors now."

"I assume they're too busy cleansing their colons and staring into each other's third eyes. Have you lived there long?"

"We moved up, full-time, a little over a year ago? Victor's company was restructuring. I had no idea Woodstock would be like those '80s teen movies about teenagers."

"John Hughes films?"

"Yes! When you're a kid, you think all those labels go away."

I could guess her meaning, but I still asked: "Labels?"

"Just those ways we categorize people . . . 'Cool.' 'Uncool.' " She was utterly disarmed. "But being a parent brings it all up again."

"So who has star quality in Woodstock?"

"Oh, you know . . . fashion photographers. Filmmakers. A few first wives of famous musicians. Their kids go to Gabriella's country day. Not that they're interested in knowing her name or mine."

I gave her an *all-in-due-course* smile.

"We have provincial attitudes in Catskill too. It's a shame. I just don't understand women who distrust new people, reject new ideas."

A grain of drink salt clung to her lip gloss. "Curiosity," she said. "That's what keeps us young."

"I agree. When I was a girl, my father used to tell me, 'Tracey, you don't have to go anywhere to travel. Every person is a sort of journey. Treat everyone you meet like your next adventure.' "

"I think so too. There's a part in *The Celestine Prophesy* I like—"

I raised my eyebrows.

"The *only* part I like. About how we don't meet people by coincidence. Anyone who crosses our path is part of our destiny. Like today! I only wish you were here last week. Abigail brought the most amazing giant unicorn raft. This California company makes them. Obscenely expensive. But you've never seen anything cuter."

"Yes, our children get on like a house on fire." I added that we ought to get together for a playdate, even though I knew we'd be gone the instant Fitz, my good-effort boy, finished the sandwich that was Melanie's treat.

I stole a long look at him. His eyes were half-closed. A thread of warm mozzarella bent and fell across his chin. I was pleased I'd filled him up with something of value. That day, at least, I'd given him more than the beans-on-toast childhood that left me famished.

CHAPTER THREE

After a full day of swimming, the children were too knackered for a bath. They arrived at dreamland smelling of chlorine and aloe.

I was shattered as well. But instead of my everyday malaise, I had the satisfying exhaustion that follows action. I was proud of myself. The children and I had gone somewhere. We'd rubbed shoulders with people who didn't pierce their infants' ears or shop in bulk. The free lunch was a reminder that I could still find solutions in the face of problems. As were the room numbers on my phone.

I stayed up a bit later and worked on the website I had promised a local taxidermist, but then dehydration hit me like an opiate. I dragged myself to bed and slept for a full eight hours. No nightmares woke me. Miraculously, no children did either.

At five the next morning, I woke to the alarm. Then I scrolled back through my phone's photo reel and dialed.

"Thank you for calling The Odell Resort," a posh recorded message said. "Please press 1 for lodging or dining reservations . . ."

When I reached someone approximating a real human, I asked to speak with the guests in Room 210. I wished I'd had a name to offer. But then, I suspected I was dealing with the night clerk, the kind of deliriously lonely young man who hadn't seen a soul since one a.m. He was apt to be wired on multiple pots of coffee and grateful for even our minor interaction.

"One moment," he said, connecting me.

"Hello? What *time* is it?" The man in 210 sounded rightfully groggy.

"Hi," I said, adopting a Yankee accent. "This is Amanda at the front desk. I'm sooo sorry to disrupt your sleep. It's just a matter of some urgency—"

"*What?*" He had an edge of hysteria, like he expected me to say a tree had fallen on his Zipcar.

"We're having a hard time with the credit card you gave at check-in."

"My Chase Visa?" He sounded slightly self-conscious. Perhaps he was expecting to be charged for a certain sort of in-room movie?

"Yes, sir. Your Chase Visa. The clerk who checked you in neglected to enter a digit."

"You need me to come down to the front desk?"

"Oh no, it's so early. I've disturbed your sleep already and, like I said, it was our mistake. If you read the numbers back to me, I can check you in again by phone."

There was a pause, and I feared he'd worked it out. But in the end, he was only fumbling for his wallet. After he recited the full number, expiration date, three-digit security code, and cardholder name—Michael P. Rondo—I thanked him profusely and apologized again.

"We'd like to offer you a discount for the inconvenience," I said. "I've deducted a hundred dollars from your bill."

When the children woke up, I switched on their favorite television program—the one with the wonky animation and bad, dad-rock theme tune. It kept them utterly static until the toy adverts, when they wailed, "Mummy! Look! Can I have that!" and I had to make another heartbreaking speech about saving our money. I felt guilty depriving them. I didn't want to raise children who were entitled and rude, spoilt beyond reason, but at the same time, I didn't want luxury to be something they only read about in newspaper supplements.

"Can I have a Popsicle?" Fitz asked.

I looked up from my phone. "For breakfast?"

"It's hot."

"All right," I said, digging through the freezer. "Here. Bring one to your sister as well."

After he'd trotted off with two sticks of Blue Dye No. 2, I fiddled with the options on my new voice-changing app. (*Effect*: Human Man; *Calling From*: Office.) Then, I dialed.

A voice answered: "Good morning. Odell Resort and Spa."

"Good morning," I said, but the reverb was all wrong.

"Hello?" the desk clerk asked while I tweaked the settings. "Are you still there?"

I used my best American accent to say: "I'm trying to reach Michael Rondo."

"Just a moment."

On the other end of the line, I recognized the voice.

"Hello?"

"Hello, Mr. Rondo. I'm phoning from Chase Visa."

"What now?" He was tetchier than he'd been an hour earlier, but he still didn't question why I'd phoned the hotel instead of his mobile.

"I'm sorry to report there's been some unusual activity on your card. Have you recently made some large Internet purchases?"

"Earlier this month—"

"Any expensive purchases in the last few hours?"

"No. No, I *didn't* . . ." I pictured him rubbing his face in agitation—his eyes puffy from a night of minibar bottles. "I gave my credit card number to someone last night. Someone from the hotel."

"Uh-oh. These schemes are on the rise. So, Mr. Rondo, I've

cancelled those transactions and refunded you. I'll also need to cancel your card, and send you a replacement immediately."

"Thank you. I'm such an idiot. I wasn't thinking."

"It happens more often than you'd think. And it's easily rectified. Now, just to be certain this *is* Michael Rondo, could you please verify your Social Security number? Great. I'll just place you on a brief hold."

That Saturday, Randy flew back to Catskill for my so-called thirty-second birthday. The date was fictional, as was my age. But I'd been bound to it ever since an early date, when Randy watched me hand my fake passport to a waiter and whooped, "Gracie! We need Champagne! Come on! You're only as old as you feel!"

So every year, I went through the motions of blowing out two fewer candles. Truly, I wasn't that bothered. If it were a crime for women to lie about their age, half of Hollywood would be behind bars.

Fitz drew me a stick-figure birthday card. Kitty plucked a bouquet of wild chamomile. And once Randy pulled his head out of the Florida real-estate listings, he chased the children around the balding grass whilst I watched them from a low-slung lawn chair.

"Gracie!" Randy called out. "Have you heard this? Kitty, sing the ABCs."

Our daughter gave a baby-toothed smile and sang the alphabet, ad-libbing at the middle point: "*H-I-J-K-Om-nom-nom-nom-P*."

"Randy?" Fitz asked, tugging on the pocket of his stepfather's chinos.

"Yeah, buddy?"

"Your name's Randy, right? And Mum's Gracie?"

Time went momentarily out of joint. I hadn't told Randy about Melanie. I'd never even mentioned The Odell. The children were so young—so impulsive and short-attention-spanned—that they usually only talked about animated squids or things that had happened in the past fifteen minutes. They never said, "Remember when . . ." They were too busy pleading for biscuits.

Randy put a hand on Fitz's shoulder. "That's right. Your mom's real name is Grace."

I nodded encouragingly.

Fitz opened his mouth again, but Randy scooped him up by the waist, flipped him upside down, and did the gladiator scream they both enjoyed.

"I'm pleased you're home!" I shouted over the ruckus. "I just read a study about the benefits of rough play! It's so much better for boys than telly or PlayStation!"

Kit and Fitz were asleep by seven, then Randy grilled steaks. We ate alone on the patio, chatting about the children to fill the silence between the nail-on-skin sound of us scratching our mosquito bites.

"Wanna open your presents?" Randy asked.

"Oh, you didn't! We're meant to be saving money."

"It's nothing big."

I accepted the package with bashful excitement. Randy had always been a sublime gift giver. But when I tore back the paper, I found a battery-operated hard skin remover for my feet. Worse, it still bore its price tag from an airport gift shop.

"Thank you?" I was still turning the gift over and over in my hands when Randy began telling me about Florida's Cuban food.

"There's this thing. Mojo and relleñas. Or maybe it's relleñas de mojo? Anyway, I've never tasted anything like it!"

I took another bite of cold steak as the conversation lulled.

"Oh, I almost forgot," I said, reaching into my pocket for Michael Rondo's Social Security number. "Here. The card's not arrived yet. But that's my social."

Randy scratched a clean-shaven cheek. At least Florida had improved his appearance. After the housing collapse, he'd initially put on a fair bit of weight. Now he was using his wifeless, childless time to *jog.* His chin has lost its conjoined twin.

"Thank you, Gracie," he said in a "sincere" tone that sounded oddly formal.

"You're welcome. So what's the latest with your deal in Coconut Grove?"

"Still ironing out the details."

"But it's going through?"

"I think so."

"Oh, thank God. When you first told me we'd missed that last payment—"

He made his standard speech about not wanting to count his closings before they hatched, then excused himself for the toilet, taking his empty glass inside to refill.

While he was gone, I tried not to look too closely at the house, with its sagging roof and gutters. Back when we'd bought it, Randy had been certain we could renovate and double its value, and I'd trusted him. He knew the local market. Only, in 2008, at the exact moment we were interviewing general contractors and having tedious debates about fixtures, the subprime collapse—that perfect storm of stupidity, momentum, and greed—burst the world economy. Our home loan evaporated and we'd had to scrap the kitchen and bathroom remodels.

After the house lost value, no bank would lend to us, which was unfortunate. But worse, banks wouldn't lend to anyone else either, which proved catastrophic for Randy's business. His buyers couldn't get mortgages. His sellers got cold feet and pulled the For Sale signs from their yards.

Randy returned, sweating all along his hairline. "Where were we?" he asked.

"We were talking about the money from these closings. So we can make up the payment we missed last month? And pay this month's mortgage too?"

He rubbed the end of his nose. "I don't know if there'll be enough for all that."

"Well then, this Florida flat you want to rent ought to wait. Keep living in the motel. We oughtn't take on more expenses until we've paid our debts. What about the rental properties? We're all up to date on those mortgage payments, right?"

His knee was jackhammering under the patio table.

"Randy?"

"I borrowed against the rental properties."

"What? When? Jesus, Randy," I said, making a fist of my napkin. "When it comes to our finances, there's no transparency."

"I didn't want to confuse you. Debating every little thing wasn't going to help us make better decisions."

"Neither was keeping it all secret. I should think that's bloody obvious now. So, what are we meant to do? We can't lose this place."

"Why not?" he asked. A question I'd considered too stupid to answer.

"Why not *foreclose* on our children's house?"

His knee was still pumping. There was an intense look in his eyes. "It's called strategic default."

"A disaster by any other name would still be shit creek." I tossed my napkin onto my plate and began to push out my chair before Randy caught me by the arm.

"Think of it as a mortgage modification that brings our payments down to zero. Foreclosure is a long process. People stay in their homes, mortgage-free, for up to a year."

"Out of the question."

"But think of all the money we'll save! Hell, we'll walk away with a nest egg—cash we can put toward a better house in Florida. It's a buyer's market."

"You really think anyone would ever give us a home loan after that? Our credit will be buggered for *years*."

"My credit will. But yours won't." He smoothed his shirt pocket, the one that contained Michael Rondo's social.

"What about values? Teaching our children to honor commitments?"

"We have no moral obligation to keep paying. The lender accepted the risk when they took on the mortgage."

"What a load—"

"Look around, Grace. Companies declare bankruptcy all the time. Kmart. United. There are times when it's just a sound business decision."

"We're not United! No one cares if we fail!"

"So we just won't tell the kids about it."

"Brilliant plan. And if we come home to a padlocked front door? What then? What explanation will you give? Foreclose on the rental properties instead. We need to keep *this* house."

"This place was collateral for those houses."

"Jesus, Randy! You didn't think to ask me before you started using our family home as a bank?"

He flexed his jaw. "Look, you've never wanted to know what actually goes on here. You just want nice things and an allowance. Like a child!"

Later, after we'd stormed off to separate corners, I was doing the washing up when Randy came in and kissed me—a gesture he seemed to think was reconciliation enough. It gave me the opportunity to see a small, white bit hanging from his nose.

"Would you like some echinacea, love?" I said, shoving him off. "You seem to have a semi-permanent cold."

"Come on, Gracie. It's your birthday. Don't be like this."

"Like *what*?"

"We're not alone. Half the mortgages in the country are underwater."

"I *am* alone, actually. Because while I'm here, waiting for the other shoe to drop, you'll be in Florida. If this is really happening, we ought to come with you."

"No. No, it's better if you stay here and pack. Tie up the loose ends."

"And what will you be doing?"

"Uh, earning a living for a start."

" 'A living'? Ha! Is that what you call it?"

"Are you suggesting I'm doing something else down there?"

"It was a reference to your low pay, actually. But now I wonder. Is there something you want to tell me?"

"Ugh! Just admit it, Grace! Admit you keep track of every shitty diaper, so you can guilt-trip me about it! Most women would say, 'Wow, Randy must miss the kids! He must be really lonely!' But you think, 'Randy, that selfish dick!' "

"Mummy?" a voice called from the stairs.

When I turned, Fitz was teary-eyed, clutching an empty water glass.

"You're fighting! *Again!* You promised you wouldn't and you *are*!"

"We're just talking," Randy lied. "I was telling your mother that some things aren't worth fighting for. Sometimes we just have to let go."

CHAPTER FOUR

I didn't get my theatricality from my mother.

Which is not to say she would have lacked the talent for it. My mam could have captivated an audience with her looks alone. She had Hepburn cheekbones, a creamy complexion, and Irish eyes that seemed to get bluer the longer you looked at them. Believe me, if I'd inherited her looks, I wouldn't have bothered learning to seduce people with language.

But like most great beauties, Mam wanted to be valued for other things. As a girl, she'd despaired that no one thought she was clever. As a woman, she hated the way other mothers harped on her bone structure; she wanted to be known for her good Protestant values.

Could she have a laugh? She must have done at the start or else she wouldn't have married a gas ticket like my dad. But by the time I was school-aged, she seemed overwhelmed by my father's impish charm. She stopped obliging when he pulled the bobbin out of her sewing machine and leaned in to kiss her. She rolled her eyes when he did his Charlie Chaplin impression, swinging her rolling pin and walking around with his enormous builder's boots on the wrong feet.

Perhaps Dad faked childlike qualities—sincerity, spontaneity, et cetera—to pull her and after she birthed a genuine child, she finally recognized the con. Or maybe she simply lacked the energy to teach us both good behavior. She only dared use the wooden spoon on me.

"Why must you both lay like maggots in bed?" she'd ask. Or: "Which one of you turned on the heating?"

See, Mam was also economical, and her make-do ethos stayed with me. To this day, I would rather break a dish than an egg. I save butter papers and hoard recycled string. I drink my tea weak and black because my parents' sugar rows made such a poor impression on me. Sweets, in general, seem like a bad omen.

Their arguments over sugar happened every Saturday. It was a part of the weekly landscape—something I could count on every bit as much as Sunday-night *Glenroe* or putting on a clean school uniform Monday morning. And it always began with the sugar my mother used in sparing amounts—the same sugar that my father stirred into his tea in quantities that made his spoon stand up straight.

After so many years, I still know the sugar rows word for word. I can recite them with the same by-heart accuracy as the songs we would belt on long car journeys: "*One day at a time, sweet Jesus . . .*" and "*We're all off to Dublin in the green, green . . .*"

"Have you used *three* sugars?" my mam would ask.

Dad: "I want my tea to be as sweet as you."

"It's not tea the way you take it. It's custard sauce."

But Dad was no audience for Mam's mottoes: *Be thrifty so you may not be grasping*, or *Enough and no waste is as good as a feast.*

He thought he was owed extravagance, having given up a creative life for the labor jobs that didn't pay much more. He'd been a poet when he and Mam fell in love. He'd attended Yeats Summer School in Sligo, where his professors had compared him to Paul Durcan. And now, thanks to her, he bore tunnels with men who could scarcely write their own names. He liked to say that without his mates and his costly, well-deserved treats, he'd be outside with the donkeys, braying with boredom.

"We'd cope with less money. If we did away with waste. Simple things make a difference." Then, she'd turn to me: "That goes for you as well. Eat up every bit of that now. If you were out in the Third World, you'd be glad of it."

At this point, Dad would thrust a fair whack of money into my palm while Mam blanched and gave me a cautious look.

"We've yet to pay the water services bill—"

But Dad would press on: "Pop out and buy yourself a new comic, my treasure. Hell, go buy yourself a Princess Di dress."

It was a relief to be halfway down the road, nudging sheep out of my path and giving a weary wave to Frank Cleary, the neighbor boy, who was usually kicking a ball against the stone wall.

The very last sugar row occurred after Cleary and I kissed on a schoolyard dare. He was avoiding my gaze either because he worried I would attempt it again or because he shyly feared I wouldn't.

"Goin' to town?" He leveled his foot at the ball, and I watched his torso twist, sending diagonal ripples down his GAA jersey.

"I am."

The ball punched the wall.

"They're on about money again?"

I nodded.

"Which one's to blame?" Cleary was an only child as well, and he shared my judicial attitude. We were both oddities in our village, where the stork visited most families four or five times.

I shrugged, feeling divided. Without Dad, there'd be no fun. Without Mam, no consistency.

"You can borrow this," Cleary said, taking a Walkman from his trouser pocket. "Parents rowing, that's what the volume knob is for."

"I'm gonna head on," I said, thanking him as I unraveled the cord.

"Good luck."

I fit the headphones over my ears, depressed the Play button, and carried on down the street, listening to Joan Armatrading's "Me Myself I." Despite the throaty lyrics and throbbing drums, I could still imagine my dad's voice, saying: "You're the one moaning about how we live on the clippings of a tin!"

But I could also feel my mam's righteous anger: "I'm not asking for a man of means, just a man of character! We've got to live in this village! Forgetting a debt doesn't mean it's paid! You owe people! What's going to happen when they arrive to collect?"

"I'm going to clear off," my father told me.

It was June 7, 1986, two weeks before the Fine Gael–Labour Party coalition attempted to lift the Irish ban on divorce, and we were at an amusement park full of ice cream cones and bumper cars. There were snaking queues. There was kiddie gambling for tokens and good-as-useless prizes.

My head was still blipping with arcade noises. My stomach hadn't found its natural landing place after the drop ride.

"I'm leaving," he repeated. "If you don't come, you'll never see me again."

He must have seen, on my face, the word I couldn't phlegm up: *Why?*

"Oh, come on. You must know why. You're a clever girl. Surely you've seen something in the papers."

The question mark didn't move from my eyes. My father always talked to me like a friend—like we were on the same level—but it led to certain errors of thinking. Like the assumption that a ten-year-old read the news.

"There's a divorce referendum being put to a vote. When it passes, your mam's gonna start the proceedings. No reasonable prospect of reconciliation . . ."

Mam. She was home, ironing Dad's shirts to within an inch of their life.

He went on, but my ears were stoppered. I was remembering the sugar rows, thinking, *Holy Jesus and all his little angels. Is this really about the fecking sugar?*

"But she couldn't. No matter—You're my dad—"

"She's made it clear she'll do whatever she bleeding well pleases."

All at once, I was too queasy to finish my sundae, hating my mother so much I couldn't stand it. I hated her rigidity and her thrift. I was fed up with her cheap substitutions and "instead of" recipes: margarine instead of butter, lamb belly instead of beef, Mam instead of Dad. How dare she cut my father out of my life?

Once my father had his answer, he aimed his beige Toyota north and drove directly to Belfast. In memory, we drove half the day, across vast green expanses that made me feel transcendently ill. I stared at the cloud shadows. I counted rainbows.

Later in life, it came as quite a shock to discover the journey couldn't have taken more than an hour. I spent the duration marveling over the way we were at the funfair one minute—my dress still bore a spot of chocolate sauce from my ice cream—and the next, I was studying the dog-eared map. I held the wheel every time Dad lit a Carroll's Number One. I nodded supportively when he lost his temper at another driver, grumbling, "Are you fecking driving it or parking it?"

I smiled and he apologized for cursing.

"It's all right," I said.

"It is, isn't it? You're not some brainless parrot. You ought to learn the full reaches of language. Swearing releases frustration. And joy."

By the time we boarded the Belfast ferry, which was destined to pass through porous, mid-'80s borders to Britain's Isle of Man, I still hadn't entirely lost that giddy funfair feeling. Metaphorically speaking, the metal bar had thudded across my lap and the ride had jerked into gear. I could either throw my hands skyward or vomit. Either way, the time to get off had passed.

It had all seemed wildly spontaneous. I didn't suspect otherwise until my father had our passports on hand to give the immigration officer, who failed to stamp them and handed them back with a dodgy wink and smile.

Night had fallen by the time we arrived on the Isle, where my father parked up on one side of a grassy track and led me, on foot, down a steep path to the fishing rocks. Shaded by a grove of trees, up to its shutters with overgrown bracken, stood a cottage. There was a beam of light in the distance, where a figure raised a torch.

"That'd be the landlady," my father said.

Looking down, I noticed he was holding two overnight bags. The trip hadn't been as spur-of-the-moment as I'd hoped. Dad had planned for it. He'd *packed.* And yet, intrinsically, I knew not to play my role scared.

I went inside the cottage and took the initiative to look for pajamas while Dad was next door at the landlady's house, discussing the terms of our rental. But when I opened the backpack, I found just a few jumpers I'd long outgrown. Dad had confused my things with the castoffs my mother had set aside for the charity shop.

So I'd lain awake in my fudge-stained dress, staring out the window at the black silk of the foreign landscape. I wanted a night-light. I missed the evening baas of our anxious sheep. I reached into my coat pocket for Cleary's Walkman and pressed Play on his mixtape. Julian Lennon filled my ears. "Too Late for Goodbyes."

Time has gone since I've been with you / We've been starting to lie.

I quickly fast-forwarded ahead to Talking Heads' "And She Was."

She was glad about it . . . No doubt about it.

Even through the walls of the house, I could feel the jagged wind the strange countryside breathing. The world was moving and I was floating above it. I had joined the world of missing persons, and there was no time to think about all the ways we were unequipped for a life in Man, without Mam.

When I think back to those early weeks on the Isle, it's the thrill, not the deprivation, that stands out. Because he no longer had to answer to my mother's accounting, Dad spoiled me. In a Douglas department store, he bought me the stirruped trousers that Mam dismissed as a passing fad, and agreed to let me pierce my ears or, as he joked, "put holes in your appendages." He set no limits on how many hours a day I could watch telly (lucky, because the one in our Quine's Hill cottage took twenty minutes to "warm up"). And at the newsagent, he regularly brought me "nobs," surprise envelopes with contents I came to know well—inside each was the same sorry assortments of tin rings, fizzy sweets, and miniature wooden goblets, which were rendered useless by my lack of dolls.

But the cash we left Ireland with must have quickly run out, because within weeks Dad was spending long days looking for work, leaving me behind.

I stared at the plasterwork.

I thought of Cleary, and scratched my infected earlobes.

I had promised my father to stay inside. The Isle wasn't like Ireland, he said. It had more ransom artists and child touchers. I oughtn't open the door, not even for the postman.

Once, I'd given him lip about it: "Dad, I *know.* If a stranger tries to take me somewhere, I'm meant to scream at the top of my voice and find a policeman."

"For God's sake, who told you that?"

"Mam."

But my mother was still a sore subject.

"Don't do that," Dad said. "If a stranger talks to you, come tell me."

But then, Dad's overprotectiveness wasn't entirely to blame for my isolation. As a tourist, I didn't know where other children hung out anyway. The bus ran occasionally, but the cryptic schedule seemed to change the exact moment I sorted it out.

In the end, I spent most afternoons alone on the couch, watching television or listening to music, so I didn't have to hear my stomach growling through my posh new clothes.

Alone, I began to fantasize in spectacular detail about my mother's corned beef and bacon sandwiches. Then my mind wandered to her Ulster Fry—runny scrambled eggs atop soda farl. And oddly, I kept thinking about her skirts and kidneys, which was a meal I had never particularly liked and thought of with a sort of belly-clenched anxiety.

Very next thing, I was in a homesick lather, thinking not only about food but also Mam's ritualized morning routine: sticking on the kettle, asking me how many sausages I wanted, and turning on the "big light" of the ceiling fan. I would turn a darkened corner and half expect to see her standing there, saying, *Go play with Cleary, I'm mopping the floor.* Or, *Will you have your ice cream in a bowl or a wafer?* Or, *That cup is too near the edge there.*

I even missed her telling me off. Once the Isle lost its novelty, I was uneasy about the way Dad didn't give a toss when I tracked dirt across the floor or skipped out into the frozen damp without a coat. Just once, it would have been reassuring to have him tell me, as my mother used to: *You'll get a chill in your kidneys dressed like that.* Or ask: *How long's that telly been on?* Or pull me in for a cuddle that was as affectionate as it was scolding: *You're terrible bold. You'll be the death of me.*

But anytime I reached the height of mammy-wanting, Dad would come home and talk to me in that delightfully adult way, which made me think I must be mad to miss Mam's patronizing sermons about the Third World.

"Have you ever noticed that ninety percent of people in public are slagging off somebody they work with?" he'd ask.

"I have," I'd lie.

"I'll bet. Everyone out there's complaining, 'I can't believe she's been promoted' or 'So-and-So in the department has been off with me from the start.' No wonder the economy's fucked. Nobody's doing any work! Everyone's in a dispute with a bleeding colleague!"

I'd tut sympathetically, knowing this was his admission that he'd gone to the pub when he failed to find work. Then I'd compliment him on his "interview outfit": a dress shirt with the sleeves rolled to the elbow, like a politician in a crisis.

"Thank you," Dad would say, turning tender and serious. "But remember, it's not clothes that make the man, it's close attention. You need to watch for openings and have a bit of energy." He reached for an empty packet of crisps on the kitchen counter. "Let's say I'm interviewing someone for the position of Head Crisp Eater."

"They've been eaten," I said ruefully, which was *my* admission that I'd licked the foil package whilst he was away.

Dad's eyes were twinkling. "Never mind that. Go on, convince me that you're the person for the job."

"Well—"

"Go on! I've seen a lot of candidates. You need to smash up the idea that you're more of the same."

"I've loads of experience eating crisps."

"No, no. Stating your case—that's the hard sell. You want a soft approach. You want to treat everyone you meet as though they're a separate country with its own culture. You can't apply the same technique to everyone."

When Dad still failed to find work, we moved in with Margaid the landlady and her tailless cats to save on rent.

In all the weeks we'd been gone, I'd never cried for my mother, but I wept like a sieve at my father's announcement: "Margaid and I have been what you'd call 'an item' for a while, and it's time, as Philip Larkin would say, to move our romance into real, untidy air." For days, my eyes were puffy and the contents of my nose dripped free.

Even as a child, I knew it was a cost-cutting measure, as opposed to true romance. My father didn't really love Margaid. She was a wrinkled widow who smelled of wet wool and kippers. Her late husband had been an accountant—he'd made a living catering to the Isle's many tax dodgers—and Margaid had passed the years since his death drinking gin and making needlepoints of Manx proverbs. The most terrifying one hung in the spare bedroom where I slept. It read: *Nee yn irrynys ta cummal ayndiu, soilshean magh ayns nyn mea*, which meant "The truth that dwells within you will shine out in your life."

Even so, I couldn't help worrying that Dad's cheating would complicate our return to Ireland. What if my mother couldn't forgive him knobbing another woman? Before Margaid, I'd been hoping, with childish logic, that absence would make my parents' hearts grow fonder. I'd been picturing the three of us reunited by Christmas. I'd been fantasizing about the holiday in lavish detail, straight down to Christmas sauce with Bird's Dream Topping, but Margaid stole the blessed baby from *that* manger.

I was no longer your average ten-year-old once we'd moved in with Marge.

Part of it was my drastic change in appearance. My father asked Margaid to trim my hair. Watching my curls hit the kitchen linoleum, I suspected the cut was really quite drastic. But when she raised a hand mirror for me to see, I found myself face-to-face with faintly afroed Joan of Arc. It almost seemed like a good thing that we weren't going back to Ireland straightaway. There was no chance I could face my mother with that pudding-bowl haircut.

But that was just the first transformation.

The day before we moved in, my father took me out to see the fairy offerings in the lane and told me he'd be speaking in an American accent from then on.

"Why?" I asked, once we were alone in the greenery.

"I rented the cottage under the pretense of being an American on holiday," my father said.

I'd noticed it and I hadn't: the way Dad spoke like a slightly slurry Robert De Niro around Margaid.

"Why?" I asked awkwardly, feeling as though my elbows were on backward.

"It's too risky to be Irish."

"Because Mam might come looking for us? Or put you in jail for kidnapping me?"

My honesty scandalized him. We never made direct mention of the way he took me. For three months, we'd been pretending we were "treating ourselves," feigning like we were on a Mam-sanctioned holiday.

"Yes."

"But you'll need to speak more if we live with Margaid. Won't she realize you're not American?"

Dad shook his head dismissively. "People like Marge, who've never traveled farther than Tesco, can't tell the difference between a fella from Dublin, Ireland, and one from Dublin, Ohio. Irish accents sound British to Americans and American to Brits."

I paused to think about that. Margaid spoke two languages: Anglo-Manx, which derived from Medieval Old Scouse, and Manx Gaelic, which she and her seething middle-aged friends only spoke whenever I was in earshot. Other accents genuinely seemed to frazzle her.

"Well, what about me?" I asked with a flare of panic. I felt like he'd covered himself and left me exposed.

He rubbed the tip of his nose and thought. "As I see it, you have two choices. One: You can work on your American accent. Or two: You can keep quiet."

I gave him the startled eyes of someone already mute.

"Don't look at me like that. You're not the first child who's been told to be seen and not heard. Read a book. A book's the best mask there is. Hide your face behind one and no one's got the first idea who you are under there. Try *The Wizard of Oz*. That's American."

Aside from the pub, my father's favorite thing back in Ireland was an ancient volume called *The Universal Self-Instructor,* which was yellowed from the cigarettes he smoked while he pored over it. Half encyclopedia and half etiquette guide, it gave concise information about just about everything: legal maxims; the history of modern nations; celebrated characters in theatre. It gave instructions for plastering broken bones, cleaning a rifle, hiring and working with an architect ("most architects are either too artistic or too practical . . ."). Dad always said a person could make himself a quick expert on anything, just as long as he picked a subject that was obsolete or difficult to verify.

"Margaid only has cookery books," I said.

"I'll see about a library card."

A cold wind churned—if I'd had hair, it would have fanned—and I realized for the first time that it must be late summer, nearly fall. I hadn't seen a calendar since we'd left Ireland.

I felt a sudden crush of worry, thinking I might have missed the first day back at school. I'd been a good student in the past, and I wasn't keen to be held back a year whilst Cleary advanced.

"The divorce referendum," I said.

"What of it?"

"Did it pass?"

"No. The voters rejected it."

"So?"

Dad pulled an angry face. "So, you're the spitting image of your mother when you look at me that way."

At least my father stayed true to his word about the library card. He convinced philistine Margaid to apply for one. Then, he flirted with the head librarian (heavy eye contact was involved, as were quotations from Elizabethan poetry) until she agreed to let him borrow books on Margie's card.

I spent weeks on end reading in bed, beneath the patchwork quilt made from Margaid's late husband's clothes, and embarked on a two-pronged course of study. On the one hand, I schooled myself on normal ten-year-olds' concerns (time travel, horsemanship, et cetera) so, should I ever see my mother again, she wouldn't suspect my Dad had filled my head with criminality. And on the other, I memorized what the authors convinced me were American sayings:

I'm very sorry, indeed. (Dorothy, *The Wizard of Oz*, page 122)
Whew! What a haul! (Frank, *The Hardy Boys Treasure Tower*, page 52)
Sure as shootin'. (Uncle Randolph, *Prairie School*, page 79)
This winter's gonna be a humdinger. (Darrell, *Prairie School*, page 87)
Criminy sakes! . . . Well, I'll be jiggered. (Darrell, *Prairie School*, page 170)

But the book I found most helpful was *Eloise.*

I'd dismissed it as easy-readerish to begin with, based on the fact that Eloise was a full four years younger than me. But the prairie books were giving me recurring nightmares that I was kidnapped by "injuns" and a story for "precocious grown-ups" struck an emotional chord, as leaving Ireland had cost me some innocence.

Straightaway, Eloise's motherless state was a comfort. So was her power—the fact that she'd turned confinement into freedom by seizing what she was owed. She disconnected strangers' phone calls. She molested their packages. She crashed their weddings. Eloise taught me that breathlessness was the key to sounding American: free-range sentences, zero punctuation. Plus, she gave me a long-lasting love of New York City and hotels, both of which struck me as morally corrupt playgrounds, where the usual sweetness and thrift didn't apply.

But above all else, Eloise gave me a heroic coping mechanism: "Here's what I like to do: pretend."

CHAPTER FIVE

For all the talk of spiritual coincidences and new friends, I hadn't intended to socialize with Melanie Ashworth beyond that first afternoon at the pool. Not because we didn't have enough in common. And certainly not because my dance card was booked up with Catskill friends. It was more that with the foreclosure and the Florida move looming over me, I hadn't needed to add more people to say goodbye to—particularly not a woman I gave a fake name to in the name of free lunch.

Even so, when she asked for my number that day at The Odell, I had done the polite thing and ponied up the digits, not raising one word of correction when I watched her type T-R-A-C . . .

It was evening when I got her first text. I was rummaging around in Randy's bathroom cabinet after he'd gone back to Florida on a JetBlue flight. Behind the Kiehl's hair products he'd paid heavily for and never used, I found an empty Altoids tin and brought a wet thumb to the barely there residue inside, debating whether it was crushed mints or trace narcotics.

I ignored her first text: "Hey Tracey! I Googled 'gin as an insect repellent,' and you're right!"

But when another text arrived twenty minutes later, it stopped me in my tracks: "I looked for you on Facebook, but couldn't find you. Are you online? I want to send you a link to that barn dance the art council puts on!"

As an illegal alien, I wasn't keen on social media.

"Sorry!" I texted back. "I deleted my account last year!"

"Whoa! A noncomformist! Go you!"

I glanced down at the bathroom floor, where a half-packed moving box reminded me of the horrors that awaited me in Florida. Randy would ogle girls in white jeans. Fitz would want to visit unlicensed alligator zoos. In the past, all of my moves had been a step up. But this one wasn't even lateral. What did Florida have to offer me, aside from sunburns and pelican paintings?

I opened my web browser and began to create a new email account. No one had claimed the address BuellerTracey.

"Not really!" I texted Melanie. "I'd just become rather addicted! Here's my email. Send the link there?"

Setting a date to meet in person is an important, delicate matter. Rather like moving from friend to lover. But Melanie was eager to jump in the sack with me, sending me an Evite to a cupcake festival (#nomnomnom #notahealthyfoodchoice) within moments.

When we arrived there days later, I made a big show of "treating" her daughter to a free pony ride whilst a distant Melanie, on a phone call to her husband, grinned like a Cheshire cat and murmured "I miss you" over and over. After she hung up, she was grateful enough to buy two dozen cupcakes for the whole lot of us, so we could try every flavor at $4 per confection. We got on so well that I invited her and her daughter, against my better judgment, to come to Catskill and play on our rusting swing set.

Inviting Melanie over was a calculated risk. Before she arrived, I tidied away the bits and bobs that could explode the name "Grace" like a bomb: the return-address stickers at the kitchen desk and the wall calendar with its underlined reminders ("Gracie: bake sale!").

As it turned out, I wasn't the only one who was anxious.

"Be careful, Gabriella . . . ," Melanie kept saying once they arrived, like a maternal nervous tic. Be careful of biting ants. Be careful you don't turn your ankle on your sandal. Be careful you don't hurt Fitz, you're a *big* girl, you're so much *heavier* than he is. And finally: "Be careful, don't throw dirt into Kitty's eyes. . . ."

Gabriella was merely sitting on Fitz's yard-sale digger, scooping broken flagstone into a sorry pile.

There is nothing like having new friends over to make a person see her surroundings with fresh eyes. From my folding chair, I noticed the dead shrubbery. My eye went to the windows' black mold. How badly I wished we owned a proper sand pit or a collection of unmaimed dolls (both arms *and* legs, their faces not scuffed off).

If Mel were another visitor, I might have claimed we owned a few extra acres and let her think crippling land taxes were to blame for the squalid, mismatched quality of our lives. But then, I suspected Melanie liked having a pet poor friend: someone outside her privileged bubble who could make her feel #blessed by comparison.

"She's all right," I said in Gabriella's defense. "You're just breaking ground, aren't you? Are you digging a foundation? Are you building your mummy a new house next door to mine?"

Gabriella smiled. "Mom! I'm building you a house!"

Melanie fanned a cyclone of gnats away from her face. "I'd looove a new house. We've considered it, but . . ."

"You wanted to *build* a house?"

She nodded. "It's always been a dream of mine. But now Victor's in London for the next year. It's too big a project. We might add an extension to our house instead. I really want a living room with a view. Something more modern. Eco-friendly, of course. That's such a selling point here."

"Your husband's *moved* to London?" The fact that she'd never mentioned it suggested we weren't as close as I thought.

"He left Monday."

I dropped my jaw. Where was the social media update about that?

"He's been going back and forth for months. This is easier. It's only temporary. . . ." The words came in monotone, and I got the sense she'd repeated them often.

Kindliness in my eyes. "So just for a short while, then."

"Depends on whether you consider a year 'short.' What can I say? His work's there."

"He's in finance?"

She nodded. "He used to manage CDOs—"

"CDOs?" Not even playing stupid.

"Don't ask. I'm not sure I ever understood what they were. And anyway, they don't exist since the economy went south. He's gone to London to work with his company's subsidiary."

She kept shrugging like a bad dancer trying to keep a beat. She took a long sip of the white wine spritzer I'd made her.

"So we're in the same boat."

"Oh, right. You mentioned something the other day, but I thought Randy was just gone for the week. You're living apart too?"

"He's a Realtor. It's been difficult to earn a living, locally, after the subprime collapse. He comes back weekends, when he can. Which is only once a month at the moment. Airfare is so bloody expensive."

"He's gone back to the UK?"

Bless. I nearly rolled over laughing. Melanie thought Randy was an Englishman. *Randy*, in a country where the word means "sex-crazed."

But for the second time in our history, I failed to correct her.

"He has," I said.

And there it was: a smile like a sigh of a relief. The mist cleared from Melanie's eyes and her expression seemed to open like a flower.

"Both our husbands abroad! What a crazy coincidence!"

"Yes, quite."

"I just love coincidences. Don't you?"

"I do."

For half a second, we stared at each other's sweat-glossed faces, unblinking, rather stunned by it all.

Then Melanie said: "Coincidences make me feel, I don't know . . . like I'm on the right track. It's like fate. So, your husband's coming back eventually? Or will you and the kids join him in the UK?"

"We'll go live with him, eventually." I lowered my voice so Kitty and Fitz couldn't hear me from the hobbyhorse swing. "This house is in foreclosure, which complicates things."

Her eyes were massive as I detailed how Randy, accustomed to galloping home sales, was stunned when the banks stopped lending.

"I can't imagine the stress. What did you do?"

"Oh, what people do. We tightened our belts, at least I did, and drained our savings."

Melanie gasped. "Your *whole* savings?"

"Gone." With my hands, I released an invisible moth. "But even worse was the emotional toll it took on Randy. He missed the buzz. You know, thrill of the house-hunt. Negotiating deals every day. He was like a stroppy teenager without it."

"Oh, Tracey. How long do you have left?"

"I'm pretty well expecting the eviction letter any minute."

My voice momentarily went thick with true emotion. It hurt to think about the wallpaper I'd painstakingly chosen two years ago, back when I used to buy fat, colorful volumes by HGTV personalities, when I cared about "injecting vibrancy" and "adding interest" to our "space."

"How's Randy dealing with it?"

Light, little laugh. "Oh, he's not. I am. Which is why I spend most evenings packing frangibles in newspaper."

Every morning, Fitz approached me with a fresh question: *Mummy, where'd the mirror go? Mummy, what happened to the books?* It was like Christmas morning in reverse.

"Please don't tell anyone," I added, an old phrase that rolled off my tongue. "It's so embarrassing. . . ."

"I wouldn't dream of it. Oh, Tracey. I feel for you." Melanie was scanning my face, her forehead cleft with pity.

"Thanks," I said. "I'm glad *someone* feels for me. Because right about now, I'm just numb to it all."

Melanie dropped her glass in the dirt, oblivious when the ice cubes spilled, and dove in for an embrace. She was so thin it was like she had no protective coating. Locked in the hug, I sharply felt her lack of bra.

When she pulled away, her face was flushed with wine. Tears had resurfaced in her eyes. They'd gathered force since the talk of London.

"Oh, come now, I'm sure we'll be all right in the end." Her expression, *Pathetic you!,* made me want to saw my head off. As did the way she kept pressing me for ugly details.

A well-concealed anger rose up inside me, and on its heels, a reckless sort of mischief. I was about to get myself in deeper, and I just didn't care. My father taught me not to let good pity go to waste. Plus, I already knew the script from the years I'd spent working with Oz.

"Actually, I've been thinking of this summer as a time to focus on myself. With Randy gone, there are fewer distractions. Maybe you could do the same. Find a project. Something like, well, your renovation."

"Oh no, I could never do something that big on my own."

"I could give you advice. I worked as an architect back in Britain. Before Kitty and Fitz."

"*Really?* You're kidding! I feel like such a fool, just assuming we're both stay-at-home moms. Haa-haah. But you had a career!"

Appearance of modesty, downplaying this new "difference" between us: "*Had* a career. It's been some time. When Randy's work troubles began, I started making efforts to go back. I've done a fair bit of domestic extension work."

"No way!"

"A country house in Warwickshire comes to mind. It sounds a bit like what you're aiming for. I'll send you my website later. You can look at the photos. Perhaps you'll feel inspired."

"Oh, yay! Please send it! I'd love to see!"

I picked up my phone, and noticed Randy hadn't returned any of my texts. With real irritation, I lied: "Ugh, the Internet's been down all day. I'll send it later. I promise."

"OK. So tell me, what was that *like*? Being an architect? In London, no less."

"It was a bit like a marriage. Time-consuming. Emotional. When work projects went well, it was thrilling. But when they didn't, I felt rather angry and trapped."

"Did you work for a big company?"

"It was a small, boutique firm. Mostly, I designed holiday homes abroad."

"Where?"

"A part of Turkey called the Turquoise Coast. Do you know it?"

"No, but it sounds glamorous! You must have been very good."

"Well, I don't know about that. Most architects are either too artistic or too practical. I tried to position myself in the middle. The technical disciplines were my real weakness. I never had much talent for things like building models."

"Oh, please!" Melanie cried, as though I were fishing for compliments. "I'm sure you were wonderful! Just look at how charming this place is! And I bet you did it on a shoestring!"

I forced myself to beam at the backhanded compliment.

"Yes," I said. "I can do a lot with very little. I really am quite resourceful that way."

After the Ashworths left, the children were knackered. Fitz crashed by seven, nodding off with a sketchpad full of doodles. Kitty messed about with the pillow she was convinced had a "bad dream side" and a "good dream" one—as if horror could switch to heaven with the flip of a seam—then fell asleep, facedown, with splayed legs.

Leaving their room on tiptoe, I glanced at my phone. Randy still hadn't texted. So I decided to ring him.

I took my phone outside and sat by the river in the humming darkness. Out there, it was easier to remember the way Randy and I used to hang our feet over the water, talking for hours and laughing like the gulls overhead.

I'd seduced Randy thoughtfully, much the way I was charming Melanie, identifying and filling his unspoken needs. He'd lost his single mother to cancer the year we met, so I presented myself as extra maternal, playing up my ready-made one-year-old. He'd also had a self-loathing streak, so helping him gain confidence, I had pretended to be more baffled than I was by Yankee ways. "Why do Americans refrigerate eggs?" I'd ask. Or: "Who's Helen Keller? What's so great about her?" Randy would puff up his chest, feeling smart and superior as he nattered on about salmonella or Keller's triumph of the human spirit over adversity.

"Hello?" Randy said, over the sounds of conversation and booming bass.

"Hi, darling. You all right?"

"Oh, Gracie. Yeah. I'm just working on my online licensing course."

"Is it an interesting unit?" I asked through gritted teeth.

There was an evasive pause. In my mind's eye I could see him shouldering through a happy-hour crowd. His phone swished with wind when he reached the door.

"Uh—yeah, sort of. I'm learning about unlawful detainer complaints—how to evict commercial tenants."

And I was stuffing duvets for orphans.

But our marriage didn't work if we were rigid about these things. We had an implied agreement: I pretended Randy's hangovers were stomach bugs and in return, he accepted that it was "easier" to file our taxes separately and "more secure" to keep our marriage certificate in a safety-deposit box that he'd never seen.

"Sounds knackering."

"It is," he confirmed over the sound of women's laughter.

"I've been texting all day. Our Amex card was declined when I tried to use it at Aldi. When I rang them, they said there was an outstanding balance of four thousand—"

"Yeah, I know. I'm just waiting for that check for the South Biscayne condo to clear. I'll pay it tomorrow. Sorry, Grace, I've got a chance to check out this corner residence on Fisher Island—"

"Right. Fine. Go. You don't want to miss the boat."

"Literally. You should see this guy's yacht."

After we'd said goodbye, I fortified myself with a cup of tea and sat down in front of the computer. I knew the password to Randy's Facebook account, but hadn't snooped in ages, being so fed up with his talk about Florida that I couldn't be arsed to look at the mojito-and-palm-tree photos he posted online.

But during his last visit, Randy had done his own laundry for the first time in recorded history. Like a daft mark, I'd merely assumed he was doing me a favor on my birthday. But in light of that night's conversation, I couldn't help assuming something more sinister. Something involving small-skirted girls from Miami.

Logging into Randy's Facebook account, I found no messages in his Sent or Received folders. And that was a change. I wondered when and why he'd begun deleting.

I checked the archived messages next. And in amongst conversations between Randy and his Floridian real estate friend—blah, blah, "distressed housing stock," blah, blah, "prices going up at a pretty strong clip"—I found a string of messages between him and a woman named Vanessa.

Before my heart could fully thunder, I told myself Vanessa might be a client.

I clicked her profile: Junior agent at the real estate firm where Randy used our remaining cash to rent a desk. Single. Barely thirty. Three dress sizes smaller than me and attractive in a tits-out, heavily made-up fashion. Her picture showed a woman with spidery eyelashes and foundation so thick it likely stayed on until sandblasted.

One of her captions—"Bitch please, I'm Cuban"—triggered a memory from my birthday dinner. What was it Randy had said? "There's this thing. Mojo and relleñas . . . It's like—fuck! Gracie, I've never tasted anything like it!"

I returned to the message exchange:

Her: "Thank you for earlier! I feel a lot better now!!"

Him: "Yeah, me too. We can meet up Wednesday for a follow-up if it helps."

Her: "How can I make it up to you?"

Him, with a winking emoticon: "I'm sure something will pop up."

Her: "How are your knees and feet now?"

Him: "Well, no carpet burns! How are you? We've been thinking about you."

Did "we" include Randy's todger? Were the burned knees the product of shagging on carpet?

Somewhere in the universe, there was a Wilhelm scream.

I understood why Randy would do it: aging, money woes, career stress. But at least Oz had asked for a separation before bedding another woman. Randy had put half the East Coast between us and blamed his career for the emotional distance. He'd gone behind my back, assuming I was too busy with the children to care, or even notice.

It occurred to me that I could phone Randy back and ask him, straight out, "Who is Vanessa?" I could warn him that if he lied, I would leave and go for full custody of Kit.

But then, that was a bluff. I had what one might call "identity issues." Plus, I'd overstayed my visa. If I tried to face Randy and a solicitor, I was apt to lose *both* children and be chucked in an American prison. I'd spend the rest of Kit's and Fitz's youth dressed in orange, serving time for identity fraud, eating the mayonnaise scones Americans call "biscuits and gravy."

Stiff upper lip. I had work to do. I switched over to the Mid-Hudson Library System and requested books on Randy's account, including *A Field Guide to American Houses.*

I already had the bare bones of an architectural website I'd designed years earlier, when I was helping Oz with his fraudulent holiday homes, and I still remembered a lot of my lines:

"Living rooms ought to be positioned on prominent corners."

"I blame Pierre Chareau for this bloody fascination with glass blocks."

That said, I had to buy myself the domain name Bueller Architecture.com. Then came the matter of cutting and pasting JPEGs to make the website look current. The last time I'd used the thing, Fitz was a fairyfly in my gut and interior columns were in fashion.

In a trendy sans-serif font, I typed: "I aim to bring a fresh perspective to my new builds and domestic extensions. I offer my clients a high level of design integrity . . ."

It was time to bank some social security.

CHAPTER SIX

"I *love* your website!" Melanie texted.

It was another scorcher of a day, and I was in the Catskill post office, buying postage for a prison letter to Oz.

I sent all my correspondence to him by way of my British friend Seema, who had taken over the London council flat where Fitz and I used to live. At that time, she was the only one back home who knew I had moved to the States. Keeping my whereabouts secret was a preventative measure. That way, Oz couldn't dob me in to lighten his sentence, no matter how he tired of prison gangs and ice-cold showers.

The letter itself was short. Mostly, I just sent quick updates about Fitz: "He has his first wobbly tooth. He pronounces 'rainbow sherbet' as 'rainbow pervert.' He's very keen on geography and Harry Potter. The other day we discovered Google Maps blurs out 10 Downing Street as though it's invisible to Muggles."

"Where are you?" Melanie texted again when I didn't send a prompt reply.

I tried writing back, but Kitty was tugging on my trouser pocket and autocorrect kept changing "architecture" to "Archipelago." On top of it all, I hadn't been able to stop imagining Vanessa smoking Randy's "Cuban cigar"—an image that burnt my throat with bile.

The clerk gave me a disapproving look.

"I need the rectangle!" Kitty shouted. Then, in a siren wail: "The *rectaaangle*!"

I realized she meant Seema's envelope and lifted her up so she could thrust it through the mail slot.

Then, I'd given her my PO box key and let her remove the stack of envelopes she found inside. In amongst the offers for debt consolidation, there was a new foreclosure letter—the most menacing yet:

> YOU HAVE TWENTY CALENDAR DAYS TO FILE A WRITTEN RESPONSE TO THE ATTACHED COMPLAINT. A PHONE CALL WILL NOT PROTECT YOU. IF YOU DO NOT FILE A RESPONSE ON TIME, YOUR WAGES, MONEY, AND PROPERTY MAY THEREAFTER BE TAKEN WITHOUT FURTHER WARNING BY THE COURT.

The heading, BANK OF AMERICA Plaintiff(s) vs. RANDALL MUELLER Defendant, made me hallucinate the horsehair smell of British courtrooms.

Tucking the envelope under my arm, my fury flared anew. No wonder Randy wasn't panicked about the foreclosure. He had a stress ball. Two of them, in fact. On Vanessa's tattooed chest.

Stabbing my keypad with angry thumbs, I texted Melanie: "You're kind! Site's under some construction. It's a tip!"

Behind a past-due cable bill, I found an envelope containing Michael Rondo's replacement Chase Visa card.

A chipper customer service representative had helped me when I'd telephoned. Using the voice-changing app, I'd dropped my voice, breathed from my diaphragm, and fumed about the call wait time with "manly" resonance. Then, I reported my "lost card" and changed my billing address.

In the post office, I peeled the plastic card off the clear tack that affixed it to the letter, and felt a moment's triumph.

My phone rang. Melanie.

I answered: "My dear friend, Mel."

I used the F word in strategic and cyclical ways. For days on end, I hammered Melanie with the word "friend." Then, abruptly, I dropped it. Subliminally, it reminded Melanie that my affection was conditional.

"Hi, Tracey! I'm sorry to call. Did I catch you at a bad time?"

"It's the perfect time."

"I'm in total awe of your website. But I couldn't access some of the links."

"Really? Which ones?"

"Let me see . . . The links to the main contractor on the Cockadilly extension. Oh, and also, the Haynes Orchard project."

So she'd noticed. I was planning to build sites for fake contractors later.

"Bloody hell. Probably just dodgy links. I'm beginning to lose faith in the woman I'm paying to redesign the site. Give Green-Oak-Architects-Dot-Co-Dot-UK a look. I worked there before I started my own firm."

I could picture her, hunched over her keyboard, those starved granny fingers tapping.

"Click on the manor house renovation," I said. "That was one of mine."

"Oh, Tracey! It's beautiful! Honestly. I wouldn't just say that. I love the double-height! All those windows! What are you up to today? Do you and the kids want to come over for lunch so we can talk about built-ins? I've been working on this mood board—"

"Doesn't that sound lovely? We're just at the post office. I don't know what time the next bus to Woodstock runs."

"Don't be ridiculous! We'll come get you!"

"I haven't got their car seats."

"I'll take the spare out of Victor's car. Fitz can ride in Gabby's booster seat."

"And Gabby?"

"She'll be fine just this once."

. . .

"So *why* don't you drive?" Melanie asked after we'd loaded the children into her plush seats. She drove a Mercedes SUV that looked almost like an armored Land Rover. In a sea of Subarus and pickup trucks, it was about as low-key as a spaceship.

"I know, a person who doesn't drive . . ." I laughed. "Impossible to imagine in America, isn't it?"

I glanced over my shoulder and noticed Fitz was watching me intently. He'd said nothing about my name since Randy's last visit, but every time Melanie called me "Tracey," he blinked.

"Mummy hasn't got a license," he said.

"Yes." I laughed. "There's that, as well."

The Celestine Prophecy was wedged in the cup holder between our seats, and I was pleased to see the bookmark was still stalled in the early chapters. The fact that she'd abandoned it—and presumably, with it, her efforts to befriend the burnt-out Woodstock types—told me she was committed to our growing friendship.

"Truly?" Melanie said. "You don't have a license?"

"Not yet. American roads . . ." I gave a convincing shiver.

"They scare you? Really?"

I nodded and said more about how I couldn't get over the lack of roundabouts. I said I was scared I'd revert to habit and drive on the left.

"Isn't that a dreadful excuse?" I self-deprecated. "It sounds childish, doesn't it?"

"Oh please." Melanie swiped her hand dismissively.

"Randy always said it was." I remembered the hypocrisy. Him calling me "overly dependent" on him, as he smugly sat surfing the MLS, watching me fold his underpants.

Over the ticking of her indicator, Melanie asked: "How did you two meet?"

Through the windshield, her tasteful bronze mailbox came into view, capital letters spelling ASHWORTH under the address.

Beyond it, a landscaper was hard at work corduroying a large lawn with fresh mow lines. We entered through the gate—the entire property was deer fenced—and rolled up the driveway, where a pricey mountain view emerged. A big, bland house rose out of the greenery.

She thought Randy was British, so I couldn't tell her the truth: that we met on an international dating site.

"We met on the coast of Spain, actually."

"Ooh, have you seen that series with Gwyneth Paltrow and Mario Batali?"

I tried to imagine whether Randy and I would have got on as instantly if we'd met in real life. Somehow I doubt it. The Internet—a place where men are men, women are men, and little girls are FBI agents—had been the perfect venue for our fast-and-loose relationship with the truth.

I had hated the transactional feel of Internet dating. Most men online hadn't seemed interested in a long-term relationship, no matter what they claimed. Ironically, I'd gone online to cancel my account when I saw Randy's message. Unlike my other e-suitors, he didn't write in text-speak or send me pictures of his one-eyed appendage. Plus, his real estate firm had a sister office in Manhattan, a city that had appealed to me ever since I was a girl.

As an added bonus, Randy was really quite cute, in his flash way. He wore adventurous shirt colors. His Jaguar convertible made inherent promises about sunshine and freedom. Plus, it was easy to gauge the effect I'd had on him: "I was on the Forbes yacht last night, gushing to everyone about this fabulous woman I met online . . ." His American directness suited my English mystery.

"The odd part is Fitz and I were meant to have left Spain that day, but he'd caught a sniffle so I postponed our flight. I wonder, now, what would have happened if we'd never changed our plans. No way of knowing. Women don't get to time travel, not unless you count books with rogue Scottish blokes."

"Aww, if you'd made your flight, you wouldn't have fallen in love."

"Yes, but I also wouldn't have received this." I reached into my purse and took out the foreclosure letter. It was risky, but also unexpected. It was exactly the sort of bold move I needed to keep Melanie pliable. Angling the paper away from her, I read in a whisper: "'The Plaintiff BANK OF AMERICA gives RANDALL *BUELLER*, Defendant, twenty calendar days to file a written response to the attached complaint . . .'"

"Oh, Tracey," she said, her voice rising in pitch. "Let me see."

I looked backward at Fitz, and quickly tucked the letter away. "I'm sorry. I shouldn't have taken it out with you-know-who here."

"Taken what out?" Fitz asked on cue.

Inside a virgin-white kitchen, Melanie oversaw the housekeeper, Janisa, as she served the kids gluten-free ravioli and a kale puree billed as a smoothie. Kitty and Fitz, with their processed-food palates, gave me a look that said they didn't know whether to eat it or return it to the compost pile from which it had come.

I played my part as the gracious guest, washing the children's dishes. I was pulling open kitchen drawers, trying to find the space for children's cutlery in amongst half a dozen bottle openers, when Janisa shooed me away.

Chastened, I made my way to the perfectly appointed living room, where Melanie was putting on a Mandarin children's DVD called *Mei Mei.*

"Totally neurotic, I know," she said. "But I only let Gabby watch TV in Chinese or Spanish."

On the eighty-inch telly screen, a panda bear in dungarees clapped emphatically.

"Wanna tour?" Melanie asked once the children were settled.

"Love one."

For the next quarter of an hour, I admired the leatherette furniture and shaggy hemp rugs. The style was confused and, occasionally, really horrible. The house was a disorientating mix of Jersey gilt and the fair-trade Indian imports that the Woodstock types favored. But I was genuinely impressed by the newness of it all. Gabby owned a life-size stuffed horse and had a massive mural featuring a Maya Angelou quote ("Be a rainbow in someone else's cloud"). Melanie's bedroom had boxes of online shopping on the floor and an aerial yoga hammock that likely doubled as a sex swing.

"Have you been to India?" I asked, in front of a cabinet that was one of Melanie's touches of ethno-eclecticness. It was a beautiful old thing, painted with images of Krishna and Radha.

"No." Expression like she had no idea why I was asking.

"Oh, you must. You'd love it."

"You've been?"

"In my late teens. With a rucksack, and a copy of *Siddhartha*. One of those youthful quests for life's truths."

The book spoke to me in ways that still haven't worn off, particularly the part that says language fails—everything becomes a lie the instant a person puts words to it.

Returning to the living room, I examined the south-facing wall. I paced back and forth slowly, pretending not to notice Melanie watching me as she twiddled her lips. I nodded to myself. I rapped on the drywall with my knuckles.

Finally, when Melanie looked like she was ready to shake an answer out of me, I announced that the wall wasn't load-bearing. I said, yes, absolutely, in my professional opinion, she could "bump it out" and extend into the garden.

She bounced up and down with girlish enthusiasm.

"Have you considered a direct-gain sunspace?" I asked. "Something to collect and vent heat into the rest of the house?"

"Like a sunroom? I should know what that is. Hah-ahh."

"I have something more integrated in mind. Some large windows with the right glazing." I threw out words like *heat loss* and *winter*, which instilled fear in the heart of even hardened upstaters.

"Yeah. Sure. Eco," Melanie said. But she seemed distracted by the array of paint swatches going through her head.

. . .

"Come on," Melanie told me the next time we visited her house for a playdate. "Our Airbnb-ers just left. I want to show you the guesthouse."

She led me and the children down a footpath that cut through a wooded slope. It was thickly shaded, lined with firs and bruise-colored hellebore.

"It looks like Ponyville!" Kitty cheered when we arrived at the house.

When she pushed in the door, the Thatcher-era decor gave me something of a shiver. It had the same floral ruffles as Margaid's house. The green-glass lampshades were identical.

"Ta-da!"

I smelled Shalimar—not Melanie's scent—and wondered if it was her dead mother's perfume.

"This was one of the reasons we bought the house," Melanie went on, as the children scrambled up the stairs to the loft. "My mother wasn't well at the time. We'd had bad luck with nursing homes. She's passed now."

"I'm so sorry."

"She wasn't well," she said again, as though that settled it. "It's still filled with her things. There's only one bedroom. Although, there's a daybed in the loft."

"You're thinking of an extension here too?"

Melanie shook her head. She pulled out a kitchen stool, and the leg screeched awkwardly against the slate tile.

"No, this doesn't need any work. It's not very modern, I know. But it's comfortable . . . And I was thinking, you and the kids can stay here while Randy finds you a place in the UK." She rambled on, rapid-fire, full of plans and advice. If I lived there, we could help each other with child care, she said. (She could afford babysitters, but didn't know any local ones.) Plus, I could keep an eye on the Catskill house. And I wouldn't have to worry about the kids coming home to find menacing notes from the bank on the door.

Now, it was one thing to let a woman call me the wrong name, but it was quite another to move into her house under the misconception that I was an underemployed architect whose husband was on the other side of an ocean.

"Oh, Melanie. You're such a good friend. You're so generous as to offer. And it's obvious you've gone to a lot of effort."

"Pish, I didn't do a thing. It was already set up."

The children were sliding down the stairs on their backsides.

"Can we go swimming today?" Fitz asked.

"Absolutely!" Melanie said, dismounting her stool and bending down to my son's level. "In fact, I'm trying to convince your mommy to move into this house. In which case, you could come swimming in the river every day! Wouldn't you like that?"

Fitz beamed. "Yes! Mum, can we?! Please!"

"I'll think about it. In the meantime, we ought to get home and make dinner. Why don't you visit the potty before we leave? It's just there, behind you."

As he closed the door, Melanie leveled her eyes on mine. "Tracey, think about it, wouldn't it be a nice way to transition the kids from Catskill to London? So the change isn't so abrupt?"

I could see the eagerness in the scythe edge of her sculpted eyebrows.

"I wish I could accept," I said. "But it's just too much of an imposition. Besides, I could never find a way to repay you."

"Oh, but you would!"

I had seduced her *too* well.

"I couldn't possibly."

"Follow me." She led me up the stairs to the loft, where a drafting desk stood beneath a stained-glass window. "So? What do you think?"

"This is for *me*?"

The heavy oak desk screamed *potential.* There was no doubt Melanie had bought it in the time I'd known her, probably at one of the Hudson antique shops where the price tags were so steep one always hoped they were printed in yen.

"Oh, Melanie," I said, lighthearted, teasing. "This brings me straight back to uni. All those painful communal-living conflicts. What if this gets to be a gross imposition? It really might. You may come to feel I'm taking advantage. You might want to chuck me out."

"I won't," she said, idealistic, firm, and desperate to avoid being alone. "Besides, it'll be your own space. Janisa will clean it, but you can do whatever you want with it. You can stay here, rent-free, and work on the plans for the extension."

It was worth considering. For the past two weeks, I'd been playing the architect, hoping to earn a couple grand that I could set aside to fund my future separation from Randy. But moving in with Melanie meant I could leave him even sooner. It was almost as though I'd been scraping away at an escape tunnel with tooth-picks and plastic spoons, and Melanie had just handed me a shovel.

"What about school? Fitz is supposed to start kindergarten this fall."

"So? We can register him at the Woodstock public school. I wish I could say he'd be there with Gabriella. But I'm probably going to keep her in country day."

"No," I said. "Absolutely not. You're much too Zen about this. It's a big thing, taking people into your home."

She tossed her hair and shrugged, enjoying the airy, Earth Mother figure I reflected back at her. "I really don't see the big deal. If I have something, I give it."

"You promise we'll talk out any conflicts? Open communica-tion?"

"I promise," she said, flinching. "Total honesty. If anything comes up, we'll work it out."

I gave a long pause for suspense, then cheered: "OK! Let's do it! Let's be neighbors."

"Yay!" Clapping her hands. "Wanna go to your house tonight and move some boxes?"

"We only need a few odds and ends," I said. "Nightgowns. Toothbrushes. You stay here with Gabby. I'll phone a taxi."

"You can take Victor's car," she said automatically. Her giving was compulsive, unthinking. She caught herself a few steps later. "I'm so sorry. . . . It completely slipped my mind . . . you don't have a license."

"It's not far. It's a shame I'm not bold enough to risk it."

"But I know it freaks you out . . ."

I'm not certain she realized she was shaking her head *yes*.

I told her I could manage. Just as long as I didn't get myself pulled over in my excitement.

She grabbed my hand awkwardly, trapped it in both of hers like a frightened bird. "You're going to get through all this . . . you and Randy. I *know* you will."

I nodded stoically.

"I'll get Victor's keys. There shouldn't be many police on the road this time of day."

Back in Catskill, I gathered up some toiletries, nappies, the children's security blankets, the laptop, which was *my* attachment object, and the contents of the full laundry basket (either my architect act had made me neglect the washing or it had been spawning whilst we slept).

I hadn't drunk a drop of alcohol all day, which was rare for any playdate with Melanie, but I still needed a sobering glass of water. I went back and forth between thinking it was mad, moving into an outbuilding that smelled vaguely of my mark's dead mother, and thinking it wasn't much different from the way other adult women run home to recharge at their mum and dad's house when their marriage hits the skids.

I filled crinkled Walmart bags with Kitty's favorite snacks: juice pouches, toaster pastries, and the kinds of chemical-rich fruit leathers that would never make it onto Melanie's fair-trade, free-range shopping list.

Then I shredded every bill addressed to GRACIE MUELLER.

I thought at length about whether to destroy the family photos. If I hauled the whole lot to the Ashworths' house, Melanie was apt to notice certain inconsistencies in my story. But if I left them, there was a chance I'd lose them if the bank boarded up the house while we were gone.

I flipped through the snapshots: There was Fitz in his baby pictures, his face a Jackson Pollock of pasta sauce. There was Kitty at eight weeks, curled like a millipede in the bend of a breast-feeding pillow. Shoving them through the hatch of the woodstove would have felt like inflicting bodily harm. So instead, I packed them into Randy's Gucci shoeboxes, loaded them into the car boot, and hoped I'd find a safe hiding place at the Ashworths' cottage.

After I'd filled a few contractor bags with essentials, I activated Michael Rondo's new credit card, logged into the voice-changing app, and contacted a few customer service reps of my own.

"Hello, Hudson Savings Bank. How can I help you today?"

"Hello," I said with male resonance. "My name is Randall Mueller. This is the second or third time I've called. My wife's name is spelled incorrectly on my joint checking account. It's not Mueller. It's Mullen. M-U-L-L-E-N."

I employed the same scheme at the credit card companies, where I had never needed a Social Security number to share Randy's exorbitant debts, but couldn't make changes to the account because I wasn't the primary cardholder. "My wife's surname is Mulligan."

While I was at it, I changed my address, in all cases (right down to my Price Chopper loyalty card), to the local battered women's shelter. My father learned the trick from the mysteries he read in bulk and used it to prevent landlords from seeking us out for back rent. "When a paper trail ends at a police station or a punched-up women's shelter," he told me, "a PI starts to look suspiciously at his client."

CHAPTER SEVEN

With lying, as with sex, an excess of confidence means a high probability of disaster. If anything threatens to undo a shameless liar, it's too much self-certainty, which was exactly what happened to me on the Isle of Man.

I'd been studying American novels and feeling reasonably good about my new syntax and expressions. My Yankee accent wasn't anywhere as slick as my dad's (his muses were characters on *M★A★S★H* and *Get Carter*), but I still sounded reasonably authentic. I thought. At least until I joined my father and Margaid at their local pub, where the barman introduced us to a pair of American tourists.

They were directly beside us at the bar, complaining about the smoke and requesting "cold" beer.

My father fingered his collar. In all the time since we'd left Ireland, we'd never encountered actual Yankees, in khaki trousers, puzzling over the meaning of eighteen o'clock.

"Hi, folks. Having a good trip?" Dad asked.

"Heck yeah," the woman responded with a showy smile and flick of her hair. Surely, her accent couldn't have been as thick as that. But in memory, she spoke like Catherine Bach on *The Dukes of Hazzard*.

"Sure is nice to meet you," her husband said. "Where y'all from?"

Dad wasn't his usual chatty self: "California."

"You're a long way from home!" the American woman said. "We're from Tennessee ourselves. Oh, look at your darlin' daughter!"

Dad had the look of the Sphinx.

The woman bent to face me. Her mouth was bright pink around the edges like she'd chatted off her lipstick. "Tell me, darlin', do you miss home?"

My father gave me a *go-on* nod. He was always trying to convince me I had "magnetism." He liked to say all children were charming—it was something to do with their disproportionately large heads.

But I was panicked to the brink of illness. Numb-faced, thinking of *Eloise*, I stuttered something about how "Pop and me" missed *Howdy Doody* and the revolving doors on the hotel where we lived. But my plummy accent didn't read "California" at all.

The Yankee man shook his head and spilt a bit of beer in the process. "*Howdy Doody* hasn't been on TV for twenty-five years!"

"Give the girl a break, Phil," his wife said. "She musta had it on tape."

I tried to say yes, that was exactly it. But my accent was half "gee whillickers" and half "top o' the morning." My eyes filled with tears.

"Oh, bless your heart," the woman said.

Her husband muttered something about a rigmarole and the barman "poking fun." They refastened their bum bags and left.

My father set to work on a sermon about how much he hated encountering Americans outside of the States. When people failed to understand them, they just spoke louder. Knowing the entire turning world hated them, they stitched maple leaves onto their backpacks and tried to pass for Canadian.

But Margaid just folded her arms. When the bar tab came, she'd called on Dad to pay our way for the first time ever.

We stayed on at Margaid's for a few weeks following that incident in the pub, but instead of dragging each other to the bedroom by their belt loops, she and Dad stayed in the kitchen debating the cost of petrol, TV license, council tax, et cetera.

She never outright called him an imposter. It was more like the Americans had planted some seed in her mind, and from that moment on, she was stingier, convinced that Dad was abusing his power as her lover.

Mute with guilt, I spent long days in the library.

"Come along," he told me when he found me there one afternoon. "We need to clear off while Marge is visiting her sister in Port Saint Mary."

At last! I thought. My father had finally tired of Margaid's kipper breath and the Isle at large. He was ready to exchange Man for Mam.

I stumbled to my feet and followed Dad at top speed back to Marge's house, where he rummaged through the cupboards and drawers.

"What are you doing?" I asked, watching him examine her tarnished wedding ring by the light of the window.

Dad shrugged. "I gave it to her. Now that we've split up, I'm taking it back."

I recognized the lie, but didn't much care. I was jittery with excitement, making beds and tidying up behind us. I hoped, when we got home, Mam would make me toast soldiers and runny boiled eggs. I hoped Cleary hadn't got a girlfriend. I hoped I'd find my friends on the green, playing kerbs or kick the can. And I hoped none of them would have a gawk at my short hair.

Before we left, I cleaned the house, hoping fresh sheets would stop Margaid phoning the constabulary. Now that my homecoming was finally in sight, the very last thing I needed was a policeman to ruin it.

We traveled to Peel, a fishing port on the west side of the island, and checked into a basic hotel. My father liked it for its value-for-money carvery, which included a bottle of wine. I loathed it for its shower, which ran like a hot-and-cold watering can.

"You look knackered," my father told me.

"I do?" I was going home, at last. I felt the same wild mania I always had on Christmas Eve.

"Uh-huh. You look dead on your feet. Margaid took it out of us, didn't she?"

Out of nowhere, I felt uncontrollably beat. Maybe it was the power of suggestion. Or maybe Dad knew my feelings better than I did. I fumbled with my shoelaces, crawled into bed in my shrunken clothes, and slept for the better part of two days.

My dreams were one unending holiday. In sleep, I sat beneath papery palm trees. When I woke up, I expected striped awnings and the smell of saltwater. Instead I found my father draping a damp washcloth over my forehead.

I jumped. "What are you doing?"

He blew his lips out. "You were burning up. I reasoned I had to do *something.* I got you a flat 7 Up as well. That's what your mam gives you, isn't it?"

I took the bottle he passed me and took an awful dose. "When do we leave for Douglas?" I didn't want my illness to delay our trip by a minute. I couldn't wait to leave behind those three-legged flags that looked like swastikas.

"That hole? Why in the name of Jesus would we go back there?"

"To get the ferry."

Dad looked at me sideways.

I clarified: "The ferry to *Belfast.*"

"Oh . . . come here to me. See, the thing is. Margaid might have reported us for rent arrears. For any number of things, really—"

I argued that was all the more reason to leave quickly, but I was groggy with illness and the words came out wrong.

My father grew agitated. He paced the room, making an unfocused racket as he counted out bills and stomped into his shoes.

My tongue felt like sole leather. I wanted to apologize for

bringing up Ireland. But before I got the chance, Dad had stormed out the door.

He was gone all night. I still had an achy fever and a deepening worry that he might never come back. But in the morning, I felt improved and worked on self-education.

I sat so close to the goggle box that its static electricity made my bad haircut stand on end. As late morning passed into early afternoon, I watched *Question Time* and *Antiques Roadshow.* The cathode ray tube gave me a calming sense of purpose. I didn't absorb the content. I wasn't *watching* TV so much as letting it colonize me, allowing word choices and pronunciations to fill the empty suck between my ears. I *tawwght* myself to broaden my "aw" sounds. I learned to pronounce "home" with a bloated *o* sound: *hohmm.*

I was repeatedly saying "laugh" with a short a—*laahf*—when my father finally returned.

"I'm sorry," I said. "For bringing up—well, for misunderstanding the plan. I've been giving my accent a rethink as well. Maybe I can pass for English?"

"Let's hear it," he said.

I began imitating the presenter on *Blue Peter:* "And now for something completely different. You'll want to ask a parent or guardian for sticky-backed plastic and some blunt-nosed scissors."

He looked at me a moment and then put two fingers in his mouth. He whistled. "You beauty!"

"Really? It's good?"

"Is it ever! Here, have some lunch."

He opened up a vast spread of takeout containers. There were lamb burgers, chips, mushy peas, and dozens of containers of brown sauce and other condiments. It was a deconstructed feast. Even the burger buns had their own Styrofoam coffins.

"How did you afford all this?!" The moment the words were out, I clasped a hand over my mouth, worrying that I sounded too much like Mam.

But this time, Dad didn't mind being challenged about money.

"Complicated orders," he said, opening a bottle of twist-top wine. "Then, you examine it all in a huff and ask the kitchen to reconfigure it. By the time you hand over your cash, they're too scattered to count it. They're ready to pay *you* to take your food and get out. Interrupt people enough—chop things into enough pieces and repackage them—and no one even suspects you've robbed them blind."

We carried on that way for weeks. Dad had little ways of making pocket cash. One of his favorites was stealing ice chests of mackerel from amateur anglers and selling them to the fishmonger. No one on the Isle seemed to mind Dad's scamming, just as long as he only preyed on the mainlanders.

In pubs, Dad played Houdini for motocross tourists who bought him free drinks in exchange. He'd do the jumping-toothpick trick. Or he bet someone he'd finish three pints of beer before they could down three shots. Most impressively, he could snap his fingers and produce smoke—a feat he accomplished by burning a matchbook strip and rubbing his thumb in the residue.

In grocery stores, Dad and I had a bank-heist routine. He'd fill a backpack with food and abandon it in a deserted aisle. Then I'd go in, pick the bag up, leave through the entrance, and take the horse tram back to the hotel, where he'd meet me after one or two drinks.

Peel wasn't awful. It had the Isle's best sunsets and ice cream. It had a fort with the hilarious name Magnus Barefoot. Dad wanted to see the waterfall at Glen Maye, so we dipped our hands in the heavy downpour. Dad wanted to see the museum devoted to Manannán, so we went and learned the myth about the sea deity's special chalice, which broke anytime someone told three lies over it.

"Well, we'd be buggered, wouldn't we?" Dad joked.

I squinted and smiled, but the longer my father kept me from other children, the more I began to confuse his crimes for mine. I scurried through the streets like a thief, staring forlornly at the girls who wore school uniforms or rode bicycles together with playing cards in the spokes.

"Go on. Join in," Dad urged one afternoon when he caught me eyeing a group of children. They were painting turnips as part of something called *Hop tu naa* (I'd be eleven years old and on the Isle another year before I realized the Manx word meant "Halloween").

I felt my cheeks go scarlet. I shook my head, a hopeless case.

"What's wrong?"

"I'm not like them."

"Why not?"

In no particular order:

1. Lack of money.
2. Lack of school.
3. Lack of mother.

The trifecta obsessed me. My thoughts were an endless loop of: *Cash, school, mother.*

"Come on, tell me," Dad pressed. He was in high spirits, wearing the musky smell of lunchtime beers, so it seemed safe to confide my grievances.

"Is that all?" He chuckled. "Well, I think we can resolve those easily, don't you?"

I nodded and beamed, thinking now, finally, we'd return to Ireland.

"Well, what are we waiting for?" Dad asked, stubbing out his ciggie. "Let's make a move."

I was so busy dreaming of Wexford strawberries, Wicklow lamb, and Gaeilge signposts that it almost didn't register when I looked up and realized we'd walked inside Glenmaye Primary School. Dad leaned against the front desk and ran through his favorite monologue: he was "American" by birth; I was English (as was my "dead" mother); and we'd moved to the Isle for tax reasons (he reckoned this made us sound posh).

"I'll just need her birth certificate," the secretary said.

"We mailed it last week," Dad said with hundred-watt confidence.

"*Gogh*," the woman huffed, rifling through file cabinets. "I'm sorry. I just took over this office. It will turn up. I'm confident of that." She passed my father a sheet of paper. "Here's the address to the local school uniform shop. You'll want the green kilt, not the blue one. Because she's in the lower school."

"The blue kilt. Got it."

She laughed so hard her bosom wobbled. Then she reached out and "casually" touched my father on his arm. "I said, the *green*."

"Right. Sorry. Us single dads are hopeless. Write your number on the back, will you? Just in case I try to buy her the bronze cardigan."

In memory, all the girls at Glenmaye Primary merge into one composite Manx friend. She was blond in a green school cardi. Her cheeks were fat from her mother's cooking, and her hair was tidy because she had someone sober to plait it.

My Manx schoolmates thought me a "rare one," and not because of my "English" accent. (My efforts to Henry Higgins myself had left me fairly well Doolittled.) No, I was the token freak because Dad and I began to attend Peel Cathedral, and there were about as many Catholics on the Isle as there were sunny days.

After Margaid, my father realized it was easier to find self-sacrificing women in a place with an actual Messiah on the wall. Like most of Dad's schemes, it worked. Catholic Mass provided, well, *masses* of women who wanted to believe in something. You could even say that religion—which emphasized "belief" over rationality—groomed them for him. Once we began going to Mass, we never lacked for food or transportation again. The church women showered us in freezer meals and chauffeured Dad around like he was the duke of Edinburgh. They even organized a parish singles mixer for his sake, where Dad pulled a woman named Ninian. (Dad called her "Ninny" behind her back.)

They went on a few dates, alone at first, and then with me in tow. We went to a pub, and I drank cola whilst Dad wooed Ninny by pretending he already knew everything about her.

"I bet you like children," he said.

"I do. Especially yours." Ninny turned to me. "I'm so glad you could join us today." Then she turned to my father. "She's so grown-up. Such a little lady."

I chewed my crisps and looked at her out of the corners of my eyes.

"I bet you like drinking red wine on the beach," Dad said.

Ninny laughed and corrected him. "White, actually."

"And I bet you like handsome, blue-eyed American men. Now, I know I'm right on this one!"

"Ha-ha. You're right!"

"So I guess it's a plan. White wine, the beach, and guessing games with a blue-eyed American and his adorable daughter."

Then, when we got together at the seaside, Dad grasped Ninny around the waist: "If we're going to be exclusive, you should know . . . I have one rule."

"What is it?"

"Two rules, actually."

"*What?*" Ninny said with a girlishness she had too much height and too many crow's-feet to carry off. She was a "handsome" woman, by which I mostly mean tall. Her legs were like German architecture (Dad's description).

"Rule one, there will be as much kissing as possible."

Ninny complied, stooping slightly so she could nuzzle his ear.

I skimmed stones at a short distance and pretended not to listen.

"Secondly, we can't possibly move in together. But I'm flexible on rule two, if you must."

The reverse psychology worked a treat, and in no time we were moving into Ninny's pricey barn conversion in a hamlet called (brace for irony) Poortown.

It was ironic, obviously, because Ninny wasn't poor. Her divorce and subsequent alimony had left her with a house full of

’80s flash. She had multiple telephones, golfing equipment, and modern furniture with a white plastic finish. She even had a microwave, an unthinkable luxury, and every morning she used it to high-speed cook the baked potato she wrapped in aluminum and packed in my sack lunch. The meal felt like a betrayal of my mother’s ham and butter sandwiches. So every day, I shoved it in the back of my desk and left it to rot.

As I recall, my school reports from that time spoke a lot about my “unwillingness” to fit in and adapt. And there was probably some truth in that. Leaving Ireland had left me with a strangeness I hadn’t learned how to conceal. Rather than trying, I played up the aberration, pretending to be the scary, starey ginger girl who was lonely by choice. I cultivated eccentricities like prominently reading my father’s poetry books and scorching the plastic backings of the bus seats with a lighter. I wore my hair greasy and my school cardigan tight enough to advertise what I hadn’t eaten that day.

Because food was the thing that made me most homesick for my mother, I subsisted on Wrigley chewing gum and air. The hungrier I got, the more amnesiac I became—the more my undernourished brain cannibalized itself. I couldn’t remember the sound of Mam’s voice, or even what she’d given me for my last birthday. And given all that, it seemed entirely possible that I’d wake up one morning and forget how to contact her if I dared.

So one day, I lifted up the top of my school desk and used my maths compass to carve my old phone number into the underside. I felt better once the digits were there, staring back at me in cold, institutional oak. My history no longer felt like a moonbeam. It had staying power and shape.

The phone had a different tone when it rang that evening. Rationally, I know that’s not possible, but I swear to God I heard it, and in a flash of crystal-clear omniscience, thought: *That’s my teacher.*

My father tolerated authority figures with the bemused face he made at the seafront, watching people clean up after their dogs.

Listening to my teacher, he seemed entertained by my infraction, not angry. At least he did until he asked: "Just curious, what was this number? The one she scratched into her trash-filled desk?"

There was a long silence—presumably my teacher read the digits aloud—and the pantomime of concern fell from his face in a sheet. Shortly after, he dropped the phone and asked me to join him upstairs, away from Ninny's punchable look of concern.

He closed the door to my bedroom and I expected his belt. But instead, he sat down on the bed and rested one elbow on his knee. All the anger had left him. And I could see him being careful, very careful, with me.

"You've been such a good girl since we left Margie's. I know the past year hasn't been easy." He bid me to come curl up under his arm.

His shape had changed so much in the time we'd been on the Isle. He was doughier in the face. But putting my cheek to his chest, the rest of him felt all bone and gristle. A new fear lodged itself in me: What if I looked different as well? I resolved then and there to dig in my heels and stay *me*-enough for my mother to recognize me when I returned.

"You've become an English girl right before my eyes," Dad went on. "You've gone at it wholehearted. You've done me proud. And I didn't want to ruin it by discussing your mam. But I have to now. Because you went and 'vandalized' your desk, in the words of your teacher."

I wanted to say something, but the words were stuck in my throat.

"You can't ring her," he told me. "She's gone."

My first thought: *Gone where?* If Mam had moved, I wouldn't know how to reach her. Unless it was possible to find an Irish phonebook on the Isle—

Time skipped like a record, and I had no idea how many minutes of dialogue were lost. A tingle of fear overcame me. My father looked like a stranger.

"Are you following?" he said, waving his hand in front of my face. "Your mother's dead."

I was sick to my stomach. Beneath my school cardi, my skin prickled with sweat.

"How?" I managed to ask.

He looked at me baffled, overcome with emotion. "She took her own life. Drowned herself. Do you understand?"

"Where? When?"

He paused, like he knew the details would hurt me: "Waterford. A few weeks ago."

It smacked of blame: the site of so many family holidays. Suddenly, I wished Ninny owned a piano. I would have pounded out a song that turned everything else to white noise.

"How do you know?" I asked, shivering all over.

"You remember James? We've kept in touch."

I remembered James. He was the thickest and dodgiest of Dad's builder mates. Mam despised him. But Dad had a sort of anthropological devotion to him—like Jane Goodall loving chimps without ever confusing herself for one. It would have broken Mam's heart that bit extra, having James tell us the news of her death.

"We'll have to go back for her funeral."

"It's already happened."

"No."

"Yes. I'm sorry, love. It was last Saturday. But James said it was everything she would have wanted. There were vases of yellow archangel. And the priest read that Psalm she liked. You know, the one that starts 'Lead me into your truth and teach me?' "

I wriggled out from under Dad's arm and did a foxhole-crawl to the head of my bed. I closed my eyes to a thick wave of nausea and disbelief. I didn't sleep so much as fall off into a sort of seasick, vegetative state: eyes closed to the heaving world around me.

Sleep couldn't burn off my deep-seated guilt. I woke in the same spot the next morning to find a gift from Ninny on my pillow. It was a prayer card. The illustration showed a saint in a blue hijab with the stunned, stunted face of a child: Mariana, the patron saint of lost parents.

That did it.

I stared at the orphaned saint, and realized it was too late to confess my sins. I hadn't just abandoned my mother once—the day of the funfair. I deserted her every day that I saw a policeman and didn't flag him down or every time I kneeled in the confessional and claimed my biggest sin was taking the Lord's name in vain. My mam's death was my penance, and the punishment fit the crime. Having left my mother, I deserved to lose her.

TRACEY BUELLER

There are high places
that don't invite us,
sharp shapes, glacier-
scraped faces, whole
ranges whose given names
slip off . . .

—Kay Ryan, "No Names"

CHAPTER EIGHT

In the old days, at the Catskill house, my sleeping children usually had spit bubbles on their lips and the air in their shared bedroom was thick with the smell of sweat and sodden nappies. But in Melanie's guest cottage, where the central air con fanned its refrigerated air, they looked like Baroque cherubs on a down comforter cloud.

And it wasn't only the children who were more relaxed at the Ashworths'. Aside from fielding Randy's phone calls (Fitz was usually too antsy to speak long and, as always, Randy was too preoccupied to really listen), I was relieved from almost all of my daily concerns. I didn't need to clean, because Janisa did it, nor cook, as Melanie constantly texted to ask if we'd like to join her and Gabby at the main house for kale pizza or quinoa "macaroni." In Woodstock, I could laugh, joke, and, best of all, genuinely listen to the children. Together, we explored the property, chased frogs through the mud, and picked wild blueberries, which were pie-hot from the sun. We played with toys that didn't belong to us. We read the Ashworths' books, lathered ourselves in their organic soaps, and watched their two hundred high-def TV channels.

Which is not to say Melanie wasn't fine company as well. In satiric moods, when she was poking fun at the part-time hippies, she could even be good for a laugh. Her energy awed me, especially when she was out in the back garden doing the yoga she was too spry and bouncy for, bounding in and out of Warrior Two like an American cheerleader. And I applauded her defiant glamour: the way she spent a full hour on her hair in a community where other upper-class women eschewed shaving and smelled of ghee.

For the better part of July, I made an advanced study of her during evening swims in her private swimming hole, after the kids were in bed, when we would wade into Saw Kill River with wineglasses held aloft.

Melanie was an awkward swimmer and she complained often about the racing current, having grown up in suburban YMCAs (big, pearly lane dividers and a lifeguard at her elbow). She tended to skinny-dip near the shore in calmer waters. She'd float on a foam noodle, putting the "bosom" in bosom friend, while I averted my eyes and let her chat my ear off. I listened attentively while she described her childhood summers at the Jersey Shore. I clutched my heart when she confided in whispered tones about being raped by her twentysomething boyfriend, despite the fact that she'd told him she didn't feel ready for sex. She told me. She told me. About how devastated she was when her mother died. About all the things she played "modest" about when she was sober.

"I loove you," she'd say at the close of each confession, always in that nasal drawl that set my teeth on edge.

I reciprocated as best I knew how. After all, the obsessive study I made of her *was* a kind of love. After she finished with the latest issue of *O Magazine*, I discreetly snatched it up, reading about the "best self" that she strived for. I studied Melanie's playlists, treating them like keys to her subconscious. And frighteningly, in between all the ladies'-night anthems, I found multiple tunes about deception: Katy Perry in the dark, falling hard with an open heart, and Taylor Swift chirping, "How strange that I don't know you at all."

"My wedding was off the hook," she blustered during one of our evening wades, as a pink sunset formed a mushroom cloud behind her.

"Off the hook?!" I asked, as if the only definition I knew meant *escaping incrimination*. Like Randy, Melanie liked explaining American idioms to me. It added to the idea that I was a clueless immigrant without the tools or the daring to deceive her.

"I *mean*, it was the best wedding I've ever been to. That sounds terrible, I know. Really competitive and shallow. But three of my friends got married the same year, and I couldn't help looking at their food and flowers and thinking, *Ours was nicer.*"

Conversations with Melanie often centered on "stuff." Thus, she began describing her fish-bowl centerpieces and fourteen-grand wedding dress, boring me to the point where I found myself studying the sandstone cliff that stood farther upriver, on the opposite shore.

"Well, weddings drag on," I said. "One has to think about *something.*"

She was standing in waist-high water, trying to use Gabby's kickboard as a cocktail tray. "What was *your* wedding like? I was on pins and needles at mine, waiting for it all to fall apart. Victor seemed too good to be true."

"How's that?" I asked.

"Well, Vic was just sooo attentive, you know? And full of these grand gestures. Granted, this was back before he dropped me like a bad habit and moved to London. Which is a grand gesture in a way. Haa-aah. Were you just deliriously happy on your wedding day?"

"Our wedding was lovely," I said, still eyeing a massive rock ledge.

In truth, I had been in a cold panic on my "wedding day," going through the motions of a small, no-frills ceremony having never told Randy that I was still married to the incarcerated Oz. Randy, battling cold feet, had entrusted all the legal proceedings to me, and I kept waiting for him to turn around and ask the more serious questions about the marriage application I'd nagged him to fill in but never returned to the town clerk.

"We had the ceremony at Poet's Walk in Rhinebeck. Randy's work colleague officiated. Fitz was the ring bearer."

I could still remember Randy, quaking with nerves, saying:

Gracie, you gave me family when I needed it most. Your charisma moves me, your mind challenges me, and your honesty delights me. Ha.

To my great relief, after we exchanged rings, Randy felt so stunned by the commitment he'd just made that he'd poured a jeroboam of Champagne down his throat and danced the night away at Gigi Trattoria, which we'd rented out for the reception.

"Was your mother there?" Melanie asked. "Did your father give you away?"

"Have you ever jumped off that?" I asked, gesturing to the cliff face.

"Jumped into the *water*? Are you crazy?"

"How high is it? Twenty feet, you reckon? Maybe twenty-five?"

"Sure. I guess."

"I'm going to try a cliff jump."

My father had made me an adrenaline junkie. He always did his best parenting at funfairs and water parks—the sort of places that made one's pulse scream with excitement and fear.

Oz, as well, had fancied risky fun. That was one of the main reasons why we'd got on so well. As newlyweds, we'd squatted in empty London flats. Later, when we had money, we bungee jumped off London Bridge. We brought a few intrepid "clients" skydiving in Istanbul.

"Nooo!" Melanie squealed, loving it. "It's too high!"

"Height doesn't accelerate your fall. Gravity actually has less pull at higher elevations."

"Really?"

"Didn't you take physics at uni?"

She shook her head. She'd only done two years at Rutgers.

"Relax," I added, joking. "I won't sue you if I break a rib."

She stuck her tongue out. "It's not my land up there anyway. The property line ends mid-river."

"Well, I won't sue your neighbor either. I'll make certain it's safe." I told her I'd done far bigger dives off the Turquoise Coast, which was true.

The river was deep, but when I reached the far side, I still swam down to the bottom to make certain I wouldn't snap my neck in the dive. The cold depth seemed more than sufficient, so I heaved myself up the nearest boulder and scrambled up a steep, wooded incline that made my calves ache.

The water looked calmer from that height, rippling with lattice-shaped waves. Downstream, Melanie was on the opposite shore, melodramatically covering her eyes with one forearm.

"I can't look! Oh, Tracey! Please don't!"

But I was already making my gleeful descent. My legs were straight, toes pointed, but as I neared the surface, I looked down—a rookie error. Hitting liquid, I felt my head snap back. The impact brought a white flash to my vision. After what felt like a long submersion, I burst to the surface, exhilarated and terrified, rubbing my neck.

"Oh my God! Oh my God! Are you OK?" Melanie called.

"That was brilliant!" I called back. "You should try it!"

I was swimming ashore for an encore dive when I stumbled into a large submerged rock. It was only a few feet from my splash-landing. *I might have hit it*, I thought, feeling a second, stronger rush of adrenaline. If I had done, I might have had to face a hospital, where a nurse would have denied me treatment (if I withheld my photo ID). Or (if I didn't) Melanie would have found out my name wasn't Tracey.

My head rang at the thought. I had a moment's paranoia. "Did you know this rock was here?" I called.

But Melanie, in a drunken tizz, couldn't hear me. Flapping about in shallow waters, she shouted back, "Oh my God! I could *never*! I was scared to death just watching you!"

I swam toward her, but when I arrived downstream at the opposite shore, it was difficult to get a word in edgewise. Melanie was still blathering on, saying: "You're so brave! If you could have seen yourself!"

Short on breath, I decided to drop it. There was nothing to

gain by showing her how shaken I was. Far better if she saw Tracey as the sort of powerful woman who executed everything with confidence and ease.

"It looked like you were levitating!" Melanie continued in a gush of awe. "Or doing yoga! Mountain Pose! You were so graceful!"

"Oh yeah," I said, dripping sarcasm as I wrung out my hair. "Miss *Grace*, all right. That's me."

Evening swims were one of my more pleasurable obligations as Melanie's houseguest. There were plenty of others I came to dread, including applying to the Broadly Experienced Foreign Architect Program, which was meant to certify me as a US architect, based on my "foreign qualifications."

"Everyone says it's easy," Melanie would say, forcing a casual look into her hard, dark eyes. "No pressure, of course. If NCARB denies your application, I'll just find an engineer to apply for the building permit."

There wasn't any indication—aside from Melanie's grating persistence about BEFAP—that she doubted my CV or online portfolio.

On the contrary, she insisted that she had only looked up the eligibility requirements for my betterment: "Our project might give you the design bug! If you get certified in the US, you'll be all ready for the next job!"

She even offered to cover the $5,000 dossier-review fee with the same spirit of generosity she had when she offered us a place to stay: "*Please*, Tracey. Let me do this for you. It's not charity. I'm just one woman helping another overcome—what do you always call it?—'maternal-leave career death'? And weren't you *just* saying how much better you'd feel if you and Randy had two incomes?"

True, I *had* confessed as much, but only because I wondered if she'd offer me a small cash loan that I could add to my escape fund.

I considered asking Melanie to pay the application fee directly to me, but decided it was too risky. As things stood, I was going to accept a five-grand deposit for the extension. Taking another five on top of it was too risky. Oz never accepted large lump sums unless he planned to change aliases and leave town the next day.

So instead, I made an unhurried production of filling out the certification forms every morning at the breakfast table. Then, when Melanie was in an especially empathetic mood, I broke the news that I wasn't eligible.

"Oh my God, Mel. How did I miss this? I don't meet the requirements. I don't believe it."

"Which one?" she asked, peering over my shoulder, looking directly at the clause that said I ought to have "good character, verified by employers."

"This one. Over here. It says I ought to have practiced architecture for eight years. I've only done six."

"Oh no! Well, don't let it get you too down. There's gotta be another way. You're a professional. You're experienced." Her upspeak sounded questioning.

"I just wish I hadn't wasted all this time. I might have been working on the site data for our project instead."

Melanie looked despondent, reading the guidelines through over and over. "This is all my fault."

"No . . . ," I said, purposely unconvincing.

CHAPTER NINE

We left for the mainland when I was twelve. My father never told me why. Possibly, he got into deep trouble with the church, or Ninny or my school.

Or maybe the Isle was just too wholesome and wee. It didn't have enough competitive drinkers. It was short on shopgirls with American-fantasy fetishes. My father's empty-promise lifestyle had a magical ability to shrink vast spaces to the size of port-a-loos. And in time, we had to avoid more and more people and places, until we were washing out our pants in the bath because we might see one of Dad's exes on the way to the launderette.

In the five years that followed, we ricocheted from one built-up area of the nation to the next. The cities changed, but the faded industrial landscapes didn't.

I was nearly grown by the time I saw the Britain of landscape paintings. There were no dappled, chocolate-box villages. No plump, rustic sheep. In place of country lanes, I got the forgotten side streets of Manchester, Huddersfield, and Leeds. My Britain smelled of rotten eggs and sounded of bin bags fluttering in the wind. My scenery was graffiti and wet cement. My neighbors were teen mothers, using car bonnets as changing tables, and drunks on a wall (sometimes my father included) singing "Fly Me to the Moon" through a traffic cone.

Up north, people distrusted the Received Pronunciation I'd worked hard to learn. My schoolmates, taking the piss, called me Lady Ponsonby.

Unable to master the region's blurred vowels, I went temporarily mute (or chewed off my tongue as a preventative measure). This selective mutism concerned my teachers. In Trafford, I was even sent to the educational psychologist and asked to point out if and where I'd been touched on a doll.

But I generally changed schools before the six-month mark, around the time my teachers would refer me to the special education needs coordinator. Typically, this event coincided with the head office taking issue with my lack of paperwork (Dad always claimed to be in the process of replacing originals that were lost in a fire).

Then, one night in Liverpool, Dad got to talking to a man during a pub quiz. Both men insisted (rightly) that *North* Yorkshire is the largest county in England, and ended up in a blazing row with their teammates, who disagreed. The losing answer (Yorkshire) went on the team sheet, after which my dad and his new mate set to work getting pissed and sabotaging the others. They couldn't believe how much they had in common. Both hated the way the media made it out like every dead child was some sort of saintly prodigy. Both thought Tony Blair was a smug prick. And neither of them was a nationalized citizen.

In between spitting on the floor, Dad's new friend mentioned he knew someone who sold forged birth certificates and passports, and he'd be happy to "facilitate" a meeting.

If memory serves, the high-quality documents cost £2,000 and came with advice to avoid airports and excess luggage. The middleman who sold them also gave us this mystifying guarantee: "If, by bad luck, you get caught at border control, we'll give you the next ones free of charge."

Having new passports meant we also had new names.

"Don't look at me like that," my father said. "Like W. C. Fields said, 'It doesn't matter what they call you, it's what you answer to.' You think I'm taking the name your mother gave you? Don't you? That's what this is really about. But this here passport is a gift. It's the freedom to travel beyond the confines of where you've come from. Instead of acting like a little mare, you could say thank you—"

Dad's freedom speech was bollocks in the end. He didn't dare test our new passports by leaving the country. But we did move south, because Dad finally had an ID that could stand up to the more competitive rental property market. Plus, he said "money floods to London," implying there'd be better "employment" for him there, by which, of course, he meant posher victims.

We arrived in the capital the year rogue trader Nick Leeson brought down Barings Bank. It was the same year the Young British Artists, exhibiting rectums and cocks, brought *Brilliant!* to America and the queen wrote to the Prince and Princess of Wales, advising them to divorce as soon as possible. The unconventional had become ordinary, and the cobbled streets heaved with aggressive vitality. Blur was performing "The Universal" on a rooftop above the roiling hellscape of Oxford Street. Angry youth were stabbing a teacher to death outside of St. George's School. And forgive me, but I started to see my life's troubles from a different perspective.

I was seventeen. My mother was gone, as was the name I'd been born with.

I remember sitting in our barely inhabitable bedsit and reading Bridget Jones's first *Independent* column—"I shall disgust myself with my own greed by smoking forty cigarettes"—and thinking, *How lovely, to journal without fear of criminal repercussion. What a privilege, to say "myself" and feel ownership of the word.* Whoever *my* self was, I'd succeeded her. And not wanting to keep on as a despondent ghost, rattling my chains in life's attic, I decided instead to rise up and walk through walls.

I was beginning to appreciate my father's less-than-legal approach. It expedited things. In Dad's words, lies might be more difficult to swallow than the truth, but they were almost always more digestible. Life was messy. Lies simplified.

During a time when most teenagers were flashing their parents two fingers and hitchhiking 'round the M25 looking for raves in fields, I did the opposite. I stuck close by my father, studying the methods of his lost-boy madness.

Looks didn't factor into who my father pulled. I watched him turn down, with decisiveness that bordered on rudery, women with bouncy-castle chests and no bad angles. Dad chatted up all women, but he applied extra effort to the ones with lowered chins and rounded shoulders, their hands skittering between the tables and their laps.

In this order, he looked for: women who spoke poorly of themselves; women who rejected compliments or favors; and women who were too polite to object when he intentionally brought them the wrong drink. And if he found one who drew all her self-worth from her exterior—if she looked like she'd spent the better part of an hour tormenting her hair and varnishing her nails to match her cardigan—then we'd be moving our luggage into her flat within the week and Dad would be playing her handyman butler.

His script was formulaic, but engrossing:

First, he'd nick a piece of her backstory and use it to forge some connection with her. If she was divorced, so was he. If she'd survived a bout of lymphoma, him too. If she'd gone to a prestigious law school, he'd attended its rival and dropped out.

What a coincidence! she'd trill. They all did.

Next, in his brilliantly persuasive way, he'd share some "personal" or "private" information. Something he didn't tell just anyone, only people he valued and trusted. Sometimes it was a small admission: he was adopted, or devastated after the death of my mother, or bored to death with some fictional desk job that paid him thirty-five quid an hour. Then, while she was still struck dumb by his emotional "honesty," he'd swear her to secrecy.

On its own, the guilty secret didn't matter for much. But if a woman kept it, she was as good as snared.

The first time I tried my father's method, my motivation was pure loneliness. I hadn't had a real friend since Cleary. I kept to myself because Dad's fear of exposure was catching. The closer people got, the more likely they were to guess the crimes I played accomplice to.

Which isn't to say I was bullied or sniped at. The head girl wasn't above having a laugh with me in the lunch line. And I wasn't chosen dead last for sports teams (even if the captain struggled to remember my name). In my estimation, the problem was this: I was so skilled at mimicking the people around me that I'd become entirely forgettable. No matter my small social triumphs, I walked the corridors in a cloak of anonymity, speaking in my Nowhereshire accent.

Deciding I needed a friend, badly, I marked Seema because she had the sad, fixed expression of a bedside dolly and that warped posture that always worked so well for Dad.

Better still, there was no competition. Seema's only friend in the world was a fat paperback, *QBasic by Example,* which she pored over the way normal girls read magazines like *Sky* and *The Face.*

After searching every bookstore in South London, I found *QBasic by Example* at Foyles and nicked it. Shoplifting was not generally my cup of tea. In fact, I avoided any criminal activities that might cause someone to ask me for ID. But I'd failed to find the book at the library and my father didn't hold on to money long enough to lend it.

"May I ask you something?" I asked Seema at lunch the next day. "Don't look so worried. I don't want your kidney. It's a *programming* question."

"All right." Her eyes were enormous behind her purple spectacles.

I sat down and delivered the speech I'd rehearsed all morning. "Well, having worked out how plus signs perform concatenation, I reckoned minus signs extract substrings—"

"You know Basic?" she asked with skepticism I hadn't planned for.

"*Know* is an overstatement. Just mucking about, really."

"I thought the same when I started." She seemed to be warming to the idea that we shared an obscure interest. "But there's special string-handling functions to extract."

The air went thin with anticipation. Was this the same sense of triumph my father got when a woman gave him her phone number?

As we spoke, I learned Seema's father was the one who'd taught her QBasic. Together, they had written a game for their MS-DOS 3. Then, on her own, Seema had modified two games—Nibbles and Gorilla—and taught herself more advanced programming in the process.

As she told me all this, it wasn't a challenge to act interested. Other humans had become an odd, alien race in all those years I'd kept myself separate from them—not wanting them to come to our flat or pry into my past. Sitting opposite Seema in the lunchroom, I was more plugged into a teenage mind-set than I had ever been. I smelled the baked beans on her breath. I studied the constellations of acne on her cheeks. And yet, I felt painfully separate from her and everything she represented. I felt, sadly, like a method actor studying a part.

At peak pain this caused me, I leaned in and said, "Seema, if I tell you something, do you promise not to go blabbing?"

Over the next year I would practice programming with and *on* Seema.

She was the baby of the family—a late-in-life girl. Her two brothers were already grown and married. And her graying mother tolerated our computer-speak with a kind of thin-lipped malevolence, serving us Bhujia toast with a look that said she wished we were watching the latest Amir Khan film instead.

Seema's flat smelled of rose petals and her father's Majmua 96 Attar. Her dead granny stared at me from a picture frame wreathed in plastic garland. And after I'd helped Seema with her chores, the two of us were drawn to the beacon of the PC, where my clever friend, stern and soft-spoken, taught me functions.

"You can replace LEFT$ and RIGHT$ with a call to MID$," she'd say, watching over my shoulder.

My interest in programming didn't come close to Seema's blinkered zeal. She had little else to do. Premarital dating was off the table and her parents wouldn't even let her go to the newsagent alone. Were it not for school, she would have sat there, day and night, writing code to a new game of her own design, while her muscles and people skills atrophied.

Personally, I didn't see coding's appeal until the day she explained to me, in terms that any five-year-old could understand, that a computer couldn't do anything on its own.

"It needs a person there," Seema said. "To give it commands."

"Debug yourself," I joked, aiming a finger at the screen.

We'd been at it so long my brain had stalled in angry befuddlement. I was kicking off about how tedious and infuriating it was, saying I wanted to chuck her precious computer into the Thames.

"It's just logic," she said. "We're only asking ourselves, is this true? And if so, how do we use that knowledge to make it do what we want?"

And in a lightning bolt, I understood. It was the same thing I'd been doing with Seema herself. I'd been lightly emulating my dad, trying to find the best way to exert some influence over her. Faced with another Friday night of object-code files, I tried to calculate whether she'd agree to the school dance if I complimented her ("You'd look so lovely in this dress!") or took the piss ("We can resume our posts as resident saddos tomorrow").

It wasn't that I programmed Seema so much as she programmed

me. Every time she bristled or submitted to something, I wrote it into my code for our next encounter.

Seema had some useful triggers. She lost her nerve if I stood too closely to her. And she'd do just about anything I asked if it meant avoiding an angry outburst or being called selfish.

But like most people, a sob story was the thing that turned her to putty in my hands.

That was where my fake confession came in. Aware of the irony—lying about a secret when I had loads that were true—I'd told Seema that I was depressed, even suicidal on occasion, on account of my old, girlhood love affair with the maths teacher at my previous school, who'd improved my failing marks in exchange for the sort of "favors" not even fit to print in the *Daily Mail.*

It was plausible enough, a teacher shagging his student. Plus, the archetypal youth fantasy gave Seema something she couldn't get anywhere else, especially given the way her mother (a more ambitious liar than me) had told her she could get pregnant by "cross-pollination" if she made eye contact with men on the bus.

The erotica I told Seema wouldn't have worked on anyone with an ounce of experience.

Even I had suffered from a lack of research. I'd lost my virginity at fifteen to the landlord's son in Dad's local—a chaffingly painful experience that had just about put me off sex completely. I'd yet to find a male friend I trusted half as much as Cleary. I particularly hated the way most boys went from tongue-tied reticence to clumsy boorishness with the help of vast quantities of alcohol.

And of course, there'd been no Internet as we know it for research. So mine were utterly implausible tales of the "spiritual, magical, electric connection" this fictional teacher had felt for me. I gave atrocious descriptions of our "hungry tongues . . ." "Trembling with desire and anticipation . . . ," I said. "He took my hand in his warm, pale one and gently positioned it down below . . ." " 'It seems quite difficult in the beginning, doesn't it?' he told me . . ." "The heat of his breath driving me insane . . ." "Delicious agony . . ." "Misbehaving for hours on the copy-room floor . . ." Seema would mouth-breathe as she listened, chin in her hands, eyes wild as she listened for the sound of her mother's keys in the door.

Seema liked her erotic monologues with a side of melodrama. She was used to Bollywood, with its suffering of innocents. But grief was easy enough to drum up. I told her my dream teacher had stayed with his "wife" and threatened to fail me if I told anyone what we'd done.

It wasn't easy to time my depressions. Typically, they had to strike when Seema's mum was out at the shops, when I shut myself in the bathroom, claiming to have a hold of her father's double-edged razor.

Really, I parked myself on her fuzzy lavatory cover, read fifty pages of *Siddhartha*, and didn't come out until Seema, sitting on the other side of the door, had exhausted every suicide-hotline cliché: *It will get better; if you can't live for yourself, live for the people you love; the way you feel is temporary, dying is forever.*

Eventually, I did feel better. Playing on Seema's emotions made me feel as though I had a little more charge over my own.

One afternoon, Seema had her face against the doorjamb, telling me I ought to convince my father to buy me a dog: "A lot of lonely people get pets. . . ."

"You don't understand," I said, cracking the door and presenting myself for her life-affirming hug. "I can't concentrate in maths anymore. Everything we do makes me think of him. Our mark this term is based on three exams, and I've already failed one."

Hopefully, Seema reminded me: "Two more chances."

"Wait," I said, fake spontaneous. "We have these graphic calculators . . ." Pretending they'd just popped into my head. "Before every exam, the teacher checks them for saved equations."

"Mine does the same," she said, not getting it.

"Well, then, you can tell me . . . I think the calculators run on a simple form of Basic."

She nodded and shrugged. Then, in a flash of understanding, her face changed with horror. I'd seen that expression on her once before, when we'd watched a cyclist get struck by a lorry.

"So," I said, "let's write a program that emulates the calculator's clear-memory function. Only, it won't wipe away anything."

CHAPTER TEN

It's official!" Melanie said one evening as I was prepping lamb for curry (it was Janisa's night off.) "Victor just booked his flight home for Labor Day!"

I smiled, as if facing a strong headwind, worrying about all the ways Victor might reassert himself as the head of the house.

"Oh, listen to me. I'm so sorry. I shouldn't gloat. What about Randy? Can he come visit soon?" She was about to leave for a summer meeting of the country day PTA, wearing skinny jeans and troweled-on makeup.

If I'd truly been on my game, I would have mentioned Randy more often: given Melanie false updates, relayed "his" funny stories and frustrations in "Britain," and pretended to find opportunities for them to meet. But I wasn't in peak form. I had been distracted by architect research, deciding on the best pay schedule for my contributions to "the extension project."

"It's difficult. Deals collapse more often in Britain. There's all this stupid chain malarkey. If he took time off now, four or five sales would fall through."

Thankfully, I'd convinced Randy to postpone his monthly visit for August. I'd moved most of our belongings to the Ashworths' house or sold them at the Kingston pawn shop that prominently advertised WE BUY GUNS, and it would have been impossible to stage the Catskill house so it looked occupied. Plus, I was concerned that the children would let our new location slip. (Fitz had told Randy about "sleepovers" in their phone conversations, but I'd been able to make out like these were the episodic sort—one Friday night a week, with a group of boys and some mum friend dishing out popcorn.)

We had talked a bit about the status of the foreclosure—the bank had recorded a "lis pendens" with the court and served Randy with a summons and complaint—and then I'd talked in metaphors, substituting women for states. I told him I didn't blame him for loving "Florida." "Florida" was sexy and cool. Florida made him happy in ways "New York" couldn't. I gave him a free pass to stay where he was until September, sidestepping his obligations to "the house."

His shaky voice had suggested my double meaning got through. "Thank you, Gracie. I've felt so selfish and immature. Like such a bad man. I'm going through something—"

"Coming home to 'Catskill' is the selfish thing," I'd said. "Plane fare is a big expense and we're meant to be saving money. Besides, if you're not happy, the children won't be either. And you're your happiest and most productive in 'Florida.' " ("In" up to your bollocks, that is.)

"Can't he ask someone to service his clients while he's away?" Melanie asked. "An assistant or something?"

"Plus, we're really quite skint. We agreed we can't afford the airfare right now."

She tapped her car keys on the counter, considering that. "Well, I'll be paying you the first deposit for our project soon. Victor really thinks we should draw up a contract first."

"I'm happy to draw up a letter of intent. I've said that from the start."

"Victor thinks it ought to be a real contract."

My stomach dropped. "That's what a letter of intent *is.* A contract. It's all there. Proposed services. Terms and conditions."

"Victor compared it to a written handshake."

"Sorry. *What?* A 'written handshake'? That's illogical."

"He says a letter of intent doesn't provide enough legal coverage."

Legal coverage, meaning the ability to sue me.

I kept sawing through the lamb with a little too much violence.

"Are you quite certain Victor understands how this process works?"

"Maybe you two want to speak directly? By videochat?"

"No. It's fine. I'll give you a contract. Just expect it to delay the project. That's all. I'm up to my neck in work and child care. The children and I were just down at town hall, chatting about building permits with the code-enforcement officer. That's why dinner's late."

"I didn't *ask* you to watch the kids tonight, Tracey. You *offered*."

"Assertive Melanie" had a ring of hollow theatricalism.

"Very well, Mel. The town official thought the existing structure might be in violation of code. Does that make you happy? Is that what you'd like me to say? Ruddy hell, I've been trying to protect you from these daily fucking headaches because, nine times out of ten, it's wasted energy. It turns out all right in the end. But if you *want* the stress, by all means. You can bloody well have it. Let's see how *you* fare."

The corner of her mouth twitched, but she refused to back down. "Speaking of things that stress me out . . . Victor and I discussed it, and we don't want you driving the car anymore. It's a stupid risk, driving without a license. I'd think it would worry you too."

It was very well by me, really. The last time I drove the Lexus, I had a near heart attack when a toll collector informed me the front headlight was out. I'd spent the whole drive back to Woodstock hallucinating police lights in my rearview mirror.

At that moment, the girls came tearing into the room. Gabby was sobbing, holding a gluten-free biscuit. Kitty was stuck to her like a barnacle, clawing for the cookie.

Melanie forced them apart. "Kitty, listen to me. Stop! Everyone gets *one* cookie. That cookie belongs to *Gabby.* In this house, we don't take things that don't belong to us."

Kitty ran to the larder, wailing, "I want *my* house! And I want a cookie!" Then, beating on the pantry door in despair: "*Cookieeee!*" Each refrain was more earsplitting than the last.

I was tempted to give in, but Melanie stood firm: "You already ate one. It's not fair if you have more than anyone else."

Melanie, talking equal distribution of wealth. That was a laugh.

Kitty scratched at the doorframe. "My dad *always* gives me a cookie!"

I tried to pick her up, but she was doughy and defiant, melting onto the floor.

Melanie ignored the tantrum and gave me a beseeching look. "Victor says you should have applied for a driver's license ages ago anyway. If you're a permanent resident, you're required by law to apply for a Social Security card *and*, within thirty days of moving here, a state-issued driver's license."

I turned to Kit. "Would you like some crushed ice?"

To Kitty, ice was a close relative of ice cream.

"OK," she sighed, sitting up and accepting the raw deal.

After Kitty was calm, and the girls had flittered back to the living room, Melanie came at me again. She just wouldn't let the issue about the car drop.

"I'm not trying to be a pain. I'm just setting some boundaries here."

I wiped my hands on Mel's I KISS BETTER THAN I COOK apron, and pulled out a kitchen stool. Then, I looked deeply into her eyes, waiting for what my old acting professors used to call a "living cue." I needed some real connection, a sign that she was prepared to hear me out.

"What is it?" she asked finally. She reached out and touched my wrist, avoiding the mess of ice and lamb's blood on the counter.

"It's over."

"What's over?"

"My marriage." Honesty rarely strengthens a friendship, but I needed Melanie to drop her defenses. "That's why I'm behind on our project. It's also the reason I've been avoiding Randy. I haven't gone to the DMV because I don't know what name I'd even put on a license: my maiden name or Bueller."

"Oh my god, Tracey." Her body language hadn't softened, but the angry strain (or, as she put it, the *not*-angry strain) had left her voice. She didn't seem to notice it was the same distraction technique I had used moments earlier with Kitty and the ice.

"I don't know why I've put off telling you."

Real tears welled up in my eyes, and I felt a little like I was breaking character.

"You're *sure*?" Melanie's voice, for the sake of my kids, was a whisper.

"I read his messages," I said, accepting a hug.

She had the same panicked expression she always wore when she had to comfort me instead of vice versa. "Who is she?"

"Some cheap woman he fucks, then sends giggly messages to on social media. It's my fault."

"Do *not* blame yourself. Fidelity is so much harder with the Internet. Not to excuse what he did—"

"If only I'd made more time, been more invested. I didn't want to think the distance was a challenge . . ."

"Show me the ow."

"Show you where it hurts? It hurts bloody everywhere."

"Sorry, the OW. You know, the other woman's profile. Have you looked her up?"

I waved the phone away. "No. No—I can't bear to look at her."

"Were there any signs?" Melanie asked. "Did you suspect?"

"Well, he's always been surgically joined to his phone. But then, most Realtors are."

"Oh, honey," she crooned. "Tracey, I had no idea. If I did, I never would have jumped all over you about the car."

Switching topics: "Victor must hate me. He really must. He must be wondering, 'Who is this nutter you've taken in off the street?' "

"He doesn't. Not at *all.* And he thinks it's a great idea to pay you in lump sums at different stages."

It wasn't my idea. That was the pay structure back when Oz and I were selling holiday flats that didn't belong to us. There'd been a 15,000 lira deposit. Then, 30 percent when our clients signed the Turkish contract (the British "translator" we recommended also worked for us). Clients paid another 30 when "the foundations were complete" and an additional 30 when "the roof went on." I sent them links to a live video feed of another company's building site. Until it came time to hand over the keys, no one ever realized we didn't own the condos we claimed to represent.

"Oh, good," I said, sniffling. "So, you'll give me ten percent when we have a signed contract. Another fifteen when we have the sketches."

It pained me to mention the sketches. I'd never bothered with drawings the last time I played the architect. Back in London, Oz had provided floor plans, square footage, and all the details he'd got when he'd met with the developer he'd gone on to impersonate. By comparison, I didn't have anything to give Melanie. I planned to take her first payment and leave town before the "project" entered its "next" stage.

"Victor was really impressed by your quote," Mel said.

Appealing to the Ashworths' greed, I had quoted them $20,000 less than the cheapest competitor.

I kept quiet, still wiping tears. Having given myself permission to cry, I found it difficult to stop.

Melanie noticed, and reached for a tissue, dabbing my eyes: "You've spent so much time analyzing our requirements, dealing with the permits. I *know* you have. I didn't mean to suggest you've been slacking."

"Thank you." I reached for a napkin and noticed an old-fashioned flip phone. As I was picking it up, Melanie said, "Ugh. I bought that for Gabby so she can take it to school in the fall."

"Great," I said. "Now Fitz will want one too."

"How have you managed to work on the project at all with all this going on? Could you ever forgive him?"

I shook my head. "Never."

Melanie momentarily turned away, her eyes welling up. "Yeah. I could see where it would be impossible to trust him after this. Victor has this saying. He likes to tell Gabby: never trust someone who lies and never lie to someone who trusts you."

CHAPTER ELEVEN

Custody dramas stir up a lot of strong emotions: anger, possessiveness, insecurity, fear. And I experienced all of them when Abigail Wheeler returned from Cape Cod.

The children and I arrived at the main house one morning to find Melanie and Abigail in the kitchen. They were fresh from dropping off their girls at the day camp my children were priced out of—the one that was the feeder for the day school that was the fast track to the only kind of university that mattered.

Moments before I announced myself, I saw Melanie leaning against the kitchen counter, talking in hushed, conspiring tones to a tall woman in khaki shorts and a pair of rubber hiking sandals.

"Good morning!" I said brightly, pulling the screen door aside.

Both women jumped a little. Abigail turned to face me with a look of residual disapproval, left over from whatever she and Mel had been discussing.

"Oh, hi!" Melanie said, pretending I hadn't interrupted them in the midst of something heavy. "Abigail, this is Tracey—the friend who's staying out back."

Abigail gave me a brisk "hey," then launched in on the kind of esoteric school conversation that left me standing there like a gooseberry. "Did I tell you they're looking for someone to redesign the PTA website?"

"It needs it," Melanie said, going on to complain about how difficult it was to find the online staff directory.

Too late, I realized Fitz's ears had pricked at a familiar word. His face flooded with enthusiasm. "Mummy! You—*You* make websites!"

He was beaming, full of pride at his contribution to an adult conversation.

I fought the urge to give Fitz a look that said he'd dropped us in it. Instead, I smiled and hoisted him up into the kind of monkey hug he was getting too big for. "You little darling," I said. "You mean your mummy *has* a website. I paid someone else to make it for me."

Fitz's eyes narrowed in disagreement, but he accepted my kiss.

As quickly as I could, I redirected him and Kitty to the playroom, where the Ashworths had a massive set of magnetic blocks. For a few minutes, I sat with them and spoke loudly in architectural terms. *This is what's called a column. Kitty, why don't you find me another column, and we can put it under this arch?*

"Some of the kindergarten moms have formed a playgroup," Abigail was saying when I returned. She was a "handsome" woman with blokey mannerisms. For weeks, I had been expecting someone fashionable—a person who made my hostess feel glamorous by association. Now I was forced to consider other ways Abigail might bolster Mel's self-image.

"No!" Melanie gasped. "A playgroup? No one told *me*!"

"Well, believe me," Abigail said. "I didn't get an Evite either. So, there are these rules, right? You have to attend two playdates a month to quote *form close connections*, otherwise you're removed from the group."

"Isn't that a bit gestapo?" I joked, putting out feelers, trying to see whether Abigail was adaptive or funny. "Do you suppose they come for you in the middle of the night?"

"Ha," Melanie laughed.

Abigail gave me a watery smile. "You also have to come to a *trial* playgroup to see if you're a match before they let you in."

Melanie's hand inched toward her phone. "Do they have a Facebook group? Should I 'like' them?"

"Don't you *dare*," Abigail said. "I'd sooner start my own fucking playgroup. Only requirement: wine."

Melanie repeated her strangled-cat laugh, but she looked bereft.

"It's mad, isn't it?" I asked. "The way mothers can be so judgmental? It's a playdate, not a country club. I wonder if you have to submit a CV for your child too."

Abigail still hadn't looked at me directly. "I'd give them Isabelle's résumé all right. It would have three-inch bold font that says: *I'm a fucking toddler.*"

I just stared, stunned by her rudeness and profanity, the way she used "fucking" like a comma.

At the very least, I was beginning to understand my rival's power. Abigail gave Melanie the hot-and-cold treatment, and my hostess responded to it. How stupid I had been, playing Tracey on the luke side of warm.

"Mum?"

When I turned, Fitz was back.

"Can I have apple juice?" he asked.

"Of course," I said, eager to get a drink in his mouth before he could mention web design again.

As I was opening the fridge, Abigail turned to ask Melanie, "Have you seen that picture on the Internet of the juice box filled with spores? I guess it happens *all the time.* A little bit of air gets in and the *whole thing* ferments."

"What's 'ferments'?" Fitz asked, listening with big, worried eyes.

"Makes alcoholic," I said, handing him a juice box. Then, joking: "Good news for your playgroup. You won't even need the wine."

Abigail gave a low-effort smile. "You're funny, Tracey."

Straw between his teeth, Fitz said: "Gracie."

I patted his head. "Yes, that's what Abigail said. 'Tracey.' "

"She *said* Tracey, but your name is *Gracie.* Melanie says it wrong all the time."

Abigail raised her eyebrows. Melanie retracted her chin. Fitz must have felt the slow ripple of surprise because the very next thing, he'd dropped his juice box and the drink was squirting all over the engineered hardwood.

"Yes," I said a little breathlessly, bending to pick it up. "I'm Tracey."

Fitz shook his head. "*Gracie*."

The silence was loud and getting louder.

Pulling off reams of kitchen roll, I said: "Yes, I'm Tracey. With a *t*. Like 'tender' or 'toast.' Listen, go wait in the living room. I'll bring you a fresh juice box in a moment." Once it was just us mums, I made my well-rehearsed speech: Fitz mixed his *g*'s and his *t*'s; a speech-therapist friend said it's a stage; mostly, we tried to ignore it.

Only Abigail didn't appear to sympathize. She crossed her arms and asked: "So you're new to country day?"

"No," Melanie stepped in. "Tracey's son, Fitz, is going to the public elementary in the fall."

"So how do you two know each other?" Abigail asked.

"We met at The Odell, actually!" Melanie said.

Abigail dropped the carabiner that held her car keys on the counter with an emphatic thump. "Ugh, The Odell. I'm really pissed off with them at the moment. They're trying to shortchange us on guest passes. I brought my nieces yesterday and they told me we didn't have any left. I said, 'OK. Fine. Give me an itemized list of names and dates. Everyone I've brought and when.' "

My heart beat double-time. When I'd given the hotel clerk the name Tracey Bueller, I'd never imagined it would become a long-term identity.

"That's not right," Melanie said. "Did they give you the list?"

My throat dilated.

Abigail rolled her eyes. "They're working on it."

Then an idea struck. "So you and your husband live in Woodstock?" I asked casually.

Abigail's nod said, *Obviously.*

Prodding for a name: "And what does he—your husband—do for work?"

Melanie interrupted, derailing me: "Tracey's husband, Randy, is working in the UK too. Isn't that an insane coincidence?"

"Yeah," Abigail said. "Insane. My husband owns a zip-line tour company."

"Oh really? I think I've heard of it. What's his name—your husband?"

"Steve."

Steve Wheeler, I thought, committing it to memory.

"We should bring the older kids sometime," Melanie said. "It's eleven miles of zip lines through the Catskill Mountains."

"And rope-line bridges," Abigail added.

Melanie: "The liability insurance is crazy."

"Speaking of legal issues," Abigail said. "What's the latest with the lawsuit?"

Melanie cleared her throat. "We just filed."

"Filed what?" I asked.

"Melanie's taking the public school to court," Abigail said. "They didn't catch Gabby's auditory processing disorder. Which has really affected her prognosis."

"What does that mean? Auditory . . ."

"Processing disorder. It's difficult to explain," Melanie said. "The important thing is they were convinced it was a speech disorder."

"Which put her really behind on reading and numbers," Abigail said.

"So this is the *Woodstock* public school?" I asked. The same school she'd suggested Fitz attend?

"Just because we had bad luck there, doesn't mean you will—" Mel turned to Abigail for help.

"Yeah." Abigail shuffled her feet a bit. "It's a fine school."

Fine for other people.

At peak awkwardness, I excused myself, pretending not to care that my children didn't share their spawn's same fast track to progress.

I was carrying the hoover to the sliding-glass door when Melanie said, "Leave it, Tracey. Janisa will vacuum the cottage when she gets in. Speaking of, I've asked her to clean the last of my mother's things out of the closet. She started the other day, but then, she didn't want to disturb your things."

The sketches were the biggest threat to my Woodstock existence, but Janisa was a close second.

Twice, I had come home to find her foraging around the loft like a cat burglar. I assumed she was looking for proof of my "work." So I had been cluttering my work space in ways I hoped were convincing. I'd used Melanie's spare printer to print off reams of building codes. I'd scrawled big lists of contractors and daily crossed some out, writing illegible notes to myself in the margins. In time, I hoped to build some fake websites for the ones I planned to recommend to the Ashworths, and leg it from Woodstock before Melanie invited them to the house.

Back in the cottage, I went to work cleaning out the closets, looking for a new place to hide my dodgy-looking pile of cash. (I'd told Melanie I'd put her check in the bank.) Making certain it was all there, I counted it over again: $5,000 in slick, barely circulated twenties.

It had been a pain in the arse to get. I'd had to have "Tracey Bueller" sign the Ashworths' check over to "Gracie Mueller." Then at the check-cashing shop, I gave the clerk my dodgy green card. I went to Walmart immediately afterward and began the slow, conspicuous process of putting some of it onto the prepaid credit cards I'd bought with Michael Rondo's Chase Visa.

Looking at the remaining cash was an agony. It got me thinking I ought to just pack up and leave straightaway before Fitz unmasked me again.

I took out my phone and Googled: "How much money do I need to leave my marriage?"

The common consensus was $10,000 to $15,000. One sad little website even offered pathetic ways to save up:

1. Collect cans and turn them in for cash.
2. Take online surveys for cash.
3. Sell household items on eBay.
4. Ask neighbors if you can do odd jobs like weeding, washing windows, etc.
5. Use coupons to get free shampoo, toothpaste, and soap and store them in a box at a friend's house. That way you won't have to spend money on toiletries when you leave.

I had already filched loads of Mel's organic bath products. I was also in the habit of skimming off the odd tenner when she sent me to buy groceries in town. But it was nowhere near enough to begin life afresh, with no steady income or support.

If only I could draft up some sleek-looking sketches, I thought. *Then I could collect Melanie's second payment installment.*

Willing to take a gamble on technology, I fetched my computer, took out my prepaid credit card, and spent $100 on a month-long subscription to a computer program for architects. But it only took a few minutes before I realized the software was going to be a time-consuming nightmare to learn. It took me over an hour to sort out how to change the digital blueprint from "model" to "paper," and even longer to unbugger the command line when the open-box became unresponsive. So I took a break, remembered the problem of Abigail Wheeler's guest passes, activated the voice-changing app on my phone, and dialed.

"Good afternoon. Odell Resort and Spa."

I said hello with male authority and asked to speak to the membership department.

"Just a moment."

"Hello?"

"Yes, hello. My name is Steve Wheeler. I'm calling about my guest passes. I need to resolve an issue. It's delicate."

"No problem, Mr. Wheeler." There was a short pause. "My computer tells me you're out of guest passes. Would you like to add more to your account?"

"Yes. But I'd like to do it without my wife's knowledge if possible. Also—" I cleared my throat, indicating embarrassment. "The last person to use the guest passes was a friend named Tracey. I'd prefer not to trouble my wife with that transaction."

CHAPTER TWELVE

I kept working like a madwoman on the architecture software, hoping to produce a reasonable sketch by mid-August. And by "reasonable," I mean one that had enough schematic-looking design stuff to get paid.

I chose the deadline because that's when Mel planned to bring Gabriella to Newport, Rhode Island, for a visit with her grandparents, and in their absence it would be easy to pack up the cottage and slip away.

But the drafting software wasn't as intuitive as I hoped. The interface was clunky. The viewport was baffling. Maybe the real problem was: I didn't have any legitimate experience with drafting, so it was taking me twice as long to sort out the commands. You can't ask a program to do something unless you know what to ask. I considered outsourcing—hiring a real architect and plagiarizing his work—but I couldn't afford the expense because I'd lowballed the Ashworths in order to get the job.

Meanwhile, Melanie found more and more excuses to come down to the cottage. She thought I could use an espresso. She wanted to give Kitty some Stella McCartney dresses that Gabby had outgrown. And the most ridiculous excuse of all: she wanted to say sorry for all the noise the children were making outside—disrupting my work to apologize for "disrupting" it.

"Soo . . . ," she always asked, segueing into what she'd really come down to say.

Sometimes she was coy: "When do you think I'll be able to take a peek?"

Other times, she acted playfully "exasperated": "What are we gonna do about these sketches, huh? I want you to finish before school starts so we can have a girls' weekend in Cape May."

"I hear what you're saying, Mel. You're a fast thinker. I understand that. I'm a fast thinker too, and I don't want things to take longer than they take. But projects take time to develop. I imagine my buildings so completely. I unconsciously live in them. I thought I had it perfect when I went to bed last night, but then I woke up this morning and realized, 'Something's wrong. There's this corner that doesn't work.' That isn't slowness. That's the artistic process. It's how I need to work, and I need a client who understands it."

"Show me the problem then. On the old sketches."

"They were rubbish. I tore them up."

"Tracey," she groaned. "Stop being such a perfectionist!"

"It's not perfectionism. It's method. I'm being methodical."

"Well, the next time there's an issue, show me. We can argue it out together."

"A finished building is the best argument."

There were less than two weeks left on my software membership, and I could just about draw a brick. Every day I considered cutting my losses and leaving Woodstock with the tiny nest egg I had. But something wouldn't let me—an ambivalence. One moment, I would be re-counting my money and filling suitcases with Melanie's guest towels, and the next, I was online, ordering reams of tracing paper in the hopes that I could do the sketches by hand.

In the end, I missed my deadline, but arrived at a better idea, a more old-fashioned sort of theft.

Melanie, bound for Rhode Island, loaded Gabby into her Mercedes. And I spent the day up at the main house, rummaging around in her jewelry box whilst Kitty and Fitz jumped on her bed. Disappointed, I realized the real jewels were in a safety-deposit box somewhere. There was some valuable art, hideous abstract expressionist stuff, but it would be a nightmare to unload; gallery owners would want to see its provenance.

In her nightstand, I found a few sentences she'd jotted down on a notepad, probably during a conversation with her lawyer: *Evidence: personal knowledge of the witness, photos and video . . .*

It was nothing to do with me, I reassured myself. It was just for the case she was building against Gabby's old public school. Regardless, I had difficulty sleeping that night. I tossed and turned for hours, my brain on trial.

A day later, Melanie returned from Rhode Island without Gabby. She seemed sad and listless, squinting into the sun like a Mumbai street child.

Without her favorite doe-eyed distraction, I expected her to throw herself ever more deeply into micromanaging me. But to my surprise and mounting concern, she didn't.

In fact, I watched all her pet projects grow stale. Her yoga mat gathered lint in the entrance hall. She stopped texting me ceiling fans she'd found on her Houzz app.

I knew for certain she was out of sorts the afternoon I found her sunbathing on the deck. No hat. Aiming for a real suntan instead of the one she paid top dollar to have aerosoled on. Even more alarming, her cell phone was nowhere in sight.

"You all right?" I asked.

The casual, English greeting typically worked like truth serum on Melanie, who took it as an invitation to divulge every thought in her head.

"I'm fine."

Oh dear. I moved closer, and saw she was reading her previously discarded copy of *The Celestine Prophecy.*

"Reacquainting yourself with the Divine?" Affectionately snarky. Using the pimp psychology that worked for Abigail so well.

Nothing. Melanie turned a page and brought a scholarly knuckle to rest near her mouth.

"How's the lawsuit coming on?"

For a split second, she looked rather stunned. We never spoke about the lawsuit.

"We won," she said flatly.

"*What?*" I was speechless. "But you've never mentioned—*When* did you testify?"

"We settled out of court."

I had so many questions, including the most relevant one: *Settled for how much?* But I didn't dare ask, because she had these shipwreck eyes. She showed no hint of triumph.

"Victor must be pleased. Have you started making plans for his visit?"

Melanie rested the open book on its spine. "Not yet." She rolled away from me, onto her stomach, and unclasped the back of her leopard-print bikini.

"Well, let me know." Ultra-accommodating. "I'm happy to clear out with the kids. You can have the place to yourselves. Get in some family time."

"You're happy to clear out," Melanie repeated with a snide chuckle.

"Yes, I reckon I would be," I said, enduring the passive aggression. Reluctant to show weakness. "Well, I'm going to go inside and get a start on dinner. Roast chicken. Organic, of course. Do you think Abigail would like to join us tonight?"

"Let's make it just the two of us," Melanie said, eyes averted, staring into the pile of her beach towel. "If that's OK with you. I love Abigail. You know that. But I'm tired of giving so much of myself to other people. Especially when I don't get anything back in return. Sorry."

And that's when I knew how much trouble I was in. Because when Melanie said *sorry* she really meant *fuck you.*

. . .

That evening, Melanie drank her body weight in alcohol while I chopped and stirred my way through a small arsenal of Nigella Lawson recipes.

Given her foul mood and her reliable appetite for gin, I took the opportunity to introduce her to the Queen Mother Cocktail. I made a double batch, stirred it up in her fat-bottomed pitcher, and set it out on the deck table, where she could top up her drink with trademark enthusiasm.

By the time I brought a chickpea salad to the porch, Mel was already on the wobbly side of drunk, regarding her crossed knees with bewilderment.

"Why's this called the Queen's Whatsit?" she asked, her fingers stumbling on the lip of the olive bowl.

Serving her: "She's said to be a fan of gin. And Dubonnet. Have I made it too strong?"

Script was crucial. Improv would lead to feelings, and feelings were a distraction. I'd decided to stay cool, run the lines I had thought of in advance, and watch Melanie closely for cues. Her reaction would tell me what part to play.

"We need some more ice, I think. Haa-haah." She slammed her hip into the table upon standing.

I dropped the salad tongs and put a hand on her shoulder. "You do so much. I'll get it."

I didn't intend to let her go anywhere. Not until I got her so hopelessly drunk that whatever was troubling her came up in a spray of expletives or vomit. She was furious, I could tell, and the risks compounded every moment she pretended she wasn't.

"I guess so. I mean . . . I know. I *am* generous. Victor always says so like it's a bad thing . . . like fussing over people makes them feel incompetent. God, I'm such a mess. Half the things I do are crazy." Gesturing to her temple, she nearly poked herself in the eye.

Tension had crept into my shoulders.

"Ahh." Things like taking in a woman she met in a whirlwind.

"I never would have fallen for a thing like this back in New

Jersey. I just didn't know anyone else here. Victor left. Being so lonely . . . it made me naïve."

A crest of fury broke over me. But getting defensive was the worst thing I could do. It was far better to play stupid.

"What exactly did you fall for?"

Her eyes were wet with tears and unfocused on account of the booze. She looked so placid and innocent, it came as quite a shock when she began shouting. Her voice rose like summer heat, scaring off the hummingbirds in the butterfly bush.

"I thought we were building something! And I felt *happy*! Like I'd found a whole nother side of myself! What an idiot I was! I put my family at risk! Who brings a person into their life without knowing the first thing about them?!"

My stomach clenched. I set down the pitcher, fearing I might drop it.

"Slow down, Mel. Don't start doubting yourself. You're a good judge of character."

"I'm *not*, actually."

"Yes, you are." Pretending she was talking about someone else, I made the clumsy assertion: "You found *me*."

Her weak smile had a tinge of disgust.

God, her anger-avoidance really hadn't made this easy. I resented being the one who had to acknowledge the elephant in the room. *Why*, I wondered, *does it fall on me to out* myself*?*

I pulled out a chair and faced her squarely. "I get it. It's all happened rather quickly. And you feel like you misread signals—"

"*Misread* them? More like they were *misrepresented* to me!"

It was worse than I imagined. And I wondered what had brought it all on. I worried she'd gone to see the town code officer. If so, he'd have said he had nothing on file for 16 Byrdcliffe Drive.

"All right, fine. If that's how you feel. But that sounds more like emotion than logic to me. Perhaps you don't feel worthy of deep connection, so you convince yourself that anyone who wants to get close to you has an ulterior motive. It's a trust issue. Quite common."

Her eyelids gleamed with humidity and sparkly makeup. She kept squinting, narrowing her eyes like she was trying to see through me. "The only trust issue I have is that I'm *too* trusting! I believed the horseshit! All of it!"

I fought the urge to raise a shushing finger. She was speaking unbelievably loud, even by American standards. Janisa had left for home hours ago, but I couldn't rule out the possibility that someone else might hear. A neighbor. Or a night jogger. I snatched the baby monitor off the table and brought it to my ear. Silence, thankfully. Melanie was howling like she meant to wake my children.

"I think you've had quite enough to drink," I said, paradoxically refreshing her glass. "Start at the beginning, all right? Is this something to do with Victor?"

"Of course it is! He's livid! He's already calling lawyers!"

There was a long pause. I couldn't speak for panic. I finally overcame lung paralysis to say: "Melanie. Look at me. What exactly does he know?"

"All of it. Well, almost. I didn't name names. But I should."

And then it hit me: Melanie had gone online, searching for proof of my foreclosure. She knew the house was registered to Randall Mueller instead of "Bueller."

"Oh, Mel, have you been sleeping? I know you're upset that Victor's gone and, now Gabby's away as well. But you're not yourself. You're acting paranoid."

She was crying, reeling with anger and alcohol. "No, it's been right in front of my eyes this whole time! All the proof I needed to know this was never going to amount to anything! I was just looking for justifications to do what I wanted to do! And now I've paid this huge price, and I have absolutely nothing to show for it! I *never* will! I've been used! And it's humiliating, OK? I'm embarrassed and I'm—I'm *fucking* angry!"

I rubbed her back, tentatively, and she seemed to stand for it, suggesting I might be able to talk her down.

"There, there," I said. "We're going to sort this out. There's more to any situation than meets the eye. Look, I'm going to clear away these dishes. Then, let's go for a walk and talk this through. Maybe down to the river where we won't wake the children."

According to my father, fresh air could improve any argument.

Ahead of me on the path, Melanie's gait was looser and faster than usual, owing to her anger or blood-alcohol content. At every turn in the path, she trampled ferns and veered into the jewelweed.

It was eight in the evening. The sun was mostly set, and the sky had a band of deep orange. Under other circumstances, it might have been beautiful. But my bones hummed with nerves, and I watched the last stripe of horizon burn.

We reached the river's edge, and Melanie waved me closer. She'd progressed to the broken-record stages of drunk, repeating words: "*Now* can we talk, Tracey? I'm ready to talk."

"That's why we're here."

Up close, she smelled strongly of gin and body odor. She stumbled a step, even after she'd ordered me to stop.

"You have doubts about me, Melanie. I get it. I rather wish you'd spoken to me sooner. I could have helped you talk it through. We might have had a chat *before* it ruined our friendship." Letting the blame sink in, I slid off my shoes and waded, ankle-deep, into the water.

She bent jerkily to take off her shoes.

"You're the last person I wanted to talk to about it!"

"Why?"

"You *know* why."

I ignored that one in favor of hitching up my trousers and wading into the current. "Mmm, the water's lovely." The water, which was Cornish in temperature, hit my calves with a painful sting. "Come in. Come on, join me."

"I don't want to swim. I can't even look at you." She turned away. "There's no way we can be friends after this."

"Mel, come back. Listen to me." I stepped out of the water and ran after her, loosely grabbing her scrawny upper arm. "You're a good person, all right? And our friendship is something quite special. Let's not compromise it. Can we agree on that?"

She nodded, indulging me. Eyes full of ginny tears.

"So what, specifically, is the problem? What's it going to take to ease your mind?"

"I know this is hard for you to face too," she said, slurring. "But just imagine for a minute that Randy found out the truth about the lies you've been telling all this time! What do you think he'd do? He'd divorce your ass, of course! And go for full custody of the children! He'd be right to! Who could defend you when you've been so selfish?!"

"Hold on, Melanie. Let's be clear here. In this little scenario of yours, I'm an *unfit mother* just because I couldn't walk on eggshells anymore? I lied, yes. I made promises I couldn't possibly keep. But I was dying in my marriage, Melanie. So I brought things to a head. I did what I needed to do to get out."

"Well, I know better than that. I hold myself to a higher standard."

"Right. Well, you're just perfect, then. What do you want? You want your deposit back?"

"The deposit? No. Keep it. I haven't even started worrying about money—"

"Yes, I get that. It's about the principle."

Melanie prattled on about morals and ethics, saying how wrong it was for me to use her just because I needed affection, validation, and care. Saying that I should have properly left one life before I embarked on another one. But I cut her off.

"Look, I really don't think anyone's used anyone else. And I think what you want is still possible, given some more time. The real problem, as I see it—and as I've been saying all along—is your practicality. Embarking on this type of thing takes daring. You need vision and guts."

"You don't think I'm brave? I'm brave."

"I suppose by some standards. I just think, in this particular instance, you put up too many walls. Literally and figuratively. You spook easily. It doesn't make for a functional partnership."

"You're such an expert on me. Everyone's such an expert on me. What I'm 'like.' Where I'm 'flawed.' I don't have to be like you . . . I don't have to leave my home country or jump off a cliff in order to be brave and open to life." Very suddenly, she took her hairband between her teeth and began piling her hair on top of her head.

"Are you all right?"

She nodded combatively. "I'm going to jump off that cliff. The same one you did."

"That's silly."

"Now I'm silly? Silly and a pussy?"

"I've never used that word. I don't like that word."

But she wasn't listening. She had already pulled off her tank top and stumbled into the river, which was high on account of the rain. She dunked to her shoulders and wet her hair, smoothing it into a sort of skullcap.

"Come back, Mel. It's late. You ought to be sleeping, not leaping off a bloody cliff. Let's just go back up to the house and continue this in the morning."

She was mid-river, doing a remedial breaststroke. After she arrived at the opposite shore, she scrambled pitifully up the incline, all palms and knees.

I scratched my ankles. The mosquitoes were out in full force.

"Look, if you insist on doing this, you'll want to take a running start and leap out at least two feet! There's a rock you need to take into account!"

I could see her thin outline, in spite of the distance and dark. She was bent over with her hands on her knees, catching her courage like it was breath. "Stop hover parenting!"

"All right! Just remember the rock to the right!"

Or was it the left?

Her bent-kneed silhouette careened toward me, one arm flailing. Holding her nose with one hand made her fall at a slant.

She hit the water with a loud, disorganized splash. I expected her to surface, brash and triumphant. But there was a gaping silence, as though the fall had knocked the breath out of her.

A pair of mating dragonflies swarmed my head, and I waved them off.

"Mel?"

Amidst the ever-present rush of water, there was a mewling sound.

I stripped off my clothes and swam in the direction of what had become a whimper. By the light of the slivered moon, I saw her a short distance off. She was near the bank, in a pocket of still water, struggling to keep her head above water.

"Mel?!" I shouted. "Are you hurt?"

Swimming closer, I found her doing a lopsided back float.

"I . . . it's my—"

I tried to put a foot down, but I was still out of my depth. Water skimmed my nostrils, and after a choking inhale, I went back to treading water with a raised chin.

"All right, listen. We need to sort out where you're injured." The words were meant to inspire confidence, but my voice was shaking.

"OK." She gulped and spat a mouthful of water.

"Come on." I nudged her the short distance to the nearest large rock. "Can you hold on?"

"I—I don't think so."

I lifted her arm to help and she made a small, intense sound. I tried again and realized her forearm had a sickening joint in the wrong place. Her hand pointed forty-five degrees in the wrong direction.

"Bloody hell." I was clinging to the rock with my left hand, and bracing Mel's back with my knee.

"What?"

"It's your arm . . ."

Anesthetized by her shock: "What about it?"

"Well, it's not meant to be swan-shaped. You've broken it." *In multiple places*, I almost added. At least it was a closed fracture. No blood. Little risk of infection.

I'd wanted to scream, knowing I had buggered myself even worse. Now Victor was apt to sic a personal-injury lawyer on me, blaming me for letting her jump drunk. He would strip away my false identity from one side, and Randy and his divorce attorney would do it from the other. Worst of all, I would lose custody of the children—the great loves of my life, the only people who didn't disgust or disappoint me.

I wished to God I never met her—that I'd never gone to The Odell.

In a moment of paranoia, I thought I heard the snap of twigs. *Deer*, I reassured myself. *Or wolves. A bear.* I turned away from it, back toward Melanie, sending a small wave crashing into her face.

"No." She coughed jaggedly. "It's my leg."

"This one?" I asked reaching.

"The other one."

I wedged her body between mine and the rock, reached underwater and traced the slippery length of her thigh with my palm. All the way to her knee, it felt right as rain. But continuing downward, my hand caught the jagged edge of a stick. Melanie gave a high, arcing scream.

I had a stupid thought: *Shite luck, impaling herself on a branch.* Then the next horrible instant, I realized I'd actually brushed the jutting bone of her fibula (or possibly, her tibia). With a mute gag, I hoisted her shin to the surface for a better look. What I saw was the protrusion of an open fracture—less leg and more orthopedic erector set. Water and gore erupted from the wound. My hand went oily with blood. The sight of it brought a fizzing sound to my ears.

My scalp goose-fleshed.

"Tracey?" Melanie asked, frenzied. In the moonlight, I watched her push her breasts out, struggling to float unsupported.

I couldn't answer. My jaw wouldn't unclench. I couldn't distinguish my face from its dark reflection on the water.

Melanie reached for me with her good arm and missed. Her jerky splash startled me. I couldn't hold her any longer. I couldn't look at her.

I ought to have gone for a kickboard. Or anchored myself on shore and fished her out with a pool noodle. But by the time I broke my fugue and looked back, she had rolled onto her stomach. The waves caught the lower half of her and spun her by the feet, carrying her downstream, headfirst, faster than she could fight it. The current became her sleigh, knocking the humpbacked X of her every which way. Water poured over her head, and presumably into her lungs.

That old conversation with Oz went through my head like a snatch of a song.

He's dead.

Don't joke.

I drowned him . . . In the river . . .

I had an eerie sensation as I swam the last few yards to shore, almost as though Melanie's wraith had shivered out of her bones and was watching me from the woods. It was an idiotic notion, of course. I didn't *do* unearthly.

But just as I was hobbling out of the water, onto the pebbles, I heard a cough and a child's singsong voice, asking, "Mummee?"

"Kitty?" I called, in a stage whisper. "Kitty? Are you here?"

Another cough. And I realized, with breathless relief, that the sound was coming from the baby monitor in the nest of my discarded clothes.

"I'm coming," I muttered, a mother's unconscious habit. I was slipping my feet into my shoes when she said it again.

"Mummy?"

The only name I had ever been afraid to lose.

CHAPTER THIRTEEN

I used my clothes to towel off, then ran back through the woods in my wet underpants, scarcely noticing the pebbles and pine needles that stuck to my bare feet.

Again and again, the monitor in my trembling hand mewled, "Mummy?"

I opened and slammed the cottage door behind me, unintentionally making a fair bit of racket in the process. When I turned the corner, I saw Kitty, half-awake, sitting on the steps to the loft.

She was still dazed with sleep. "Hi."

I hesitated, sickened by the *drip, drip* of my wet hair onto the slate floor.

"Have you had a bad dream?" I asked, pulling my damp top over my head.

"I need water."

"Water," I repeated, looking at my pruned fingers.

I accepted her outstretched cup and held it distractedly under the tap. The sound of running water made fine hairs gather at the back of my neck.

I watch her drink with a series of deep, suckling sounds, then said, "Come on. Let's get you to bed." As if the nightly ritual was enough to restore our lives to order.

Kit stumbled toward the bedroom, and I followed close behind, wondering whether I ought to wake Fitz and leave immediately.

I even had a thought to call the Woodstock Police Department. It would be far less bother to report an accidental drowning than it would be to scrub the house of DNA evidence and create a trail of fake emails that said the children and I moved out weeks ago. But then, if I reported the death, I would need to show law enforcement my dodgy green card. It had been good enough to fool Randy, but a police force wouldn't share his emotional blind spots. They would see the poor text alignment and glaring typos a mile off.

Fitz was sound asleep. I bent to kiss his cheek, but my wet hair dripped on the duvet, and I instinctively pulled back.

Kitty collapsed facefirst into her pillow, and I rubbed her back until I was certain she was down.

First thing, I found and attached my wristwatch. As Oz's murder accomplice, I'd learned just how important time was. It would all matter: when we left Woodstock, how long the body was submerged, the time stamps on any incoming texts to Mel's phone.

Of all these things, Melanie's phone was the most important. Even though it wasn't in use, it was still in constant communication with the nearest cellular antennae, meaning police would use it to map her final whereabouts.

I didn't have a Faraday bag, but I'd read somewhere that an empty paint container can inhibit wireless transmissions. So I ransacked the cottage shed, found an old can of Benjamin Moore, and rinsed it out as best I could with the garden hose.

Still shivering, I wheezed up the hill to the main house and found Melanie's phone on the patio table, directly beside her empty glass. Just before I shoved it inside the can, I had a thought that I could toss in a heap of rocks as well and sink the whole thing in the river. But then, if phones were anything like computer hard drives, they could be dried out by specialist recovery companies. If police employed one, they'd recover all of Mel's data regardless: her Java applications and the whole of her SIM card, including identifying photos of me, Kitty, and Fitz. I fitted the lid on the can and hoped to hell Seema could help.

In the Ashworths' home office, I swiveled in Victor's desk chair and clicked "Menu" on Melanie's laptop:

History.
Show All History.
Today.

Her search history was incriminating to say the least:

The Character Assassin: Cheaters, Con Artists and Sociopaths
"Red Flags" for Unhealthy Relationships—Self.com
Dear Nice Girl: This Is Why You're Always Getting Played for a Fool

I felt myself glazing over. I could blitz Melanie's entire search history, but any halfway decent computer technician would be able to recover it.

OK, I thought. *Think.*

I could still taste creek water. I looked again at my watch. My brain was overbaked and the later it got, the more likely I was to make critical mistakes.

In the end, I reset the passwords on Melanie's email and social media accounts to a long string of numbers and special characters that Seema and I had devised years ago when we challenged each other to find the strongest password possible. With a little luck, it would present a challenge for police cryptanalysts, who would try to guess Mel's passwords by using birthdays and pet names and, when they couldn't get in, try to subpoena her email service.

I took her laptop as well. I knew full well its absence would make Mel's death look suspicious, but then, there was no avoiding it, so would ours.

New York City was only a temporary stopover. That's what I told myself the next morning as I helped the children board a bus to

Port Authority. We would stay one month, maximum, while I made and saved enough money to finance a move to Denver or Los Angeles (somewhere far west of the Ashworths). Britain was still out of the question, along with the rest of the EU, because there was still a chance my name occupied a place on the National Crime Agency's Most Wanted list.

For most of the ride, I felt false and labored, playing the part of the superefficient working mum in the event any of the passengers were the sort of crime watchers apt to dial police tip lines. I'd even dressed in a smart-looking pantsuit that Gracie/Tracey rarely wore. Anyone who saw me on my phone was apt to think I was "reading reports" or "responding to clients." In reality, I was searching classifieds for short-term rentals.

To begin with, the children and I stayed in a twenty-dollar-a-night "emergency overnight crash" that I found advertised on Craigslist. It was located in Sunset Park, Brooklyn, in the basement of Finger Joy—a filthy nail salon that sounded like a filthy massage parlor. It was neither comfortable nor pretty. The children slept in pedicure chairs and I lay awake on a deconstructed massage table, staring alternately at the Chinese Coca-Cola posters on the wall and the exposed wires that hung from the ceiling. The next morning, I cut Kitty's hair to the nape of her neck and slathered mine with indigo, dyeing it to match Fitz's.

"Ew. What's that?" Kitty squealed when she saw me with a head full of mud and cling film.

"Henna. Well, indigo, actually. It's dye."

The smell of it brought me straight back to another dark transition in my life.

"Die?" She dropped her crayon. She'd been using a Mexican takeout menu as a coloring book.

I got her meaning instantly. "No. It's *hair* dye. Made of vegetables. Like paint for your head."

"Oh." She giggled through her palms in that way that always brought me immense joy, even there, in the basement of a salon with very low standards for hygiene.

"Can I play a game on your phone?" Fitz asked.

"No, love. Not now. Sorry."

I was desperate to turn on my phone and Melanie's as well, so I could find out what precisely she'd told Victor about our architecture deal. But if I did, police could use it to track our location. So instead, I left both phones in the paint can.

Our first week as fugitives passed quickly. At night, we ate in dim-sum restaurants with golden drapery. During the day, we haunted fast-food restaurants. Kit and Fitz ate cheap, stinking, mass-produced food off the "Summer Break Menu," and I drank black coffee and used the free Wi-Fi to execute phase two of my Randy plan.

It took me less than a week to do the research and understand how a death certificate was processed through the Electronic Death Registration System. But once I did, I realized with cognitive dissonance that there was no verification.

It was an absolute shock: Both doctors and funeral directors had do-it-themselves access to the online portal, and it was easy to find their licensing numbers from other online databases. I knew Seema would lose it when I told her. It was the biggest data breach in the history of the Internet: anyone with basic computer skills could impersonate a doctor or funeral director and declare someone dead.

I glanced up from my laptop to check on the children, who were in the McPlay area. Fitz was making guns of his hands in a way I'd warned him against a million times.

"Peeew! Peew! You're dead!" he taunted.

Kitty let out one of those little-girl shrieks that could peel the remaining red paint off the walls.

Quieting them, I returned to my open Internet tabs. It had been four days and the news outlets still hadn't reported anything about Melanie. Maybe her body hadn't been found. Or maybe the tragedy had passed for suicide, and Victor was struggling to write her obituary. But I couldn't rule out the possibility that police were interviewing witnesses and gathering evidence on Tracey Bueller, in which case, I was not keen to publicize our bloodlust.

"You're dead!" Fitz repeated at top volume. "I've slayed you to death!"

"That's redundant," I said. "'Slay' *means* 'put to death.' And it's not nice. It's sad, when someone dies. You understand that, don't you?"

My eye twitched.

The children seemed to listen with more reverence than usual.

I returned my attention to my computer screen, wondering if I was truly prepared to commit digital matricide—to exile my children, forever, from the names Katherine Mueller and Fitz Jabbur? I glanced between the screen and Fitz's rapidly maturing face. I looked at Kitty's long eyelashes, which glowed auburn beneath fluorescent lights. Taking their names, I risked taking their identity and self-worth, as well. After all, to name is to love.

I took a deep breath.

It took me five minutes to "become" a "doctor." Ten more to fashion myself as a "funeral director," and only short time longer to complete our death certificates. I used doctorly jargon, plagiarized from other documents that I found online, and entered my own anonymous email and burner phone number in place of a Dr. Marvin Koutsos in Catskill, New York. In all three cases, I listed the cause of death as natural:

> Accidental auto fatality. Occurred in a taxicab, approximately one mile down a private, nontraffic road.
>
> Crushed skull with avulsions of the cranium and brain.
>
> Multiple lacerations of the hands and lower extremities.

Digital death wasn't an endgame, only a way to create misinformation and complicate an already complex paper trail. In time, the Woodstock police would still link Tracey to Gracie. The real

Dr. Koutsos would say he never examined us. And of course, the cops would reach out to Randy in Florida, who'd confess he never found our remains.

But I had a little something up my sleeve that I hoped would help on this last point. I was insured for $500,000 in life insurance. It was one of those monthly bills I had always prioritized, because with the foreclosure and Randy's dwindling income, it had seemed more than likely that one of us would kill the other or drop dead of stress.

We'd been skint a long time, and half a million dollars would go a long way toward clearing our debts. If Randy used it to pay off credit cards and reverse the foreclosure on the Catskill house, then he'd find it very difficult to phone in an AMBER Alert once he began to suspect we weren't dead.

I devoted the following day to buying good-quality passports online, something I'd never been able to afford back when I was living with Randy.

Victor Ashworth had a subscription to *BusinessWeek*, and back at Byrdcliffe Drive, I'd read that major banks had begun to offer Bitcoins—the digitally generated currency that wasn't controlled by any of the banks that caused the subprime collapse or managed by any of the countries whose economies were going tits-up. So I marched (rather ironically, it seemed to me) into the same national bank branch that was foreclosing on the Catskill house, and converted the cash I'd saved in Woodstock to digital currency.

From there, the children and I visited Duane Reade for passport photos, and then the Brooklyn Public Library, another free Wi-Fi hotspot. While Kit and Fitz attended children's story hour, I gave my Bitcoins to a tumbler site, which charged a fee, but laundered the currency, exchanging them for Bitcoins that couldn't be traced back to me.

After that, my online shopping spree began. After two years' austerity, dropping large sums of money was more thrilling than

I care to admit. I downloaded the TOR browser, the doorway to the dark web, and visited a popular online black market, where I could browse anonymously. The site was mainly known as a platform for illegal drugs, but it also offered a range of other products. And I scrolled through them all—Armory, Computer Equipment, Credit Cards, Erotica—until I came to Forgeries.

The top-rated vendor offered real, doctored US passports for Ƀ203,703, somewhere in the vicinity of $1,100 each. But buying a fake ID online was riskier than purchasing guns or drugs. I needed to provide photos, and I knew that might incriminate me if the seller turned out to be law enforcement.

But the shop's reviews were encouraging and mostly literate:

"Ten working days to Mexico. Wish every vendor was this good."

"I was worried when I bought this. But don't be. Your [*sic*] in good hands with these guys."

The biometrics matched the old owners, so if we ever used the passports to cross a border, we'd be buggered. But I reckoned they ought to serve us well domestically.

When I sent an encrypted message to the seller (ensuring he and *only* he could read it), the names he messaged back—Marianna, Catarina, and Giovanni De Felice—felt oddly fated. Mariana was patron saint of my youth. Catarina could be shortened to Cat, a close relative of Kit. The only real loser was Fitz. "Giovanni" sounded like a Casanovan footballer, but then, I was confident we could think of a nickname.

I added the passports to my cart and used the library's scanner to send the seller JPEGs of our passport photos. From there, my Bitcoins went into escrow.

By the time story hour had finished, I had a remaining Ƀ1,229,629 ($6,640) to my name. It seemed like a lot until I added up the price of additional expenses like birth certificates and Social Security numbers, which I would need to secure health insurance, rent a flat, and enroll the children in school. I couldn't do both—buy more documents *and* move us out of Finger Joy—and after a week of breathing in fingernail glue, a new flat was my main priority. The dust emitted by the nail files was affecting Fitz like seasonal allergies. The phone, which rang constantly, gave me a headache, as did the woman who picked it up and responded, over and over: "He not here right now." So I literally went for broke and used my remaining Bitcoins to buy 340 stolen credit card numbers in the same online black market.

Moments after I received the seller's message (he sent me the card numbers, expiration dates, names, and addresses), I did one last check of the *Daily Freeman* and read that authorities had recovered a woman's body from a "remote location along the Saw Kill River":

> Investigators matched the drowned woman to the description of a 39-year-old Woodstock woman reported missing Thursday. The body was turned over to the Ulster County Coroner for an autopsy to determine foul play, but according to police: "We don't believe the general public or anyone else is in harm's way, but we are treating the area as a crime scene until further notice."

Waiting for police to release the details of Melanie's investigation was an exercise in patience, much like profiting on stolen credit cards.

The following day, I bit my cuticles and ate antacids like candy. I tried to supervise the children at the park, but I was distracted, habitually ten seconds slow to respond to a skinned knee or a request to push Kit on the swing. I couldn't stop wondering why it had taken almost a week for anyone to find Mel's body or report her missing. I refreshed the *Daily Freeman* site again and again, inventing reasons to explain why an update wasn't forthcoming. But I convinced myself that police were waiting for Victor, traveling from Britain, to identify the body rather than drafting a press release that named me as a suspect.

As for the credit card fraud, I researched. I was careful. You could even say I approached it in a rather mumsy way.

It worked like this. I made fake listings for eBay products I didn't actually own. Big-ticket toys were my favorite: Razor scooters, electric motocross bikes, et cetera. Being a mother, I knew their worth. And they sold quickly when I listed them below market value. After a buyer completed their purchase (say they deposited $200 into the PayPal account I'd registered to a foreign address), I used my stolen credit card to make an identical purchase from a reputable vendor at full retail price ($280), then had it shipped to my buyer. The toy arrived. The consumer got a bargain. The credit card company refunded the money on the fraudulent purchase. And I walked away from a relatively victimless crime, earning $200 on a $20 investment.

By the time our fake passports arrived at the FedEx Ship Center where I'd rented a mailbox (no ID required), I had transformed ฿1,229,629 into ฿7,266,481, or $6,640 into $39,239, and the *Daily Freeman* had redacted Melanie's name out of respect for her family:

> The woman pulled out of the Saw Kill River on Friday afternoon appears to be a suicide, Woodstock Police Captain Noah Harriott said.
>
> The 39-year-old woman had been reported missing by her housekeeper when she didn't return home from a trip to Rhode Island, where her in-laws hadn't seen her since the previous week. Detectives suspect the death was caused by suicide or accidental drowning.
>
> "She was in crisis," said her friend Abigail Wheeler. "She was the type of person who believed the best in people. Unfortunately, that also meant she blamed herself for their bad behavior."

It should have been good news all around. Police didn't think Melanie was murdered and whether or not Tracey Bueller was a person of interest, they hadn't named her in the press. But despising Abigail, I couldn't help worrying what she'd told police about *my* "bad behavior."

Giving myself more escape options, I bought three US birth

certificates (฿132,388); three Social Security cards (฿145,488); and a top-of-the-range fake green card (฿277,777). The bill came to nearly $3,000, but I still had more than enough left in liquid assets to buy the new smartphone I needed to finalize my fresh start.

When the documents arrived two weeks later, I took the children upstairs to Finger Joy and left them with the owner's thirteen-year-old daughter Niu, who charged the obscenely low rate of $5 an hour to babysit and had already taught Fitz more Mandarin than the Ashworths' *Mei Mei* DVD. Even Kit had picked up the phrase *bu yao* ("do not want"), which made her two-year-old tantrums seem cultured and, almost, charming.

Then, I was off to the nearest wireless retailer. My British accent made it easy to pretend I was fresh off the boat from the UK and had never had an American cell-phone plan before. But the twentysomething clerk was so naïve or stoned (or both) that he asked very few questions anyway.

I felt a rush of fear, entering Marianna De Felice's Social Security number into the electronic keypad, but the machine appeared to accept it. And after paying a $400 security deposit to make up for my lack of credit history, I walked away with a top-of-the-range status phone.

For the day's final challenge, I found myself back at Finger Joy, thrusting another $5 at Niu in the hopes that she'd keep the children a little longer.

"No problem," she said.

The children were having a raucous good time gluing cotton balls onto emery boards.

After I thanked her, I rushed to the basement, hoping the reception was good enough to download my favorite voice-changing app. In order to finish things, I needed quiet solemnity. The streets of Sunset Park, with its whipping flags and honking horns, weren't going to do. Neither would a tea shop filled with howling babies.

. . .

"Randolph Mueller," Randy answered in the mock-professional tone he used when he didn't recognize a phone number. (I had watched him field enough phone calls to know he was probably reaching for his laptop and opening the file where he tracked his real-estate leads.)

"Mr. Mueller?" I repeated.

"Yes." Tapping keys on his laptop. "Is this Mr. Morales?"

"No. My name's Tucker." The voice-changing app gave me a decent B-movie man's voice.

"Mr. Tucker," Randy repeated. He sounded hungover, his primary mood beyond angry, drunk, or high. "Oh, right, this is about the ranch house on Chattahoochee Street? Are you ready to make an offer?"

"*Paul* Tucker," I said. "I'm a police chaplain with the Ulster County Police Department."

"You're from New York? Is there a problem with the foreclosure?"

"No, sir." I was subtle and serious. "I'm phoning today with deep regret. It's my sad duty to inform you of the deaths of your wife, Gracie Mueller, and children, Katherine and Fitzpatrick."

I was expecting tears or curse words. Instead, he said: "Oh."

"There was a traffic accident. Your wife and children were pronounced dead at the scene—"

"Gracie doesn't drive."

"They were in a taxi. The driver also died in the collision."

After a long pause, Randy asked: "Where were they going?"

"According to the dispatcher, the taxi was bound for the Colonie Center."

"What's that?'

"It's a shopping mall, sir."

There was a deep silence, followed by a whir of activity on Randy's end of the line. It sounded like he was opening and closing drawers, rummaging around. "We've been having money problems."

I began saying it was just a standard traffic accident—no indication "Gracie" had been under distress—but midway through my speech, there was a heavy thud as though Randy had laid his phone on a table.

In the distance, he murmured something I couldn't make out. I distinctly heard a woman say, *Oh my God.*

I looked at my watch. It was nearly six o'clock at night. There was a chance he was still in the office.

"Sorry," Randy said, picking up the phone. "I just . . . This is—" He paused, giving me time to register the sound of chopping.

"Listen, shock is a normal response. As a chaplain, I'm here to give you twenty-four-hour assistance."

The phone dropped again. There was a long snuffling sound.

"Should I come back to New York?" he said, too loudly. "Are they there now? At a morgue? Do I need to . . . identify them? I don't know how this works."

"A friend of the family has already done that. When the time comes, I'll liaise between you and the funeral home, and I'll let you know how to get copies of the death certificates. But today, I just want to make sure you have the necessary support and emotional care."

He gave a groaning sigh and sniffed. "My friend is here."

A woman's voice filled the background. She was speaking in a soft, breathy tone that offered as much allure as it did comfort. Straining my ears, I heard her say: "We're gonna get through this."

We'll get through it all right, I thought. The children and me. She and Randy could go have coke-till-dawn sex. I, for one, was going to get a grip on something more meaningful than a man's meat and two veg.

"This is so surreal," Randy said, his euphoria at odds with his words. "I can't believe I wasn't there to say goodbye."

"I'm deeply sorry for the loss of your children."

A part of me meant it.

CHAPTER FOURTEEN

University pressure drove me into the arms of employment. Everyone in upper sixth was worrying continuously about their futures, rating the positives and negatives of schools like St. Andrews and Warwick. But I wasn't certain I could afford to enroll anywhere. Hoping to earn enough cash to cover some fees, I marched into The Royal Chemsworth, an impeccably restored old four-star hotel (my father sometimes crashed its corporate cocktail hours) and requested a job application.

"Are you honest?" my potential boss asked.

"Yes," I answered, a sickening fear in my stomach.

"Do you have a boyfriend?"

No idea which answer made me more employable, I lied: "Yes."

"Good," he said, satisfied. "That's what we like here. Honest, honorable girls."

He handed me a gray housekeeper's uniform and launched into a little orientation speech: I should knock three times on a door before entering; I should surrender any items guests left behind to the front desk; and I was permitted to accept tips, but not money for "propositions" (by which I assumed he meant sex).

I nodded, then went to the toilet to change into my ill-fitting and oddly porny uniform, which zipped, top to bottom, down the front, leaving the zipper dangling between my knees. It only occurred to me as I was riding the lift to the top floor that I'd transposed myself into the pages of *Eloise*.

I can't say I enjoyed cleaning hotel rooms. But I learned much from its ideology.

"It's about the *illusion* of clean," Reina, the sweary woman who trained me, said, as she ate a pillow chocolate.

During my first shift, I watched Reina wipe down the water glasses with the same sponge she'd used on the tub. She explained that the comforters weren't washed, "bloody *never*," unless there was "bleeding blood." She told me that, in spite of my *yoof*, making forty beds a day and cleaning up bodily fluids at warp speed would break my back.

The pay was small but steady. Each week, I collected a check for one hundred pounds and took it to the dodgy check center, where a clerk pretended to scrutinize my passport and turned it into cash for a twenty-quid fee. Then, back at the flat, I hid the remaining money between the pages of *Eloise* and, when that was full, the Jackie Collins books that inspired the erotica I told Seema. (Dad was too much of a literary snob to read them and his latest girlfriend, a home-care worker named Chardonnay, was all but illiterate.)

Speaking of my father, my job changed things between us. When I arrived home every evening in my maid's uniform, he gave me the disapproving look other fathers reserve for love bites and nose rings. To this day, I don't know whether he objected to maid work specifically or the idea of employment in general.

"How much did you make today in tips?" he asked one night with a drunken sneer.

I was in the kitchen, devouring the uneaten half of a room-service sandwich and reviewing a shoplifted book about how to prepare for university interviews. (The author's number one "useful hint" was: "Be yourself." *Brilliant*, I thought. *Because* that's *a possibility*.)

"No tips," I replied honestly. "It's not really a service position. Hotel guests don't see or interact with the maid."

The only "tips" I ever got were the piles of sick that drunk guests left me on the carpet. During one memorable shift, I discovered one had spewed into the ice bucket; he'd also turned up the thermostat to 27°C, and the heat of the room had baked an aromatic sick-cake.

Looking to offset the balance of power, I was drawn to the guests' possessions that were meant to be off-limits. I couldn't help it. It was late March by that point, and I'd begun hearing back from universities. I'd already been accepted to St. Andrews and Edinburgh, and so far I'd barely earned a quarter of the cash I needed to see me through my first year.

So I began working harder and faster, scrubbing out the bathtubs at double speed, specifically so I'd have five spare minutes per room to hunt for valuables. I found small luxuries. Atomizers of French *parfum*. A pair of nude suede pumps, lying like twin virgins beneath the tissue paper of a Jimmy Choo box. Once, I found a talent agent's address book and copied down John Cleese's number for the sheer enjoyment of knowing I could ring him if I dared. But for all my rummaging around, I never found anything I could resell at a massive profit.

In April, I was tidying up a guest room and finding more of the same. Leaflets for art exhibitions served as coasters on the nightstands. There was a suitcase like a box of weeping loneliness, filled with tweed blazers, stained carpet slippers, comfort undies, and a sketchbook filled with crap portraiture. So imagine my surprise when I nudged aside a Mason Pearson brush and found an embossed invitation from Her Majesty.

I lifted the thick ivory card by the edges and stared stunned at the occasion (lunch) and the suggested attire (day dress or lounge suit). The name on the addressee line was Albina Penn-Cox.

I'd like to say I was cooler, that I wasn't the sort of person who used my time in the break room to pore over the aristocrats in *Tatler.* But in truth, I devoured every article about the queen's personal glove makers and the supposed "etiquette of farting." I reread each issue so many times my imagination grew edges and textures. It was almost as though the painful thought, *My life would be better if I'd had my mother,* had been replaced with a more bearable one I'd absorbed from Dad: *My life would be better if I had money.*

"What's that?" Reina asked, popping her head in to check my progress.

"It fell out of the bed while I was changing the sheets."

"Posh twat," she said, reading over my shoulder.

"Does she stay here often?"

"The queen?"

"Albina Penn-Cox." Seeing no sign of a man in her room, it seemed to me that she might make a very good mark—far more lucrative than Chardonnay ("Charlie," Dad called her), whom we'd been living with ever since he fell out with a public-relations executive over a suspicious credit card transaction.

"Oh yeah, whenever she's down from Clacherdon."

"Clacherdon?" My *Tatler* knowledge wasn't as encyclopedic as I thought.

"Her estate in Scotland. Or her husband's, before he dropped dead in a muddy field. Heart attack during a pheasant shoot."

"Where, specifically, in Scotland?"

I was getting the first glimmer of a mad idea. Maybe, just maybe, if I set up Albina with Dad, I could halve my living expenses by staying at her massive estate. Instead of four years of Pot Noodles, I could eat formal, lavish dinners off porcelain. Instead of the cheapest flat available, I could have thick wool boutique rugs, original oil paintings, and majestic sculpted gardens.

"I don't know. In the south. Aren't most Scottish castles in the south?"

"How old is Albina, do you reckon?"

Reina's look told me I ought to shut up and empty the blooming bins. "You've seen her. Toff with no eyelashes. Takes her tea in the restaurant every afternoon."

I frowned and shook my head.

Reina was growing as exasperated as she did when I tried to strip and wash the sheets that didn't look slept on. "You know the one. Likes her headscarves. I don't think she knows how to brush her hair."

I was quite certain I'd never seen Albina Penn-Cox before.

The very next shift I spotted her striding down the corridor toward me: not a wide woman, but an utterly hipless one, and she looked rather like a nutter in her shapeless shearling coat, which she wore like an unbelted dressing gown. Reina was right about Albina's hair; behind the china-pattern scarf that framed her forehead, her blond-gray curls swelled in freeze-frame explosion. Seeing her in the flesh, I worried she might be too old for my father. But then, in matters of sex, Jackie Collins had convinced me that women can outlast men half their age.

Closer and closer she came with shuffling feet and a proudly cocked chin.

I was under obligation to bid her a good morning, as I was every guest. But I had other plans. So instead, I rounded the corner and ducked behind my housekeeping cart, pretending to arrange the same miniature bottles of shampoo that my father was always trying to convince me to steal and sell on Camden High Street: "The bloody students on Camden High Street. They could do with a wash."

"Buy you a pint, Dad?" I asked that evening when I arrived home from work.

He was in the front room of the basement flat we shared with Charlie, whom he was "in love with" because her sixty-hour workweeks left him with plenty of unsupervised time to drink her wine, eat her ready meals, and gather his strength for more lucrative conquests.

"Sure," he said, American as a pancake house.

. . .

I've forgotten the name of Dad's regular pub at the time. The Stab Inn. Or the Fox and Hound. I do remember its pervasive gloom—the dark panels, blacked-out windows, and a disorientating number of decoy doors.

Once inside, it was impossible to glean the weather or season, whether the sun was up or down. It was not the sort of establishment you'd go to natter after work or even *think* about using the loo. The men were scruffy and hard, apt to facially disfigure anyone wearing another team's football colors. And the female clientele was tits-out and cellulitic, sporting forty-eight-hour-bender hair.

I waited while my father greeted his mates.

"So, to what do I owe the honor?" he asked as we found our way to an open table.

"Got left a tip," I lied, lightly coughing on the charred smells of burnt sausages, stale cigarettes, and dried-up Jack Daniel's. "So I thought I'd buy you a drink and this . . ."

I held out a John Singer Sargent book.

He took the book from me and began flipping through the portraits.

"Thank you?" He gave me an incredulous look.

"There's a guest at the hotel," I said. "A widow. Not necessarily the type to brush her hair or wash behind her ears. But she has a title and, from what I gather, a sizeable pile. She likes Sargent."

"How do you know?"

"She went to the exhibition at the National Gallery this week. I found the brochure in her room."

"Well, how do you know she liked it?"

"Because she's an artist as well. I found her sketchbook, and it's filled with derivative shite. Nineteenth-century French traditions and the like." I tapped the book cover. "I thought you might read up and become a fan as well."

"Ha!" my father said, running a hand through his hair. "You're playing matchmaker? Awfully Jane Austen of you, isn't it?"

"Come on, Dad. If anyone can fake it, it's you. Besides, a lot of toffs go for Americans. It's easier to pair off with a foreigner than it is to find a mate with the proper background."

"And what do *you* get out of all this?" Dad asked, bringing an elbow to his chair.

"A finder's fee."

A bigger laugh. Flash of his yellowing teeth. "How much?"

I could see he was enjoying himself. Oddly, I was too. I felt as close to him as I had those first few days on the Isle, when criminality felt less like something he'd thrust on me and more like a choice we'd made together.

"She has an estate near St. Andrews. It's a castle, really. I want to live there whilst I get my degree." The demand landed like a whisper, but the look in my eyes said I meant it.

He howled with laughter. "That's completely ridiculous."

"Why? Is it really that different than the way we've been living the past decade?"

"I'm tired, and comfortable where I am. Maybe I don't want to go fucking it all up on some half-brained scheme you haven't bothered to think through. Why are you so worried about living expenses anyway? You're earning money."

"Not enough."

"Apply for a grant, then."

"I can't. Not without a National Insurance number."

It was one thing to use Seema's number to work a minimum-wage job and quite another to take out a student loan with it. Especially now that Seema's father had agreed to let her take courses in computing and IT.

He lit a cigarette and exhaled. "Look, it's just, you bring me here to tell me that you've met this ripe mark, but how do you know for certain that she's as rich as you think? Because she has a posh accent? Accents can be faked. You ought to know that better than anyone."

"Albina Penn-Cox is proper Old Scotland, descended from an

iron magnate, with a clan and everything," I said, pushing back my chair and putting my messenger bag over my head. "I've done my research. She's worth millions of pounds on paper, and I've only offered you a cut of it because I felt sorry for you. Living with Charlie. Eating off TV tables. Not to worry, I'll do it myself."

"*How?* Big plans to turn your widow into a late-in-life lesbian? Gonna hope she has a thing for freckles?"

"Fuck off," I said, turning to leave.

"I see what you're doing. And your game isn't half-bad, for a beginner. You know the value of what you're offering, and that's good. But you need to use less emotion and more patience. Don't ask for your opponent's faith, demand their action. Remember, negotiation is just two people mutually taking advantage of each other. You want to set yourself up in Scotland. Fine. I'll help you. But you need to slow down, sit down, and tell me something about this woman that I can actually use."

My father claimed he needed a room at the hotel in order to do the "scheme" (by which he meant sex with Albina) properly. He couldn't very well bring her back to Charlie's flat. Nor could he rely on Albina, with her good breeding and Ladies' College etiquette, to invite him up to her room.

"What makes you think she'll come to *your* room? If she's such a lady?"

To which Dad replied, "That's just how it works, treasure. Blame Neanderthal double standards."

And so, during my next shift at the Chemsworth, I found myself poring over the cleaning schedule, searching out a vacant room. On the chart in the break room, I spied a free junior suite on the near-empty upper level. Soaking tub. Four-poster bed. I could clean it myself once my father was finished.

And access wouldn't be a problem. I could lend Dad my skeleton housekeeping key—the one that unlocked all the guest rooms—and take off work with a fake illness in the interim.

. . .

For two full days, I lay awake in Charlie's dingy sitting room. Twice, I watched the sun set and rise on the breeze-block view. Like a self-fulfilling prophecy, I had made myself rather ill. My clenched jaw ached. Time felt off-center. Over and over I imagined Reina and a manager pushing in the door to find my father sleeping (or worse) in a suite that cost more per night than Charlie's weekly rent.

Would they give him a chance to explain before they called security?

I had told him not to hand over my key card no matter what. But when he was piss drunk, my father could be forgetful, maybe even enough to leave it out on the bedside table. Would he be arrested if it was found? Would I? And would our fake IDs survive the scrutiny?

I was about to go to the Chemsworth and see what was keeping him when I heard a noise at the door.

"Dad?" I called out.

But it was merely Charlie, back from her night shift.

"You mean he's not home yet?" she asked.

I lied and said he'd popped out for bread.

"Right." She stared at me ten seconds too long. Long enough to make me realize it would have been far more convincing if I'd said he'd gone out for booze.

After Charlie walked off to draw herself a bath with a bottle of her namesake, I ventured out into the frozen rain to wait for Dad beneath the bus shelter.

It was nearly nightfall when I caught sight of him through the windscreen of an approaching bus.

My first impression was: *What sorcery is this?* Dad'd had a louse-ectomy. I hadn't seen him as smooth-shaven since our churchgoing days on the Isle. He was wearing a dog-toothed jacket and toff-red trousers I'd never seen before. And impossible as it was, he looked trimmer. Give him a belt and a decent night's sleep and he gave the impression of a man who ate egg whites and swam a hundred lengths a day. He was chatting up two female passengers—one who looked like she was trying not to throttle him and another who looked like she'd happily have his babies.

He stepped off the bus, laughing like a naughty schoolboy, and I babbled hello with relief.

"You beauty!" he said. "It worked like a dream!"

A smile tore through me. "You *have* got my key?"

"It's right here. Come on. We need a celebratory drink. This time it's on me."

I was expecting another visit to his regular place. But instead, I found myself sitting opposite my father inside a posh gentleman's pub I'd never noticed before. Inside, it was filled with attractive, well-dressed couples.

Dad set a cider in front of me. He was effervescent.

"So much has happened."

"Start from the beginning," I said, eagerly.

"All right. Tea." He sipped his drink and put his weight on one arm of his chair. "I complained about my table. Requested the one next to Albina Penn-Cox. And she's so close I can smell her Earl Grey. Her teapot is practically steaming up my glasses."

I felt giddy. I was going to have housing at university. Better still, I'd attend polo cups and garden parties.

"I'd just ordered a glass of Champagne when a very posh voice says, 'So I see you've been to the exhibit at the National Gallery.' She'd noticed that book you gave me."

I nodded, self-satisfied.

Dad crossed his legs. "I said, 'So, you've been too. What did you think?' Because remember, you have to let these people get an opinion in. Then, you agree enough to make them feel understood. Or play stupid enough to make them feel special. Best yet, some combination of the two."

I affected a pupil's expression. Being noticed by my father felt better than it ought to. I felt like his equal for a change.

"And what did she say?"

"She said she loves the way Sargent painted hands—on and on about how ferociously beautiful and expressive they are. She's a painter. Your Albina Penn-Cox."

"I *told* you that."

"Well, it was important to let her tell me herself."

"You invited her to your table?"

"Modern woman, after all, your Albina. She asked *me* to join *her.* So I'm sharing her toasted tea cakes, and she's complaining that her own watercolors are too saccharine. And I'm matching her body language, smoothing my napkin same as her, tilting my head when she tilts hers. I'm saying, 'Aw, you're just being modest. I'd love to see them.' And she starts joking, 'Well, I would show you, but they're in my studio, back in Scotland, and I've just run away from there.' "

"Let me guess, you claimed to be a painter as well?"

"Me? I couldn't paint a fence. But I said I was a fugitive too, that I left America because I didn't want to run the family business."

My face fell. "So she's not going back to Clacherdon? Do you think, in time, she'd let me stay there anyway?"

"Maybe eventually. Who knows? She's leaving for six months in France, then another four in Spain. She'll go home after. Thing is, I'm her muse now. I *sat* for her last night." That old dirty twinkle in his eyes. "And she's asked me to come with her abroad."

My tongue had gone dry. A retching feeling was upon me. "You're leaving England?"

"Wasn't that the kind of thing you were hoping for?"

"Ha." Less like a laugh and more like expelled air. "No worries about your passport, then."

"I won't know how good it really is until I try."

I stared at the dregs of my cider. "What about me? Chardonnay's not going to keep me on as a flatmate. Should I move up north early? Would Albina lend you some cash? Enough to cover rent in a student flat?"

He shook his head dismissively. "I've got to work up to that. At least to start, I need to make a show of paying my own way."

I was lost in my own thoughts, thinking how foolish I'd been to make myself in my father's image.

"Why don't you stay with that friend of yours?" Dad asked.

"*Seema?*"

Seema's mother forbade sleepovers. She looked at me like I was the human embodiment of everything she found improper (dance classes, bikinis, washing men's and women's clothing in a communal laundry load). I'd have better luck kipping at work, in the closet where we stored the spare pillows.

"You just haven't hooked her properly. You need to make yourself indispensable—"

With Seema's name still hanging in the air, I made a decision.

"India," I said.

Dad's confusion looked genuine. "You're asking if I'm going to India with Albina?"

"No. If you're traipsing around Europe, then *I'm* going to India. I'll defer my enrollment and take a gap year. I have enough in savings."

"Impossible."

"I'll do it cheaply. Ironically, travels in Asia are more affordable than student housing. It's a wonder anyone goes to uni at all."

"That's not what I meant." He made a lighthearted gesture with his cigarette. "I had to dip into the Jackie Collins Savings and Loan. There were clothes, for a start. I had to look the part—"

His red trousers were suddenly the color of violent crime. "You *took* my money?"

"I needed spending cash, plane tickets—"

I stared with horror at the drink my father had "treated" me to with my own twenty-pound note.

"You *stole* from me!" Loud enough to make the knobs at the neighboring table look my way.

Why was I so surprised? He was a crook. But he was my father as well, and up until that moment, I'd had no trouble reconciling the two.

Dad leaned forward. He looked halfheartedly (or quarter-heartedly) earnest. "It was a *loan.* Better still, an investment. Once we're out traveling, I'll tell Albina that my money is tied up. Or claim my elderly mother needs my help. I'll pay you back, I promise. Now, I'll tell you what I'm offering as a repayment plan . . ."

CHAPTER FIFTEEN

I researched a lot in the beginning, reading up about the best way to break divorce to children. Unfortunately, the one time I'd attempt leafing through *The Truth About Divorce* in the stacks of the public library, Fitz, who was an increasingly good reader, caught me and sounded out the words:

"*The Truth About Di—*"

"*The Truth About Diving*," I said, shoving the book back in its place.

"*The Truth About Dying?*"

An older gentleman cocked his newspaper to stare.

"Never mind that," I said. "Let's go look for *Waiting for the Magic*."

According to online reviews, the book taught children that "love and magic" were all it took to cope with the announcement of what they must have already suspected—that we had found ourselves on the wrong side of the divorce rate.

"No," Fitz said, his eyes darkening with resistance. "The only magic I like is Harry Potter."

Given the children weren't in any hurry to address the reason why Randy and I were living apart, I decided to plot our move out of New York City before I broke the news about the so-called "divorce."

In addition, our dream city had to be a fair distance from Florida and Woodstock, where my daily Internet search turned up Mel's obituary:

> Melanie Ashworth, a Woodstock mother, passed away unexpectedly at home last week. Her friends in New Jersey and Woodstock will remember Melanie as a vivacious and determined personality who lived for her daughter.
>
> "She always said her daughter helped her find purpose in her life," Melanie's cousin Shaina Ursola of Matawan, N.J., said. "She loved being a mom, and she was good at it."
>
> Melanie will also be remembered for her commitment to education and justice. "Melanie had become a champion for learning disabilities," said her husband, Victor. "Her work in this area was cut tragically short, but she laid a groundwork for children in this community. Her power and self-assurance will inspire them to speak up in the face of injustice and do anything they set their minds to."
>
> The community at large mourns Melanie's loss, especially Hudson Valley Country Day, where she was a valued volunteer. Her service will be held at Woodstock Reformed Church this Saturday at 12:30.

The old suicide-euphemism "died unexpectedly" reassured me. But then I reread it and lost some confidence. "Unexpectedly" didn't automatically rule out murder. Plus, Victor's words—"cut short"—implied violence.

With the help of *BusinessWeek*, I made a list of potential new cities, far away from the Ashworths and their grief:

Dallas
Chevy Chase, Maryland

Suburbs of Chicago: Kenilworth, Glencoe, Winnetka
California: Hillsborough, Woodside, Los Altos Hills
Colorado: Castle Pines, Cherry Hills Village

Moving to most of those cities without a car was like going into deep space without a rocket, so I decided on Chicago for its public transportation. I told myself the children would play lacrosse. I would move up the social strata by claiming close ties to Obama.

The week of the divorce announcement, I phoned the Plaza Hotel and offered them a feature article and a free banner ad in exchange for a comped night in the Eloise Suite.

Officially, I was a journalist there to "research an article" for a travel website I'd made up called "Go There."

Unofficially, I planned to use the luxurious, kid-friendly weekend to take the sting out of my separation from Randy.

The suite itself ordinarily cost $2,000 a night, but the hotel didn't stop at a free night's stay. Fitz was also given a complimentary etiquette class in the tearoom. The manager gave Kitty a replica of Eloise's monogramed bathrobe.

As I was phoning room service, the hotel's PR rep rapped on the door.

"Oh, hello," I said uncertainly, worried she'd found out Go There's average click-through rates were rubbish.

But to my relief, she was only there to give me free Champagne and truffles, as well as a hot-pink folder filled with press releases. And I reciprocated with questions about Betsey Johnson, who'd designed the zebra-print carpet and candy-striped walls.

"What's *your* name?" the woman asked, crouching down to address Kit.

"Kitty!" my girl enthused, because I hadn't yet found the courage to tell her that she would be Catarina from now on.

"That was Kay Thompson's nickname too!" the PR lady said. "The author of *Eloise*!"

I popped a truffle into Kit's mouth before she could say more and told the PR woman I would contact her for final approval before "the story" ran.

Close calls notwithstanding, it was easier to feel optimistic in posh surroundings. The children and I spent the afternoon cocooned in Egyptian cotton, watching pay-per-view against the pink leather headboard. We napped. We ate room service with our fingers. On occasion, we stopped to smell the vases of pink roses that bedecked every surface.

At dusk, I pulled back the argyle curtains, saw the city lights reflecting off the pond, and proposed a walk in Central Park.

But stage fright set in, and I struggled to get the words out. I tried and failed to say "divorce" after a short, moonlit play at Billy Johnson Playground. I got gun-shy again as we ate soft-serve from Tasti D-Light.

As a last-ditch effort, I agreed to a carriage ride with a driver who looked a little like a young Oz.

We were trotting past the Time Warner Center when I looked up at the dark glass towers.

"Does it always look that way?" I asked the driver. "With whole floors standing empty?"

"Uh-huh," he confirmed, looking up from a text message. (For ten minutes, he'd been holding his phone with one hand and slapping the reins with the other.) "They're owned by, what do you call them, shield corporations?"

"Shell corporations?"

"Yeah, that's it. Shells. Greeks and Russians, I think. Chinese too. No one lives there, though. The owners got arrested in their home countries."

"For what?"

"War crimes, I think. Also, fraud?"

That was the moment I realized Manhattan *itself* had become the Plaza: an iconic landmark with a standard of luxury that only foreigners could afford. Vast quantities of foreign money were flowing unchecked through the city, and no one seemed to know or care where they came from. I ought to have been scared off by the words "arrested" and "fraud," but I couldn't help feeling encouraged.

Marianna and Gracie/Tracey were shell corporations in a sense. They'd left spotty, complex paper trails, all the while protecting my real entity from litigation. Now that Gracie Mueller was dead, it would take skip tracers ages to trace her back to my Christian name. They would have to review business records and court documents from three countries, affording me more than enough time and warning to escape.

Fitz was staring up at the construction lights at 15 Central Park West.

Kitty was snuggled against my side, wearing a perma-grin.

Why leave? I wondered. What New York City lacked in distance from Woodstock, it made up for in anonymity. In Manhattan, Kit was just another stroller to dodge. I was just another middle-aged woman, invisible except to the lower-class men who catcalled: "Hey Mama!" Or: "Love to get me some of that pretty white pussy."

The next morning, as we were eating apple-fritter French toast in bed, I asked the children directly if they knew why we left upstate New York.

"We're here for vacation," Fitz said.

"Well, that's part of it. We're also here in the city because Randy and I have decided not to be married anymore. It's not your fault. We can just love you best when we live in different houses. It's OK to feel sad and angry. I just want you to know that you're not to blame."

Fitz looked at me for a moment. It was a deep look, soul-searching, before he went back to raking a fork through the maple syrup on his plate.

"You'll always have someone who loves you and takes care of you when you're sick. But for right now, for a long time, actually, that's going to be me. I'm going to be your mother and your father while Randy sorts out some grown-up problems. Don't worry about him. He's safe. He has people to keep him company. He just needs some time to learn how to look after himself, so he can be an even better dad."

"So we're going to stay here?" Fitz asked.

"In the city? Yes."

Kitty began jumping on the bed, bouncing the room-service tray.

"I'm glad that excites you. But sit down. There are other changes to come as well."

"Like what?" Fitz asked, deadpan.

"Like your names."

The idea was so outlandish it widened my son's dark eyes. He dropped his jaw comedically.

"No."

"Yes."

"Do I get to pick it?"

I gulped cold tea from my cup. "I wish you could. But it hasn't worked out that way." I turned to Kitty. "From now on, your name is going to be Cat."

She beamed, as though I'd given her permission to spout whiskers.

"You like cats, don't you?"

"Yes!" she said, bounding to her feet again.

"Excellent. So from now on you're called Cat. You understand?"

"Yes!" she said, jumping on the bed. "I'll be a cat who's called 'Kitty'!"

Fitz laughed convulsively.

"Or—you can be a kitty who's called Cat. Fitz, my love, you are going to be called Gio De Felice."

"*No*," he said with more conviction than I'd ever heard before.

"Yes. You're Gio. You have to be."

"No way."

"Well, perhaps you can be Gio most of the time the way Superman is Clark Kent—"

"Fitz!" he said in monosyllabic defiance.

I had expected some initial resistance. But I'd been so accepting when my father renamed me that I'd never imagined Fitz and Kitty might refuse.

"What if I said you must be Gio if you want to go to school?"

Fitz enjoyed pre-K, but evidently school was not the emotional necessity it had been for me.

"I'm Fitz!" His dark eyes sparkled, giving his anger an edge of enjoyment. It was as though it had just occurred to him that his name was sovereign territory.

I dropped my teacup and put an arm around him. "Fair play. But in fact, you have four names. It's something they do in India, where I met your dad."

"Oz?" he asked, keeping his arms rigidly at his sides and swaying a little in my grasp.

"Yes. Your father, Oz. We loved the idea of an Indian naming ceremony—a *namakarana*—so we had one for you, eleven days after you were born. We covered your left ear with a betel leaf, and we whispered your name, Fitzpatrick, into your right ear three times."

"You did? What's a beetle leaf?"

"It's a vine leaf." Actually, we'd used an oak leaf. Culturally appropriating and doing it all wrong. "We gave you four names, total: your first, middle, and last names, plus a constellation name, which we kept secret from everyone."

"Really?" He was smiling. Everyone loves a secret.

"Uh-huh. And do you know what that secret name was?" I paused for effect. "Gio."

"OK," he said.

"Really? You'll be Gio?"

I didn't trust the change. It seemed too sudden.

"Yeah. OK. If it's my consolation name."

"Constellation name," I corrected.

I looked out the window, where the city was awash in shadows and diffuse gray light. Before it was Manhattan, it had been New Amsterdam. Before that, Nouvelle Angoulême. Before that, Mannahatta. New York has always been synonymous with rebranding.

CHAPTER SIXTEEN

While Dad and Albina Penn-Cox toured vineyards and art biennales, quaffing French bubblies and name-dropping Baroque portrait painters, I embarked on my tour of Southeast Asia with the thousand quid that Dad hadn't found in my copy of *Eloise*.

I traveled alone, experiencing all the things hapless youth are meant to find transcendent: the holes-in-the-wall and hostels, the motorbikes and tuk-tuks and *songthaews*, the mushroom omelets and ten kinds of diarrhea. I ate red bananas, fetal duck eggs, and intestine hot pot. I drank baht shots, and Imodium, and fresh-pressed sugarcane juice. I washed elephants and had a monkey steal my sunglasses. I befriended other gap-yearers, dreadlocked people who wore Ali Baba pants, took incessant pictures, and used "chill" as a descriptor. Caught in a downpour in Luang Prabang, I was laughed at by monks. At Wat Phan Tao Temple, I read a warning, posted in English—BEWARE THE SCAMMER IN THIS TEMPLE. HE IS A THAI GENTLEMAN, WELL-DRESSED.—and felt unexpectedly homesick for my father.

Mostly, I looked for cashpoints because I lived on the threshold of absolute poverty and because my father had promised to repay the money he'd taken from me by making regular deposits to a bank account he'd opened for that purpose. In Cambodia, I withdrew riel at Phnom Penh Market, amidst the smell of durian and fried tarantulas. In Bangkok, I followed a group of backpackers through the sticky-floored bars in Nana Plaza, and withdrew baht while the others watched a woman launch Ping-Pong balls out of her fanny. On Ko Pha-ngan, a working ATM brought me more euphoria than the monthly dreadlocks-and-douchebags party on Haad Rin Beach.

I felt nervous every time I went to take out money. I didn't know how my father was coming about the cash, embezzling it from Albina or whatnot. And with no guarantee what the bank balance would be—all through Chiang Rai, Chiang Mai, and into Laos, the deposits had been shrinking—it was impossible to stick to a budget. My ability to buy essentials like Deet spray, double-entry visas, or hepatitis booster shots at the local Red Cross was always in question.

Feeling like my own ransomer, in Vientiane, I tracked down what had to be the only Internet café in the whole of Laos and emailed Dad at the account I had set up for him:

Dear Dad,

Will you be paying by check, charge, or cash?

Joking. I'm writing to thank you and Albina for your last financial contribution, without which I might still be in Bangkok, taking bar girl jobs.

As per your suggestion, I have recorded every purchase, no matter how small. To date, I have logged four hundred and eighty-six (four hundred and eighty-seven, if I count this Internet cafe). My largest expenses are illegal drugs and admission to the sort of full-moon parties where foreigners vomit and copulate on the beach. Joking, again. I spend approximately nine pounds a day on food, five on housing, three on transportation, and a mere ten thousand on Imodium.

Relatedly, I met a lovely German bloke while I was motorbiking through the mountains in Pho. And then I ate the uncooked greens. His parting words were: "This might have been really romantic if you were in control of your bowels."

Speaking of romance, I hope you and Albina are well. I look forward to hearing about your trip and understand if you are too busy to write. I imagine you are feeding each other steak frites and gazing into each other's eyes. Or maybe sipping aperitifs on the mountain in those Cezanne paintings she likes.

Laos is lovely. Friendly people. Spicy, utterly delicious food. The only challenge is transportation. It's quite mountainous, and I find myself rather limited in how I get around.

So if you could stick to our agreed-upon budget, I can take a bus to Luang Prabang instead of relying on my Thai-Laos dictionary for hitchhiking phrases. One car passes every six minutes on the A-road (mostly dirt, with random sections of pavement) and I am not keen to experience it in the back of a farmer's pickup.

Very sincerely,
Your discreet and loyal daughter

But no reply was forthcoming. Not in the "Computa Café" on Bangkok's Khao San Road. Not in the queue-for-an-hour "email suite" in a basement in Paharganj, Delhi. And arriving in Varanasi, India, I discovered there had been no further deposits. I had a mere two thousand rupees to my name, approximately thirty pounds.

I still remember it as though it were yesterday: there at the Bank of Baroda, standing powerless before an ATM draped in cheerful plastic garland, staring at the dismal numbers on the smeary screen.

"American?" asked a voice behind me.

"British," I said, bending to remove the heartbreakingly small stack of bills.

"Good," he said, one brow barely lifted. Holding this almost-smile between his teeth.

"Is it?" I asked, straightening. I slid the cash into my money belt, flapped my shirt over it, and turned to look at him.

Despite his looks, I was in no mood for any more male attention. As it was, I'd spent most of my time in India being hissed at.

"Yes," he said, his smile broadening. "That means I can tell you a joke about the American traveler in India."

He was the lucky kind who could blend in on that subcontinent. His dark, velvet hair was his passport to anonymity. For that matter, so were his eyes, which reflected light like black ice.

"The American traveler in India asks, 'Will I be able to see elephants in the street?' And guess how the concierge answers. True story."

I smiled in spite of myself. "I don't know. What does the concierge say?"

" 'That depends how much you've been drinking, sir.' "

I laughed, punch-drunk with despair, and he began another one.

"The American traveler asks, 'Can you give me some information about hippo racing?' And the concierge says, '*Africa* is the big, triangle-shaped continent south of Europe. *India* is the big triangle in the middle of the Pacific and Indian Oceans, which does not . . . Oh, forget it. Sure, hippo racing is every Tuesday night on the Ganges. Go naked.' "

I laughed again. "Funny." And my stomach did an odd rabbit kick it hadn't done since the German bloke.

"You mean, funny, *Oz*."

Beyond him, in the labyrinthine lanes of the old city, there was drumming, singing, monkey screeches, pilgrims' metal plates clattering, people elbowing their way to Vishwanath Temple, carrying water from the holy Ganges. Dusk was on its way, adding a level of risk to my solo travels. Every day, sunset fell like a sentence. It left me doom-laden.

He, Oz, was still studying me. His mouth had fallen slightly. His eyes were tearing in the wafting incense, the smells of human piss and cow dung.

He reached down and lifted my hand, which up until then had been hanging limp by my side. "And this would be the part where you tell me *your* name . . ."

. . .

I let Oz lead me to a rooftop restaurant with an attached guesthouse he recommended.

Under any other circumstance, I would have hesitated to trust a stranger based solely on his taut abdomen, dreamy eyes, and claim to know the best palak potatoes in town. But even if I wasn't utterly skint, I hadn't been in Varanasi long enough to get my bearings.

A few feet away from our table, a man played the sitar—a sweet buzzy drone.

Below us, the open sewer of a river was quieting itself. There, in the lower light, its holiness finally shone through in ways I could appreciate and see. The bazaars were lighting up, women organizing their goods in the flickering light. Behind tiny windows, families were kneeling down to dinner, heating tea on charcoals.

"Have you figured it out yet?" Oz asked.

I adjusted the shawl I wore for modesty. "You mean, why I'm sitting here with you?"

His laugh said, *fair play*. "I meant, have you had your revelation yet?"

I gave him the *are-you-mad* look I reserved for backpackers who tried to tempt me with "happy milkshakes" made of magic mushrooms.

"*Darshan*," he said. "It's the divine insight that happens to a lot of people in Varanasi."

"Hmmm," I said. Under other circumstances, I would have balked at that sort of earnestness. But amid the sandalwood incense and the golden bloodred sky, I was willing to try sincerity. Or at the very least, entertain more than snark.

"What does that mean, *hmmm*?"

"It just means that makes sense *here*." I cast a downward look at the dusk crowd, which was washing themselves and praying. "Back home, epiphanies are kind of lowbrow."

"Lowbrow. Ah." Oz wiped his mouth. "I get it. Your parents are rich assholes, and you've come to Varanasi to escape them. Good on you."

"Ha!" I laughed, overly pleased I'd disguised my naffdom.

"What?"

"Nothing. It's just—my father likes to say accusations are confessions."

"You think I've run away from something?"

I took my chin in my hand, play combative. Smiling, of course.

Given his looks, I was imagining he'd got some posh girl up the duff and been driven out of town by her politician dad. So I was quite taken aback when he described a festering cesspool of child abuse that was midway between *Jane Eyre* and *Matilda.* His mother had died in a minibus wreck. ("She had a crushed skull with avulsions of the cranium and brain. Trust me, you don't want to know what that means.") Being clueless in the ways of children, his father had passed him off to his aunt, who lived in the Eastern Anatolia region of Turkey and used to lock him in the dog kennel some days because he "behaved like a dog and belonged with the dogs."

"I spent every waking moment planning my escape and left home the minute I turned sixteen."

"Do you still speak to them? Your family?"

"Why would I? In life we are obligated only to ourselves. What? You're judging."

"No. The opposite. I've never considered breaking contact with my father. I feel a bit like you've given me permission."

"You're going to drop-kick the old bastard?"

"No . . ."

"Why not?"

"He's good fun when he's not being a dick—"

He made a face. "And you always have to be there for your family."

"Oh no, I've left family before."

I had said it without meaning to, and when Oz pressed me for details, I went ahead and described the way Dad and I had left Ireland. I was so far away from home that the risks felt reduced. Plus, something in me wanted to show Oz I was as world-weary as he was. I hadn't traveled as much in the geographic sense, so I had to work harder to prove I'd seen some misery.

Oz shook his head. "He sounds like a waste of space. I mean, you live in *London*? And he's mooching tenners off divorcées? There's no limit to the schemes he could be running: courier scams, boiler rooms. I mean, if you're going to scam, do it properly. Criminality's no excuse for poor work ethic."

"Well, he has a well-off older woman now. Scottish aristocracy. Not that it's helped him pay back the money he owes me."

"This breaks my heart," Oz said, his hand spider-crawling across the pink tablecloth toward mine.

I flushed as he stroked my inner wrist with his thumb. "*Heartbreaking* is a little much. It's challenging, maybe."

"Yes, very challenging for me. I'd been hoping you'd pay for dinner."

We were drunk on White Mischief vodka and the magic of travel. I nearly fell over laughing, my shawl slipping in the process.

"And here I was hoping this meal was on *you*. I spent my last rupees on that dreadful hotel."

In the end, Oz worked out a deal with the restaurant's owner, paying our bill in hashish—the same dark, sticky stuff we later smoked from a pipe on the banks of the river.

I listened, nodding dumbly, in smoky delirium, while he talked.

"Is Oz a typical name in Turkey?"

He nodded. "Short for Ozgur."

"What's the best thing you've seen in Varanasi?"

"The pyres. I like the idea that we've all had a million identities before this one, and we'll have another million after it. So what's so special about this particular body? Why put it in the ground like the Christians?"

"And the worst?"

"I saw it during a sunrise boat ride on the Ganges. The bottom half of a dead baby floated to the surface. Hindus don't cremate infants."

The hash tingled in my bones and I felt a tear roll down my cheek.

He smiled, tickling my face with the fringe end of my shawl.

"I want to kiss you," he said, but cited Indian attitudes about public displays of affection. "There's a Ganga Aarti ceremony about to start. Come brave it with me."

After so many months wandering lost and alone, I liked the way Oz demanded action. He didn't ask questions. Instead, he told me where to go.

We squeezed through the crowd to where five Hindu priests were chanting in a barrage of color, waving cobra-shaped oil lamps. And the whole time, Oz stood behind me. His breath was twinkly soft in my ear, commentating: "These are offerings to the deities . . . The flower for solidity . . . The water and handkerchief for liquidity . . . The flame because light destroys the darkness of ignorance . . ."

We cupped our downturned hands over the *aarti* plate and raised our palms to our foreheads. Singing "Om Jai Shiv Omkara" in the crush of the crowd, Oz brushed my curls off my collarbone, leaned down, and—so discreetly, so briefly—put his lips there.

After the ceremony, Oz and I were smoking more hash, sharing a chillum with two ash-smeared sadhus, bells jingling from the pierced privates beneath their loincloths. And I was thinking, in stoned fashion, just how deeply I understood them: their haunted eyes, the way they relied entirely on the generosity of others—begging for food and hash—the way so many had been orphaned, then set out wandering, with no hope to live or wish to die.

"Let's go over there," Oz said suddenly, breaking off another chunk of hash to give to the sadhus. He took my hand and guided me over to a crowd that was gathering near the Asti Ghat.

"What's happening?" I asked.

There was an elderly man being carried down the steps to the shore.

"He's dying," Oz said. "But he's accepted it. He's having a small ceremony with his family. When a person dies in Varanasi, all their sins disappear. Even the sins they accumulated in their thousand past lives."

And from the top of the steps, we looked down and watched him collapse, a holy man massaging the old man's back while Oz rubbed mine. The ground breathed unsteadily beneath me, and my legs jellied with a second wave of hashish.

My half-averted face was wet with tears.

Beside me, Oz's voice sounded very far away: "You're sad for him?"

I shook my head. I was happy for the man to die blameless—pure. "Just thinking about my past lives," I said.

They rolled the corpse onto a stretcher, and made certain the man was really dead. The family cried. Finally, a man moved it to the pits and stacked it with wood, the man's head and feet still exposed.

The dead man's son circled the pyre and lit it with a burning reed. As the wood caught, a gray plume of smoke wafted over us. The son filled a clay pot with river water, splashed it on the pyre, and threw it to the ground with a smash that caught me off guard.

I felt like my chest had tectonic plates, and they moved.

Oz said: "He breaks the pot to symbolize the end of the relationship."

It made such sense. Even to my stoned mind. Someone died, and you experienced it with all five senses. You felt the smash. You heard the feasting flames. You coughed on the thick, hazy smell of their dust. You watched this person who had meant so much revert back to nothing right in front of you.

The dead man's face was utterly extinguished of life—a graying black coal. But the burning kept up.

And the one thought in my mind was: the scorched silhouette, trembling in the force of the flames, reminded me of my mother—a woman I'd never bothered going back to, not even after her death. It struck me as a betrayal even worse than leaving Ireland. I'd never done any of the things a better daughter would have done—remembrances like finding her obituary, tending to her possessions, visiting her grave. Why?

Being just as estranged from my emotions as I was from my Irish vowels, it occurred to me, for the first time ever, that maybe it wasn't loyalty for my father that had kept me from tracking down my mam all those years. Maybe I was angry with her. Maybe, all these years, some obstinate little voice in the back of my mind asked, *Why? Why should I hunt her down when she'd never bothered doing the same for me?*

"What is it?" Oz asked, watching with concern as I dragged my palms across my face.

And I could only say: "I think I've had my revelation."

MARIANNA DE FELICE

(Five Years Later)

All an actor can play is himself. Himself in the thousand-and-one variations dictated by a thousand-and-one roles.

—Charles Marowitz, *Stanislavsky & The Method*

CHAPTER SEVENTEEN

City living is like raising children in the sense that the days are long, but the years pass quick. Five weeks became five months, which gave way to five years.

An overheard conversation at the nail shop led to a cash sublet in Red Hook, where we lived in a basement studio until I decided to move us to Manhattan, no matter the cost.

Moving was more difficult than I anticipated. Manhattan real-estate brokers made Randy look honest by comparison. I read the classified ads religiously, prepared to swoop on anything that fell within our tiny budget. But every time I showed up for a "viewing," the apartment on offer turned out to be a brokers' office. I'd go inside and find young people in clip-on ties, packed in like dairy cows.

"Which apartment are you here about?" they'd ask, shifty-eyed.

"The two-bedroom in the Flatiron District."

"Oh," they'd say, then clumsily explain that the "two-bedroom Manhattan apartment" they had advertised was actually a Queens studio with "good transportation lines" and the landlord's permission to put up drywall.

After two weeks of duplicitous bullshite, I was crying in frustration. The whole bait-and-switch was designed to make me hire a broker for an outrageous fee, and I refused to give in to their grift.

I reconnected with the slimiest listing agent I'd met—the one who had offered me a no-fee studio, then, when I met him there thirty minutes later, claimed it had just been rented and offered to show me a "different one" just down the street that carried a $1,500 broker's fee.

I emailed him an application and packed the attached file with a key logger and computer-monitoring software. After he'd opened it, I saw everything he did on his computer: his passwords, his messages, the bizarre ninja porn he watched when his boss wasn't looking. In amongst his emails, I found a landlord who was prepared to pay him a fee to bring him potential tenants for a studio on Seventy-Second and Second. So I emailed the landlord my application directly and moved in the same day.

I changed my business model once the children were in school, leaving me more time for "work." For the next four years, I created a series of websites for phony SEO service companies, offering small businesses a "special discount" on a $499-a-year service package that would improve their websites' chances of being found and ranked by search engines. I accepted electronic money transfers and sat on the bogus website for a month, periodically emailing clients with filler newsletters. Then, I closed down the website and bank account, took a day or two to rest, and began the whole process all over again. It wasn't the most secure way to earn a living, but then, acting had prepared me for the endlessly repeating cycle of paychecks and poverty.

Work is a distinctly adult pleasure, and there are times when I felt like I was missing out. In Midtown, I glanced up at the high-rise office buildings and felt a searing envy for the men and women inside, who were deriving meaning and identity from their jobs in addition to cold, hard, reliable cash. Yet, even with my Social Security number and bogus green card, I didn't dare put myself up for an honest job. Instead, I used motherhood as an escape hatch—a graceful and convenient exit from the workforce.

The parents at Fitz's public school, which I came to think of as PS 666, worked forty-nine-hour workweeks and still managed to volunteer for field trips and cafeteria duty. When the PTA stalwarts leaned over the bake-sale table to ask, "Do *you* work, Marianna?" I shyly referenced the modest payout I'd received after my "divorce," then pointed to someone else's cupcakes and claimed they were my contribution.

Playing the alimony mum satisfied questions, but it also gave me something of an inferiority complex. And the year Gio turned ten, I could tell my insecurities were rubbing off on him.

He nurtured self-doubt like a secret pet puppy. I tried discussing it with him. I asked whether any of the other boys were unkind to him on account of his single mother or his hazy background. But he just scratched a dark eyebrow, shook his head, and returned his attention to YouTube, where his favorite videos asked the irremediable question *Where in the World Is Carmen Sandiego?*

Presumably he was interested in geography because so many of his classmates were multilingual. Gio described their fathers—Korean grocers, Bangladeshi cabdrivers, and Serbian plumbers—in voyeuristic detail, and yet he'd made no friends. He watched other boys from a scholarly distance.

That is, he did before he got himself into serious trouble during a class field trip to the Intrepid Sea, Air, and Space Museum.

I wasn't there at the time, which felt like another strike against me when I rushed uptown to meet his teacher and the school principal. As a "stay-at-home mother," I really should have volunteered to chaperone the field trip. Instead, I'd spent the morning writing dozens of fake five-star reviews for my latest dodgy "SEO company," following a close call with a Roto-Rooter who'd hired me because he thought I could do the impossible and make him the first result when one Googled "plumbers in Queens."

The principal was a woman about my age, with a low ponytail that accentuated her large, rounded forehead and lovely skin that shined like a samovar. She gave me a bright greeting that matched her blindingly orange dress.

"Mrs. De Felice," she said. "Please sit. I know this isn't the news you were hoping to get today. I've just been sitting here with Ms. Ingarta, trying to get a clearer sense of what happened."

As I sat and crossed my legs, I noticed a fish tank in the corner. Inside, a pair of silver fish darted in and out of a ceramic shipwreck.

"The message I received said Gio nearly caused an accident? But both children are fine?" Every time the school phoned, I panicked, thinking they'd discovered his birth certificate was a fake.

Gio's teacher Ms. Ingarta ran her fingers through her short, frosted hair. "'Accident' sounds accidental. This was *intentional*."

"My son would never hurt anyone," I said in the Yankee accent I had more or less perfected in five years. I didn't even think of it as "speaking American" so much as doing a scaled-down impression of my dad. Our first year in Brooklyn, Gio used to ask, *Hey Mom, remember when you used to call me "old chum"?* Or, *Mom, remember when you used to say things like "jolly good work"?* Every time, I told him the same thing: *I lived in Britain for a while, remember, Gee? But I'm an American now, and I want to sound that way. Like those nasty bumper stickers say: "Welcome to America, Speak English."*

Ms. Ingarta put a heavy palm on the principal's desk: "Gio trespassed, for a start. He crossed *two* barriers that said the flight deck was closed. To say nothing of the fact that the children are supposed to stay together as a group!"

"So that's the problem? My son went onto the flight deck when he shouldn't? I'm not condoning his actions, but surely any boy would be tempted to see the airplanes? I don't really see how that's putting his—or anyone else's—life *in danger*."

Ms. Ingarta balked.

The principal shot her a let-me-handle-this look. "The thing is, Gio convinced his field-trip partner to go with him."

"Isn't that a good thing? That Gio's finally making friends? Besides, aren't they supposed to use the buddy system?"

"In this case, it could be seen as coercive."

"*Coercive?*"

Ms. Ingarta leaned forward emphatically, addressing the principal instead of me. "When I came up, Gio was luring the other child onto the ledge! I've seen a lot in my career, but this chilled me to the bone. It was deliberate! I shudder to think what would have happened if I'd found them even one moment later."

"Let's not be overly dramatic," I said.

"Dramatic! We're talking about a seventeen-story drop into the Hudson River!"

The aquarium bubbled.

I crossed my arms and shook my head. "When you say 'luring,' you mean what, exactly?"

"He was saying, 'No. You can't see from there. Climb over. I'll lift you.' "

"You make him sound like a sociopath. What I hear is a ten-year-old kid having a naughty adventure with a friend."

"Gio has no friends," Ms. Ingarta said. "You implied as much yourself."

"Does Gio have any positive male role models?" the principal asked.

"My ex isn't in the picture. He had some . . ."—I hesitated for effect—"addiction issues."

Research told me Randy might not be the blooming alcoholic he was back when I had the distinct pleasure of being his "wife." The last time I'd checked his wish list on a popular book-selling site, I'd found a number of recovery books, including Alcoholics Anonymous's *Twelve Steps and Twelve Traditions*.

"I'm sorry," the principal said. "Goodness knows, there are all kinds of families. Have you looked into big-brother programs? Or boys-only summer camps? Registration's probably passed, but between us, we can pull strings. I have a list of resources here, somewhere." She pressed a button and asked her assistant to fetch a flyer. She added: "Boys need to see that men can be gentle too."

I nodded in agreement.

Rather than looking for his daughter, Randy had indeed taken the life-insurance payout. And from what I could tell, he hadn't even used the money to save the Catskill house. Instead, he'd invested it into his own Miami-based real estate firm. Mueller Realty. *For All Your Coral Gables and South Florida Real Estate Needs.*

"I understand," the principal said. "So we need to decide how to address this situation. Right now, I think it's in everyone's best interest if Gio leaves class."

"You're suspending him?"

"I prefer the term 'out-of-school discipline.'"

After the meeting, I retrieved the children from the aftercare program in the school gymnasium, where Gio was sitting forlornly on the bleachers, watching the "well-adjusted" boys pull down one another's trousers.

"Sorry, Mom," he grumbled when he saw me.

"It's all right," I said.

"They told you what happened?"

"They did. But I'd rather hear your version."

"I didn't see the sign."

I gave him a dubious look. "Your teacher said there were *two* signs. And a barrier."

"I like being up high," he said to his sneakers. He was dragging the toe across the floor, working the spot where the sole had begun to separate.

"Come on." I sighed. "Let's go to the newsstand. I'll buy you both a Snickers."

As a malcontent London teenager, I used to do the same thing: use the newsagent as therapy, binge reading magazines in order to avoid thinking about my own shabby, exhausting life. When we arrived, Cat found a book of word searches. Gio paged through *National Geographic.* I lost myself in *Star* magazine, glancing up from the extramarital affairs of famous people only when I noticed Cat had knocked a copy of *Tatler* onto the floor.

Still fuming—there was no way Gio had intentionally tried to drown a classmate, he was tearing up over an article about endangered condors, for fuck's sake—I bent down and found the magazine was open to a guide to international schools. There in the first column was a description of the Boulevard School:

> BOULEVARD: The hype heard 'round the world: it's a celebrity pit; impossible to get into; the trendiest school in New York (ergo, the US?). Honestly? "It's the most nurturing place you can imagine," reports one Manhattan mother. Top-notch tech. Brutalist architecture. Tate-Modernish art. Brainboxes are very welcome, but creative mojo and strong language skills are a must. Register from the maternity ward. Jet, set, go! Education in first class.

Staring at the glossy mag in my hands, I thought maybe Ms. Ingarta had a point about Gio not fitting in. Even with the children's fake documents, we still stuck out like sore thumbs in the public school system. And I was fed up with feeling like an outsider—Irish in England, British in America, peculiar at PS 666. But almost everyone at Boulevard was foreign. It sounded less like a school and more like a tax haven. Like Monte Carlo or the Cayman Islands. I pictured rhinestone royalty. Nouveau riche sizing up nouveau riche. Everyone too preoccupied with "Don't you know who I am?" to ever stop and ask "Who are *you*, really?"

Plus, the school was practically a good-mark convention. So many bored billionaires, all cut off from the sort of personal support systems who might warn them about people like me.

But then, we would never have the money or connections to get in. You had to have legacy, or be enrolled from kindergarten, or give a $20 million endowment.

That, or you had to work out some other less-than-meritocratic admissions scheme—shag someone on the admissions board, maybe.

In general, sex wasn't part of my seductive repertoire. Not since Randy.

The role was too easy. That was part of it. Any idiot can play the sex siren given the right assets: Marilyn's doe eyes; Brigitte Bardot's chest; a big, filthy laugh. You play to men's visual weaknesses and protective instincts. You make your mouth titter schoolgirl innocence and your body exude all-caps SEX. There's no skill. Therefore, no thrill.

What's more, gold-digging is the most insecure con. In time, a man always wants different pleasures. If my father hadn't convinced me as much, Randy certainly did. It had been bad enough, being cast aside for Vanessa in my mid-thirties. I wasn't keen to set myself up to be discarded again, in my forties—left with nothing but my nightly wrinkle regimen.

But the goal was admissions, not full financial support. Guttingly, a little research revealed all the admissions officers were married. But the board had a teacher-adviser who appeared to be single: Francis Blake.

Francis, I thought, clicking on a link to his video-conferenced writing workshop. *Let's pray he's more sexually suggestible than the pope.*

In his blogs, Francis began a great many sentences with "Hopefully," which fact alone suggested he'd be a very good mark. Plus, he was tech-savvy, strewing himself all over the Interwebs, in the name of using technology as a teaching tool. He tweeted teaching tips ("Chances are the genius in your class isn't the kid you think it is") and posted a daily #selfiewithastudent who was working exceptionally hard in his class: "This girl can write one mean topic sentence" and "Meet your new lit. journal editor! David Remnick's got nothing on this guy!"

I clicked repeatedly through his photos, memorizing his cowboy's jaw, his warm hazel eyes, and his Woody Allenish way of pairing dress trousers with trainers.

Then, I sat back for many weeks, stalking his social media accounts.

. . .

I found my "in" on a lazy Sunday in late May when Francis shared a photo of Jane Austen's longhand and geo-tagged it to the Morgan Library.

My stomach fluttered. If lovestruck characters have cartoon hearts and birds buzzing around their heads, mine was aswarm with Boulevard logos. (A little boat with a sail shaped like the letter *B*.)

I left the children with a babysitter, changed into my clingiest day dress, and taxied downtown at top speed.

I was imagining a classic professor type: gnawing physical insecurities, easy to seduce with pure sexuality. But when I arrived, and bent to adjust my shoe at very revealing angle, I found Francis was too busy eyeing the display cases to look.

I began to wonder if I'd read him all wrong. In person, he had a quiet confidence and the dreamy look of a romantic. *What if he doesn't want a sex siren?* I thought. What if he wanted someone who shared his sensitivity and intelligence—a partner who, as the woman on display would say, could meet him "in conversation"?

I hadn't read *Pride and Prejudice*, only seen the film, and for the life of me, I didn't remember a thing beyond Mark Darcy's wet shirt. I had a thought to pop out to the toilets and read the SparkNotes on my phone, but if I did, there was a chance I could lose him.

"Wouldn't it be fun to have a Jane Austen–themed meal?" I asked, winging it.

Francis did a polite double take, as though he were unclear whether I was addressing him.

"What would that look like exactly?" he said, after a moment's consideration. "Like, Pies and Prejudice?"

I hadn't the foggiest idea what I'd meant. I'd just been looking for a cue from him, something to guide me.

"That's it exactly!" I said, aiming for playful.

He gave a guarded smile but made no move to say more.

I had come on too strong and jarred him. That, or he just wasn't attracted to me. It occurred to me how foolish I'd been, assuming

I could just go out and pick up a man, no problem, after five years' absence from the dating scene. Especially when I had bags under my eyes, and two children from two previous marriages, not to mention no job—

"Might be a little ostentatious," he said.

I reddened at criticism, but just at the moment my cheeks flared with self-reproach, I focused on his hazel eyes. They were the browny-blue of agitated water. Glittering with humor.

His meaning hit me all at once, and I doubled over laughing with a soft volume that implied intimacy. "With an *A*, right? Austentatious?"

His small smile brought nice flashbacks from my student days. Rather than reveling in his own intellect, he seemed delighted that he'd made *me* feel clever.

After the Morgan Museum, I invited Francis to join me for a coffee at Madison Bistro.

Like I said, I was hoping to use him to get the children into Boulevard, of course, nothing more. But as I was sitting there, working hard to fill the troubling first-date silences, it occurred to me that his benefits package must include free tuition.

I mentioned just enough of Gio and Cat to seem forthcoming without blathering. "So judging by the way you've listened so patiently to me, you have kids too?" I asked. "Do they attend the school where you teach?"

"No. I mean"—Francis cleared his throat and sipped his mug of tea—"I like children. But I don't have any of my own. Even if I did, my school is one of the city's most expensive. I doubt I could afford it. How's that for irony?"

I was secretly crestfallen. "You don't get free tuition, as a teacher?"

"Just a discount. I don't want to call the headmaster *cheap*." He smiled with playful diplomacy. "He's just—business-minded. He worked in the corporate world before he turned his sights to education. Where do your children go to school?"

I told him about PS 666. Described the way Gio's teacher thought he didn't "fit in."

Genuine sympathy. Francis listened with his whole face. "If you want to teach children anything, you have to model basic kindness, and it sounds like this woman isn't doing much of that."

"Yes," I said, thinking of my father. "I learned that early on too."

Francis's eyebrows shot up. "You teach?"

His eyes went as soft as an approaching touch, and I saw an opening.

"Well, I used to teach. Back in Britain."

The vibe between us had been pleasant enough, but my supposed background in education raised the temperature. Francis looked agitated, in the best way. He wanted an Austenian partner, all right: kinship, intellectual equality.

"What subject?" he asked.

Targets with active minds are worrisome. My father liked to say an intelligent mark is a dangerous mark. But then, Francis had other assets—things I'd never known I wanted until now, sitting opposite them. His administrative sway at Boulevard was a large part of it. But I admired his sense of purpose as well. God help me, he said "pedagogy" with such passion that I heard the word "orgy."

"Dramatic arts," I said instinctively.

I watched his smile form in the lines around his eyes first. He touched his spoon tenderly, as though it were a substitute for my hand. He had nice hands, despite his bitten fingernails.

We talked more, and my thoughts wandered to how much Gio would love attending Boulevard if Francis got him in. He would resurrect the Mandarin he'd learned at Finger Joy. He'd meet other spindly boys who spent all their time on Google Earth.

Francis paid the bill with quiet chivalry (that was promising) while I took his phone and added the contact "Marianna."

. . .

During the long subway ride home, I wondered: How difficult could it be to play a teacher? It had certainly improved Francis's opinion of me. And I remembered a lot of lines from my student days.

At home that night, I listened to teaching podcasts about subjects like "The True Identity of an Educator" and jotted down sound bites that I could use as a starter script. Teachers today spoke an entirely different language from the ones I'd grown up with. They talked about something called "growth mind-set" and "project-based learning." They commiserated about burnout—that feeling of "living" the role of the teacher, but going through the motions in the classroom. I almost forgot they were talking about education. They sounded like actors trying to galvanize their audience of students, and they convinced me that my theatre background actually made me incredibly well suited for the job.

The terminology was going to be the main challenge. Discipline was "classroom management." Discussion was "active learning." A teacher didn't say "truth"; she talked about "belief," "acceptance," "verification," "justification," and so on. I learned just enough education-speak to put it down. To my relief and growing credibility, it worked a treat. Francis said he admired me for bucking drab educational trends.

He carried the torch high for me in other ways too. When he finally kissed me, he did so with passion, pinning me against my apartment building's front door with the starved intensity of a man who had grown up wanking not over his father's *Playboy* but reading his mother's copy of *Delta of Venus*. It was not difficult to see the nerd in him—the bookish chap who had been slow to shed his virginity. He feared and revered women. We were mysteries to him. We were holy days. Maybe that was even why he'd entered the female-dominated field of education. To worship. I'm generalizing, of course. Describing only the way it was between us in the beginning. But he was a romantic: crazy about love in general, and then too quickly, me specifically.

"You really miss the classroom, don't you?" Francis asked me, early one evening at the dollar-book rack outside the Strand, where he had caught me thumbing through *The Ignorant Schoolmaster*, a book that argued a person needs no prior history with a subject to teach it.

"I do," I said honestly. "I didn't have the most conventional upbringing. School always felt like my home, in the absence of a healthy one. I suppose in a way it still does."

"Well, I'll keep my ear to the ground for openings."

"Oh, no. You don't have to do that."

"Why wouldn't I?"

"I'm just thinking I might consider a different path. I've been applying for months and I haven't been on one interview. My résumé is beginning to feel like a list of things I never want to do again anyway." I stepped closer to him, out of the way of a pair of NYU students who were loudly sharing their thoughts about capitalism.

"You don't mean that, really."

"No, I don't. I just remember how tired I used to be."

"Teachers dream of sleep," he said. "That's one of the main reasons my last relationship failed."

I laughed, a mistake, given how nervous he was around me, as if waiting for me to unmask *his* insecurities. "You broke up because you were too tired for"—I reached for an ed-speak euphemism—"*explication*?"

He chuckled. "Among other things. It's hard to commit your life to someone who falls asleep in a pile of papers every night at nine p.m. Or doesn't make it home for dinner because there's a J.V. volleyball game."

"Ah, so you were engaged."

"Were . . . Was." Pretending it was the grammar that troubled him.

I doubted their breakup was really down to his profession. It sounded like dumped logic, which is to say: too cheap and tidy to be real. But I agreed anyway: "Civilians don't get it. When you marry a teacher, the school community becomes family."

His crow's-feet deepened as he smiled. "You said it."

Lest I overstate my prowess, I should say that timing played a role. He was post-breakup, but pre–playing the field. Not yet thwarting love by looking for it.

"What do you think of this?" I said, reading aloud from *The Ignorant Schoolmaster*: "People want to be near a teacher who has 'worked in the gap between feeling and expression . . .' The teacher who has tried to 'give voice to the silent dialogue the soul has with itself, who have gambled all their credibility on the bet of the similarity of minds.' "

He approached me from behind, wrapping his arms around my waist and stooping to rest his chin on my shoulder. "I think I can't believe you're reading that."

"Is that a good thing or a bad thing?"

He smelled my hair and said, "What do you think?"

His two-bedroom apartment on Thirty-Fourth and Tenth was the Taj Mahal compared to ours, which barely accommodated the children's bunk bed and my futon, but there were also touches of long-term bachelordom.

For instance, lined up beside the door with psychotic precision, there were *five* pairs of running shoes and even more loafers. I mean, there were gray suede loafers. Loafers in khaki linen. Tasseled lawyer loafers. And loafers with moccasin toes, the sort that hip, young downtown men wore with rolled-up jeans. It was the United Nations of loafers, and I couldn't begin to understand why a schoolteacher needed so many shoes.

"Can I get you something to drink?" he asked, opening his refrigerator wide enough to reveal the horror show inside. I saw foil takeout containers, half-drunk Snapple bottles, even a liter of Mountain Dew.

I shook my head and pulled back the kitchen curtain, looking out onto a litter-choked air shaft.

"It's not much to look at," Francis said.

"I like it. I had the same view at every hotel in India."

His eyes were attentive and, possibly, sexually anxious as he asked me the obvious questions about where I had traveled and whether it was true that journeying around India was like seeing the world with the lid off.

I ignored the inquiry and pulled him in for a kiss. I touched my tongue to his and inhaled the teacherly scent of him: Xerox ink and peppermint tea. In educational terms, I took an "attitudinal assessment" of the "emotional growth" that was happening in the broken-in chinos he wore to work. Then, I pulled away and asked him to show me the bedroom.

As I've said, sex isn't the most effective method of seduction. If you want your mark to reveal his true character, just about the worst thing you can do is undress him.

People aren't defenseless when they're fucking. Just the opposite. They're strategizing.

First sex with a new mark is the worst sex of all because there's no way to identify and fill his emotional voids straightaway. Depending on the person, "sex" can be code for any number of things: obligation, escape, power, submission. The man slipping it up you might make polite, delicate love whilst porn music plays in his head. And the inverse is true as well. It's quite possible for a man who treats you like a disposable orifice to entertain marriage fantasies; he might turn around and invite you to meet his mother before his male secretions have dried between your legs. Compared to the feminine seductions I excelled at, sex was not a straightforward exchange of cues and acting.

At least Francis's bedroom was a tidy, suitable set. The walls were decorated with photos of New York landmarks—the Chrysler Building, sunbeams in Grand Central Station, and whatnot, the sorts of things that sweet, clueless men hang when they're making an effort. Books were stacked on the windowsills. The duvet was that particular shade of "single man" that is neither blue nor gray. The air conditioner was blowing and spitting, and like all New York flats, the temperature in the room bore no relation to the season.

I took a carnal approach right from the start. I pressed my lips against his. I drove my pubic bone into his thigh, pretending to be bold because that's what I suspected he needed—this shy, undemonstrative man, the first I'd let touch me in five years. I forced a tender flush of excitement into my cheeks. I thought of the sense of belonging that Gio would feel at Boulevard and all the clever and influential friends he would make once Francis got him in.

I positioned myself astride him on his blue-gray bed, and saw a look in his lamplit eyes that I couldn't quite interpret. I arched my back and moved my hips as the air conditioner gasped and rattled. I dropped, disjointedly, to my knees and took him in my mouth. After a few seconds, he drew me upward.

"I want you close to me," he said. "Is that all right?"

He turned off the light, and we embraced in the sweltering darkness.

Stroking my hair and cheek, he said: "Let me learn you." His head met my waist, and my lower half experienced a wet lurch of expectation, but my head was still all ambition and strategy. I didn't want to receive. I wanted to give, so I could get what I wanted.

I felt his breath as he pressed his mouth to me, sending an involuntary shudder through me. As his tongue found its mark, I attempted to keep my mind on the con. I made the appropriate sounds. I ignored the tender angle of his head. This was not going to be sexual oblivion, some communion of souls or ruinous love. He pushed my knees up to my chest, and the gesture was so unexpected that I made a sound of surprise. To see him at school, wearing his Boulevard lanyard and his tie with the little swallows on it, you would never expect him to be so spirited between the sheets.

Still eager to strategize, I became slightly distracted by the amplifying sound of my breath. Francis had this tenacious curiosity.

He was noticing patterns, tracing things back to their origins. My legs fell open. My stomach hurt, as though I'd been laughing for hours or braced for pain just as long. I wasn't a woman, I was a body of water—wet and trembling all along the surface.

He rose and fucked me like he was reading Tennyson: totally engrossed, treating me like I was this moving and complex piece of literature. It was unsettling how present he was—the way he could see me through his own pleasure. If only he'd quit holding my jaw and doing that deep gaze into my eyes. I feared, from that close angle, that he might finally recognize what I was all about.

He grabbed at my heart through my left breast. He kissed oxygen into me. It was a *violation*, that's what it was. I had not consented to anything like real love. Yet, there I was, clutching at the sheets, in a state of intimate duress over his little inarticulate half whispers—"Mmm baby, oh God." It had all gone too far. I wrapped my legs around him, wanting every particle. Wanting far more than I'd come for. It was wonderful, which was petrifying. But just when I reached peak terror, pleasure turned on pain. My sticky, shaking body betrayed me, and I was seized by an eye-watering orgasm. A moment later, I was lying, traumatized, in a twitching pool of my own fragility. The sweat between my breasts turned cold and I felt utterly exposed.

CHAPTER EIGHTEEN

Oz and I spent the night of my *darshan* in the guesthouse he'd recommended—a tiled room that opened onto a patio covered with monkey feces and syringes.

Under other circumstances, the housekeeper in me would have been scandalized by the bloodied light switch, the coffee rings on the nightstands, and the showerhead crusted with rust. But I was distracted, shivering under the weight of the realization that I'd missed my mam's funeral and Oz, who unwrapped my traveling clothes with rough boldness.

We did it all night, for an impossible six or seven hours, and in between we smoked hash, kissing each other with the lingering taste of the drug on our lips. Insects buzzed in our ears. The air was heavy with sweat. Sometime in the blue-black twilight, the joints we passed between us took on a taste like coffee and dark chocolate and the sex began to seem less like a test of psychological and spiritual endurance.

"Sync your breathing to mine," Oz urged me at the start. "You'll feel it. The transfer of energy between us." And sitting up in bed like Shiva, he pulled me astride him so we were chest-to-sweat-damp-chest, his inhale filling my chest, my exhale withdrawing breath from his.

The choked little breaths I'd been taking at the ghats turned into great, cresting waves of emotion that never seemed to break, just moved slowly and continually between us, from our chests to our bellies to our mouths, which still tasted of earthy smoke. The way Oz licked my upper lip inspired me to suck his lower one.

With Oz, everything was sex. Stroking was sex. Scratching, tapping, and compression were sex. Anticipation was sex. Aggravation was sex. Occasionally "good," "productive" pain was sex.

Nothing was straightforwardly sexual, and everything was. He fucked me with his thumbs, his tongue, his dick, the heels of his hands, even his forearms, all of it wet with previous submersions, and every time I felt myself trembling and about to climax, he would put a calming hand on my pubic bone or my heart and bring me down from the surge. Grief overtook my bliss. My whole body pled. I took another hit of hashish.

"You like that, do you?" he'd say. Then he'd begin the delicious agony all over again.

Sometime around dawn, Oz—who seemed more interested in holding sway over me than actually getting off—was looking into my eyes with all the energy of his life force and I was so overloaded with sexual frustration that, I swear, I came without him touching me.

"Was *that* my revelation?" Oz asked, tracing a figure eight on my breastbone. "Because it feels like it was."

I groaned, "Please don't say I'm your goddess."

"Aww," he said, roping my hair around his hand. "Would it really be so bad to be worshiped? To be like Lakshmi, with me banging pots to fend off your dark relatives?" A cheeky smile crossed his face, and he wrapped an arm under my thigh, forced it up to my chest. His face grew serious. "Stay here with me. Forever."

"In Varanasi?"

He nodded.

"Me, here, forever. That's a distinct possibility now that I've run out of cash."

"You can't go. I won't let you." Like a drug dealer: "I'll get you whatever you need."

"Very chivalrous. But from what I've seen, you don't have a pot to piss in either."

"So we'll make some money together," he said, his mouth wet and velvety on my collarbone.

"How?"

"I'll show you."

I was worried that Oz meant prostitution. I pictured my photo in the local newspapers: red lips lined with black kohl to dissuade clients from kissing me. I imagined trying to find a way to separate my body from my soul, trailing Oz to a bar, drinking toddies while he negotiated price with my john—some man with strange desires who'd try to pay me in bangles.

But thankfully my new boyfriend didn't want to sell me for sex. And once that knowledge fully sunk in, it made his actual proposition seem far less unseemly. On the contrary, it was second nature.

"You ready?" he asked once we arrived at the bus stand the next day.

"Ready," I said over the honking horns. Rickshaws and cars with mildewed paint jobs stirred up dust. Exhaust shimmered in the midmorning heat.

A local coach, sky blue and lightly dented, was approaching. I knew the sort well. Like a children's school bus, only fuller, with people hanging out the windows and doors. It was so full in some cases that half the passengers had to disembark before a sharp corner so the whole thing wouldn't tip.

A pair of young blond tourists stepped off and fought their way through the crush of human bodies, carrying their sleeping bags and day packs, plus the cycle locks they'd likely used to secure them to their seats while they slept. They both had backpackers' expressions: self-conscious exhaustion. The bloke still wore the head torch he'd used aboard as a reading light. The girl had a traumatized look like she'd woken up mid-journey to find someone sitting on her lap.

A throng of Omni drivers instantly enveloped them, all frantically gesturing with one hand, shouting, "Taxi! Taxi!"

Oz, with an amused face, waded through the crowd in their direction, tugging me along behind him by the hand.

"Don't you wish Indians did queuing?" he asked them. "You Swedish?"

"Dutch!" the bloke shouted over the noise. He was reading over his girlfriend's shoulder, trying to make sense of a map and list of travel contacts.

"Do you know where Jyoti Hotel is?" the girl asked me. Her eyes were bloodshot, her nose sunburnt and peeling.

Oz glanced down at her papers from his tall height. The encouraging squeeze he gave my hand caused my stomach to leap.

"Yes?" I said, pointing to a spot on her coffee-stained map. "That's the one—"

"On Luxa Road," Oz said. "We nearly stayed there. Remember, love? But we opted for OK International. Very nearby. Shall we share a taxi?"

Their faces flowered with relief. The bloke nodded. The girl returned her papers to her forward-facing backpack.

"We'll need to withdraw money," she said.

"There's a cashpoint just there." I pointed helpfully. I looked to Oz. He was watching me under his dark lashes with a look of admiration that made my heart titter.

"Just beside the Life Bakery," he added.

I held out my hand to the girl. "We'll wait by the taxi with your rucksacks."

A quick look passed between them. They seemed to be wondering if it was wise to leave their packs with total strangers. But the day was hot, and the bags looked heavy. Plus, they were exhausted from what appeared to be an all-night journey.

They nodded their agreement, then thanked us and walked off in the prescribed direction. No sooner had they vanished into the rolling tide of cows, babies, bindis, and bellies, we scurried off with their packs in the opposite direction.

We ran laughing through the muddy lanes, by the man selling sweetened yogurt in clay pots, past the flower vendors and signs for yoga schools. Everything was even more dazzling than it had been the previous day: the trim of every sari glinted like sunshine. A mural of Ganesh on a pale-pink wall called to mind my long-ago Irish bedroom. I ran weightlessly, like a child, laughing so hard my stomach jellied and no sound came out of my mouth—until I was coughing on the dirt, smoke, and ash, the rank smells of garbage and sewage. Half-blinded by it all, I narrowly collided with a cow.

But most vivid of all was Oz: his lightning-bolt forearm, the firmness of his hand in mine. The forceful way he steered me to a sari shop with pink pillars. Inside, the walls were rainbowed with bolts of silk. Mannequins struck haughty poses in Banaras brocades.

Oz greeted a woman wearing a white sari and an unwieldy amount of jewelry—what looked like 15 percent of the world's gold. "Nafi here?"

She waved in the direction of the back room.

Oz pulled aside a violet silk curtain and immediately we found ourselves in a tight concrete box. A man sat on the floor, unpacking merchandise between his knees.

"Nafi!"

"Hello, my friend," Nafi said, standing. "What do you have for me?"

"Here." Oz helped me out of the Dutch girl's rucksack and swung the one he was wearing onto the floor. "Lots of nice things inside."

Nafi loosened the drawstring and pulled out a few items: hiking boots, headphones, a top-of-the-range camera. "Four thousand," he said, looking satisfied.

"Five."

"Forty-five hundred."

"And a box of henna powder," Oz said.

Nafi laughed. "I'll ask Lata." He pretended to notice me for the first time. "You have a new friend."

Oz took the outthrust stack of bills.

"My *jigri*," he said, as though I needed no other name.

"What if we run into them?" I asked. We were back at the guesthouse, drinking whiskey and Thums Up cola in the dimly lit bathroom, which was thick with the muddy, vegetal smell of henna hair dye.

"The Dutch pair?"

I nodded. I was shivering in a stained bath towel, my hair slathered with the natural hair dye that had come without English instructions. "We didn't ask how long they were staying. What if we go out to a café and they're there, eating vadas?"

"It will be more difficult to pick you out in a crowd after *this*." He stuck a finger into the greenish-black sludge in the sink. "And the way I see it, we have food, drink, money. We can cuddle up here for days. If we run out, I'll go get more. I'll bring it all back to you like offerings to the goddess."

His eyes shone with triumph. He dropped my towel an inch and used his hennaed finger to write his name over my heart. When I turned to face the mirror, it read in reverse, black as a branding: ZO.

His hands spread in front of my face, and I flinched before I realized he was clasping a silver necklace around my neck. Then came another and another. Gold. Then, strands of glass beads. He parted my towel, let it drop to the filthy tiles. And I stood there, in so many necklaces, bare and bejeweled like the women in the Asparas paintings.

"Where did you get these?"

"I found them in the front pocket of the Dutch girl's bag. While Nafi was going through her boyfriend's rucksack."

"When you called me your *jigri* . . . what did that mean?"

"My beloved."

"Like your girlfriend?"

"Yes, very much like my girlfriend."

There was an odd pressure in my throat. "Why didn't you scam *me*? Were you going to? Back at the ATM?"

"I watched you enter your PIN number, if that's what you mean. But then we went to dinner and you told me that you had no money. And you had this orphan's face. You were so sad and beautiful."

I rolled my eyes.

"Really. You had those eyes that said you'd seen things I couldn't understand. And me, with my wanderlust, I want to see everything. How much longer till you wash this out?"

"I don't know. I have an idea I'm supposed to leave it in for hours."

Oz bent to grab my hips. "I know a way to pass the time."

I let him lean me against the crime scene of a sink, tug at the new necklaces around my throat, and progress in his rather authoritative style. I was nineteen, and no one had ever touched me with as much domineeringness.

Plus, Oz was fully committed to me from the very start. He wanted a partner in crime, drugs, philosophy, travel, and of course, sex. He wanted to drive me batty with anticipation. He wanted to lay me on my stomach and make me shake or brace myself.

By the time I finally stepped into the shower three hours later, Oz and I looked like oversexed swamp people, with dye streaked across our faces, chests, and hands. The *OZ* on my breast had become a henna tattoo. The air in the room was a dialogue of hash, dye, and afterglow.

Even after I washed it out, I still smelled like the sweet rot of henna. Weak-legged and snoozy with exhaustion, I stood before the mirror. My hair had come out far too dark. It was the pitch-black of death, and failing to recognize myself, I felt utterly reborn.

For almost four months, well into the summer of 1999, Oz and I ran schemes in Varanasi. Sometimes we stole luggage, same as we had with the Dutch couple. But we were, essentially, stealing underpants, trainers, and Western bath products, and the risks vastly outweighed the rewards. There was better money in money, so to speak.

"So why don't we steal PIN numbers?" I asked. "The way you were going to nick mine?"

"Well, all that's much more difficult now."

"Why?"

Oz frowned. "Because we're a couple."

And because I was beginning to think like Oz, I understood. Once he memorized his marks' PIN numbers, he must have followed them back to their hotel rooms and done the sorts of sexual athletics that left them too stupid and knackered to notice when he left with their wallets.

"There might be another way," he said.

"What? A threesome? Fat chance!"

"I didn't mean *that.* I was thinking more along the lines of a doctor's visit."

So, one gray afternoon, I went to see the corrupt physician who occasionally sold Oz ecstasy and speed. We waited for an hour in the busy waiting room, inhaling the smells of body odor and damp clothing. And the whole time, I fiddled with my dark hair (still a novelty) and rehearsed my lines in my head, feeling my mounting stage fright. By the time my name was called, I had reached such a level of nervous anguish that it wasn't even a lie when I looked into the doctor's spectacled eyes and complained of anxiety.

"Yes," he said. "You're in quite a state." And he sent us away with a script for lorazepam.

From there, we proceeded to the Indian chemist (also dodgy), who dispensed a shockingly large quantity of little yellow pills and did his best to mime the side effects. And I stayed in character, twitching nervously, nodding my understanding.

. . .

At nightfall the same day, Oz and I went to a café attached to a youth hostel, popular with backpackers for its Western-style toilet.

The gap-yearers were out en masse. They were consulting their *Lonely Planet* guides. Rubbing their scabby new lotus tattoos. Reciting the only word they knew (bīyara, *beer*).

Oz and I ordered two Kingfishers. I sipped slowly, pretending to watch a paan-chewing man play the tabla, while Oz crushed three lorazepams with the back of his spoon.

Over the sound of a harmonium, Oz said: "Find the drunkest people here."

I surveyed the crowd. There were a few stoned-looking Canadians. There was a large group of Israelis, probably fresh out of their time in the army. And there were American backpackers, girls, who hadn't yet changed out of the pajamas they wore for travel into the tight, bright outfits they wore at night.

Finally, I settled on the Australian-looking blokes two tables away. One had floppy blond hair. The other had sari fabric sewed to the hem of his jeans. Both looked like they'd been drinking since nine a.m., like it was only a matter of hours before they'd be skinny-dipping in a public fountain.

"Probably them. Over there."

Oz nodded. "Good call."

"What if they overdose?"

"Unlikely," he said. "If anything, we have the opposite challenge. We need to get it down them as quickly as possible." And calling the waiter over, he ordered four shots of Bagpiper whiskey (Gag-piper, we called it), two of which he spiked with the yellow powder from his side of the table.

"Go talk to them," Oz instructed.

"Hi there," I said. "Excuse me."

"Hey. Us? How ya goin'?" the blond one said. Both their eyes went to Oz as though they needed his permission to speak to me.

"Could you do me a massive favor and help us drink these whiskeys? The waiter brought us two too many. We'll be legless if we have all this."

"Ace," his friend slurred with an expression like he'd just won on a scratch card.

"He needs this like he needs a third armpit," the blond said. "Wanna join us?"

I sat. Oz pulled a chair up as well, and told a few cricket jokes that went straight over my head, after which the Aussies confided their full itinerary, just like that. Between them, they had saved up fifteen grand working at a video store.

It became clear the drug was taking effect when the bloke with the patched trousers gestured too close to our neighbors' plate, sending a plate of goyazas crashing to the floor.

Oz suggested we go smoke hash in their room, and it was clear from the start that their accommodations were far nicer than ours. We moved through the tiled reception area, past the morning muesli bar and the activity board, and up the challenging circular staircase. We ended up playing Sherpa, taking them up one at a time, me climbing ahead and pulling each bloke by his wrist while Oz held up the rear and braced them.

While we were doing the sari bloke, a pair of descending American girls gasped, "Oh my gawd! Is he OK?"

My face went numb, but Oz looked untroubled.

"Oh, he's a happy bastard," he said.

The girls laughed tentatively and flashed each other meaningful looks.

Once they'd gone down the stairs, the blond fumbled his room key out of his pocket and onto the floor, and Oz corralled the boys into the room that matched the number on the key chain.

There were two mattresses on the floor inside. And it was only a matter of seconds before the sari bloke melted sideways onto one of them. The blond did a sort of folding collapse into a circular rattan chair.

Oz tore open a cigarette and poured the contents into a drinking glass. He used his fingertips to flake and combine it with the hash, then carefully sprinkled it into the bowl of his massive chillum. He wrapped a wet cloth around the bottom and passed the pipe to the blond.

"Come light this," he instructed me, observing the custom that the person who prepares the chillum should not light it.

I took the lighter Oz gave me and brought it to the bowl. I watched the blond take a few hits, his suckling mouth like someone at a hamster bottle. His transformation was startling. The lorazepam had turned his sunburnt face a frightful shade of greenish white.

"*Bom Shankar,*" he just about managed to say, as their bedroom filled with the soapy smell of hash.

I pressed my scarf to the underside of the door, worried the smell might draw the other backpackers out of their holes.

"Leave it," Oz said, coolly. "It's no problem."

It was the sari bloke's turn. But he appeared to have trouble finding his mouth, and twice he coughed at the moment of inhale, turning the chillum into a blow-dart gun, blanketing his mattress with hash and smoking embers.

Oz patiently patted out the sparks, repacked the pipe, and held it to the sari bloke's slack mouth. He looked oddly paternal doing so. Or doctorly, like he was nursing the pathetic lad back to health.

We sat in silence for what felt like ages, trying not to eye our watches, waiting for both boys to make their final descent into sleep. Finally, with Oz talking some nonsense about Brahma, both blokes closed their eyes. They looked like they were meditating, but after five minutes, it became clear they had passed out.

Oz motioned to the curtains, and I drew them shut. Then, with impressive quietness, he moved the bottles atop the suitcase and opened it. "Check their pockets," he instructed me in a whisper.

Nervously, I crept over to the sari bloke, who was looking far too gray for my liking. I remember thinking, darkly, if he'd passed out that way down by the ghats, someone would have stacked him with firewood. But I put my left hand on his chest, and was reassured by its rise and fall. My right hand found its way to the square-shaped bulge in his pocket.

I tried to move my hand as slowly and fluidly as I could, but the stiff fabric balked every time I got the angle wrong.

"Ay," he croaked, changing position.

I can't do it! I mouthed to Oz.

But he just gave me a look that said I wasn't trying hard enough. He had the contents of the boys' suitcases spread out on the floor around him: sheets of travel itineraries, cameras, and music players.

There were footsteps in the corridor.

"He does this all the time," a whiney voice said on the other side of the door.

My eyes shot to Oz, who had eased the blond out of his saucer-shaped chair. He was holding the sleeping fellow upright, struggling against the weight of him, while he fished through his pockets. "Take off your clothes," he whispered.

"Are you crackers?"

"Just do it," Oz said. "It will be all right. I promise."

There were silhouettes on the other side of the curtain-clad door. And the sound of the American girl's baby voice: "You didn't *see* him. He was *shitfaced*."

Fear shot through me. I fumbled the wallet onto the floor, tore my shirt over my head, and ripped down my trousers as though there were a trapped spider in the leg.

A knock sounded at the door. Polite first, then annoyingly frantic.

"Take off the rest, and answer it," Oz whispered, looking concerned for the first time.

I stripped off my underpants. My trembling hand found the clasp of my bra.

I unlatched the deadbolt, and cracked the door wide enough to see two pairs of heavily made-up eyes blinking at me.

"Hello?" I said, trembling, making a fig-leaf of my scarf.

"Ohhhh. Sorry," a ponytailed girl said. And her friend took off down the corridor, clutching herself in a fit of squealing giggles.

CHAPTER NINETEEN

"PTA" was for plebs, evidently. At the Boulevard School, it was known as the PAC, or parents' advisory council, which pretty well set the stage for the caste system at play: *We are the parents and you are the help.* It was a minor miracle the board didn't make the teachers check coats or fill seats every time a high-net-worth person stood to take a phone call.

The meeting was in the glass-and-steel cafeteria. The space had fake Gerrit Rietveld chairs, real Keith Harings on the walls, and a pervasive smell of lemongrass and almond milk. The full industrial kitchen was in the basement and connected by dumbwaiters so the children could eat their high-class food without looking at the lower-class faces who'd prepared it.

It was my first meeting, but straightaway, I recognized the proscenium arch.

The three co-presidents were center stage, alongside the headmaster, Henry Upton. They were joined by the guest stars: a downy nutritionist from the *Today* show, on hand to speak about the school lunch, and a top-dollar "Ivy League adviser" who edited college applications essays for the "reasonable" fee of eight grand per draft.

The committee chairwomen sat at tables on either side. They were the heads of euphemistically named boards like "Development" (i.e., fund-raising); "Enrichment" (field trips and jollies);

"Assemblies" (expressly, celebrity visits); "Beautification and Upkeep" (interior design); and "Community Outreach" (in other words, party planning).

A table of catering platters including an elaborate sushi spread, formed the stage apron. Silky slices of fish closely matched the shades of ivory, nori-black, and blush worn by the exotic downtown crowd.

And beyond it all, barely an afterthought, was an audience of industrialists' and princes' wives, clumped in groups of like with like, gossiping in Cantonese or Arabic.

"There's a seat there," Francis said. Hand on the small of my back, escorting me to an empty chair.

"Hi, Mr. Blake," a Carla Bruni type lilted, moving her It-bag so he could sit.

"Please, call me Francis. Lily, I'd like you to meet my girlfriend, Marianna De Felice. Marianna, this is Lily Forhman. She's on the PAC's Audit Committee. And her son, Marceau, is one of the most promising young writers in my sixth-grade writing workshop."

She laughed, cheekbones jutting. "Oh goodness. We could only hope. Paul has him pegged for Yale."

Francis's look told me Lily's husband was a man of some importance. "Marianna's son, Gio, is in the fifth grade. And her daughter, Catarina, is in third."

"I'm surprised we haven't met before." The lamb's fur of Lily's jacket brushed my arm as she shook my hand. My senses reeled with the florals of her perfume.

I told her we'd just enrolled.

"Wow, newbies," Lily said. "I didn't know they existed with so much sibling priority."

"We got lucky." I gave a conspiring smile to Francis, who had spent the summer working his magic with admissions so the children could begin immediately, at the start of the school year. We had only been dating four months, but it felt right. My children idolized him for his encyclopedic knowledge of fart jokes and Roald Dahl stories. And we ourselves felt it was less challenging to blend families than it was to live apart. On this point, Francis liked to paraphrase Anais Nin: "Staying tight in a bud is more painful than blossoming."

Cleaning his Ira Glass glasses with a pocket square, Francis returned my look with a small wink.

He had been supportive in every sense of the word, securing the children spots at Boulevard and moving us all into his modest flat. On weeknights, he played chess with Gio. On weekends, he made heart-shaped pancakes for Cat. In his remaining spare time, we went to retro revival classic cinema together and ate popcorn from the same bag. Plus, every evening he helped me revise my résumé, helping me try to find a teaching position with the same smoldering care that he applied when he was positioning me on my back with my legs in the air.

"So, do you like the school?" Lily asked with a directness I found intrusive. She sidled her crossed knees in my direction, and I could feel her marking me, enjoying the idea that she might get juicy gossip from the teacher's new pet.

"What's not to love?" I meant it. The children had come to associate the word "school" with guest lectures from NASA astronauts. When it rained, they had indoor recess in an architect-designed "green" playroom where real climbing trees grew through the school roof.

"I know," Lily said. "It's divine."

My father taught me to talk to every woman as though I loved her and every man as though he bored me. It was like Lily got the same advice arse backward. I wondered if there was a bit of a con artist in her too. Reformed siren, I reckoned. Missing the thrill of the chase. She'd netted a billionaire and hadn't felt powerful since.

Her gaze flitted to the door, where an actress with a very droppable name had wandered in wearing leather trousers and a messy ponytail. I recognized her instantly as the postmodern Sophia Loren. Her name was just on the tip of my tongue. Lately, she appeared in more tabloids than films.

One could feel it: the rubberneck that refused to rubberneck.

The rich mummies were overcompensating, trying *too* hard not to look at the woman of note.

Her name came to me then, like a marquee flipped on: Ainsley Doyle. Or, rather, AINSLEY DOYLE. The cold shoulder had the reverse effect of spotlighting her. She stood in bull's-eye stillness, shunned and luminous, scanning the tables and fiddling with a cashmere scarf that was as large as a baby sling. She ducked into a nearby table, where two Frenchwomen were griping about the low inventory of New York apartments and how co-ops discriminated against foreigners.

Remembering me, Lily hit me with the city's ubiquitous question: "So what do you do, Marianna?"

"I was a teacher. Back before I had kids."

"Marianna is a very accomplished theatre teacher," Francis said. "She's taught at some of Britain's most prestigious prep schools."

I smiled. I *was* very accomplished at building complex webpages. I'd applied myself since Melanie. I put in longer hours. I called on Seema for help. My latest work had dynamic content and heavy storage.

The crux of the CV I'd showed Francis were websites for two "British boarding schools," where I'd "taught" theatre as an "American expat." Each was filled with descriptions of an "excellent all-around education" and stock photos of ginger pupils in crested blazers. Each had email addresses that I checked myself (I turned away one prospective student a week), and a Guildhall-era photo of me on the staff page. I'd Photoshopped my hair black, for good measure.

"Have you met Brent Esnad yet?" Lily asked.

"Our lower-school dramatic arts teacher," Francis said.

"No, but I hear good things."

Lily shimmied out of her Lamb Chop coat. "Oh, Brent's the best." It was a mindless coo. She was scanning the room, hoping to look casual as she eyed Ainsley Doyle.

Ainsley's presence, insular as it was, spurred the meeting into action. The key players began clicking through PowerPoint slides.

Everyone else bent to follow the virtual itinerary on their phones, pink diamonds twinkling in their earlobes, their arms toned and bare.

The exclusive company really had its own climate. It was an unseasonably chilly September, and beyond the walls of Boulevard, the lower classes were wrapped in down, complaining about the rising price of coffee and bread, selling off gold for cash.

By comparison, the financial portion of the meeting revealed the PAC had enough in its bank account to buy a Manhattan penthouse with a southeast exposure. The decimal point where millions meet thousands gives me a jangly feeling that was either excitement or high-stakes fear. And there they were, talking like it still wasn't enough. Still planning benefit auctions and for-profit galas with performances by Justin Timberlake and Pharrell.

"I know no one in this room likes discussing tuition hikes," a woman said to an audience of snickers. "But I also know we have the resources and we love our school."

The word "tuition" made my ears chirp. It sent anxiety itching up the back of my neck.

Francis could get us discounted tuition, but he would have to take a pay cut as a result, making it impossible for us to carry on in the city.

Francis was "willing" to move for us, he said. He was "happy" to ship us all off to Tarrytown. But deep down, I knew he'd resent it. He'd miss the city's friction and grit. Francis loved Manhattan. He'd grown up there, and his history was written on every cross-street. If I lost him every morning to the Metro-North line, I knew it would only be a matter of time before I lost him for good.

So, I'd lied and told Francis that I could cover the tuition myself. I had scraped together Boulevard's deposit and two months' tuition using savings from my old SEO scams. And when it still wasn't enough, I'd supplemented with online classified cons, in which I "accidentally" sent my mark a check for ten times the price of the item I'd promised to collect and instructed them to deposit it and wire the difference to a British account that Oz, fresh out of jail, had opened for me for that purpose. But it was unreliable income. I had to cast a wide net because three-quarters of the people I contacted caught on halfway through. And on top of it, Oz took a cut.

Even worse for me and my marks, all the scams played on the lower classes as opposed to the rich. So did all of the desperate-times ploys I could think of. Theoretically, I could have targeted people with bad credit, accepting deposits for apartments I didn't own. Or I might have searched job boards for prospective "employees," promising stay-at-home jobs and accepting wire transfers for office equipment I would never send. But contrary to popular belief, a parasitic lifestyle *is* work, and sucking the poor's lifeblood crushes the soul.

Francis and I kept separate checking accounts. What he didn't know was: mine had just enough cash to cover tuition for one more month. After that, the children were out on their arses, back to PS 666. If I was going to keep them at Boulevard, I either needed an ingenious way to make vast sums of money or I needed Upton to hire me to teach drama.

But there was the problem of Brent Esnad. *Brilliant* Brent Esnad. Over my chirr of money anxieties, I heard his name clear and bright.

"Talk to Brent," a PAC mother with a takeaway cup of kale juice said. "I'm sure he'll have more time after the world theatre assembly tomorrow."

"World theatre assembly?" I whispered to Francis.

"It's a big undertaking. Lots of pressure to be cutting-edge. You know Boulevard. God forbid you just stand behind the lectern and talk into a microphone. There has to be streaming video and the director of the Bolshoi Ballet conferenced in."

Another hour dragged past, and the meeting wasn't remotely close to finished. The billionaire mothers were just getting started on the great school-lunch-menu debates, passing motions to buy something called an "alfresco flatbread hearth."

Francis took my hand under the table. His lips brushed my ear.

"You drowning?" he asked in whisper.

"Sorry?"

"The first meeting of the year always runs long."

"Oh, right. I'm OK." I checked my phone, saw the Wi-Fi icon in the corner, and had a brainstorm: "Can I go up to your room for a few minutes? I'd wanted to revise my teaching statement tonight. And this meeting is endless."

"Sure," he whispered back. "Do you want to use my laptop? It's in the bottom drawer of my desk."

"That would be great. Thanks. Will you write down the Wi-Fi password?"

"I'm already logged in to the network. But text me if you have a problem."

Because this was Boulevard, Francis's classroom wasn't a classroom. It was a "teaching station." It had a view of the High Line and a Loretta Lux portrait that was worth nineteen grand.

I found Francis's laptop in his desk and installed myself at the marble conference table that served as a collaborative school desk.

His computer was logged in to Wi-Fi and the Boulevard file-sharing network all right. So I did an ARP spoof for a MITM attack between Brent and the router. It was hardly advanced hacking—more like child's play. I scrolled through Brent's recently visited pages—Boulevard homepage, a video conferencing site, and a YouTube video of traditional folk theatre—and injected it with some well-packed Java that executed shellcode straight into memory. I had barely closed out the file when I heard men's voices in the corridor. When I looked up, I saw Henry Upton.

He was slapping Francis's back appreciatively. They were discussing something I didn't entirely catch. But I heard the words: "São Paulo" and "seed funding."

As they were about to part ways, Francis said: "Henry, this is my girlfriend, Marianna De Felice."

We both made the same back-and-forth gesture. *We've met before, briefly.*

From the doorway, Francis added: "Marianna's a drama teacher. A staple on the English prep-school scene."

"Is that so?" Henry said politely. "I'd love to hear more about that sometime."

I nodded, my expectations stalled at zero. *Let's do.*

"OK, Francis," Henry said. "Good stuff. Let me know if you hear from that *New York* magazine reporter."

New York magazine was doing a profile on Henry Upton. So was the *New York Post.* He was making waves as an "education entrepreneur."

"Will do," Francis said. After Henry was gone, he asked: "How'd it go with the teaching statement?"

"Not well. I've scrapped the whole thing. I'm totally stuck."

Francis pulled up a chair. "Back when I was job hunting, I had the world's most simple idea. I thought, 'At the end of the day, I'm the same as every teacher I'm competing against. We all have more or less the same training, technology, and skills. So why do some people get hired when there are others out there who would do a better job—who are more driven to help their students succeed?' "

"God yes, Francis, *why*? It's driving me bananas."

"Well, 'why' really is the magic word. Every single teacher out there can describe what they do, one hundred percent. Some can even explain how they do it. But very, very few understand *why* they do it."

"To help students build confidence," I said. "Or to understand the material."

"Well, yes. Only, that's the result. By 'why,' I mean, the ill-equipped teachers don't know their purpose or cause. So what do you believe in?"

I hesitated, trying to think two or three steps ahead. What would Francis want me to believe in? What would Henry Upton?

"Don't even make it school-related," Francis said. "We can do that later. For now, think about what you believe in a broader sense. What are your philosophies about life?"

"Well—I suppose I believe in challenging the status quo. And I believe information is worthless unless you use it to separate appearance from reality."

"Good." Francis went to his desk and began jotting notes in his Moleskine. "And how do you act? Not on the stage"—he chuckled—"in real life, rather. What's your process of doing things?"

"How do I like to do things? *Anything?*"

He nodded.

"Well, I guess I try to act with speed. It builds momentum and garners a fair bit of awe. And I try to strategize. Strategy is the best defense and the best offense. Also, I believe in ingenuity; when you don't do things the usual way, you have to have unusual power."

His pen kept moving. "And how about socially? What's your approach to people?"

"Well, relationships are important. *Really* important. Because it's hard to make your way in the world alone. Does that make me sound weak?"

"No. It makes you sound collaborative." He was flipping pages and scribbling like mad. "Just hold on. Look at this." He passed me the little notebook. "How does this look?"

"I'm not an educator who does things the usual way, which gives me unusual power . . ." As I read the rest, Francis watched me, doing his teacher's lean against the desk. He cupped his chin thoughtfully. His eyes were smiling.

"It still needs a little revision here and there," he added, "but that's what I'd call an inspiring teaching statement."

"Thank you, Francis. This is perfect. I love it."

If everything went to plan, I'd be needing it soon.

"While I have you here," he said, "will you take a look at this six-word memoir?"

"Of course."

He passed me the canvas, upon which the student had painted a couch on fire in addition to her one-sentence history.

"Is 'trill' a bad word?" Francis said. "I asked the student and she said no. But the eighth graders all giggled when I hung it up."

"*Trill*? I think that's a typo. I read it as 'thrill.'"

"OK. Whew. I'm relieved."

I laughed. "It's the other part that's raunchy."

"Which part?"

"'Netflix and chill,'" I read aloud. "'Only gonna thrill.'"

He just stared at me, utterly clueless.

"Francis! *Netflix and chill.* That means 'fuck.'"

"No." He bent over laughing, but when he straightened up, he had the expression of a man who'd been hit with a hammer. "I can't believe she lied to me. She lied to my face."

I asked which student it was and he named the daughter of a Russian metals magnate.

"So what are you going to do?" I wondered whether he would schedule a parent meeting or file an incident report.

But he just quietly took the canvas from my hand, put it in the bottom drawer of his desk, and never spoke of the incident again.

CHAPTER TWENTY

The day after the canceled world theatre assembly, we were running late.

Inside the flat, as outside on the city sidewalks, personal space was a rare privilege. Gio and Cat had to be staggered. One put on Boulevard's gray-and-black uniform in the cupboard-sized bedroom they shared while the other spat toothpaste into the stubble Francis left in the sink. We couldn't afford school lunch (it cost $24.99 per tray), but two people couldn't pack lunches in Francis's galley kitchen. The toast couldn't be depressed if the blow dryer was in use, lest the fuse go kaboom.

Overcrowding wasn't my only problem. Gio had begun acting like a teenager, fluctuating between taciturn and backchatty. "Cool story, bro," he said in response to anything he deemed boring. "Boom!" he said when he thought he'd bested me in a verbal joust.

"You can't tell me what to do!" he howled at me, locking himself in the toilet after I asked him to put away his tablet and dress for school.

Secretly, I thought it was healthy, suitable behavior. It was far better than the silent way I'd moved through childhood, clinging to my anger like a death pact.

"I didn't tell you what to do, sweetie. I *asked*. I even said please. Didn't I?"

Cat nodded supportively. She was eating strawberries from the half-pint box.

Maybe Gio was just flush with hormones. He'd had another growth spurt and it seemed like any day, he'd be too old for Nerf guns and sleeping with the light on.

I wanted to comfort and support him through pre-adolescence, but one moment he had shut himself in his room, hollering, "You're not the boss of me!" and the next, he was regressing, crying on my lap because Cat had hurt his feelings. I couldn't decide whether to treat him like a child or a young adult.

Back in the kitchen, Cat was admiring her reflection in the stainless-steel side of her half-packed lunch box. "Can I get a mani?"

"A *nanny*? No. For now, you have your mom to take care of you."

"Not a nanny. A *ma-ma*-mani. Nora's mom brings her for manis *every week*."

"Not a chance." They were the New York way, but I still equated nail salons with Finger Joy. "What you want are short, trim nails with a slick of Chanel topcoat."

" 'A slick of topcoat,' " Francis said thoughtfully. "That's a funny expression, isn't it? I've never heard that before."

"I guess you aren't up on your beauty terminology." I wondered what Americans said instead. *A coat of polish?*

"True enough." He had his bag over his shoulder and a travel mug of green tea in hand. "Do you want me to talk to Gio? I'm about to brush my teeth."

It was killing me that he hadn't said anything about Brent. Gio had told me the world theatre assembly hadn't happened. But Francis hadn't uttered a word. Perhaps he was waiting to see if Brent would be fired.

"I'll take care of it," I said. Pressing my face against the door: "Gio? Can I come in?"

His grunt of assent was surprisingly low. Before long, his voice would break like a thundershower.

"Thanks, sweetie, but you'll need to unlock it."

The door opened on a face that was pure Oz. Dark lashes framing intelligent eyes.

I stooped to hug him, but his hands stayed balled in his pockets. I threw a towel over the bathtub's damp edge and invited him to sit. "You're hurting. I can see that. Is it a Francis problem?"

He shook his head no.

"Is it your new school? Is someone there picking on you?" I was already down $17,000 in tuition, so it pained me to ask: "Do you hate Boulevard altogether?"

He made a noncommittal sound. "It's just different. I have *Japanese* class, and I can't even say 'yes' right. Every time the teacher says it, it just sounds like a weird hum. Like *Mmm-mm*."

"Japanese is tricky."

"At least I can say 'hello.' *Shi de*."

"That's Chinese," I said with a little edge of panic.

Sometimes I wondered if Gio remembered watching *Mei Mei*. If so, that meant he might remember other snippets of the Ashworths' house. I used to test him when I was feeling brave and we were alone, asking if he recalled how we used to make blueberry jam. (Subtext: from the Ashworths' blueberries.) Or saying, "Do you remember the time Cat got her hand stuck in the upright mixer?" (Real question: Did he remember the Ashworths' posh kitchen tools?) But Gio either said no or imagined they took place in the Catskill house. I stopped this line of inquiry after we moved in with Francis.

A despairing Gio hung his head. His dark fringe fell in his eyes.

I had been so certain he'd feel at home at Boulevard, with its language-immersion programs and four global campuses. I'd overlooked a massive blind spot.

"I understand why you might feel different from the other boys. Francis and I don't have jets or superyachts. It's unfair that this country doesn't pay teachers like it's a proper profession."

Gio looked up. Reluctantly, his eyes met mine. "Carter's having a birthday party."

"He *is*?" Carter was meant to be one of Gio's most promising new friends.

"I didn't even *know* until Elijah asked if I had my costume."

I was heartbroken on his behalf. "Let me talk to Carter's mom. Do you know when the party is?"

He shrugged. "This weekend?"

"Where?"

"It's a Harry Potter party."

"So Hogwarts, then."

No smile. *Fan* was an understatement. Gio had a PhD in Potter.

"Sorry to barge in on you. I'll only be a minute," Francis said, Flat-Stanley-ing himself to reach his electric toothbrush.

"Gio, why don't you go make sure your backpack is good to go?"

I loved using that American expression. Good to *go*. It spoke to me for obvious reasons.

After Gio had gone, I turned to Francis.

"Have you heard anything about Carter's birthday party?"

Over the buzzing of good oral hygiene: "A few murmurs, I think."

"Do you know where it is? I lost the invitation. It would be so embarrassing to have to call his mom."

"Hmmm . . ." Even the way Francis spit seemed considerate. "The Gansevoort? The Standard?" He plunged a finger into the drain and pulled out a slimy, hairy lump. "What is this? A Barbie head?"

"Ugh, Cat," I sighed. "She keeps doing that. I told her to just tell me if she feels like she's too old for them. She doesn't have to hide them every time she has a playdate."

"There's something else."

"Something down the drain?"

"No. I've been hesitant to bring it up. Cat's been the topic of conversation in the teachers' lounge. I thought you deserved to know."

"The teachers are discussing *Cat*?" Francis didn't usually interfere in matters of child-rearing.

"She's been doing the other girls' hair. Whether they want it or not."

"What? Forcibly giving them ponytails?" I laughed. "Be serious, Francis. If the girls don't want Cat playing with their hair, they're free to speak up. Use their words."

"She can be very coercive."

"And if it wasn't Cat, it would be another girl. Instead of tearing Cat down, why don't the teachers work on the other girls' self-esteem so they're more assertive or something?" We were on the verge of a massive falling-out. "Ponytails. Right. Is that all?"

"Some of Cat's fictions—"

"Sorry, *fictions*?"

"Remember Cat's lost tooth? The one that supposedly fell down the drain?"

I folded my arms. "Of course."

"There's a rumor Cat gave it to her friend Nora."

"The Nora who gets two hundred dollars a tooth?"

"Evidently, Cat proposed a hundred-dollar split."

I smiled in spite of myself. The most I slipped under Cat's pillow was a fiver.

"The staff got a good laugh out of it too."

"So if Cat's such a problem, why haven't her teachers talked to me directly?"

Francis was giving me his "parent-teacher conference" look—the one he reserved for women who thought their demon spawn were precious snowflakes.

"It's Boulevard's policy to overlook a certain amount of disruptive behavior. The school would rather focus on rewarding good behavior instead. The thing is, Mari—" He thought for a minute. "Parents have certain expectations. It's important to preserve the fantasy that there's very little bullying or disruption. I'm not saying it's right. It's just the price of doing business. It keeps enrollment up."

"We had a similar policies at my last boarding school."

"Then you can guess how much Boulevard likes making examples of people. They turn a blind eye to the smaller stuff. But in the event of a big incident, they'll come down hard on her. The school will sacrifice Cat to defend their own interests. The same behavior that's excused in a diamond merchant's kid won't be tolerated in the daughter of two lowly teachers."

"So it all comes down to class, then? The rich are held to different standards? A rich kid manipulates the system for profit and he's smart. A poor kid does it and she's a threat to society."

"Listen, it's my experience that the quote-unquote controlling students are experiencing a momentary absence of trust. So let's make a plan. What do you say? Let's figure out how we can give Cat the emotional security she needs to trust that her friends like her for who she is?"

He was giving me that *you're safe* look that took me out at the knees.

"OK. I'll talk to her. On a completely unrelated note, what happened to yesterday's theatre assembly? Cat was looking forward to it."

Francis gave a heavy sigh. "Brent was preparing yesterday morning with the AV tech. Henry Upton brought an investor into the auditorium. He was trying to show Boulevard in its best light. You know, borderless education, exciting new programming, but—"

I bit my lip, lest my expression let on that I knew what was coming.

"Instead of whatever clip Brent was hoping to play, his computer played pornography."

BAFTA-worthy look of horror. "It *played* porn or it projected it?"

"Projected it. Onto the big screen. It was really horrible, Mari. He couldn't close it out. It wasn't just pictures, it was video. *Loud*, graphic video."

"Surely Henry understood. Don't all men indulge in a bit of—"

"Gay porn?"

"Regardless. Surely all men, from time to time—"

"The website mentioned schoolboys. That's the part that makes it even more problematic. And it could have happened in front of students."

Yes, it could have happened in front of the students. When I'd embedded the code, I hadn't made light of that risk. But I also knew the politics of Boulevard. Francis had told me countless stories of Henry Upton's helicopter leadership style. Things at Boulevard rarely happened without a dress rehearsal.

"If you don't want me applying for the job, I understand," I said, my voice going pitchy.

Francis's chin did something odd. "No, I'd be thrilled if you apply. I'm just not sure there is a job, yet."

Fair play. But there would be. After Francis and the children left for school, I used a throwaway email address to send what he'd told me to tips@nypost.com.

News of Brent's scandal traveled faster and farther than I'd hoped. Come Monday, a story appeared in the *New York Post*, then spread like cultural Ebola through the regional news and gossip sites. *The Daily Beast. Gothamist. Gawker.* By Wednesday, a story had made it all the way to the online versions of the British papers. Mummies the world over were gobbling up the celebrity angle (every headline named Ainsley Doyle's daughter as a pupil) and the schadenfreude (it was the worst cock-up at an exclusive private school since the girl who caught tick-born encephalitis during the Hotchkiss School's trip to China).

On Thursday, the same week, Oz emailed my prep-school account to tell me he'd video conferenced with Henry Upton, pretending to be the headmaster of the last school I'd worked at. He recited, verbatim, the reference I had penned for myself: *Marianna De Felice engages students; Marianna De Felice is a creative curriculum developer; Marianna De Felice is a brilliant role model; I highly recommend her.*

By Friday, I was in Upton's office, wearing clear-glass lenses and my most suitable interview attire, my hair smart and serumed, explaining the power of musical theatre: "Our culture does so much digitally, which is great. But the idea of human-to-human interaction has become foreign to a lot of children. Theatre is about live interplay. Drama can't be accomplished alone."

"And why do you want to teach at Boulevard, specifically?"

Publicly, Henry's image was a little "Steve Jobs." Newspapers described him as a "scrappy genius," a "charismatic" whose ambition and egotism were his Achilles' heels. But in private, the PAC mothers called him "the golden retriever," on account of his sandy coloring and his panting eagerness to do anything they asked.

"Well, excusing for a moment that my children are students, I'd say the school and I are a very good fit. I've always taken a cross-cultural approach to the way I teach. There's a reason music and theatre exist in every culture on earth. They establish a collective identity."

Upton looked stress-battered. He lifted his glasses and rubbed the bridge of his nose. "Yes, Brent used to say the same thing."

"I've created my own presentation on *Wayang*. Indonesian puppets, that is. I hope that's not too presumptuous."

"Is that so?"

"It's just a draft, of course." I picked up my phone and emailed the file I had at the ready—the one I'd been working on ever since I added twinks and jocks to Brent's presentation. "I'm sure it would improve with your notes."

His phone dinged. "You're proactive. I admire that."

"Well, it was the protective mother in me, more than the ambitious teacher. Cat and Gio were looking forward to the presentation. And I thought our children deserve a seamless transition. The Brent incident wasn't Boulevard's fault. And there's no need for it to define us. It can only help the school's standing to show everyone—our children, the parents, the press—that we can bounce back, and quickly."

The smile he gave me was both devastated and grateful.

From that point on, Upton was phoning it in. He kept the questions rolling, but the forward pitch of his posture gave me the sense that almost any answer I gave would cut the muster.

"Tell me about the last obstacle you overcame."

Alcoholic husband? I thought. *Visa issues?*

"What are your weaknesses?"

Cream buns and women with low self-esteem?

"Do you have any questions for me?"

"Yes. Do you have any concerns about me? Any reasons you doubt my suitability for this position?"

He brought an elbow to his desk. "I don't typically lay all my cards on the table like this. But you seem like a pretty good match. I just need to make sure the PAC and the board feel the same. So here's what I'm willing to do. I'd like to give this a trial period, and instate you as our *acting* dramatic arts teacher."

How apropos.

"It would be an honor," I said.

He gave me a foot-in-door speech: "The salary isn't much to start. Although, chances are, it will lead to a more permanent position. If we approach it this way—"

"It will give the parents time to get to know me. Makes good sense. I see the design. I just have one housekeeping question. Will my position impact my children's tuition?"

"Yes, they'll be covered."

I took the children to the carousel at Pier Sixty-Two. They were too old for it, but we needed a place to speak privately. Or that New York paradox, in the privacy of public.

Only, we reached the carousel at peak wait time and had to queue for twenty minutes. "There's something I want to run past the two of you," I told them while we waited.

Run past was another expression I loved. Why were Americans always racing straight by what they were trying to say?

"*What?*" Gio asked. His mouth looked cynical. His eyes were concerned.

"I've been offered a job teaching drama at your school."

"Yes!" Cat said, throwing her painted fingernails in the air.

"But you're *not* a teacher," Gio said with a conviction that made me wonder why he'd never said as much in front of Francis. For months, he'd sat watching us make ed-talk. And yet, he'd never raised one word of objection. Maybe he'd kept quiet out of loyalty to me? Or maybe he wasn't keen to lose another dad?

"I used to work," I said, vaguely. "You were too little to remember. Time was, I was more than just your mom. Your principal found me more than qualified."

"We're gonna get double recess! And free dessert!" Cat did a jumping jack, but her foot grazed the wheel of someone's stroller and propelled it into a nanny's broad backside.

We got a wealth of dirty looks.

"No, honey. Everything will be almost exactly the same. But I'll teach you acting once a week."

"So what do we *get*?" Cat asked mystified.

"My new job will help pay for your school."

"What?" she said with a little shriek. "You *pay* for us to go to school? But it's sooo boring!"

"And you also get a mom with a sense of identity and purpose. A role model . . ." Even as I said it, I knew they didn't care about that.

Staring at the Hudson, Gio karate-chopped the dividing rope, which snapped and retracted back into its metal pole.

"What?" I asked.

"Nothing."

"You look like you have an issue."

"I *don't*."

But when we finally climbed aboard the ride, which was custom designed with animals from New York state, he narrowed his eyes at me and beelined directly for the eel.

. . .

For over a week, I sat alone in the flat, attempting to prep for work. I reread Francis's copy of *Teach Like a Champion*. I brainstormed lesson plans and picked out teacherly outfits. I reviewed Bret Esnad's phonetic seating charts (there were *three* Petras, with three different pronunciations). I went online, searched Marianna De Felice's name (which defied Google for the millionth time), and hoped the real one, wherever she was, wasn't a convicted child toucher.

On the tenth day, an envelope arrived from the New York State Education Department. Tearing it open, I found, of all things, a clearance letter.

CHAPTER TWENTY-ONE

On Monday morning I found myself in the auditorium, which was officially the Darius B. Monte Theater for the Performing Arts. It was as state-of-the-art as everything else at Boulevard: nine hundred seats; acoustic engineering; bowed walls that gave a good impression that the luxe world was closing in around you.

Atop the piano bench, I had four manila folders, one for each class, a school-issued tablet, and a Delaney book.

I also had an idea I should have some red pens handy, to keep a hit list of students who did naughty things. But I hadn't bought any, meaning juvenile delinquents got first-day amnesty.

I stood behind the lectern to start, then decided it looked defensive. Francis's teaching books said body language is 90 percent of successful communication.

It had been a mistake to get to the theater so early. My stage fright had too much time to gestate. I could think of nothing besides the students filing down the aisles and sizing me up, comparing me to "brilliant" Brent Esnad.

I decided to meet the children outside instead, and hurried up the aisle. If teaching was anything like being a student, then the hallway was an important performance space. I decided it would be where I forged my reputation.

The door opened as I reached for it.

"Sorry," Francis said, colliding with me in a way that was inadvertently sexual. "Just coming to give you a kiss for luck."

His lips found my face just as the Japanese-style school bell began playing Westminster Quarters in a bright tone.

"Marianna?"

"Mmm?" My heart was as loud and disorderly as the feet in the halls.

"Are you OK?"

"Just a little first-day impostor syndrome. I think a part of me is still waiting for Brent to waltz in and take his class back."

"It's yours now. Believe it. If you don't, the kids won't either."

"I'm not as qualified as Brent. I hate that."

"Hate is a strong word. Besides, you're the one who always says, 'Teaching is the art of sharing not just what you know, but also what you don't know.' "

"Do I really say that?"

"Shush. You're walking in with a mind-set of curiosity and a desire to learn from them too."

Behind him, students were pouring down the hall.

"Right. You're right. We'll grow together. What was it they used to say in teachers' college? 'A good teacher is really just a good student'?"

And with that hope, I faced a second-grade teacher, who was holding a leaf of paper like a court foreman and leading a jury of obscenely wealthy seven-year-olds.

I swear, the period was half-over by the time I got them seated. They shoved, squabbled, and sang under their breath. They picked and chewed the contents of their noses, then flapped up and down on the folding theater seats.

"Hi," I said for reasons I couldn't fathom. I had been reading up on pedagogy for six months, but all the convincing lines had gone out of my head.

After some early disasters, I decided to use my own approach.

I stood in the hallway, radiating positivity, as Gio's class of fifth graders arrived fresh from recess with chapped cheeks and hair dancing with cold-weather static. What's more, I had plugged my laptop into the theater sound system, hoping to use music to blast them into submission. Cleary and I enjoyed Wham! when we were their age, so I played it at top volume while they streamed into the auditorium.

"Call me good, call me bad / Call me anything you want to, baby."

It was like I'd flipped a car. They'd been reared on Bach and Chopin, plus singsongy French and Mandarin. They were so unaccustomed to synth pop that they filed onto the stage and sat in a swift, orderly circle. The ones who weren't grinning in devious approval looked like they were about to cry. I had their attention, 100 percent.

I recited the theater rules to them, which I had pared down to just two: "come prepared" and "show respect." Then I asked for a volunteer.

"Preferably someone tough," I added. "Someone who's not going to cry."

A smattering of hands went up. Mostly it was boys nominating one another, thrusting one another's hands up on a dare. I settled on the boy who stood up in superhero stance, hands on his girlish chinoed hips.

"Thank you. What's your name, dear?"

"Faddei."

"Fatty?"

"Fadd-*ieee*," he reiterated. Later, I learned it was the Russian form of Thaddeus.

"Great, thank you, Faddei." With my next breath, I hollered: "Faddei! What did I say about bothering the children next to you?! Would you *like* me to lose it?!"

Faddei had the look of someone who was on the verge of soiling himself. The other children clutched their mouths in horror.

But just at the moment when the tension became unbearable, all my anger dropped away and I made my voice matter-of-fact: "Because I don't like to lose it."

The cleverest ones laughed like hyenas on helium. Then the others caught up and realized I'd been joking the whole time.

"OK, who can tell me why I just shouted at Faddei?"

No one raised their hand. The fake tirade had earned me the floor, and no one was keen to take it from me.

"I shouted at Faddei because I want you to know that I can behave terribly if you do. At the end of the day, I have an objective and we're going to achieve it. If you're in the way, there's gonna be a problem. I *also* shouted at Faddei because anger is a private emotion, and drama class is about teaching you to be private in public. Very soon, you're all going to have the skills to do that."

They looked up at me with a mixture of intimidation and awe.

I'd barely segued into the subject matter when a girl began crying.

In American teachers' parlance, she appeared to be the class "*that* kid"—not shy, not artsy, not trying to fit in, wearing her face like a kick-me sign, getting everything just wrong enough to make everyone impatient. A few of the other pupils rolled their eyes.

I hadn't the first idea what to do. None of my classroom-management books said anything about children who begin crying out of clear blue space.

So I busied the others with a basic theatre exercise: "Who here knows the mirror game?"

No one answered. They were all whispering to one another about the crying girl, who was still bawling at me with a look of accusation.

"Pick a partner and copy everything they do and say. You know how to copy, right? Excellent. Find a friend."

I invited the crybaby down to the orchestra pit, where we could speak privately, side by side on the piano bench.

"Are you OK, honey?" I asked, wishing very much that she'd stop kicking the $70,000 instrument.

"No!" she said, nonspecifically.

I glanced up at the stage and found pairs of children mimicking each other's inappropriate words. One pair was giving each other the middle finger.

"Do you have a fever?"

I reached out to feel her forehead, but she screamed in resistance and angled her body away.

"OK, see, the thing is, this isn't working out, honey. We're making our introductions and you're interrupting my flow. So what do you say you tell me what's wrong?"

But she gave me nothing but silent indignation.

I opened my Delaney book: "What's your name?" Admittedly, I should have asked this first.

"Gab-*beee*." In a rambling whine.

"What's your last name, sweetheart?"

"Ashworth."

My vision tunneled. My ears roared with white noise. I told myself it couldn't be. I looked at her, squinting, trying to make her features cohere. It took a moment, but eventually I recognized her sloping, bewildered eyebrows. Her bottom-heavy cheeks. She had the damp, dark eyes of a kicked puppy.

I was shivering all over, disproportionately shocked. In my mind, Gabby Ashworth was as synonymous with Woodstock as my mam was with Ireland.

"You're not on my class list." Anxiety gave my voice an aggressive edge.

"It's my first day."

I reached for my phone, checked my Boulevard email address, and found her new-student notice from the head office, along with something called an Individualized Education Program.

Shite, I thought. That was that. There would be no more worries about taking my thing with Francis too far. No more asking myself how I would know when to stop. Melanie's daughter went to Boulevard, which meant it was time to leave it all (dream job, dream city, dream man) behind.

I tried to focus on the situation at hand: getting Gabby out of the theater before she recognized me.

"OK, Gabby Ashworth. Do you remember what my name is? I'm Ms. De Felice. I know this is the first time we've ever met, and you don't know me very well, but I'm here to help. But I want you to know that I get it. I've felt the same as you. From time to time, everyone does. Can you describe what you're feeling? Anger maybe? That's not a bad thing. Anger helps us survive by overcoming obstacles. Or fear? Fear helps us survive by avoiding danger."

Gabby's tears stopped, but her expression was hard.

I turned around and realized two boys were trying to stick a pen into the AV switchboard.

"OK, what do you say we get you down to the school doctor?"

Being Boulevard, a lowly school nurse was not good enough. The school *doctor* had five diplomas on her wall and an assistant professorship at NYU School of Medicine.

"Gio?" I called

"Yeah, Mom? I mean, Mrs. De Felice?"

"Never mind."

I couldn't chance Gabby recognizing him either.

"Petra? Could you please walk Gabby to the doctor's office?"

"I'm *Pay*-truh. Yeah, sure."

Five years earlier, I was in the habit of Internet stalking Victor and his daughter on a daily basis. Given Manhattan was only a hundred miles from Woodstock, it would have been wise to keep it up. But I had let the city convince me, in its persuasive way, that I was both invisible and invincible.

It pained me to admit, but I'd also been so excited about my new life that I quit keeping tabs on my old one. What's more, there was an element of denial. The same magical thinking that made it easy to suspend reality and play a role had a downside, and that was overlooking the limitations of mind over matter.

Don't get me wrong, I wasn't deluded. I didn't actually believe the Ashworths didn't exist just as long as I didn't think about them. It had just been easier to function when I *wasn't* typing their names into an Internet search every day. I'd been living in the sweet spot between forgetting and avoidance.

After my run-in with Gabby, I couldn't put it off any longer. That night, after Francis and the children went to sleep, I faced my laptop squarely and typed Victor's name into the search bar with a toque of dread.

My stomach dropped. Victor Ashworth had been in Manhattan for at least a year. Maybe he sent Gabby to public school before Boulevard. More likely, she had defected from Dalton or Spence.

The search engine recalled a photo of Victor at last year's New Yorkers for Children Spring Dinner Dance. Then another of him at the Tribeca Film Festival. By the time I got to a photo of him at an Hermès event (the photographer had snapped him saying something that made Viggo Mortensen laugh), my heart was halfway to my esophagus.

But the most damning photo of Vic was on *Guest of a Guest.* There he was at Project Sunshine's annual golf classic, literally rubbing shoulders with Boulevard headmaster Henry Upton as they smiled for a photo with too much flash.

I was horrified. Not only because Victor knew Henry but because I had *seen* the photo before. I'd been slack about Googling Victor, but I *had* been researching my new boss in secret for months. The fact that I'd looked directly at Victor and didn't recognize him seemed to prove I had some a massive cognitive blind spot. I'd *avoided* the truth. I'd *willfully* kept myself in the dark.

Victor had joined a private-equities giant called Spring View Group and become a partner in its "secondaries" division, which persuaded pension funds, hedge funds, and other investors to buy stakes in private-equity funds. I wondered how many millions per year he collected in annual compensation. According to the *Wall*

Street Journal, Spring View had recently closed a transaction that earned the company $1.5 billion in capital.

But that wasn't all. According to the "Vows" section of the *Times*, Victor Ashworth had got himself some "social security" as well. Six months ago, he'd married the heiress to a French cosmetics empire—a woman named Camille Dumont, her net worth in the billions:

> . . . After Mr. Ashworth's financial services company transferred him to Manhattan, he avoided revealing his status as a widower. "It was my deep, dark secret," he said. "I wasn't sure I even wanted to date."
>
> Fortunately for the couple, Ms. Dumont, a tall, dazzling woman with an expressive manner, defies comparison. A widow herself, she knew very well what it was like to lose a spouse. "Before Victor, I'd met a lot of men who just didn't understand that death is different than breaking up. They'd tell me, 'I felt just the same after my divorce.' No. When you bury a spouse, you're left with all the love you had when they were alive . . ."

Dumbstruck, I stared again at the headline: THEN BECOMES NOW, TWO HEARTS CARRY ON.

The children would have to leave Boulevard. That was a given. But I would also have to lose Francis and leave New York.

I heard Francis's snores flag. So did the ambient music that soothed him to sleep. I quickly closed out my windows and cleared my browser history while he trudged down the short corridor.

When he arrived, his bleary eyes looked smaller without his glasses.

"I'm sorry," I said. "I'm keeping you up."

"No. You're not. I just wanted to get a look at the landscape."

I didn't know what to say. The photos of Victor had stunned me stupid.

Francis clarified: "I wanted to find out what's keeping *you* awake. Give me some landmarks. I'm not sure I can read the signposts."

Francis was brilliant at applying the Socratic method to my problems. After his ex-fiancée had accused him of being emotionally closed off, he'd become very good at talking about feelings (at least other people's). He dismantled even my most vile moods with patient precision. He'd quote me back to me. He'd break my bloody nightmare down into outstanding problems and key assumptions before bandaging me up with a bit of humor or optimism. You can call it "mansplaining." That's in fashion. But he never explained me to me. He just waded through my problems with his teacher's style of listening—*Tell me more, I'd like to hear about that*—the one that always made me feel pleasantly squishy.

I told him I was just obsessing about the failures of my first day.

"I'm disappointed in myself," I said. "My inner perfectionist is kicking my ass. There was this incident. At the start of class, one of the fifth graders started crying out of nowhere. She was hysterical. I had to send her to the doctor."

"So, she probably had some sort of incident in her previous class. Who had the fifth graders before you?"

"Before drama, they had recess."

"Well, there you have it. One of the other girls probably left her out of a game. What did the front office say?"

It hadn't occurred to me to check in with the front office.

"Mom?"

There was Gio, with sleep-crusted eyes and bed head. The dark patch on the front of his pajama pants told me he'd wet the bed again, a problem he was far too old for.

"I had a nightmare," he said.

"Oh, honey, you've had an accident as well."

"Don't worry," Francis said. "It happens to the best of us, Gee. Come on, let's get you some clean shorts."

I stood. "It's OK. I've got it covered. Maybe we can finish this conversation tomorrow?"

"Sure. Let's have a date night."

Francis was the only man who'd ever successfully made me warm to the phrase *date night*, which had always sounded too close to *playdate* for my taste.

Francis clapped a reassuring hand on Gio's shoulder, then kissed me on the cheek. "If you still feel down later, wake me up," he whispered. A few moments later, his deep-sleep music returned.

I rummaged around in the "linen closet," which, because it was New York, also housed books, dishes, bottled drinks, and sporting equipment—a whole life stacked with Tetris-level precision.

I climbed the ladder to change the sheets on Gio's top bunk.

"Do you want to tell me about your bad dream?" I asked.

"There was this computer. It's hard to explain. . . . It wanted me to do something. I *had* to do something, or you'd die."

"*I'd* die?"

"Yeah," Gio said. "But I couldn't figure out which buttons to press. I kept choosing wrong. And every time I hit the wrong thing, scary things flashed on the screen."

"What kinds of scary things?"

"I don't know."

"Well, that computer's not allowed to frighten you. If you were back in your dream, you know what I'd tell you to do?"

"What?" The hair around his temples was damp with sweat.

"Call for me. I'll come and turn that computer off, then turn it back on again. If you want to fix a problem, that's the first stage. You reboot. Hey, can I ask you something about class today?"

"Sure."

"That girl who was crying—"

"Gabby?"

"Yes, Gabby. How does she treat you?"

"I don't know. She's weird with me, I guess."

"Weirder than she is with anyone else?"

He shook his head.

Testing him: "Do you think you could have met her before? Someplace else?"

"No."

His denial seemed genuine, which was a comfort. I'd read up on studies about infantile amnesia. If Gio didn't remember living at the Ashworths' house now, there was a good chance he wouldn't ever remember. By age ten, childhood memories are crystallized. The few things Gio *did* recall, he would keep and draw his identity from. He was unlikely to unearth any others.

"Do you know anything about her parents?"

"What's the big deal about Gabby Ashworth?"

"I just want to know my students. So I can be a good teacher."

He was too tired to be sarcastic. For a change. "She lives with her stepmother, I think. Some of the other kids say her real mom is dead. Was that why she was crying?"

"I don't know. But you're right, it's very hard to lose a mommy so young. It's not for us to judge how she behaves."

As I was stuffing Gio's wet sheets into the laundry hamper, I found one of Francis's little Moleskine notebooks at the bottom and felt almost breathless with loss. That sounds sentimental. But having resigned myself to the coming breakup, I knew I would never know another man who whispered Lord Byron's "She Walks in Beauty" to me after he watched me cross traffic. And I sure as hell would never have another man tell me (as Francis once did): "My love wasn't just hanging around, waiting for someone to attach itself to, Mari. *You* helped make it. I never felt particularly good or affectionate before you came along." I got into bed beside him and cried mutely like Meryl in *Sophie's Choice*. I watched him sleep, memorizing the musculature of his face like a habit I was about to give up.

But then, did I really have to leave New York? To my knowledge, Victor Ashworth wasn't even looking for Tracey Bueller. And if he ever did, he would lean on heuristics. He'd look for a "con woman," someone slick and grandiose who earned vast sums of money by lazing about on her backside—not a schoolteacher who earned peanuts. What if, instead of splitting up with Francis, I just avoided places that attracted visiting upstaters: the Natural History Museum, Lincoln Center, and the High Line? The decision required thought. It called for research.

On Monday morning, I went back to work and reviewed Gabriella Ashworth's Individual Education Plan. Sinister motives aside, I was meant to sign off on it for the head office. It was a contract. Legally binding. Obligating me to bridge the "learning gap" that Gabby suffered as a result of her auditory processing disorder—the same condition that led Melanie to sue the public school in Woodstock.

According to Boulevard's special education assessor, as well as Gabby's pervious one at Horace Mann, she had a very poor working memory. In math, for instance, she couldn't remember more than three or four digits at a time. And when we put on class productions, I was forbidden from making her memorize her part and instead must allow her to read from a script.

Gabby's education plan also said her functioning decreased with background noise. She could hear all right. If you gave her an ear test, she'd pass. But her doctors had determined that she had difficulty understanding people with high- or low-pitched voices and—I nearly pinched myself—speakers with "prominent accents."

If the educators who'd assessed Gabby were right, then there was a good chance she hadn't picked up on half of what I'd said that summer in Woodstock. *Problems with background noise?* Kitty had been in a near-constant state of screaming. *Difficulty with accents and figures of speech?* It was no wonder Gabby used to look at me with those big watery eyes. To her, I must have sounded like the Beatles, played backward.

I read it all—the diagnosis, the symptoms—with a delicious relief that intensified my guilt. Not only had I taken Gabby's mother, but there I was, glad for the condition that blitzed her memory. I was a monster. A 9.5 arsehole. As I signed Marianna's name to Gabby's I.E.P., I vowed to do whatever I could to support her in school, without drawing undue attention to myself and arousing Victor Ashworth's suspicions. I couldn't bring back her mother, but as some small consolation, I could give her the arts and, therein, an intellectual and creative home that would be there for her no matter what.

CHAPTER TWENTY-TWO

The Australians' cash seemed to smolder in my pocket. Once we were mercifully back at the guesthouse, I stood barefoot on the cracked tiles, watching Oz pour me a drink.

"You did brilliantly," he said, putting his arms around me.

My head wobbled. "I didn't do much at all."

"Oh, feel you shake. Are you sorry we did it? Look at all this pretty cash." He opened the blond's wallet and made a fan of rainbow bills on the unmade bed.

I was woozy. In such vast quantities, the bills looked oddly worthless.

"I wonder how they'll get to Kashmir after this."

"The kids? They'll be all right. I bet they already paid their tariffs. Put them on credit cards."

I opened the sari bloke's wallet, and to my horror, a family photo fell out. I stared at Oz accusingly.

"What?" he said. "That's proof they have parents they can phone for help. Do I have that? Do *you*?"

"No."

"No," he affirmed, sitting beside me on the bed and smoothing my hair to one shoulder. "But we have each other. We have our resilience."

I looked again at the photo. The sari bloke's family wore

matching T-shirts and smiles. His father had a supportive hand on his mum's shoulder.

I confided: "There's something I really want to do. It may sound mad—"

"You want to get married?"

"Ha!" I crunched a bunch of rupees in one fist and chucked them at him.

He flung some back at me, until the room was aflutter with airborne bills.

"I need to leave India," I said, once the money settled. "I want to find where my mother is buried. I don't think I can forgive her until I do."

"Forgive her for what?"

"For never coming to find me."

Considering that, he fiddled with a starched pink bill. "Well, then, we'll have to go back," he said sitting up, eyes on mine.

"Really? You want to come to Ireland?"

"Why not?"

"We'll need more money, for one."

"So we'll do a few more backpackers. We have more pills. We can raise the cash."

"No," I said. "No, let me get the money another way. Or at least let me try."

It was pouring as we ducked into an Internet café. Oz and I had walked miles to get there, weaving around women in wet saris and dodging the splash of passing motorbikes, huddling under the umbrella we'd nicked from the hotel's reception.

Inside, it was homely and dry, gecko stickers on the walls, the smell of tobacco and aromatic spices. Oz and I claimed a PC.

He had choreographed the plan at breakfast that morning, over papaya lassi. The day set a new precedent for our relationship.

From that moment forward, I was the visionary, dreaming up new schemes, and Oz was the director/choreographer who saw them through to completion.

"So the story is: we're planning a trip to Nepal," Oz said. "We're going to talk loudly about it, wildly excited. Make price comparisons aloud. Think *American volume.* Yes?"

"Yes," I echoed.

"I'm going to mark time near the printer, ready to create a distraction if I see anyone watching you. And you'll be . . . Explain to me what you'll be doing again?"

"I'll be searching the Internet history and cache."

"What for?"

"Email addresses. Hotel and travel websites." Travelzoo had just launched. Expedia was a healthy three years old. "If I find an address, I'll email it, pretending I'm the hotel or train company they've been looking at. 'Sorry, we lost your reservation. Can you send me your credit card details again?' "

"How will you create the email address?"

"I have this friend Seema, back in London. She taught me how to use Telnet to write an email spoof. Once, we sent an email to her father from tonyblair@gov.uk."

"Good deal," Oz said. "Let's give it a try. Afterward I'll bring the information to Nafi."

"Will he give you a fair price?"

"Should do."

At the café, it was better pickings than I'd hoped. The last person to use AOL had even left herself logged in, leaving me to read all her travel reservations, as well as her mother's passive-aggressive emails. Long before our prepaid hour expired, I had sent off two dozen email spoofs.

Admittedly, it wasn't any more ethical than Oz's method. Although one could argue we were stealing from the credit card companies, who were apt to reverse the charges after the reported thefts.

But at least it was anonymous. No one we stole from could pick us out of a lineup. They'd never tasted Oz's hash or noticed the rather memorable way my black hair stood at odds with my freckles.

Oz had never taken a computer course in his life, and he wasn't thrilled about surrendering so much creative control to me, given he was used to scamming "slowly and alone." What's more, he didn't fully understand my methods. He still typed with two fingers and hadn't the foggiest idea you could attach files to emails. But after we'd stolen a few credit card numbers, even he could agree that frittering the day away in Internet cafés was much less work than running around the hot, busy streets.

It took a heap of stolen credit card numbers to raise the cash for two tickets to Dublin. We spent so much time in Internet cafés that the owners grew suspicious of us and Oz began to give them weekly bribes, passing money over the counter in an empty Gold Leaf cigarette box. But in time, we pulled together the money, helped in part by a surprise deposit from my father.

Oz understood the terms of the journey. He was to come to Ireland, help me find where Mam was buried, then leave me alone to pay my respects. And he was happy as a lark to be seeing a new part of the world. He spent the flight from Varanasi to Delhi—as well as the one from Delhi to Abu Dhabi—sipping duty-free whiskey and asking me questions that made me squirm like a captive, willing the captain to turn off the seat-belt sign.

"Is it true that everyone says 'aye'?"

" 'Aye' is Northern Irish," I snipped with irritation.

Ever since the trip had become a reality, I had little attention span for anything beyond recollections of my mother. Alone, I had flashbacks of laying my head on her knee for de-nitting, or top and tailing gooseberries together. I thought fondly of her big jar of pickling vinegar and her homemade curtains with the massive hems. These were the warm-duvet memories that I pulled around me, and as much as I loved Oz, his incessant questions detracted from my nostalgia.

He pulled one headphone away from my ear. “What’s the Irish drinking etiquette? Rounds?”

I nodded. “Someone’s likely to buy you a drink. It falls on you to get the next round in.”

“I see,” he said happily. “Like a pyramid scheme.”

“Or a system built on friendship and trust.”

“You’re too nervous!” he said, lowering my meal tray for the flight attendant I’d failed to notice. “Paying your respects to your mum, after so many years! It’s going to be great!”

“I just want to honor her memory,” I said, fighting an airy feeling, an odd mental draft.

It was after midnight when we touched down in Dublin.

It was too late to thumb a ride or book tickets on the rail. So we checked into a hostel near the airport bus stop.

“Is it spider breeding season or something?” Oz asked, looking at the corpse of one someone had squished against the wall.

“My mother used to say if you have spiders, you don’t have mice. I would rather have spiders.”

Oz produced a small bottle of booze he’d nicked from the flight attendant’s trolley and stashed in his carry-on bag. “You have spiders in Ireland that kill mice? Fucking hell.”

I didn’t have it in me to laugh. My stomach was sparking with air-pressure pains. The damp cold stupefied me after months in subtropical climates.

For a time we sat in bed, eating takeaway gravy and chips.

Or rather, Oz ate. I watched him in a fugue.

“You should eat something,” he told me. “Have some. They’re very good.”

Just looking at the heap of beige food churned my stomach. They were my father’s favorite hangover cure.

“I’m too knackered,” I groaned, stripping the bed of the duvet

I knew with certainty had never been washed. Then, so tired I was reeling, I curled up, chattering, beneath the cardboard sheets.

I slept. I must have. Otherwise, Oz would have practiced his tantra on me. But from my perspective, it didn't feel like sleep at all. Every third second, I jolted awake to the sounds of footsteps or voices. A clang of a pipe. Running water. Wind. The too-close sound of the bed creaking in the room next door. Back in India, I'd discovered that the squealing crescendo of Oz's snore could sound like a scream, given the right levels of sleep deprivation. And in my lover's breath, I heard wailing all night. When I nodded off, I fell directly into a night terror, imagining a pair of guests had taken a wrong turn on the way to the shared toilet and stood, silhouetted, staring at us from the foot of the bed.

When morning came, I was shattered. A kiss from Oz hit my neck like a trickle, shocking me awake, forcing me to register the painful gash of light between the curtains. I sat up. I lay down.

It had been over a decade since I'd set foot in my hometown. Surely everyone there knew I'd run out on my mother. Even worse, they'd heard how she'd killed herself as a result. What if we arrived and Cleary and his parents hated me? What if they all thought I had blood on my hands?

I drifted off to sleep again and awoke shivering with chills.

"You're white as a sheet," Oz said. "And you whimpered with nightmares all night. We shouldn't travel."

I made my way to my rucksack. Everything we owned smelled of incense and the hash we'd smuggled in the cartridge of my portable CD player. "I'll cope. We'll go today. But there's something I want to do first."

"Anything. What do you have in mind? A visit to the chemist?"

"It's a tummy bug. I'll soldier on."

Oz tossed the sheet to one side and joined me over the bags that were spewing filthy laundry and various international coins.

"Then what?" Oz said. "Breakfast at the café across the street?

So much time in the land of sacred cows. I want to eat Irish back bacon!"

Outside, there was a storm in progress. I could hear water running down the drainpipes and sloping roofs.

"I don't want food." I let Oz grab my hip and pull me in for a cuddle.

"So what *does* the goddess want?"

I looked up at his intense eyes.

"She wants to get married."

"What?" He had a look of smirking joy. "No! You?! I don't believe it! You're the one who is always so constipated about marriage! Making me feel like some pervert for wanting a wife—"

I kissed him hard, like he was an extra lung. "Well, you are amoral. But then, I am too."

CHAPTER TWENTY-THREE

It reached new levels of absurdity, holding a fifth grader's birthday party at dusk. As did having it at the Top of the Standard. Carter's mummy was trying to shoehorn an adult's Champagne disco into a child's Dementor piñata. But then, Gio, seemingly the only child in Manhattan who didn't get an invitation, was heartbroken, so I decided to use my special skills to his advantage.

I'd had to mask him. I had tricked him into a Voldemort costume by telling him Halloween Adventure was entirely sold out of Gryffindor robes.

Unearthing the details of Carter's party had been fairly simple once I knew the potential locations. I'd inquired about booking my own party on the same date at both venues—the Standard and the Gansevoort—and only the Standard was booked.

Internet research told me the space had its own entrance with a straight-shot lift to the roof. But I was hoping to avoid the velvet rope and attendant clipboard Nazi, so I steered He Who Must Not Be Named through the revolving, yellow door of the main hotel.

We couldn't have picked a more perfect time to sneak in. Reception was clogged with wheeling luggage and Euro tourists waiting to check in. A few chuckled at us as if to say *New Yorkers are mad*. We quickly turned the corner toward the stairs, and Gio's black robe billowed behind him.

"Can't we take the elevator?" he asked in the muffled parseltongue his rubber mask created.

"It's broken. Didn't you see the sign?" I asked, huffing. I had lost nearly a stone in five years, ever since we moved to the city, but I still wasn't fit enough for the climb. We'd gone ten floors and had another eight to go.

"The present!" Gio said when we reached the sixteenth floor.

I heard his stomach growl as I was bent over, catching my breath. He'd skipped lunch. He'd been too excited about the party to eat.

"What about it?"

He peeled his mask up over his face. "We forgot to bring one!"

"You thoughtful boy," I said, replacing his mask. "Not to worry. I bought it online and shipped it to Carter's house."

"What'd you get him?"

"A marble run. Think he'll like that?"

"Maybe."

Maybe not. It was no skin off my nose. I hadn't really sent it.

"Shall we? Are you ready?"

He nodded.

"You go on ahead of me."

Once he was plodding up the final steps, I reached into my handbag for the empty glass I'd brought from home. (A Champagne flute, combined with a little black dress, are the only props one ever needs to crash a party.)

At the back door, the bouncer sat on a folding chair and stared at his phone. I smiled softly as we passed, but he didn't notice or stop me pulling open the door. He was an ostrich with his head in the sport scores.

We stepped inside, and the room swelled around us in a twisting vortex of rose-gold columns and crystal tiles, all set into champagne fizz by the high altitude and the Hudson sunset. Even the carpet shone with golden bits of lamé.

"Whoa," Gio said.

A cocktail waitress darted toward me. She had features like a porn star and an expression like a government worker.

"Excuse me," she said sharply.

"Hi." The thought that she was about to eject us in front of Gio's new mates was enough to send sweat pouring through the fabric of my dress. Which was a shame because I'd left the tags on, planning to return it to Barneys.

"May I refresh your glass?"

"Lovely. Thank you." My hand trembled a bit as I held out my glass. Once she'd gone, I bent down to Voldemort. "Shall we mingle?"

He made a *come on* gesture with his pointed little wand.

I let him lead the way. On the east side of the party was an ice-cream bar and a real-life snowy owl on the gloved arm of a handler; the poor creature looked only slightly less uncomfortable than the real-life Daniel Radcliffe, who was also in attendance, gritting his teeth for pictures. In the west, there was an open bar—oysters, Champagne, and deconstructed gin martinis—and the alpha-women from the PAC, who were sucking olives and flashing the red soles of their shoes. The two worlds collided on the dance floor, where Brooke Shields and Katie Couric were laughing in high-def loveliness, cutting a rug in a sea of Harrys and Hermiones.

Gio spotted a friend and wandered off to explore a table of nonalcoholic "potions"—shot glasses full of "truth serum" and "dragon spit"—and so I gravitated to the adult bar with my eye on the canapés.

"Marianna!" a voice called, just as I was enjoying some quality time with a quail's egg on toast.

A nimble little claw pinched my bicep, and when I turned, I saw Lily of the PAC, wearing a bright little frock I'd seen in the window of Intermix.

"Hi!" I said, accepting her air-kiss, dodging flying wisps of her hair.

"Oh my God. I *loved* the fifth graders' short film! And having them speak Japanese? Sooo brilliant."

"Well, it *was* Kabuki theatre. Masaki"—the Japanese teacher—"translated the script, and the students did the English subtitles in postproduction."

The students had played characters like Shōjō (the drunk orangutan), Genkurō (the shape-shifting fox spirit) and Ishikawa Goemon (the outlaw hero who stole gold to give to the poor). I had painted their faces with geisha makeup and taught them to use a green screen to set the scene at a Shinto shrine. In the process, I learned the quiet pupils were only quiet with their mouths. Given the right role (be it makeup or film editing or drums), they were just as comfortable onstage as they were on a sporting field.

"Lily, help me out here," a man said suddenly, too loud and bumpingly close. "I can't catch this bartender. I need bait."

Charming. I turned and full-body flinched at the sight of Victor Ashworth. He was wearing a gabardine sport coat and a chesty western shirt that could use another popper done up. From the looks of it, he'd already had maybe one drink too many. But like everyone else, he was drinking it all in: not only the raw oysters and Belvedere vodka, but also the preposterously beautiful skyline.

Lily wasn't bothered, playing the worm on his proverbial hook, wriggling around in her fab little dress until she caught the barman's eye.

When Vic turned to look at me, drink in hand, his expression changed in a way that made my heart clap in my chest. Maybe it was my imagination, but he looked a little startled. For the first time, I wondered if Janisa had worked with a police sketch artist—

"Hello," I said. "I'm Marianna."

"Victor." He extended his hand. "Victor *Ashworth.*"

Was it intentional? The way he accentuated this last part?

He squeezed my palm slowly, as if prolonging the gesture, giving him time to study my features one by one: eyes, nose, mouth, chin.

Lily seemed to notice as well. "Marianna is Francis Blake's girlfriend," she said, scanning the room with a bored-flat face as though she were looking for someone more influential to talk to. Someone, maybe, like Ainsley Doyle.

There was ice in my veins and a cold little panic taking over.

"Marianna's the new drama teacher," Lily told Vic.

"*Well,*" Victor said. "Good time to be a drama teacher."

"So I hear," I said. "Poor Brent. Who knew his world theatre was so heavy on moans."

Vic laughed, but I could tell he hadn't stopped trying to get a read on me. If anything, he seemed to be paying even closer attention. But then, wasn't there a chance he was like that with everyone? The superrich closed themselves off to everyone else.

"Your daughter is a joy to teach," I said, firmly positioning myself as an educator. "She's an observer, as you know. There's a quiet power in that, especially for an actor. Besides, lots of students feel awkward singing and dancing onstage at the start."

Halfway through the speech, I realized I was working too hard to prove myself, treating a cocktail party like a parent-teacher conference.

"She probably gets that from me," Vic said. "I've never liked musicals. The way actors are talking one minute and bursting into song the next? Feels kind of phony, don't you think? I don't like phony."

A tingling feeling crept up my left arm, a mock heart attack.

Vic moved closer. "I heard Gabby had an incident in your class, early on."

"It was my first day. Change is difficult for children. Difficult for all of us, really—"

"And you didn't contact me. I suppose I shouldn't be surprised."

My neutral expression felt painful now, my mouth quite misshapen. "I wanted to review her I.E.P. before we spoke."

He chuckled mutely, as if he didn't buy it. "Gabby can't process verbal information if there's background noise—"

"Yes. So, I've learned—"

"Listen, Ms. . . . *Remind me?*"

"De Felice."

"Right. Okay, Ms. *De Felice.* Your position at Boulevard is temporary. So I'm going to stop pretending for a minute and level with you. I had high hopes for this school, and it isn't making the right accommodations for my daughter. It's doing her an injustice. And we've all suffered quite enough injustice in recent years."

Lily rubbed his back in a gesture of sympathy. Did she know about Melanie?

Getting misty in the manner of someone who had definitely had too many martinis, Vic said: "I won't have Gabby giving up because a broken system gave up on us. Shit happens. But it's never too late to stand up for what you believe in, am I right?"

"You're so right," Lily said, stupidly sipping her drink. "That's the problem in the world today. There's no accountability. I said the same thing at the dry cleaner just this week. I left a pair of Thierry Lasry sunglasses in the pocket of my coat and, of course, when I went to pick it up, they were gone. I told them just because you didn't get caught, doesn't mean you haven't broken the law."

Vic set his drink down on the bar and looked me dead in the eyes. "I believe in karma. I think neglecting someone in need always comes back to bite you in the ass. That's why I've talked at length with Henry. We've laid out a plan. I want people to see the truth for themselves."

I grasped for educational buzzwords: "Well, I can't speak for the other teachers at Boulevard. But in my class, Gabby is a part of our *community.* I've worked very hard to *empower her* and form a *strategy.*"

Again, the draw of his brow said he didn't quite believe me. He steepled his fingers to his lips as though he were holding something back.

"Sorry," he said, finally. More to Lily than me. "I've let my anger get the best of me. As you can tell, I've been carrying this around with me for quite some time."

Lily squeezed his shoulder again.

Vic looked at me, then picked up his drink. "There's Regina, Carter's mother. I should say hello. Unless you two want to join me?"

I shook my head weakly.

"Oh! Kelly's here!" Lily said. "I'll catch up with you in a minute." The fame-crazed look in her eyes told me she meant either Ripa, Rutherford, or Preston.

I watched Victor Ashworth disappear into a sea of short, spangly skirts. Moments later, he emerged in the sunken seating area that had become the party's unofficial VIP section. Regina was air-kissing him. The owner of the Middle East's largest flour mill poured him a drink from what I estimated was a $600 bottle of vodka. Vic took a Cuban from his pocket with that ridiculous phallic reverence all men have when they handle cigars.

Had he been trying to provoke me? Hoping I'd incriminate myself?

No. I was simply being paranoid. Victor didn't have any dirt on Marianna. Gabby didn't remember me. And I'd cleared all the background checks. Plus, the longer Marianna stayed at Boulevard, the more character witnesses she would have: powerful parents and respected teachers like Francis.

Besides, if Victor went into school saying I resembled his late wife's dead architect he'd look mad. No, worse, he'd appear sad. And the only thing that makes people more uneasy than the idea of a killer in their midst is someone, especially a man, airing his unprocessed grief.

My phone vibrated in my black leather clutch. Checking the text, I found a photo from Francis. It was a snap of him and Cat. She was laughing uncontrollably. And his short hair was gathered into what must have been eight or ten ponytails.

Before I could respond, he sent another text: *Don't worry. It was consensual.*

The dance floor was clearing for a game of Quiddich. Gio, now with his friends, was hopping in place with excitement and joy. He was an entirely different boy from the unsuccessful, invisible lad he had been back at PS 666. He was happy. Cat was happy. I was in love and employed. I didn't wear my scars prominently, front and center, on my forehead, but I too had overcome the evil that beset me. No matter the ghosts that haunted Hogwarts by way of Boulevard, I was not going anywhere.

CHAPTER TWENTY-FOUR

At the General Register Office, the clerk with hair as red as a beetroot informed Oz and me that we needed to live in Dublin for fifteen days before we applied to be married. But it was less of an impediment than another box to tick. Oz made an arrangement with the scabby-faced teen who worked the hostel's night shift, and an exchange was made: hash for a sworn letter, avowing we had lived at the Tristan Hostel for over a month. We were back at the GRO two hours later, where we presented our passports (mine fake, Oz's presumably genuine) and were given a date for a civil ceremony in one week's time.

Inside Busáras—soot of bus fumes, tramps demanding cigarettes, bird shite all over the terrazzo tiles—we were over the moon, discussing vows and wedding bands as we bought ruinously expensive tickets to Limerick.

Oz insisted on carrying my rucksack in addition to his. "Before you, I'd never met a woman as strong as me," he said. "I'm going to be a good husband to you. I promise. I'll do the opposite of everything my uncle did. No daily updates on your failings. No drug binges. Well, unless we're doing them together. And I'm going to provide for you. So you don't have to scam anymore. I want to keep you out of harm's way."

"I don't care about that," I said honestly. They were others' concerns, squarer people's forward-planning. I lived in the moment. I loved Oz as he was. And I liked collaborating with him. We shared a vision for our lives (maybe a *lack* of vision, but even that was a shared outlook in its way).

Yes, I was testing the water with both feet. And I had a vague idea that our engagement was all knotted up with my mother: leaving her, holding it against her that she never came to find me, relegating her to the blackest depths of my memory.

But that awareness didn't change my tummy-sick need to have a ring on my finger. If I was going to stage my own personal funeral for my mother, I needed the security of an old-fashioned ball and chain. I wanted Oz to tether me. I needed to be held down in one place. That way, should I flee again—flee Ireland, flee myself, run shrieking from family, love, relationships, the whole-cloth human species—I could only scamper in circles, pulling futilely against the systems I had put in place.

Oz touched my face when the coach rolled into Limerick, and I awoke with a snap.

"Look familiar?" he said. Out the window, I saw St. Joseph's Church, where one of my dad's builder mates had picked someone's pocket during holy communion, followed by the city art gallery, which I always remembered framed with waist-high tulips.

"A little." I was sweat-soaked, my chest creaking, a false hum in my voice.

The streets were stenciled with the warning STADFEACH ("Stop, Look"). But I didn't want to look too closely.

Before the bus came to a full stop, I said: "I fancy a drink."

"You need to eat something," Oz said when we arrived at a Limerick pub. But the mutton stew he set down was so very wrong, I could only stare at it.

Slow and sleepy, in a fever haze, I set about getting drunk instead, downing two ciders in the time it took Oz to eat his black pudding.

I kept hallucinating my dad out of the corner of my eye. I could imagine him quite clearly, amidst all the ferns and brass, placing his flat cap over a large scotch, betting someone he could drink it without lifting or touching the hat. I could hear his voice, introducing me to the barman in that way he always did, *My daughter. Taught her everything she knows. But not everything* I *know. Harr.*

Sweaty and unsupported, almost oscillating on my stool, I went to the toilets and boked myself sober.

"You don't reckon the church would have rejected her corpse, do you?" Oz asked once I got back to the table. "Because she was a suicide? Sanctity of life and all that? In Victorian times suicides got buried at crossroads with stakes through their hearts."

"So did actors."

"Really?" He had his legs crossed, ankle over knee, as he discreetly rolled a hash cigarette in his lap.

I nodded. "I guess we'll find out when we get to the cemetery. Actually, on second thought, can we stop at the old house first? It's on the way." I hadn't brought anything to put on my mother's grave. It occurred to me that it was lilac season, and I might be able to clip a bouquet from the bushes in front of our old house.

"You're the boss," Oz said.

Outside, in the pub alley, I took Oz's joint between my thumb and forefinger and inhaled. "Is this a different type than usual?" I asked, exhaling a stream of blue-gray smoke that matched the Irish "sunshine."

"The hash? It's the same as always," Oz said, leaning down for a kiss as he took the doobie off me.

But this was not the usual body high. I was knackered, but not relaxed. My thoughts were disjointed, not expansive. My legs went numb. My mouth was dry.

Oz hailed a taxi and I settled into the backseat with grim finality.

I had to check the letterbox twice. The house looked so much smaller and washed-out than the one in my memory. It was just a sallow bungalow, four windows, one door, crouched and brooding in its own shadow. I kept searching for my mother's big-hemmed curtains in the windows. I wouldn't have believed it was the same structure if it weren't for the empty lot next door, where I remembered Mam setting up "sweets shops" for me and Cleary: a game that consisted mostly of her scales, old jam jars, plastic money, and a bag of kola pips. To my disappointment, even the lilac bush was gone.

"No one's home," Oz said after knocking on the door. "I need a piss. What's round back?"

"Field of cows. On a clear day, we could see the Limerick Flying Club."

I wondered if it had bothered my father, living in such close proximity to private jets, seeing daily proof that posher people were going better places.

"So, next stop's the cemetery?" Oz asked when he came back.

I nodded, in a cold sweat.

A flock of spotted redshank passed overhead, bound for the River Shannon. I closed my eyes and stood in an odd stew of emotions.

Just as we were turning to walk west into town, I turned and saw a woman running down the lane. She was wearing an apron and yellow washing-up gloves, a bedsheet thrown over her arm.

She slowed as she got closer, a look of suspicion on her face. Maybe she thought Oz was a Roma traveler, looking for copper wiring to steal. But then I realized her searching little look was directed at *me*.

"Erin Aelish?"

I'd always imagined those four syllables would sound like a homecoming. But there was no peace. No fulfillment. Only the rush of loss, and then a choking shame.

"Erin? Is that you?"

It was a struggle to breathe.

Oz was smiling, eager. "Uh-huh. This is Erin. She goes by Grace now."

I had the slow-motion sensation of one name colliding with the other.

"In heaven's name!" the woman said.

I was at a loss. I hadn't the foggiest idea who she was.

"Your accent! Jaysus. And your hair! I hardly recognized you! How gorgeous you are! I mistook you for delivery people. I came over, thinking I'd have to take in a package for Cait. She and her family are away on holidays."

"Cait?" Oz said. He looked at me hopefully as though she might be a relation.

I shook my head.

"Cait and her husband moved in years after you left. Erin Aelish! I don't believe it! Frank will be delighted to see you!"

So she was Cleary's mam. I looked at her more closely this time. She was nothing at all like the doorful of woman I remembered. For a start, I'd grown taller than her in the time I'd been away. Staring at her pale lips, I remembered Dad used to call her an "absolute wagon." He'd always said she could talk the teeth out of a saw.

"Come over!" she said. "I'll put on a kettle and you can visit with Frank! His father passed two years ago. Heart attack. God bless. He was a lovely man wasn't he?"

I mumbled something in the affirmative, whilst Oz expressed his sympathy.

His mother was different, but the boy who opened the door was the exact same Cleary. There was that small apostrophe of concern between his brows. There was his mouth—the one that had taught me kissing.

"Erin." He even had the same, old gentle way of speaking.

Inside, I was surrounded by the familiar scents of woodsmoke, cabbage, blue washing-up liquid, and (impossibly) the girlhood smell of my father's tweed hat.

As we took a seat in their living room, Oz interlaced his hand with mine. Cleary and his mam were on an opposing sofa, staring at us over a yellow floral rug and the contents of a full tea tray. My stomach lurched as Cleary's mum sugared my tea.

She handed me the cup. "We always wondered where you'd got off to. The house . . . well, the bank foreclosed on it. You don't want to know what it sold for. Break your heart it would."

I felt guilty. Worse, disgusted with myself. I'd always thought Mam had given up on life purely because Dad and I had abandoned her. For the first time, I realized she must have had material concerns as well. After Dad left, she'd had no way to pay the bills.

Cleary's mam passed me a plate of what my mother used to call the "going-out biscuits." Adorned with jam, they were super-fancy and therefore only for visitors. "So what brings you to Coonagh?" she said.

"We came to pay our respects to my mum," I said softly.

"Sorry?"

Oz bit his jammy dodger. "We've come to visit her grave."

His mam made a small mournful sound. "Your mam is . . . And you think she's buried in Coonagh?"

"She isn't?" Oz asked.

Cleary rubbed his clenched jaw. "No."

"I'm so sorry for your loss," she said, finding her social footing. "She was a good woman, your mam. Was she ill?"

I was in the grip of a terrible awkwardness, unwilling to introduce the word "suicide" to a casual afternoon tea.

Oz spoke up: "It was unexpected," he said euphemistically. "She was depressed."

My eyes filled with hot tears, but I blinked them away.

Cleary's mam nodded knowingly. "Yes, I imagine money was a stress after the divorce."

The word "divorce" made me feel I was on more solid emotional ground. I rubbed my nose, disguising a sniffle. "You knew my parents were separating?"

"Well, there were rumors. Your mam had discussed the divorce referendum with the priest."

Cleary shook his head with a look of stern disapproval. "Isn't there meant to be confidentiality? Seal of the confessional?"

Oz nodded like an off-duty bishop.

"When did she move away?" I asked.

"Your mam? Well, same time as you. She ran off with another man. A younger fella, in the Defense Forces. At least, that was the rumor. People judged her harshly, as you might imagine. But not me. She had a lot on her plate. It couldn't have been easy, living with your father. Evidently this young man could provide an honest living."

I stared at her, dumbfounded, unable to metabolize this new information. It brought me straight back to the role I hated playing as an only child, trying to balance my mother's side of a story with my father's, sorting out who'd behaved unfairly and who'd got what they deserved.

"Sorry, do you have any idea where Erin's mum *is* buried?" Oz asked.

Cleary's mam looked at me. "No . . . I mean, I didn't know. We always thought you went with her. Frank and his da, bless his soul, spent years trying to find you."

I turned to Cleary. "You *did*?"

"The day you left—"

Timing was one thing I could speak about with total authority. "We'd been to the amusement park that day," I said.

There was some dispute in her narrowed eyes. "No. That was some days earlier. You'd brought Frank home a prize. A pair of glasses with spring eyeballs. Isn't that right?"

"Yes," Cleary said softly.

"*No.*" I was firm on this topic. I didn't remember prank glasses. "No, we went to the Isle of Man directly after the funfair. I still had fudge from the café on my dress."

Cleary's mam and I went back and forth a few more times, in polite but robust disagreement. As we argued the particulars, I paid no attention to the dissenting voice in my head, reminding me that I dressed in clean clothes on Monday and wore them for the remainder of the week.

"Frank," she said. "Bring us the photos, will you?"

A moment later, Cleary was standing in front of me with a tin of Roses. I opened the lid. Instead of chocolates, I found snapshots.

"Cait gave them to us, along with some of your other things. We've got your mam's recipe box as well. And that book of poems your father wrote."

I stared at the glossy images in shock. I was so long resigned to the idea that everything from my past was gone.

"There's some old post Cait's saved as well. Frank, will you get it from the attic?"

I began flipping through the photos. There was my mother, looking more beautiful than I could have possibly imagined—wearing a short dress and a broad smile—leaving me to wonder if she might have pulled a young military man after all. I lingered over pictures of her, studying her the way a stranger might, and quickly skipped past the ones of my father. (In every photo, he either looked tuned-out, angry, or mischievous or had his face half-obscured.)

By comparison, there were loads of pictures of me. There I was, not older than two years old, astride a rocking horse. Me again, not much older, with yolk from my mother's fry on my face. First communion. Christmas. Another Christmas. A school play. Having a boot picnic with my mother on holiday in Waterford. Frame by frame, I watched myself grow taller and paler, as though I'd seen a ghost. My gaze started to take on an unfocused look. My smile took on the quality of someone baring their teeth.

I was thanking Cleary's mother robotically when I got to a photo that stopped me in my tracks. It was just a picture of Cleary and me playing a board game (Blackboard Jungle) on the floor of my old childhood bedroom, but a crack of terror went through me all the same.

At first, I thought it was because I looked slightly dazed in the picture. My skin was that ghostly shade of sheet white. But I forced myself to look a minute longer and realized the scary element was the wallpaper. It had a pattern of palms atop vertical stripes.

Twelve, I thought. *That's the number of feathers on each palm. I count them when I'm scared. When Dad is shouting. I can even make out the pattern in the dark.*

My skin goose-fleshed. That pattern felt like the phantom of a limb I hadn't even known I was missing.

All at once, I smelled bleach and then tasted it in the air, so thick it coated my tongue and the back of my throat. When I looked up, I saw Cleary, back with a stack of old letters, glancing downward at the photo in my trembling hands. Seeing him should have dispelled the daydream, but it only made it stronger.

Twelve droopy palms. When one fans into another, it makes a tic-tac-toe pattern. I play tic-tac-toe instead of looking at the men at the foot of the bed. As long as I don't look at them, they're not there, debating what to do with me now that I've seen what I have.

"I forgot about Blackboard Jungle," Cleary says. "Wasn't it based on that game show?"

I roll onto my side and become the palm-tree pattern. Ribs green and flexible. Curve of my spine like a stem. Still ignoring the men, I imagine something tropical—the sound of waves. I can ignore them right up until the moment one pulls the pillow out from under my head and brings it down onto my face.

A fit of dry-coughing snapped me back to the present. Oz was rubbing my back. There was a tickle in my throat, obstructing my inhale.

Cleary's mam gave me a goading nod. "Take a sip of tea, dear."

I did. It was so sweet I clenched my toes. I coughed hard enough to bring tears to my eyes. Breath failed me. There was a clamping pain in my chest.

That pillow, bearing down on me. It's so soft at first. Like the hug I sorely need. Then comes the moment I realize I can't breathe. That's when I hear my own scream—a strangled sound that pins me back in my body. My tongue's turned to fabric. My eyes ache from the pressure. My nose is close to breaking. I arch my back in defense, but my spine is still a limp stalk. The world bears down on me again. Weight upon weight, giving way to a dizzy sensation. And all the air is gone from the world. Breathing's useless. So I elect to stop breathing. As though it's a decision a person can make.

Desperate to act normal, I took another sip of tea and gagged again.

There's the underwater sound of one man's voice, telling the other to stop, saying there might be another solution.

When my eyes focused, I realized Cleary's mam was standing.

"Would you like to visit the house, Erin?" she asked me, jingling a set of keys. "I'm due down at the church, but Frank can take you. I'm sure Cait won't mind."

"That would be great!" Oz enthused, giving me an encouraging look that said the visit would be good for me.

I couldn't speak. My eyes were bleary. My sinuses brimmed with snot and ghost tears.

CHAPTER TWENTY-FIVE

The Saturday after the Potter party, Henry Upton called a surprise staff meeting.

"Are you OK?" Francis asked me as we watched our colleagues file into the teachers' lounge, which looked rather like an airline's first-class lounge. The sectionals were red-leather chesterfields. The coffee tables were supine SMART Boards.

"Uh-huh. Why?"

"I can feel the stress coming off you." He put both hands out, warming himself by my infernal worry.

I handed him a cup of herbal tea and sipped my own cooling cup of bitter coffee. "Just worried about leaving Cat and Gio in the theater," I lied. "I hope they'll be all right on their own."

"They're watching movies on their tablets. They'll be fine. And I'll go check on them at the halfway point. These meetings go faster than you think. Especially once you know how to read Henry's buzzwords. After 'snapshot data' comes 'higher-order thinking skills.' From there, it's a sleigh ride into 'I-can statements' and the 'failure-is-not-an-option support structure.' By the time Upton utters 'college- and career-ready,' the meeting's as good as done."

I faked a laugh, but my attention was flickering at the edges. I was still thinking about the vague threat Victor made at the Potter party. All that business about justice and talking to Upton.

As more teachers funneled in, the room filled with an air of friendly competition. They were ready to position themselves as team leaders. They were opening their notebooks full of ideas for service-learning projects. A few were pretending not to size up the new math teacher that Upton had poached from Saint Albans.

Speaking of Upton, when I looked up, he was striding to the front of the room. He stood, for some five or ten minutes, watching his assistant connect the computer cords he needed to pontificate. Finally, with his digital props good to go, he began by praising our energy and creativity, reminding us that we were providing the best education that money could buy.

"We've all struggled to show parents and colleagues exactly the kind of learning that is happening in class, so thanks to a generous donation, all of our classrooms are currently being outfitted for live streaming video."

Everyone who had a hand raised one.

Well, almost everyone. I couldn't move a muscle, wondering whether the donation had come from Vic. If he'd installed the cameras in order to gather evidence on Marianna.

"Is this like Periscope?" a young history teacher asked. "Are we using it to connect with our brother and sister schools abroad?"

"Well, that's one application," Upton said. "But we're going to use it on the local level too."

He pointed to the brink-of-retirement Earth sciences teacher.

"How so?" the man asked.

"Well, the benefits are far-reaching. As we all know, our students are a mobile bunch, and now they won't miss anything. No matter where in the world they are, absent students will be able to attend class. This technology turns Boulevard into a truly global space."

"So every class will be filmed?"

"Indeed. The idea is: empowering parents. With cameras, they can witness our continuous improvement and child-centered learning."

A woman near the rear said: "Does this have legal implications?

Are parents going to give their consent or, conversely, opt out? Are we going to have to worry about filming some students and not others?"

Upton reassured her. "We're well within FERPA guidelines."

"FERPA?" I whispered.

Francis leaned in. "The Family Educational Rights and Privacy Act."

"Besides," Upton said, "the camera is primarily on you all—the teachers. You're the focal point. Not the students."

My tongue was a weight. For the first time, it occurred to me that Janisa might still work for the Ashworths. What if she did, and Vic live-streamed my classroom in his flat?

Francis shook his head in a way that implied moral objection. "Henry?" he said, with a raised hand. "I understand that it might be inspiring to connect with our colleagues in this way. And I suppose having parents watch could be . . . potentially . . . validating. But what's the privacy policy? How wide-reaching is this app?"

"Anyone with a link will be able to access it. Is that what you meant?"

I tried not to look horrified. An unlisted link was hardly private. What was the point of an exclusive school like Boulevard, if Upton let anyone with an IP address peep?

Just as Upton was about to shift his attention to someone else, Francis added: "I'm just not sure we want to turn our classrooms into reality shows. When I'm teaching, I don't want to be wondering whether I ought to be connecting with my kids or with a camera."

"The technology itself is very unobtrusive. You won't even notice it. I assure you, my first priority is supporting you in your classrooms as you support our students, *live*."

The meeting ran an hour late, due to the sheer volume of teachers' questions. My colleagues were concerned about the commenting system, specifically whether students could anonymously mock them online. They were also worried about being held liable for students who were accidentally filmed after their parents opted out; after all, most of the parents on the PAC held ransom insurance because Boulevard's students were attractive to kidnappers.

"Look," Upton said, "it's top-of-the-line technology, and it's been paid for in full. I assure you, it's fast, fun, and expansive."

On the first live-streamed day, I woke too early, grinding my teeth. My hands went a bit numb as I packed up my lesson plans and thought about the beady eye of the ceiling-mounted IP camera.

But then, I wasn't the only teacher struggling to adapt.

Francis was still outraged as he packed our lunches for the day. He used his talents as a writer to pen lunch-box poems for Gio and Cat. Things like: *You learn with your brain. You love with your heart. But if your stomach's not full, then neither can start.* But that day, he just stared at his blank notepad.

"How much new work this is going to create?" he asked rhetorically. "Are we going to get home at night and have to respond to a dozen emails from parents, complaining about the lessons they've seen? Or *worse*, field phone calls with parents' suggestions, ways I can 'tweak' my methods and make them better?"

Even before the cameras, Francis had been feeling burnt out. Fed up with the heaps of work we brought home every night, he had been focusing on his time management and encouraging me to do the same. He'd made a plan for us to arrive at school forty minutes early to make photocopies, plan *only* during our planning period, and grade papers on the subway and during lunch. He was determined for us to have a life outside of our ill-paying jobs.

I leaned against his back, trying to reassure him as he slapped generic lunch meat on slices of bread. My cheek found the soft pile of his sweater vest. He smelled of shaving cream and grapefruit juice.

"I thought the same," I said. "But then I remembered that most parents can't even be bothered to sign permission slips. What are the chances they're *really* going to sit down and watch our classes? They have too much philanthropy work for that. Or they're busy outfitting their private islands."

"You're right. Thank you for talking me down from the ledge."

I leaned in to kiss him. But when I pulled away, the track lights created a glare on his glasses, making it difficult to read the look in his eyes.

"Don't sweat the cameras," I said again. "You're a good man and a great teacher. The only difference is now even more people will see it. *Streaming. Live.* Directly to their hedge-fund headquarters and megamansions."

He rested his chin on my head. "You really think I'm a good man?"

"The best. Why ever would you doubt that?"

But he just squeezed me a bit harder. "Lately, I'm less and less sure."

I had Gabby's class of fifth graders first, which did little to calm my nerves. The unit we were working on was Greek tragedy. It was a tie-in to their social studies lessons, where they were learning about prehistoric civilizations all the way up to the Roman Empire. I was barely ten minutes into the discussion about why Greek tragedy was the cornerstone for dramatic art when I felt the camera virtually bearing down on me.

I tried to smile, that old remedy for stage fright, but it didn't work. I could hear my voice rising in pitch.

"Usually, a character rises above his peers and oversteps the bounds of his greatness. Does anyone know what that means?" I realized I was using words that were well over their heads.

Nothing.

"Um, like, the character thinks he's so cool. Take Icarus, who flew so close to the sun that his wings melted. Or Narcissus, who was so in love with his own reflection that he drowned trying to touch it."

I made a clumsy transition into the way Greek characters were slaves to their fate, then I asked them to share what they considered to be their fatal flaws.

"Being allergic to horses," one of the Petras said. Rumor had it, her parents were in a bidding war over a million-dollar racehorse.

Gabby piped in with her fatal flaw: "Sometimes I don't remember stuff I've heard. I have trouble with sounds."

I nodded supportively. "That's one of many reasons why we, as a class, work so hard to make sure we don't speak over one another."

Gio surprised me by raising his hand.

"I feel like that sometimes too. Actually, it's more like I remember things, but I'm not sure they're real. Like I remember blueberry bushes at our old house, but I'm pretty sure we never had them. I remember this rainbow poster my sister used to have in her room—"

"Yes, memory's very unreliable," I said quickly.

I looked at the clock and realized with a shock that the period was almost over. So I segued into homework and told them they were going to write and perform their own "Greek tragedy" in the coming weeks, complete with a prologue, masks, speaking lines for the audience, and a "late point of attack."

I quizzed them: "What does that mean again?" Then, when no one answered: "An action that causes more action. Cause and effect. One thing leading to another. There's no memorization necessary," I reassured Vic, by way of the camera. "You can read from your scripts, but you still need to *act.*"

They were barely out the door when my phone began sounding like a real life Greek chorus. Parents were giving my streaming video a thumbs-up.

I also got a text message from Vic: *Funny, I thought the main feature in a Greek tragedy was bankruptcy. Very interesting class. Couldn't help noticing you didn't confess YOUR fatal flaw, though.*

I walked into the arm of a theater chair, and hard enough to bruise the hell out of the flesh above my knee. Was the bankruptcy thing a reference to the Catskill foreclosure? And if so, why didn't he just phone the police?

I struggled through the rest of my morning classes in a fog. During lunch period, I went and sat in the teachers' lounge, hoping to hear some horror stories. I couldn't be the only teacher who was having a bad time with the new ed-tech.

But I sat there for forty minutes, hiding behind my open laptop, silent earbuds in each ear, and in all that time, the only story I heard about parents' all-consuming entitlement had nothing to do with streaming video.

It seemed a small group of mothers objected to the school's new anti-cheating technique, which involved confiscating students' cell phones during tests.

"Ugh," one teacher sighed. "Is it really *that* outrageous to have these kids go without their smartphones for thirty minutes of the day? 'Don't take their toys away,' they say. 'Supervise them better.' How about you come and do my job, lady? You'll realize it's like trying to hold thirty corks underwater at the same time."

Two more heavily surveillanced weeks passed, and I earned more smiley-faced raves.

Even my colleagues approved. Gio's teacher Janet emailed to say: *Eeeeep! I can't wait to see the final Greek tragedies. Should we involve Ainsley Doyle? And could we invite the parents? I'm tempted to invite the whole school! It's such a good culminating activity.*

It was encouraging, it really was. Together, Janet and I drafted a presentation, and made a pitch to Upton that involved lots of cheery gesticulating and "cumulative links" charts.

"The kids really want to demonstrate their knowledge to their parents," I said. "Plus, it's a great way to celebrate their writing."

"I was going to suggest the same thing," Upton said. "Do you think you could include something like a multimedia video wall? If it fits. Just a little something to remind parents how devoted

Boulevard is to classroom technology? I'd love to see our interactive SMART projectors shine."

"That ought to be easy."

As we were packing up, he casually asked what we thought about the IP cameras.

"I didn't see the broader benefits at first," I said. "But it seems to me it's really improved the parents' satisfaction. Nothing's changed in the classroom. We're doing the same things we've always done, but now they can see it."

I'd even received an email from Ainsley Doyle, telling me: *I like that thing you told the kids today, about how performance shouldn't be their main goal. It was nice to hear someone put the emphasis on the personal process. Creating and reflecting, that's what it's all about.*

I was out in the hallway, sharing a congratulatory hug with Janet, when my phone dinged with another text message from Vic. I jabbed the green icon of the dialogue bubble.

I owe you an apology for what I said at Carter's party. I see now Gabby's very at home in your class. It's almost like she's known you for years.

"Is that text from a parent?" Janet asked.

"How did you know?"

"The look on your face. Which one?"

"Victor Ashworth."

Light-headed, I reread the message. Was it threatening? Sincere?

Well, she's very at home onstage, I wrote back. *She has a wonderful sense of action and space. It will serve her well when we get to the unit on physical comedy.*

"That one's a busybody!" Janet said. "He emails me constantly!"

"How does he find the time? Doesn't he work?"

Janet shrugged. "I think he's one of those big Wall Street hitters with celebrity investors. He probably spends half the day getting yelled at by CEOs and royalty and the other half taking his frustrations out on people like us. Plus, the girl's mother died. I think it's made him extra protective."

"What does Vic say in his emails to *you*?"

"Oh, the usual. He thinks I'm assigning too much homework. Or he wants a detailed account of my classroom-management plan. I just decided to open up my classroom to him. I gave him an open invitation to visit anytime. He even has his own special chair."

I smiled uncertainly as another text from Victor arrived: *She probably has yoga to thank for that. Gabby did a lot of it when we lived upstate. Great place, Woodstock. Spent much time there?*

"He sure is nicer to you than me," Janet said, reading over my shoulder.

"Why would he assume I've been to Woodstock?"

"I don't know," Janet said. "Hasn't everyone? It's closer than the Berkshires. And way cheaper than the Hamptons."

This was nothing to do with classroom management. Victor Ashworth was trying to get a read on me.

Well, I was not going to make it that easy for him.

Yoga's very good for actors. I've never been to Woodstock.

My phone made a swishing sound as I pressed Send.

I expected Vic to write back. He was such a fast texter, you'd think he had four thumbs. But he just let the conversation hang there, leaving me to wonder if his silence was pointed.

CHAPTER TWENTY-SIX

Cleary twisted the key to my childhood house and my heart reared up at the click of the deadbolt.

He held the door open for me, and I stepped inside, feeling claustrophobic in my rain mac. My senses were gridlocked. There was a stone-deaf whoosh in my ears.

Stepping into the front room, I thought I heard Oz ask Cleary what year Cait and her family moved in. Whatever his reply, I didn't hear. My attention was locked on the piano in the corner of the room.

Cleary noticed. His eyes had a soulful look I remembered from the afternoon I tried to bottle-feed one of our orphaned lambs. It was lying down, panting slightly, not interested in milk. When we came back an hour later, it was dead. Pulpy kidney, my father had said.

"That was yours," Cleary told me. "The piano, I mean."

My mam had taught me how to play. I could picture her beside me in a pastel jumper, its collar turned up against a red blotch on her neck. I'd learned "Danny Boy" on those keys. I could practically hear her say, "One-two-ready-play."

Oz depressed a key, and I jumped a mile. I hadn't realized he was standing beside me.

Cleary, leaning against a side table, wore a pale, serious expression.

I stared at the gold letters of the piano's maker, BENTLEY, and got a prickling sensation up the back of my neck. I knew the logo well. The exact curve of every letter. Sometimes, in the early stages of the sugar rows, I'd played "Too Ra Loo Ra" in an attempt to make the shouting recede. That, or I'd just quietly sit on the piano bench, concentrating so hard on that logo it was like I'd merged with it. Afterward, I couldn't hear any of it: parents, sugar, money, liquor, who my father was working with or for.

"I could use a glass of water," Oz said. "Which way to the kitchen?"

Cleary turned on the light in the corridor and led the way.

I followed them with a metallic taste in my mouth.

To my relief, the kitchen had been remodeled, stripped of any reminders of Mam. The Aga was gone. There was a microwave, which would have pleased her to no end. Still, I had a pain in my stomach, and a burning throb in my skull like lit filament. I couldn't lift my gaze from the floor. They were the original tiles—a complicated assortment of squares and rectangles, the sort you could stare at for hours, trying to work out where the pattern began and ended.

Oz was opening cabinets, looking for a water glass, presumably. But he found the liquor cabinet, straight off, as if by drinker's sonar.

Cleary touched my elbow. "You all right?"

"Grand." I was bloody freezing.

"Tell the truth."

There was a shadow in my peripheral vision. Oz was lifting a bottle of whiskey, inspecting its label by window light.

I gave Cleary the smallest possible nod.

But when I looked down at the tiles, I felt the same trapped sensation I'd felt staring at the wallpaper in my childhood photos.

Oz closed the cabinet door and I heard a flat boom. The sound was louder than the gesture.

"You've gone gray," Cleary said.

I could feel him staring at me with what was either revulsion or concern. But I couldn't hold his gaze. It was impossible to unfold my attention from the pattern of tiles that I knew so well—the ones that felt imbued with horror.

"Shall we see the bedrooms?" Oz asked.

But I was soaked in sweat and scared mute. There was a sharp ache at the top of my scalp. I was seeing things—tripping my arse off, regretting the cider and hash—because I couldn't stop imagining blood and something else. I was light-headed. Static tickled my ears.

"No," I said too quickly. "I've seen enough."

I did an awkward little run for the exit, trying and failing to act casual. When I flung open the door, the gray day was blinding. I stepped off the front step and felt weightless, light as a child in my father's arms. *No man ever wore a scarf as warm as his daughter's arm around his neck*, Dad liked to say. I regained my footing just in time.

Cleary was locking up behind us.

"Where do you think her mum is?" Oz asked. "If she's not buried in Coonagh, I mean."

My neck prickled. The dark-red geometry overtook my thoughts again, and I pushed it away.

"Erin would probably know better than me."

Both men looked at me, and I made a helpless gesture. I was tired. All afternoon people had been pressing me for information, then discounting anything I had to say.

"What about that church in Kilshanny?" Cleary said. "Your mam liked to go there, didn't she?"

"She did?"

Cleary gave me a sideways look.

"Is it far?" Oz asked.

We drove over an hour, then searched beneath drizzling skies, but none of the headstones in the churchyard bore my mother's name. Oz proposed a consolation trip to the pub, but I felt too travel sick. So I told them to go on without me and sat on a scarred bench on the promenade, staring at the green cliffs and islands of puffins that used to thrill me back when I was a girl.

Not long after, Cleary came back and handed me a little sealed package. "I brought you some paracetamol."

"Thank you."

"Are you all right? You had a look of childhood about you today."

"How so?"

"I don't know," he said. But it was all pretense. He seemed very clear about what he wanted to say. "You'd get this look when we were children. I don't know how to explain it, exactly. You'd get it when our das were shouting at the telly over sports. 'G'wan,' my da would shout, and you'd be scared stiff. 'For fuck's sake! Kick it dead!' yours would say, and you'd go silent. You wouldn't speak for the rest of the night. You hated when people yelled—at the telly. Each other."

"Well, I'm sorry for being so silent and spacey with your mum. She must think I'm bloody rude."

"No," he said. "No, no. Nothing of the sort. She's glad to see you. We all are. We never thought we'd see you again, you realize that, yeah?" The look in his eyes was warm and accepting, somehow it cut me even deeper than if he'd been angry with me.

I locked my eyes on the road.

"Loads of tour buses go past here, don't they?" I was willing one to come, full of gaping tourists with cameras, charging down the lane frequently enough to discourage criminals.

"Not loads. Some. Plus, I remembered the day I tried to convince you to tell someone your da broke your mam's arm. That time I found you crying in the field. So scared you didn't know where you were. I should have told my own da. I wanted to, after you went away. But you always made me promise—"

I shook my head, thinking of my mother's blue eyes. One cloudy, behind a drooping eyelid. The other round with fear. Her beautiful hair a mess of blood and what I had told myself were haricot beans.

"She ran off with another man. Everyone in town knew it. Your mam said so herself."

"But who's to say who started those rumors? Your dad could be behind it. James too. Don't you think it's more likely they split up because of the way he earned his money?"

"Jesus, Cleary. Will you just—shut up?"

He looked hurt and stunned. "I'm sorry. I know you never liked thinking about it. It was like, if you didn't acknowledge it, it didn't go on—"

"And who are you? My psychologist? You know me so well, after ten years apart. Get off your high horse."

The open air had begun to feel like a small, enclosed space. The salt air turned my stomach.

Cleary rubbed his forehead. "This is exactly what I mean. I've never wanted to hurt you. Or make you angry. I've only ever wanted to help. I thought, if I found you *before* I told my parents, I'd be there to help you through. The way I used to. Do you remember what we used to do when you got scared?"

My mind was all negative space. I could scarcely remember why we were having this conversation. Why he was giving me that look of guarded disquiet.

"I'd turn on a record for you. Or I'd give you something to hold. Sometimes that helped. You'd take that yellow ball from the Mousetrap game in both hands—"

I saw my father lifting the heavy lid of my mother's pot and wrinkling his nose at its contents. A cold prickle of pain went through my stomach, and I imagined that metallic boom again. Again, I saw the red lines lengthening. Beans or brains. Blood in the grout.

The wind sobbed hysterically.

"No . . . ," I told Cleary. "No, I wasn't scared as a child. I was a rascal. I must have been playing . . . Playacting . . ."

All at once, I was aware of my wet hair and eyelashes. It had begun raining sometime over the course of our conversation. But when? The damp feeling made my skin crawl, and I instinctively glanced down at my thigh, looking for the spot that would turn into a dark stain of "chocolate sauce." I could see my father upending the sugar bowl over the right mess of my mother's head. Sugar in her eyelashes and the crease of her neck. Clumps of wet sugar in her hair, turning from white to pink to red.

Cleary was watching me with tender sorrow, curl of hair between his bright eyes. "So the funfair is really the last thing you remember of Ireland?"

I looked again at the cliff and double-sniffed. My shoulders juddered.

Cleary's Adam's apple, in profile, did the same.

If Dad had killed my mother, it would certainly have been James who'd helped him clean up the mess. It would have been James who'd tried to smother me, the only witness to Dad's crime, until my father stopped him. It was no strain to imagine James, lit by headlights, being rough with the Toyota's choke while my father, in the passenger seat, whispered things in a low, agitated voice. They would have brought her—my mam—to the Atlantic. Possibly even the same countryside we were looking at, where big, loamy waves foretold a coming storm.

"Yes." A guilty fear was tingling up the base of my skull. My legs swayed like something reflecting on water. "There's nothing else. We left for Man the same day."

CHAPTER TWENTY-SEVEN

There was no way of knowing whether Vic suspected me until a week or so later, when I was in the staff room, photocopying scripts. Or more accurately, I was in a wrestling match with the eternally jammed Xerox machine, getting enough toner on my face to look coal-roasted in the process.

I was seriously considering using the sign one of the jokier teachers had posted (FOR STRESS REDUCTION, BANG HEAD HERE), but instead I stepped away and took a breather, pulling up a live stream of Janet's classroom on my phone. If the kids were in gym or music or Mandarin, she might be able to come help me with the machine. But she was passing out vocabulary quizzes.

Just as I was making a second attempt with the copier's paper tray, my phone dinged with a text from an unfamiliar number: *I'm wondering what a woman with your moral compass thinks of this new anti-cheating initiative.*

Sorry, who is this? I typed back. Boulevard gave us corporate phones, pre-loaded with every parent's phone number, but on occasion, I still received texts from assistants and au pairs—people who weren't in the system.

It's Victor Ashworth, texting from Gabby's phone. The nanny packed mine in her backpack today. No Supernanny, that one. It's our little family tradition, choosing the worst people to care for our kids.

The phone trembled in my hand. I gagged on airborne toner.

I typed: *The new policy isn't about ethics, but opportunity. Students will cheat if they can. That's just human nature. But Henry doesn't want to make it needlessly easy for them. It ought to be more challenging than taking their phones to the bathroom and Googling the exam answers.*

Vic responded: *Your moral perspective is . . . interesting. Do you have a free period? I'd love to talk more about this. I'm on my way to Boulevard now to pick up my phone.*

Abandoning my copies, I tore off my cardigan and power-walked the corridors. I arrived out of breath at Janet's door, an Irish flush in my cheeks.

"I hope I'm not disrupting," I whispered. "It's just, I saw on the IP cameras that you had a few minutes, and I wanted to run a few things past you for the Greek tragedy production. Would you rather I find you later, in the teachers' lounge?"

"No, it's fine." Janet waved me inside. "They'll be a few minutes longer. Come in."

"The head office really needs us to pick a date for the dress rehearsal. . . ."

While I stalled on details with Janet, I looked discreetly at the blackboard behind her. Propped up against it were eighteen iPhones, BlackBerrys, and Androids, a student's name written above each one in chalk.

"Yes, you're right. We should design save-the-dates soon," Janet said. The "soon" suggested I'd begun to overstay my welcome.

"And since we're going with the title *Modern Tragedies,* I had a thought we could print up posters with pictures of some of the minor annoyances we all like to get so dramatic about these days. Things like 'tangled earbuds' or 'My phone isn't the newest model anymore.' Although from the look of it, none of your kids have *that* problem."

There, just right of center, I spotted Gabby's name. Victor's smartphone was a lucky brand. At least for me. I was fairly certain there were security holes in its operating system, and I might be able to exploit them to gain administrative privileges.

"You're right," Janet said softly. "The things these parents consider tragedies. 'My personal assistant does everything I ask, but I have to *ask.*' "

I laughed. "Or 'Counting all these bills makes my fingers tired.' "

We giggled like schoolgirls, then hushed ourselves. I tipped my head toward the back of the room in a way that had already become code for *Mind the camera.*

Janet looked at it, stricken. Her phone buzzed.

"It's the central office," she said, with a look of genuine terror. "You don't think the parents heard us, just now, do you?"

"I doubt it. This isn't *1984.* But you better pick up anyway."

"Hello? Sorry? Gabby? Yes, I've got it right here. Is it urgent? Do you want to send someone down to get it?" Then, covering the receiver, she whispered: "Nothing to do with the camera. The front office just wants Gabby Ashworth's cell phone."

"I'll bring it to them," I volunteered. "I'm going that way."

"Marianna's here. She can bring you Gabby's phone. Great. I'll send her down."

I moved as quickly as I could, short of running, down to the theater, where my Boulevard-issued laptop and USB cable were in the cupboard.

Backstage, out of sight of the IP camera, I laid out all my supplies on the director's desk and set to work.

Step one: Opening the rooting software on my laptop.

Step two: Unlocking Victor's phone without a passcode. I had an old trick for that. I went to the main menu, clicked the timer, and held down the power button until the menu I needed appeared. Then I double clicked as though to view Vic's previous pages, held the second click, and hit "cancel" with my free hand. When I let go: *bam.* I was inside without a password.

From there, I enabled "Developer Options." Still overheated from my mad dash down the school hallway, sweat trickled down the back of my silk blouse as I enabled USB Debugging Mode.

Step three: Preparing the phone for rooting. I checked the

battery level on Victor's phone. It was 50 percent, thank God. If it powered off during the process, it would never work again. I plugged it into my laptop via the USB cable and a message popped up: "Installing driver . . ."

For ten full minutes, the message didn't change. "Installing driver . . ." "Installing driver . . ."

I tried to remember exactly where Vic lived. Tribeca? And presumably, he worked on Wall Street? I prayed for heavy traffic—the sort that makes New Yorkers threaten one another with bodily harm.

"Installing driver . . ." "Installing driver . . ."

I felt like a surgeon with a flatlining patient.

"Installing driver . . ." "Installing driver . . ."

Just when I was certain I'd fucked myself, a new message appeared on the screen: "Please allow USB debugging via your device."

I clicked "OK."

A message showed: "Connecting . . ."

Then another: "Connection established."

I clicked "Root," and watched another death wheel appear. "Waiting for device . . ."

Again, it went on and on.

"Waiting for device . . ." "Waiting for device . . ."

I looked at my watch. The school bell was due to chime any minute. The second graders would file into the theater.

"Waiting for device . . ."

I startled at the sound of my phone.

"Hello?"

"Marianna? Hi, it's Regina in the front office. Mr. Ashworth's just arrived, looking for his cell phone. Do you want me to send him down to the theater?"

"No. No—I'm sorry. I just got tied up with an email. Keep him there. I'm on my way."

I didn't know what to do. I couldn't unplug Vic's phone. I

couldn't perform any actions on it. The screen showed a lock icon. "Rooting . . . ," it said. "Rooting . . ."

And then the screen went black.

T-minus two minutes before the bell was set to ring. By some miracle, Vic's phone restarted itself. Multicolored lightning flashed across the screen. The date and time returned. Better yet, all his files and apps were still there.

"Root succeeded!" my computer said, just as the bell began to chime.

Victor's phone was now my double agent.

Slamming my laptop shut, I hoofed it down to the head office.

There was heavy hallway traffic. Children's voices bounced off the high ceilings overhead. Teachers, unironically, yelled at them to quiet down. A colleague in a far-off room said, "The bell doesn't dismiss you! I dismiss you!"

I saw Francis over a sea of Hobbits in khaki trousers.

"Mari!" He waved.

But I had to keep jogging. I ducked and weaved around a girl with a Sherpa-sized Burberry backpack. "I'm late!" I called back. "I'll come find you during lunch!"

I nearly collided with a math teacher as I tore past a four-foot golden bear sculpture (designed by Takashi Murakami and Kanye West). A few scandalized students looked at me while I raced down the same steps we always instructed them to walk down.

Very next thing, I was in the Boulevard front office, which was as massive and white as a heaven scene from a 1940s film—like it was specially designed to make you feel far away from the vibrancy and mess of real life. The chandeliers were white. The lacquer tables were white. The office staff was the only thing that wasn't exclusively white, but even then, they all had the blank, composed look of jurors you'd imagine in an afterlife court. I scanned the room for Victor and didn't find him.

I set Vic's mobile down on the vast white desk in front of one of the school secretaries. "Here's Gabby Ashworth's phone."

. . .

Once Francis and the children were asleep, I searched Vic's email for messages between him and Boulevard. Janet hadn't been exaggerating, Vic really was a helicopter. I counted thirty-eight messages between him and Henry Upton. In them, Vic mostly discussed the details of Gabby's condition and the IP cameras, which it was now very clear he had implemented. He was a wealthy version of the sort of playground hoverers I had known upstate, the ones who forbid their children to wade in steams (because of bacteria) or play in grass (because of ticks) and lurched down to confiscate anything deemed unsuitable for their children's hands. But if Upton was annoyed, he didn't let on. He'd given each email a thoughtful response, and continued to cite the "staggering generosity" of Vic's latest financial contribution.

I searched again for any emails containing the name "Marianna."

No messages match your search.

I broadened the search by looking in the spam and trash folders, and yet I found nothing.

So I scrolled through Vic's bookmarks, which he had divided into fuddy-duddy folders like "Sports," "Finance," "Funny," and—my heart gave a little kick—"Justice for Melanie."

Despite immense nausea, I clicked and found the following links:

Drowning and Forensics—Forensics Online

Six Cases of Premeditated Murder by Drowning—National Center for Biotechnology Information

Murder or Suicide (How You and a Detective Can Tell)—True Crime

I clicked the last link and began to read:

If a corpse has been in the water for an excess of forty-eight hours, the victim's epidermis will look greenish bronze, thus it's very easy to determine how long he or she has been submerged. There may also be some pre-peeling as the fat deposits beneath the skin transform into a soapy material—

I skipped ahead to the next paragraph about "degloving," a phenomenon where flesh easily slips off drowned victims' hands and feet. An ancient pain burned through my stomach. My heart thumped and I quickly closed out the tab.

I went on to read a legal article Victor had bookmarked, but I couldn't focus on anything beyond phrases like: "reopening a suicide case" and "there is no statute of limitations for murder."

I kept scrolling and came upon something even worse.

Right around the time Vic had enrolled Gabby in Boulevard, he'd bookmarked RandallMuellerRealty.com. And the property history on our old house in Catskill.

Most worryingly of all, Victor had also saved the webpage for a high-end intelligence firm called Bahram Intelligence Agency. According to the company's home page, the experts on payroll came from state and federal investigative agencies: *Our seasoned investigators have the connections and procedural knowledge to secure the concrete evidence that will support your case.* They offered technology services, like data recovery and computer forensics. Plus, they did surveillance: *Many cases require covertly following a subject, observing their every meeting and move.*

I went back to Victor's email and searched his in-box for the word "Bahram." Over twenty messages popped up, but they were all frustratingly one-sided. Vic wrote tomes to the investigators, but they themselves rarely disclosed sensitive information by email, probably on account of Internet privacy fears. I suspected the most confidential business was discussed by telephone.

Even so, I found enough bits and bobs to clue me in to the status of the investigation. In his first email to Bahram, Vic vented about the Woodstock Police Department:

Yes, my wife was feeling shaky about finances. There was the money she had spent on the extension, as well as what she stood to lose going forward. But that's not enough to determine suicide. Lots of people worry about money. Hell, most of the goddamn country is worried about money. But most people don't kill themselves. Melanie didn't kill herself. She was MURDERED. Thank you for believing me on this point.

The criminal profile you sent through impressed me. Very detailed. I couldn't agree more. From the very beginning, I said Melanie's killer walked away from her. That's what set this thing off. I'm happy the police psychologist agreed. This is a person who is braver online. Someone who can't keep commitments. Yes. All that makes sense. My wife had a way of making people, even lowlifes, feel valued and appreciated.

I found another that made me feel utterly ill:

So, let me get this straight? The Woodstock Police KNEW Tracey Bueller was actually GRACE MUELLER, on account of my late wife's phone records? But they never looked for her because of the death records? The ones that showed she died a week before Melanie?

To this, an investigator from Bahram wrote back:

The Woodstock Police spoke to the husband, Randall Mueller, who corroborated the story. The coroner was not contacted. Neither was the state trooper who attended the so-called "crash." I think we should send one of our own investigators to Florida as soon as possible. Please phone the office to discuss.

I found one more email—a disjointed revenge fantasy that Vic sent a month before Gabby enrolled in Boulevard:

You said yourself in the criminal profile that my wife's killer prioritized family. Well, I've spent the night comforting a crying eight-year-old who refuses to listen to a word her stepmother says because she misses her real mom. I want justice. It's not right that the person who drowned my wife is out there enjoying the family life that was taken from us. I want everything that can be done to be done. I want Randy Mueller interviewed. I want Gracie Mueller found and interviewed. I want digital forensics doing everything they can to recover my wife's emails. And when we have our answers, I want surveillance. My little girl will not be at peace until the truth comes to light.

After I closed out the message, I couldn't stop myself pulling back the curtain on the one window that faced the street and looking for . . . I don't know what I was looking for, exactly, maybe a Bahram investigator, paid to track my every move. Outside, there was nothing but passing traffic. Mist levitated in the streetlights. A taxi applied its brakes with a squeal. But just as I was chiding myself for being paranoid, the shadow of a dog walker emerged between parked cars and I jumped back from the window, my pulse screaming like the violins in a Hitchcock film.

I filled a glass with tap water. But the drain rejected the overflow. Before I knew it, I was staring into the hazy depths of another blocked sink. I grabbed a steak knife and poked around in an attempt dislodge the blockage, tentatively at first and then with a kind of despairing violence.

Finally, I stabbed something all the way through and lifted the blockage, now solid and visible, to the light. Another Barbie head sat on the end of my knife. A redhead this time. There was a snarl of wet hair in her eyes and a broad dent at the back of her head. I stared at her for a second longer before burying her in the rubbish bin just as deep as I could.

Returning to my desk, I listened to the angry hiss of the radiator and reminded myself that rooting Victor's phone had given me the upper hand. From then on, whenever Bahram gave him case updates, I would get them as well. If they found any solid proof on Marianna, I could use technology to intuitively adjust my plans.

The first step was establishing a strong defense by installing new, defensive applets on Victor's phone.

I began with the most immediate threat: Bahram Intelligence Agency. I found the company's contact information in an Internet search, and rigged it so anytime Victor received a voicemail from the firm, his phone would automatically transcribe the message and email it to me at TeacherTrouble@bdomainname—a throwaway email address I established for all Vic-related matters—and delete the sent message from the user interface.

Next, I set about defending my physical territory. There were a lot of ways I could make Vic's operating system work for me. Whenever he set foot inside Boulevard, I wanted to know. So I created a recipe that emailed TeacherTrouble anytime his phone's location services showed him at school.

What if Victor came to our apartment? It was unlikely. But then, I had the capability to set precautions just in case, so I established a recipe so Victor's location would make our wireless lighting dim and pulse if he ever turned up.

Finally, I used the social media accounts that Upton required me to have to follow Victor Ashworth. I set an applet that would text me anytime he made a post.

I yawned. It was half past two in the morning. My eyes burned in the false sunshine of the computer screen.

I was about to power down my computer and go to bed when I realized there was more in Victor's search history since the last time I'd looked. Vic was online at that very moment.

I wondered what woke him.

A phone call? There was nothing in his call history.

A message? He had no new emails or texts.

Noodling around on his phone at this hour had a tinge of nihilism.

I watched him check world currencies.

I stood by as he surfed CNN. Every news item he clicked unfolded directly in front of me:

A Bit of Drama: A Test of Patience at Healthcare Summit

Hero Teacher Tackled Colorado Gunman

Seven Children Among 18 Refugees Drowned off Turkey

I sat in the dark, reading the last story by Victor's virtual side. Was he thinking of Melanie as he read? "The coast guard said it recovered the bodies from a wooden boat which was heading from the western province of Canakkale to the Greek Island of Lesbos when it crashed into rocks and took on water . . ."

He must have done. Because the next moment, he was back to the search engine, hunting for more case studies in drowning forensics. He lingered on articles about a twenty-four-year-old woman from Minnesota who'd drowned in a lake (her missing cell phone was never recovered). He read about what one news source called "Albany's vanishing girls"—five disappearances where female victims turned up dead in the Hudson River.

Was it possible he thought Melanie fell into the clutches of a serial killer? But then, why was Bahram interested in Gracie Mueller? And why was it so imperative that they speak to Randy?

Another link appeared in Victor's search history:

Grief After Murder—Information for Survivors of Homicide Victims

Again, I read alongside him:

Wanting someone who was part of our life for years can become a ticking time bomb. . . . If your spouse was murdered, you may feel lonely longer and more deeply than with other deaths. . . . Give yourself permission to be alone and angry. . . .

I stared at the words in an awful daze. Francis's deep-sleep music was still going strong in the bedroom. The faint, terrible sound of water streamed relentlessly from his bedside speakers.

There was a long silence in Victor's Internet history.

I rubbed my eyes, then clutched my temples with thumb and forefinger. Just as I was reaching to power down my laptop, a new entry popped up in Victor's history:

Marianna De Felice—Google Search

Followed by my profile on the Boulevard site.

I looked on, stunned, as Victor watched my virtual interview "Introducing Marianna De Felice," which Upton had posted the week that he hired me. I plugged in my headphones and clicked the Play button as well. The sound of my own voice rose in my earbuds: *"I believe anyone can act, just as long as they're willing to be private in public—"*

Maybe I was being overly harsh on myself, but my "American" accent suddenly sounded shit.

I watched Victor search for my fake boarding school and pull up the website of my own creation.

My photo filled the screen. There was the ghost of a chickenpox scar on my temple. Would Janisa or Abigail remember it?

CHAPTER TWENTY-EIGHT

It's just here," I said as a massive house swung into view.

"That's the gatehouse," the taxi driver told me, and proceeded to motor farther down the potholed drive. A green sweep of lawn emerged from the wooly moorland. In the middle of it, a downed tree waited for someone to clear it away with a chain saw.

Finally, I saw it: Clacherdon, a sallow-colored house. It had a smear of black mold under each buckled windowpane and its chimney leaned at an alarming angle. It looked much more impressive reflected wrong side up in the river that ran through Albina's thousands upon thousands of acres.

Oz put a hand on my thigh. "You look so worried. I assure you, the rich are just like the art students you love. The less impressed you act, the more they kiss your arse."

At the time, we were living in a squatter house share in Leytonstone and earning money by stealing bank details, credit cards, and band gear. Our flatmates, who were working-class art students, made performance-art videos of themselves arguing, or having sex, or miming opera in the nude. I liked it. Together, we consumed vast amounts of vodka (for warmth) and talked energetically about the Stanislavski method. But Oz hung on the periphery, irritated and fighting about politics, dreaming up schemes for us to earn the deposit we needed to get a flat of our own.

"I'm fine," I said. "Just promise me this is a onetime event. We get in, we get what we need, and we get out."

The driver pretended not to watch in the rearview as Oz gave me a kiss.

"Hand to God." He gave my knee an excited squeeze. "You're going to be very glad you did this. Remember to play on his sympathies. Make him feel guilty for the way he left you high and dry in India. He owes you. Plus, all the years he spent withholding information about your mum, leaving you with no choice but to roam the Irish countryside—"

"No. Oz, I told you. We're leaving my mother out of this. If you mention Ireland—" I threatened things. Divorce. Interpol.

"Deep breaths," he said in this irritating, instructive way. "He's just a mark. We've done this thousands of times."

He gave me a massive kiss on the mouth, and then we stepped out of the taxi onto the cobblestone drive. As Oz hoisted our rucksacks out of the boot, we were struck by a bracing wind.

I told myself Oz was right. After one week of shallow socializing at Clacherdon, I'd walk away with a happy husband and, if my father agreed to it, a substantial loan to put toward a new flat. I could even treat the journey like a fact-finding mission, watching my father closely enough to determine whether he had it in him to do the things I'd imagined back in Ireland and staunchly kept to myself.

As I was pulling my coat tighter around me, two Labradors jumped on me from behind, stopping my spooked heart with the shove of four mucky paws.

I must have let out a small shriek because Oz was beside me the next second, patting their wiggling bottoms. "You're a good girl, aren't you? Yes, yes. Good girl, muddy girl." And then to me: "Pull it together."

I took one deep breath before I turned and saw a hint of a velvet bathrobe. It was my father, standing in the open door with a copy of the Sunday newspaper supplement under his arm. His wet hair was slicked to one side in a fashion I'd never seen him wear before.

I froze for a moment. So numb that I failed to notice that one of the dogs was sniffing the more intimate regions of my trousers.

A woman, Albina, appeared by his side. She was tufty-haired, dressed in oxblood trousers and the sort of tan, tweed jacket I remembered from my long-ago snoop through her suitcase. I'd been so worried about seeing my father I'd never considered whether she might recognize me from the Chemsworth. But I stepped forward and climbed the discolored stairs anyway, telling myself that toffs like her weren't the type who acknowledged maids, let alone remembered them.

Albina gave me a welcoming smile, but through her thick jaw, it still looked half sneer. "Lovely you could pay us a visit."

In a very good American accent: "Albina, this is my daughter, Grace. I'd like you to meet Albina."

I could tell he'd been working on his social graces, making a script of the *Debrett's Guide* the way he once had *The Universal Self-Instructor.*

Albina shook our hands.

"Cheers for letting me impose as well," my husband said.

Dad gave a chummy smile. "Happy she found a travel companion."

"It's no imposition. We're pleased for the company," Albina said. She went on to explain that their closest neighbors lived in a castle two hours away and there was still some clannish animosity there; one of her ancestors had slain theirs with a pike. More aristo-chatter followed about the bleakness of March. Albina told us they didn't expect any more visitors from the south until August, when the reeling parties began.

Inside the enormous house, the wallpaper was peeling. The windowpanes were filthy with gull shite. But my father was so stuffed up with pathetic self-importance, he expected us to be equally impressed. Leading us through the frigid great hall, he looked straight past the dead flies and bat droppings and told us about the more important oil portraits.

"Clacherdon tartan remains one of Vivienne Westwood's favorites," Albina said.

We sat at the untidy table and drank hot cocoa with cream, politely staring at one another over the less-than-hostessy touches, the centerpieces of ashtrays and empty honey jars. Albina brushed crumbs and stray tobacco into her palm. Dad lit a rollie and explained that we'd interrupted their daily "hunt for treasure," an afternoon pastime where they climbed unused stairwells and put their hands through holes in the plasterwork in search of lead cups and medieval coins. My father had even treated himself to a metal detector.

Albina terrified me at close range, what with her habit of sitting so still. She had stooped shoulders. She was engrossed with her hands—clasping, unclasping, reclasping them—a gesture very close to wringing. Eerier still, her expression went utterly blank at any mention of expense—the metal detector, for instance. It frightened me not that my father had found such a perfect mark, but that *I* had.

My heart pounded whenever I looked at my dad, remembering little snatches of the sugar rows. *Fucking battle-axe!* I swallowed and tried harder to track whatever it was he was saying, something about how much it cost per year to keep Clacherdon ticking over.

"Forty thousand pounds." Oz whistled. He tried to draw me into the conversation, turning and asking me: "Can you believe that?"

I shook my head sympathetically. *Get off yer high horse! You're no intellectual! Creative types give something! They add to the world!*

While I was deep in thought, Oz asked about Albina's heritage. He was genuinely interested in her family's earls and countesses, plus the more hush-hush descendants who'd fought on the side of the English seven hundred years ago.

As they spoke, I could feel my father examining me in minute detail. He wasn't just looking at me. He seemed to be analyzing me, trying to gauge my inner contents.

"I mentioned a lot of this in my correspondence," he said. "But then, Grace isn't much for email these days, are you? I would have thought you'd worried me enough, deferring university to go hitching around India. But then you go and fall off the face of the Earth."

Evidently, I wasn't the only one acting.

Oz leapt to my defense, laying the foundation for later discussions about a loan. "Our living conditions are somewhat substandard at the moment. We barely have heat, let alone phone or Internet. We're hoping to pull together enough cash to move—"

But money woes only got my father banging on about Clacherdon again. "Heat's on the back burner here too. Thank goodness for fireplaces. Our main priority is the roof. We need a million pounds to stop the water getting in. Fortunately, the community has been very supportive indeed. No one wants to see this piece of history slide into dereliction."

"Are we finished?" Albina asked. "Shall I show you to your rooms?"

Dad squeezed Albina's knee. "Notice she's using the plural. Anything else would be improper, wouldn't it, love? And here at Clacherdon, we're very concerned with the done thing."

Oz moved his chipped teacup aside. "Funny thing about that . . . It's probably your daughter's place to tell you."

"We've married," I said, hoarsely.

Albina clapped her hands softly, just once, then brought her hands to her thin lips.

"Well," Dad said. For all his social flair, he had no idea how a proper father ought to react. "That *is* a surprise."

"Have you any pictures?" Albina asked. "I've never seen a Nepalese wedding."

"It was an Irish wedding," Oz said.

If I weren't so stunned, I would have given him a swift kick under the table. I couldn't believe he'd violated the terms of our agreement so soon.

The hard look in Dad's eyes was at odds with his congenial smile. "You've been to Ireland?"

"Dublin," Oz said, boldly. "And Limerick."

Dad dropped his chin and gave me a warning look. It might have only lasted a fraction of a second, but it still felt like a kick in the teeth.

"And have you given any thought to how you'll earn a living?" Dad asked. Seemingly, he had found the appropriate script. Concerned. Protective. Both an utter joke.

Oz rubbed his hands together and began talking about Turkey, how it was shaping up to become the next major holiday-home and investment destination: "EasyJet just added routes to Dalaman and Istanbul. BA flies to Antalya. I'm working with some property developers. They were looking for someone who speaks the language and can help broker deals."

"So you're an estate agent?" my father said with false politeness that did nothing to mask his condescension.

"For all intents and purposes," Oz said, with this infuriating reverence like he was actually striving for paternal approval, not just greasing the wheels for a con.

"Isn't there a new golf course in Dalaman?" Albina asked, filling an awkward pause. "Yes, we've friends who've stayed there. Remember, darling? The Barranermans? They made the error of traveling during Ramadan and had to dine behind a curtain all week, so they wouldn't offend the locals."

My sense of time was collapsing. Although we'd just arrived, I felt like we'd been there forever. I wanted to go back to London. I wanted to be anywhere other than directly across the table from my father—who suddenly seemed less like a person than a physical embodiment of the pain in my chest.

"What the fuck?" I asked Oz later.

Albina had shown us to a bedroom with revolting pink walls

and left us with a phony invitation to use the electric heater if we weren't as "impervious to cold" as she and Dad were.

"What?" Oz pulled back a floral curtain and looked out at the grounds through a cracked windowpane.

"You promised me!"

"Oh, yes. I brought up Ireland. I'm sorry. Albina asked about getting married in Nepal. I panicked."

I looked at him as though he'd gone mad. Oz was a liar by trade. What was my father—Kryptonite?

"Well, please don't mention Cleary. Don't say anything more about who we saw or where we visited. As I see it, we eat some mutton, admire my father's woodpile, listen to a bit more of Albina's snobbery about the 'ghastly' bagpiper who plays every morning at Balmoral, and we're done with it. I'll ask my father for the rent money myself. I don't want you involved in the loan discussions."

"*All right,*" he said, uncertainly.

"What does that mean? 'All right'?"

"It just means, let me know if you change your mind. Your old man's a rotter, all right. You were right about that. If it comes to it, I can step in and relate to him on his level."

My heart lifted. I pulled him in for a hug. "You really think so?"

He chuckled and shook his head. "Oh yeah. He's a real lying bastard. Everything's a sleight of hand."

I watched Oz closely for the remainder of the visit, making certain he wasn't talking about Ireland, but we spent so little time together, it became difficult to gauge whether he was holding up his side of the agreement.

I'd turn away for one second, to pat one of the dogs, and Dad would sweep Oz away to the carriage house (allegedly, to "admire the new stucco") or the roof (to "see the problematic shingles"). He kept my husband up late nights drinking. He took Oz for an extra-leisurely walk around the property whilst I admired the paintings in Albina's art studio. He recruited Oz for all sorts of men-only pursuits: salmon fishing, chopping wood, hauling scraps to a bonfire site.

I tagged along when I could, watching like a gooseberry as they bonded.

Dad lectured Oz about knives, watches, motors, and incendiaries (I swear, he hit every macho topic short of foreskins) and Oz pretended to listen reverently. At least, I hoped it was pretend. I prayed Dad wasn't showering Oz with all that paternal guidance because he knew my husband's weak points. Hopefully, Oz hadn't confided his childhood.

I was checking in with Oz for what felt like the forty-fifth time, confirming, "You don't really give a toss about anything he's saying, do you?"

"What's the problem? I'm just being polite and sticking to neutral topics like you asked."

Sometimes when Dad gave me the silent treatment at dinner (fish-finger sandwiches by the light of wax-crusted candlesticks), it seemed like he was trying to send a message to me. Something like: *Nothing you say has value. Not even your husband will believe you if you tell.* And other times, it seemed like he was just leaving me out because I was acting out of sorts with *him*, gritting my teeth with rage when he spoke or spearing my peas with a tremor.

I finally got my answer when we found ourselves alone after dinner on the final night. I was doing the washing up. Oz, with his weak bladder, had gone to the toilet. Albina had got up to let the dogs out (one of them had been licking the plates in the open dishwasher). My father was sitting at the head of the table, cleaning the shotgun he used to hunt grouse.

"So. Why Ireland?" he asked when I turned away from the sink.

My heart beat incongruently, like a double-headed drum. It was the first time he'd addressed me since tea on the day we arrived. I hesitated. "Oz had never been."

"See anyone you knew?" As he fit the pieces of the shotgun together, the weapon was angled my way.

Even if I'd known what to say, I was all out of breath. Fear bore down on me. I opened my mouth, although nothing came out but a gag.

"I take that as a yes?" He dropped the ammunition in the gauge. I heard the gun make a clicking sound.

I felt that old pressure behind my eyes. I tasted the fabric between my teeth. In the past, in rare moments when I gave myself permission to think about who'd smothered me, I always imagined it was James. But for the first time, it occurred to me that it might well have been my father holding down the pillow, full force, and James who had persuaded him to stop.

There was a crushing weight in my chest. But I couldn't quit staring at him.

The very next moment, Albina returned to the kitchen and my father went back to wiping down the gun's exterior with an old tea towel, cheerfully whistling "Too Ra Loo Ra" under his breath.

"My father pointed his gun at me," I told Oz later that night in our bedroom. Dad and Albina were still awake, having their nightcap.

"Was it an accident?" Oz said.

"It felt threatening."

"Was it loaded?"

My voice shook. "He loaded it during."

"Did you ask him about the money?"

"No. I had a shotgun aimed at my face. I wasn't exactly in the ideal position to negotiate."

"Don't blame the gun. All week, you've been afraid to ask. Which is why I offered to do it from the start. We have to leave in the morning. So, from here on out, this is my grift. I'm going to go downstairs and ask him tonight. Unless you can name one good reason why I shouldn't."

Out of the corner of my eye, I saw a mouse run along the filthy wall skirting.

And I tried to put words to it: the unspeakable things in my head, the sugar rows, and the thwack, all the images that had come rushing back with the Bentley logo, the tiles and the palms on my old wallpaper. But of all the disadvantages Dad had given me, the worst was this misclassification—the idea that my reality was little more than "playacting" and pretending as though nothing was wrong was "the truth." I still wasn't positive. Plus, I lacked proof. If I told Oz, I felt certain I'd be called a liar.

"You're right," I managed to say. "I'm afraid of him. I can't ask."

"You don't have to," Oz said. "Just leave it to me."

That night, I lay awake alone in the enormous dark, listening to the sounds of what was either a tawny owl or the far-off hoot of pissed-up laughter. Oz was downstairs, talking to Dad about money, under the pretense of "one last cigarette" before bed.

The next moment, the lamp was on. Oz, smelling of whiskey and tobacco, was beside the soft, lumpy mattress, stripping off his trousers.

Half awake, I rubbed my face.

The wind let out a darkening roar.

"What time is it?" I asked.

Oz fiddled with his stolen wristwatch. "A little after four."

"Four in the *morning*?"

"Don't be mad." He bent and groped for the bed. He held the mattress down before sitting as if he expected it to slide out from under him.

"Mad about what? Fuck. Oz? You've told him more about Ireland, haven't you?"

Still in his coat, he lay on his side and crossed his arms, hugging himself.

"Oz? Wake up."

He groped around in his pocket, and continued digging around even after a messy wad of twenty-pound notes fell out. He propped himself up and tried to gather them into a pile, but his elbow slipped. He laid back against the pillow, reached for the nearest bill, and smoothed it out on his chest.

"He gave you the loan? I don't believe it."

I sat in the dim, counting the bills. "Are you asleep? There's over five thousand pounds here."

He spoke with closed eyes. "He said you should go to acting school all right. Pretending you'd been in Nepal. Just like when you were a child. The naughty girl you'd been. A right little liar." The words were so hateful, but he smiled softly. He was doing the perpetual nodding thing he always did when he was utterly trollied.

"He said that?" A wave of injustice hit me. Tears welled up in my eyes.

"He's a dreadful drunk, your dad."

"And you're a teetotaler. So why did he give you this if he feels that way? What did you have to promise for it?" Suddenly, it seemed like hush money—an encoded agreement. Maybe Dad had paid Oz off to keep me silent.

"I gave him the Aussie treatment," Oz said. "Sleepy-pells in his Bell's."

"Pills?" It took me a moment. Then I shook him roughly. "Lorazepam? Oz? Where did you take this from? His office? What if he realizes it's missing before we leave?"

He gave me another slurry smile. "He won't. . . ."

"He might—"

"He's dead."

"Don't joke."

"I drowned him . . . In the river . . ."

Emotion pulled on me from all sides. Disbelief. Panic. Anger. Elation. Even a glint of disappointment because he hadn't yet answered to or atoned for his crimes.

I was worried also about incriminating marks Oz might have left. Fingerprints on the back of Dad's neck. Traces of skin under Dad's nails.

"Where in the river?" I was panicked at the thought of two men's footprints in the mud. Signs of struggle.

But it was undiscussable. This time I couldn't wake him.

While he snored, I rummaged through our things for the prescription bottle with my name on it. The coroner would do a toxicology test. Albina would wonder where the lorazepam had come from. When we woke up in the morning, there might be police at the door. They'd question us. The missing cash would look suspicious.

I picked up the lorazepam bottle. It had my name on it, and Oz's fingerprints. My hand was shaking. My first instinct was to hide it in our suitcases, but then, what if police searched our possessions in the morning?

I stumbled down the corridor to the loo. It was a ghastly place. All the toilets at Clacherdon had audible drafts and smelled of damp. I tugged the pull string over the sink and held the bottle label under the running tap, scraping off my wet name with my fingernail. When it was all gone, I emptied the contents down the plugless drain. The pills skittered like pocket change against the porcelain. Then I tiptoed back to our room and stashed the bottle in the depths of my rucksack, resolving to chuck it someplace random on our way out of town.

CHAPTER TWENTY-NINE

I took down the website for my fake boarding school immediately, while Victor was still looking at it, along with my LinkedIn profile. I also began outlining a resignation letter.

At the ungodly hour of three a.m., my email sounded with an incoming message.

Dear Grace,

How's my wife, the urban goddess?

I've been waiting to hear if my stellar recommendation got you that teaching job. You, gainfully employed. Now, that's something I'd like to see. I wonder, when do you find the time to think? I've never understood why people value work over contemplation. Why does everyone feel compelled to be so fucking useful?

But I'm not being completely honest. The Boulevard site tells me you indeed got the job, so I'm wondering where my monthly cut is. Our usual percentage of your paycheck. Wired to my account by the fifteenth of every month.

I know I can count on you to hold up your side of our bargain. Our word's our law, isn't it? And you wouldn't want me to turn up at your posh school with my true stories. Imagine.

For richer or poorer,
Oz

It felt like a sign. One more reason to cut my losses and run before I had to explain to Francis why my absurd paycheck was getting even smaller.

How stupid I'd been, involving Oz in my interview process. There I was, trying to build an honest life and make all manner of clean breaks, yet I had leveraged my new life on my old one. I'd got myself indebted to Oz, again, and let him know exactly where to find me.

If Seema's people skills were half as good as her coding knowledge, I would have asked her to play my reference instead. But for all her other redeeming qualities, Seema wasn't charming. Her live-in girlfriend, Gwen, was; but with her fauxhawk and neck tattoo, it would have been a struggle to make her pass as the headmistress of a conservative boarding school.

For the first time in ages, I felt nostalgic for those Randy years upstate. At least when Oz was in prison, he hadn't expected more than the occasional parcel: cartons of fags, snapshots of Fitz, old-fashioned chewy sweets, books of Descartes and "Freddy" (as he called Nietzsche). I never imagined that he'd come back, demanding a share of everything I had, based solely on our shared history and the fact that his name still sat aside Grace's on a real marriage certificate somewhere.

I wrote back:

Sorry Oz,

Teaching's not as lucrative as I'd hoped. Haven't you seen "Breaking Bad"? I'm quitting first thing Monday. Thanks again for the recommendation, but I'm afraid I can't return the favor.

Grace

The next night in bed, I was spooning Francis as he fine-tuned a PowerPoint lecture about persuasive writing. I had my cheek against his shoulder, near the *Moby-Dick* tattoo he'd got in his early twenties. *He eludes both hunters and philosophers,* Francis said whenever I traced it with my fingertip. He regretted it. He got it in some manner of acceptance, after he'd been rejected from a number of MFA programs and decided that he couldn't put words to the great American novel that he saw so clearly in his head.

"As fun as it's been, I'm not sure the job is working out for me," I confessed. "The children would really benefit from more support at home, don't you think? I mean, I have a better chance of balancing on a tightrope than going between play rehearsals and Fitz's homework. Plus, there's our staff meetings and Cat's extracurriculars."

Francis turned around.

I rambled on. "The kids are getting older. There's more they need to tell me and less they want to. I should be at home more. . . . And speaking of home, the kids need more space. They deserve a *house* with a yard and a basketball hoop. We'll never get that in the city. But if we moved, say, to New Hampshire . . . There's plenty of schools just as prestigious as Boulevard there. St. Paul's and Phillips Exeter—"

"Where's all this coming from?" he said.

I ran through my justifications again.

"I hear you telling me you don't have the time and energy to give the children the attention you want," Francis said. "Well, if that's what it is . . . Is that really all it is?"

He looked like he didn't entirely believe me.

I nodded, a lump in my throat.

"Well, in that case, we can find other solutions, small steps we can take to solve the problem. Why is this coming up now? Has something happened with the kids this week?"

I hesitated, trying to shake away an image of Oz.

"It's just a feeling. Mother's intuition."

He hugged me. "I understand, but I wonder if there aren't better ways to support them without giving up something you love. The kids see how fulfilled you are. It's good for them too. They get to see how rewarding work can be."

I'd lost control of the scene.

There was something more in his eyes. "I worry about you, sometimes. I hope that doesn't sound patronizing. I don't mean it that way. In fact, I admire the free spirit in you."

"That's me. A rolling stone."

"I don't know if that's true. But if it is, then I just want to be a soft place for you to land. You don't roll in one direction, though, Mari. You seem to charge headfirst into things and back off them just as quickly. There's a lot of push-pull in you."

"I know."

"Why is that?"

Nothing judgy in his look. There was no disapproval. His eyes were filled with the warm glow of the bedside lamp. God help me, in that moment, I almost told him all of it: Dad's lies, the dodgy deals with Oz, Melanie being pulled into the current. Fortunately, the next instant, he said: "I love you. You know that. You can be honest with me."

A shadowy panic set in. I remembered, on a visceral level, just how much damage honesty can do.

"I'll stay through the *Modern Tragedies* production. Then I'm quitting come spring break. Maybe we can revisit the idea of moving out of the city then too?"

"Of course. If things don't feel better by then, we'll revisit this. I've got your back."

"You're right," I said. "About my ambivalence. It's a problem. I'm going to work on it."

He rubbed my shoulder, and I felt seen straight through, accepted across every layer.

"Can I ask you a question? What the hell do you see in me, Francis? Honestly. Shouldn't you be off somewhere with an easy wife?"

He laughed. "I don't think anyone wants an 'easy' wife."

"You know what I mean."

"But you see, someone like that wouldn't have your intelligence, would they? Nor the tender heart it disguises."

"They might."

"Doubtful. Besides, I'm an English teacher, remember? I love subtext. I need a challenging read."

The last thing I wanted was Francis searching for hidden meaning, and so I did my best to act harried and burnt out.

It wasn't difficult to fake. I worked my arse off. During the day, I organized my lesson plans. I put Lily of the PAC in charge of sourcing costumes for *Modern Tragedies* and recruited Ainsley Doyle to be my co-director, because having Boulevard's biggest celebrity on my side gave me much-needed legitimacy. Every night, I stayed up late, reading Vic Ashworth's emails and texts until the blood vessels stood out in my eyes. But most consuming of all were the applets, which I kept adding.

Oddly, instead of reassuring me, my preventative measures only raised my anxiety. I kept my phone on me at all times, set to mute.

But even then, I'd be in the middle of a lesson on stop-frame animation (the kids and I were building digital sets for *Modern Tragedies*) when I would receive an email telling me Victor had a new voicemail. I'd instantly lose my train of thought. Plus, I'd get extra exasperated with pupils who asked me to repeat things because they weren't listening. And with the ones who insisted, "I can't!" before they even bloody tried. The moment the bell chimed, I dashed backstage to check my phone.

Bahram Intelligence Agency had been ringing Vic often enough to worry me. But they never left explicit details. The email transcripts only said things like:

Victor, we've begun the background check. Expect two weeks before it's done in full. That said, there's been an interesting development already. Please call the office when you can.

I'd really thought the applets on Victor's phone would make me feel more grounded and prepared, better able to give my full attention to my job and family. But instead, they fed my paranoia. When I wasn't obsessively checking Vic's call logs and search history, I was tossing and turning in bed, trying to guess whether the "development" was a witness—whether someone, if anyone, could have overheard my conversation with Melanie. I felt trapped. There was a pinhole in my lungs and a searing ache in my chest. But the alerts and defenses I'd set only caused me to anxiously go online and set more.

And of course, at the same time, Victor was still texting me. At least once a week. Sometimes more. One day, I looked at my phone and realized he had sent me nearly fifty messages in the time I'd been Gabby's teacher.

The latest one read: *Following me on social media, huh?*

Stressed from the Bahram Intelligence Agency alerts (they'd contacted him three times that day), it was a struggle to think on my feet. I typed and deleted half a dozen texts before replying: *I've been following all my students' parents. It only seems fair, given your IP cameras. You guys get to check up on* ME *all day.*

Vic read my text, but he didn't write back, which left me with the looping thought: *I shouldn't have written that.* What if he forwarded it to Upton? It could look like I was criticizing Boulevard's policies—the same ones I'd pretended to support during the Great Phone-Free Testing Debate.

Less than twenty minutes later, Vic emailed Bahram to say: *I know you're struggling with email recovery, but I'm paying you good money. I want my wife's messages. They're going to leave no question about the person who cheated and killed her.*

He meant the emails I'd sent Melanie about the extension.

I could imagine myself too vividly on the defendant's stand. If the prosecution found my emails, they would milk them. I knew because of the quotes I read in the British papers when Oz was on trial. The prosecution cast him as a kind of monster. They called him a "dupe," "a classic cheapskate," "a frightful shape-shifter." I was surprised they didn't come straight out and call him a boggart.

If Bahram found my correspondence, the DA would use it as character proof. They'd say I was a serial imposter who killed Melanie in cold blood. They wouldn't try me for manslaughter. I'd go down for murder in the first degree.

On second thought, maybe Oz really was a bogeyman. I had barely finished thinking about him when he sent me a message:

Dear Grace,

Sorry to hear your illustrious teaching career isn't working out. Probably for the best. If you ask me, it's a waste of your talents. People like you and me aren't meant to have regular jobs.

But the thing is. You still owe me for the recommendation. For a lot of things, actually. Including that council flat I gave you. The same one you passed on, behind my back, to your cyberdykes. Even if you quit your job, those favors bear returning. And I struggle to believe you, with all your special talents, can't find a way to repay the debts. Especially now that you're mingling with the wealthiest parents in New York.

Now, I've always thought self-interest drives altruism. People say helping others gives them a sense of "contentment" or "satisfaction" and I hear the subtext. They're doing it for the buzz, helping others to help themselves.

So help yourself, Erin.

I'm in New York. Come see me at the Viceroy. We can have a drink at the rooftop bar and I can tell you all about how you can use your clever scripts to help me with this new business venture I've got going.

Or would you rather I pop by your place? Thirty-Fourth Street, right? Between Ninth Avenue and Tenth? I could come to you. Really, it's no trouble at all :)

Your other half,
Oz

The children and I were rehearsing *Modern Tragedies* with Ainsley Doyle the next day when Janet barged into the auditorium, nostrils flaring.

My first thought was that Lily of the PAC had buggered up the costumes. They were scheduled to be messengered the same afternoon. The PAC had donated close to $13,000 to the production, and Lily had the masks specially made from the same designer who did the costumes for the Broadway revival of *Pippin*.

But instead, she took me aside, saying: "Something came up today. With Gio."

I pulled Gio into the stage wings as the Greek chorus was circling clockwise around the stage, rehearsing their *strophe*. (It would be followed by the *antistrophe*, where they circled counterclockwise, and the *epode*, or after-song, during which they finally stood still.)

"What's wrong?" Gio asked. "Is it my tragedy?"

"No, honey. It's not the play. It's about Carter."

"What about him?" He stood cross-armed, defensive, but his eyes were fearful.

"Janet overheard as you were telling him stories about your real father. Boasting that he's the gang leader of an international thief network?"

He took a step backward, and the black fabric of the stage wing enveloped him. "Carter was saying his dad showed him this ATM that gives out gold bars instead of cash."

"OK. And you said what in response?"

"Just that he was lying. And Carter said, 'How would you know? The machine was in Abu Dhabi and you've never been to the Emirates. You've probably never even been on a plane because your parents are only teachers.' So I said that wasn't true. My real dad is *from* the Middle East and he has five million pounds. And Carter said five million pounds is nothing. You can, like, barely buy a Koenigsegg CCXR Trevita for that."

"A Koen . . . what? I don't know what that is."

The face he made communicated how hopeless I was. "It's a car."

I lowered my voice and stepped closer. "At what point did you tell him your father robs and kills people? And more importantly, how did you know that?"

"Who cares? It's the *truth*. And he's *my* dad."

"I care. You need to tell me if you've seen him. Has he contacted you?"

"You weren't even going to tell me that he's here in New York."

"How do you know that?"

"I saw an email on your phone. He called you his wife."

My phone. "You checked my Boulevard email address?"

"Yeah."

"What else did you see there?"

"Nothing."

"Then tell me how you felt about what you saw there."

He glanced away. "Regular."

"Regular is not an emotion, darling. It's a filler word. You can't even order 'coffee regular' anymore. Gio. Please look at me. What else did you see on my phone? How do you know my passcode?"

"I bypassed it. I clicked the timer and held down the power button—"

"You know that trick?"

"Shouldn't you tell Francis that you're married? Did Randy know? Is that why you got divorced?"

"There were a lot of reasons for that. I'd like to tell Francis in my own time. Unless you've told him already."

He shifted his weight. "I haven't said anything." He turned away from me and looked to the stage, where his classmates were reaching the *epode*.

"Listen," I said, "this is a big conversation, and there isn't time to explain it all at this moment. For now, there's just one more thing: Do you know what Oz looks like? Well, *do* you?"

"Yeah. He looks like me. I image searched him."

"OK. Well, if you see him anywhere—at the school gates or on the street near our apartment—I need to know immediately. Understood? Now, go join the Greek chorus. You're a good kid. An honest kid. I love you."

CHAPTER THIRTY

Because they never found my father's body, they never found the lorazepam in in his system. Presumably, the river washed him straight into the North Sea. Dad's watery grave suited him. If he'd been found, the unfairness of it all might well have killed me. I didn't want him to have a headstone, or a mausoleum, or an epitaph—any of those fond remembrances he had denied my mam.

Plus, it turned out Dad had been in a fair bit of trouble with the horsey set before he died. He had pocketed the donations he'd collected to fix Clacherdon's roof (hence the five grand Oz had found in Dad's billfold). Plus, he'd been passing himself off as a successful bond trader, taking investments from Albina's toff friends and guaranteeing them large returns "any day." Turns out they had begun comparing notes. Some wanted to file fraud reports.

Albina told police she didn't know a thing about any of it and, for the life of me, I couldn't decide if she was lying.

The Aberdeen police finally put Dad's death down to suicide, reckoning he had drowned himself in order to avoid court. Searching Clacherdon, they'd even found a poem that was dark enough to pass as a suicide note: *I'm hung like my father,* Dad had written. *Two feet from the ceiling.*

At the end of it all, Oz and I returned to London with a sickly sort of intimacy. We put the cash Oz stole off my father toward a sublet in Kilburn, although living in an Irish area stirred up bad memories. (I never told Oz it bothered me; I felt rather like he should have known and afforded him the proper resentment.)

We never discussed Dad's murder over a pot of tea or even during daylight hours. It was a subject we only ever broached in bed with the lights out—a secret, shameful foreplay.

Under cover of darkness, I whispered like a snooker commentator: "I'm not sad to see him go, believe me. But I can't understand where your head was. Either of you."

"I was off my face, all right? We must have drunk a whole bottle of whiskey between us."

"Well, you were still in better condition than Dad, given you'd slipped him those pills."

"Look. I can't speak for your father, Grace. But do you know the Chomsky-Foucault debate?"

"No."

"Well, Chomsky thought, philosophically, it's all right to commit a crime in order to stop or bring justice to another crime. And I agree. I vowed to provide for you, Grace. I saw the money in his office and I knew Albina wouldn't miss it. Your dad *told* me she didn't know how much money they had. She's hopeless with finances."

"You should have discussed it with me, before you did something you couldn't go back on."

"Do you think I *like* what I did? I don't. But an opportunity presented itself and I took it. Yes, I should have spoke to you first. But we haven't gone to jail. And the money helped. We're *married* now, Grace. We deserve a better life. Aren't you tired of being skint? Nicking pocket change? Living in shitholes?"

Even in the dark, I felt him bring a hand to his face. He was crying, which reassured me.

"How do you know they won't find his body?"

"I weighed him down with rocks."

"Rocks?"

"A lot of rocks. Listen, Grace. I've warned you, I don't want to talk about this. Especially not now, before bed. I have enough nightmares already. So let's *please* just shut up." He jerked the sheets over his head, made his way down the bed, and kissed me through my knickers until I stopped talking.

In time, we quit our precoital chats and stopped talking about Dad's murder entirely.

But it didn't go away. Oz imagined my silent spells were synonymous with *I'm still bloody angry at you for drugging my old man.* And anytime he got a certain grunty tone of voice, I just knew he was thinking something to the effect of *I killed the father who called you a little liar, so don't bollock me for putting out the bins on the wrong day.*

We didn't hate each other by any stretch. Nor was our marriage without intimacy or affection. We still had wailing, thrashing sex every night and sank into each other's sweaty embrace when it was finished. But neither of us felt entirely in control of ourselves when the other was around. Even though I'd taken a break from conning, I still worried myself sick about what Oz was getting up to. Meanwhile, he got arsey with me anytime I asked about the grifts he was working, saying it was no longer my business.

He had impressed his boss, a man he called the Wayfarer, by suggesting they expand their fake holiday villas to Turkey, where British clients couldn't read the language on the documents.

The model was really quite clever. The marks were seduced by low purchase prices and sobbingly beautiful photos of the Aegean Coast, then paid small monthly "dividends" skimmed off their own investments.

As the business grew, Oz even took a few whales on all-expenses-paid tours. He'd fly them private to the Turkish Riviera; stuff them full of octopus and anise-flavored raki; and then take them aboard catamarans to dance all night long. Then, at the height of the following day's hangover, he'd bring them to the rental properties "their money" had built, and tell them they couldn't tour it, as there were renters inside. Indeed, there *were* people living inside those beautiful buildings on the bay, but neither their names nor Oz's were on the deeds.

I sniffed around as he packed suitcases filled with suncream and swimming trunks, plus the expensive new suits he had tailored in Savile Row.

"Can't I come with you?"

Oz was so secretive about these trips that I'd begun worrying he was cheating on me, shagging women with umlauted names.

He rerolled an inflatable neck pillow. "We've talked about this. Many times."

I was enrolled in Guildhall at that point, onstage with real thespian chaps—most of them skinny as rakes, wearing high-cuffed boots and gelled-back hair—grunting suggestively for vocal warm-ups. To hear my professors tell it, there was a very good chance that my fellow students and I would be on film and television one day. Oz worried that one of our marks might see me, years down the road, in a new ITV series, identify me, and send me to prison.

"So I'll wear a disguise. The program has a wig closet, for God's sake. I don't mean to be a pest, but I really feel I could contribute something interesting and useful—"

Oz had been struggling to sell property to women, which was a massive blow to his ego. He'd had such success seducing backpackers in his single days.

"No," he said sharply. "That wasn't the agreement. You're meant to be in school."

Frowning, I went back to highlighting my speaking lines while Oz fielded a phone call from a client.

"Yes, yes . . . I understand. But I don't think France and Spain are a better investment. . . . No . . . Ms. Wilkinson, you're mistaken. France wants to increase capital-gains tax. I'm leaving for the Turquoise Coast tomorrow, but why don't I take you to lunch at the Ivy before I go. . . . No, I'll have no trouble securing a table. Shall we say one p.m.?"

. . .

The next day, I left uni in flicked eyeliner and the black harem pants I wore to movement class and took a taxi to West Street. Upon arriving, I stepped out into the lightning flashes of paparazzi who were standing across the street of the theater opposite, where *The Mousetrap* was enjoying its fifty-somethingth run. With my large sunglasses on and my hair (back to its natural red) in a chignon, they seemed to mistake me for an A-list celebrity.

On the other side of the diamond-mullioned windows, it was a different story.

"I'm afraid we're fully booked, madam," a maître d'hôtel said.

But I asked to speak with the restaurant manager, the color-blind one Oz had told me he was on first-name terms with. And the next moment, he escorted me past the bow-tied waiters and at least a dozen starry names to a plywood table, where Oz and an older, blond woman were eating gulls' eggs and trompette tart.

I threw off my 1920s black fur traveling coat, borrowed off a Guildhall first year in stage and costume management, and greeted him by his latest fake name.

"My last meeting ran late," I said, smoothing a pale green napkin in my lap. "Victoria is so exacting. I told her I was late to meet you, but she wanted to triple-check the measurements for the chinoiserie paper, which is fair play. I mean, it *is* hand-painted. Plus, the baby nurse kept interrupting us. And *then* David returned from Madrid."

"Victoria *Beckham*?" Oz's mark said. She was wearing lots of shadow on her eyes and an age-inappropriate dress. She looked like a *Tatler* reader and maybe worse. She might well have read *Heat*. I would have bet anything she was divorced.

I ignored her gauche question and introduced myself with a spirit of generosity: "Lovely to meet you. I'm the designer on the Turquoise Coast project." I went on to say Oz had told me quite a lot about her good taste, and I was eager to collaborate on design ideas. "I'd like to ask what you think about incorporating contemporary furniture in amongst the Ottoman ceilings? Disaster?"

She looked at me under thick, false eyelashes. After a few moments of heavy mouth-breathing, she said: "Why, I think that would depend on the pieces themselves."

The *pieces*. She was trying to speak my language. That was good.

Oz listened with a look of resigned disapproval. He couldn't stop me without blowing his cover. So instead, he hailed the waiter and requested a third Champagne glass.

I suggested we set a date to go shopping at Adam together. "I'd love to get your opinion on the pendant lamps I'm considering for the building's reception. Clear glass spheres with a five-armed light head. Are you a fan of decorative filament? It's a little too avant-garde for some."

"Oh yes," she said. "I just love it."

"I knew you'd say that!" I gave Oz's arm a playful squeeze. "In future, will you please bring me more clients like this one?" I turned to the mark, who was decidedly single. "There's so many *bachelors* buying units in this building and they're all useless when it comes to this sort of thing."

I knew I had her. She took out her checkbook before we'd even got to the baked Alaska.

Oz wanted to be angry. But he was too happy about the long string of zeros on the check she wrote out.

For a few weeks after that first meeting, Oz and I got on. We had slow, atmospheric sex in the shower, the kind we used to have in India. But before long, he was back to his dreary monologues about why I ought to stick it out at Guildhall. There were more bitter arguments. Eventually I dropped out altogether, quitting the excruciating task of what my professors called the art of "fooling my own nature."

Oz was livid that I'd unenrolled. But he still employed me off the books, promoting me from "interior designer" to "architect"—a role I played until I got pregnant with Fitz.

Oz and I hadn't been aiming to have a baby. I'd just had a moment of weakness during one of our no-expenses-spared trips to the Aegean. There had been moonlight, a forty-five-foot yacht, and enough rosé to sink it (along with what was left of my common sense).

A month and a half later, I was crying over a test stick with no idea how I could possibly play the role of someone's mother when I scarcely remembered my own. For a few days, I even considered abortion so we wouldn't have to sacrifice our high-risk lifestyle.

Oz wouldn't hear of it. "Work is important," he said. "But family comes first."

I felt a little as though I were incubating the happy childhood he'd never had.

No remedy helped my morning sickness. Not ice lollies nor ginger. And after I nearly chundered into a client's plate of sevruga caviar (we were at the Ivy, with Nicole Kidman at the neighboring table), Oz instructed me to waddle away from business for a while and take my maternity leave early.

I was home with my months-old little boy, and feeling quite newborn myself, the day the first plainclothes police officer knocked on the door of the luxury flat we were renting in Marylebone.

"Mrs. Jabbur?"

In the event of an emergency, Oz had always told me to step outside, close the door, and speak to the officer in the corridor. But Fitz was sleeping on the floor in his ergonomic baby chair and the exhausted new mother in me won out over the hardened criminal. I couldn't bear to wake him, and so I nodded and stayed where I was.

"Is everything all right?" There was an honest wobble in my voice.

They introduced themselves as detectives from the National

Fraud Intelligence Bureau and said they wanted to ask me about the investments my husband had taken to fund his Turkish properties.

I felt myself glazing over in my panic. I tried to remember Oz's emergency action plan. I was meant to ask if they had a search warrant. I was also meant to phone the criminal defender on the business card Oz had put in my wallet—the one who specialized in money laundering and fraudulent trades. But all I could do was stare at the pattern of the one copper's necktie and try to remember how long it had been since I'd removed my architecture site from the web. Would they seize my computer and recover it? And would Fitz be put in foster care if both his parents went to prison? I had no family who could care for him.

Fortunately, Fitz woke with a cry of existential angst. The high-pitched sound brought me around enough to make it clear that I wasn't going to be overly cooperative.

"Officer, I can't let you inside without a search warrant."

One officer put his hand on the doorjamb. "I think it's in your best interest to tell us what you know, Mrs. Jabbur. Your husband owes his investors a lot of money. He's looking at a number of serious allegations."

"I don't know anything about that," I said, scooping up Fitz and clutching him to my chest. "I'm just a mum, and I need to feed my baby. Please leave your card in the letterbox. My husband or his attorney will contact you."

The visit came as no surprise to Oz, who'd spent all afternoon at an emergency off-site meeting with his business partners.

"I'm covered," Oz reassured me as we lay together in bed that night, watching little Fitz sleep between us. "The company lawyers will look out for me, but you never had a formal arrangement with them. And now we've this little chap." We both looked down at Fitz, the only source of peace in the room. "We need to hedge our bets."

"OK. How?"

"I think you and Fitz need to distance yourself from me. Just temporarily. Until the charges are dropped."

The charge was fraud, which didn't seem so bad. In time, I'd find out that Oz was accused of 151 counts of it. During trial, the prosecutor would trot in fifty-nine property investors who had paid Oz's company a total of £5 million. And at least a dozen of them would reference the missing designer/architect that Oz had employed as a "tool" to gain their trust.

"Where will we go?" I asked.

"There's a council flat you can use. It's yours for as long as we need it."

Going back to a council estate felt like returning to every vile block of flats Dad and I had lived in up North. A million childhood memories came flooding back: fleas on wallpaper, a dead cat in the stairwell, a schizophrenic neighbor who had covered every inch of his walls with poetry about demons and ghouls.

I hung my head. "How will that work, exactly?"

"It will be registered in my mate's friend's name. So will the utility bills."

"Who is this mate?"

"Someone from the company." He looked shifty enough to make me wonder whether it was a woman. But then, what kind of mistress makes provisions for her husband's wife?

"And he's trustworthy?"

"Definitely. You won't get caught. The council hardly ever data-matches the tenants. And even if they do, I've been assured the old tenant isn't registered at another address."

"Does that mean she's dead?"

Oz shrugged. "The less we know, the better."

There was a terrible finality to the conversation.

"What's this mean for us?" I said.

"You and me?"

I nodded, stroking Fitz's downy head.

"Well, we might be apart some time. I know that. And you're going to need money. I want you to know you have my full permission to do whatever you need in order to live comfortably." The sad look on his face said he meant "whomever."

"You're encouraging me to *cheat* on you? Because that sounds like the kind of thing someone says when they're already getting their jollies elsewhere."

"You're asking me if I'm seeing other women?"

I nodded and crossed my arms across my chest.

He stroked our sleeping son's curled fist and gave me a heavy look. "Yes." He looked away, like a bastard. "There's someone else. We've grown close."

I might have hit him if our infant son weren't between us. "Who is she?"

"Does it matter? I'm going to jail anyway. I won't be seeing anyone for a very long time—"

"You don't know that. I'm your *wife*. And I deserve real answers. Not just you giving me permission to shag whomever to assuage your own guilt."

"Come on, Grace. It's not like that. I'm thinking practically. You're going to be a single mum, and people are *looking* for you. You need to keep a low profile. Instead of running around Internet cafés, looking for marks, you'd do better to find just *one*—a man who can support you financially."

"So you're whoring me out? I'd rather to go to prison. I'm guilty as well."

His frustrations were growing. "This doesn't have to be a soap opera or some Jacobean drama. It's just wise planning. I could be in prison nine years if the trial goes tits-up."

"So why don't you run too? We could go, all three of us, together."

Oz scratched his cheek.

My jaw dropped. "It's this other woman, isn't it? You won't leave *her*."

"It's not that."

"Bullshit!"

"If I leave, they'll go after my partners. And it was my idea, bringing the business to Turkey."

"Do you mean they're making you take the fall? For all of it?"

"It's my decision. I owe it to them."

"What about what you owe *me?* Last I checked, I was your partner. Me, your *wife*."

"They've done a lot for me."

"And I haven't?"

"They're dangerous."

It was becoming a strain to keep my voice down. "So am I. So are you."

Becoming a mum had given me a taste of the family life I'd been missing ever since I lost my own mother. I was not ready to live in hell permanently. I had not signed on to be an orphaned single mum.

Oz gave a sad smile. "Fair play. But they're capable of worse than the two of us combined."

I was defiant. "So, if you run away with us—change your name, move countries—they'll find and *kill* us?"

"Might do. Come on, Grace. Do you think I *want* to send you two away? I'm doing it for you. Everything I do . . . everything I've *done* is for you."

CHAPTER THIRTY-ONE

The fifth graders left, the lunch bell chimed, and it occurred to me that I might just have time to see Oz at the Viceroy if I left that instant and made it back to Boulevard by the end of my planning period. Enough was enough. All those years ago, Oz had told me outright to go find myself an older gentleman who would lavish me with money and gifts. If I had done, would he have left me alone? Or would he be back the same way he was now that I had a real job?

I looked at my phone to check the time and noticed I'd missed a call. It was from one of my applets. Vic's location had set off a notification. He was in the building. What's more, he'd arrived forty minutes ago and had yet to leave. *What's he doing?* I wondered. *Meeting with Upton? About what?*

Forgetting Oz for a moment, I ran backstage to the director's desk, where my laptop was waiting, and scrolled through the whole lot: Vic's emails, incoming messages, outgoing calls.

He'd phoned Bahram Intelligence Agency twice that morning. And one of the detectives had sent him an email:

Hi Vic,

I know you had some questions about the polygraph and its limitations in a court of law. Please see the attached file, The Truth About

Polygraphs. It's barred from most state and federal courts, but it gets its value as an interview aid. I think we can expect it to shine a light on some of the cracks in this case.

Read it over, and call me at the office to discuss. After that, we'll get this interrogation under way.

I stared at the screen in a state of shock. What if Vic had brought an investigator to school? What if they were meeting with Upton, reviewing my fingerprints and CV?

I reread the email, my eyes darting between the stage door and my computer screen. I was trying to decide if I ought to trigger one of my in-case-of-emergency applets. I had set one that would automatically email my pre-written resignation letter to Upton and a Dear John note to Francis anytime I made a social media post with the hashtag #curtsy. The code was a nod to the final line in *As You Like It:* "When I make curtsy, bid me farewell."

It was tempting. I had my hand on the rip cord. I began to type "#cu—" But autocorrect prompted: "#cutting?" "#curtains?" "#Cuba?"

My thumb found the *r* just as I heard the heavy metallic sound of the theater door.

"Marianna?" a voice called.

My phone clattered to the floor, and the sound rode the room's acoustics, reverberating.

"Marianna, are you back there?"

I crept toward a crack of light in the curtain, clutching my phone to my breast. It was only Francis.

"Hi," I said.

He held up a wax paper bag. "I brought you lunch."

We sat like students, shoulder to shoulder, hanging our legs over the side of the stage, unwrapping the posh sandwiches we only ever treated ourselves to when we were one "teacher look" away from running our heads through the laminating machine.

Only this time, I hadn't any appetite. My stomach was still in knots with the knowledge that Victor was in the building, doing

God-knows-what, and Oz was at the Viceroy, scheming up new ways to make me turn a profit. I considered asking Francis to go outside for a walk. But then, what if I ran into Upton in the hallway? What if Oz was stalking me at the school gates?

I threaded my fingers through Francis's, and rubbed a spot of dry-erase marker off his thumb.

"How did your presentation go?" I asked. "The one on heroes' journeys?" Francis had been up late all week, reviewing it with his heavily flagged copy of *Hatchet*.

He ran his fingers through his hair and blew out his lips.

"Oh no. I'm sorry."

He dropped my hand and made a ball of his napkin. "The lecture was fine."

"So?"

"So, Janet came to see me during my planning period. There was an issue with Gio and she didn't want to bother you during rehearsals."

"We spoke. She *did* interrupt rehearsals."

"Good," he said. "I told her to. I didn't feel qualified to speak on the issue."

"Look. I don't see the big deal where the school is concerned. No one can blame Gio for exaggerating or being curious about his real dad. Probably I should have told him more about Oz years ago. But it was all ancient history. Things that happened before Gio was even born. I thought he understood the distinction between a biological dad, someone who helped make him, and a dad-dad, who would teach him to shave and be there when he gets married." I gave a little smile. "Someone like you."

"Yes. I understand not sharing the criminal particulars. But don't you think you should have told me?"

"I told you he was in prison."

"Yes, but you didn't say he'd defrauded people out of millions."

"He didn't work alone. He took the fall for a lot of people." I wasn't being well-spoken. It felt impossible to defend myself without defending Oz.

"So I read. They just caught one of his co-conspirators."

"What? When?" I don't know how I'd missed news that big. Keeping close tabs on Victor, I'd neglected to Internet stalk Oz. "Who was his partner?"

"Some older woman. She left Dubai for France and got extradited to the UK. 'A crime ring,' the paper called it. You always made it sound like he was selling stolen laptops off the back of a truck."

"A woman, you said?" And just as I was digesting that revelation, the theater door opened.

"Here she is," Upton said.

My blood evaporated. Victor was by his side.

I watched Francis brush the crumbs off his trousers and stand to greet them, then forced myself to follow him up the aisle. As I got closer, a smile of extraordinary confidence spread across Vic's face. It was the sort of shit-eating grin that announced its low intentions.

Francis smoothed the lanyard that half-covered his tie. "I should get back before the bell."

"I'll see you tonight, won't I, at the literacy benefit?" Upton asked.

"You got it," Francis said.

Upton had a table and big plans to use it to woo investors. He usually invited people who were better connected than Francis (he usually invited people like *Vic*), but because literacy was the cause du jour, all the English teachers had received an invite.

As Francis left, Upton turned to me. "You'll be joining us tonight, right?"

"I'm afraid Francis is a solo act. Our babysitter canceled."

Vic made the appropriate noises.

Upton said I'd be missed.

"So to what do I owe the pleasure of your visit?"

"We just had a rather long meeting about you—" Upton said, removing his buzzing cell phone from his pocket. He sighed as he read the screen. "Chinese investors. Please excuse me. If I don't take this now, I'll never catch them with the time difference. *Nín hǎo.*" He pushed the theater door open.

The moment Upton was gone, Vic got a naughty glint in his eye.

"Is your passport up to date?" he asked. Big smile.

I dropped his gaze.

"Uh-oh," he said. "Better address that."

"I'm not going anywhere," I said, with something like conviction.

"Uh-uh. Think again. I just recommended you as chaperone for the Singapore trip. No getting around it. Henry's counting on you. That's not a problem, is it?"

I felt myself seizing up. Our fake passports would never hold up at border control.

Still holding my phone, it occurred to me that I could use one of my applets—the antisocial one I used whenever I'd agreed to meet a coworker after work and instantly regretted it.

"When's the trip again?" I asked.

"Second week in May."

"Let me take a peek at my calendar."

I tapped an icon ("Get Yourself Out of an Awkward Situation"), which triggered my phone to ring.

"I'm so sorry, Vic. I've been expecting this call." I spun for the door quick enough to whiplash us both. As I was turning the corner, stabbing the End Call button on my phone, I collided with Upton.

"Marianna. I forgot to mention, your old headmaster phoned today."

Oz.

"Oh? What did he want?"

"He wanted to confirm that you're still working at Boulevard. If I didn't know better, I'd say he was trying to poach you back. I just wanted to make sure you're still enjoying yourself here. I'd hate to keep you from better opportunities."

. . .

Back at the flat that night, I watched Francis polish his dress shoes. He put on his suit jacket and gave me an expectant look. "Well?"

"You look terrific."

He yawned and adjusted his tie. His nails were bitten down to the quick.

"You're mad I'm not coming, aren't you?"

"It's not your fault."

"Just promise you won't fall into the clutches of some reclusive mining heiress."

The intercom buzzed. Upton's town car had arrived.

"Farewell," he said. "God knows when we shall meet again."

"Not funny. Listen, have fun tonight."

He gave me a kiss that made Cat, who was strewn across the couch, watching *Cupcake Wars,* say, "*Eewww.*"

Francis had barely been gone ten minutes when my phone buzzed. It was the babysitter. Her "appointment" (meaning her OKCupid date) had canceled, leaving her free to watch Gio and Cat.

I ran around, slapping on heels and lipstick. I gave the apartment a quick tidy and rounded up the children for a lecture about going to bed on time.

I found Gio in the bedroom, playing computer games.

I climbed the ladder to his bunk bed and rested my chin on the mattress. "Hi love, I'm going out for a bit. But Brittany's coming to babysit."

"OK."

As I was kissing him goodbye, the lights began to dim and flicker.

My organs turned to stone. I could tell I had a bug-eyed look of horror by the way Gio asked: "What?"

"Stay here," I said, my heels stuttering on the ladder. "It's nothing to worry about. Just a brownout. The electricity fluctuating." I was thinking about the applets I'd set. The ones that were meant to flicker the lights anytime Victor was in the building.

I heard a knock at the door.

"Cat?" I called. "Cat, come to your room!"

"Mom? Do you know someone's at the door?"

The knock returned. It was all knuckles. An assertive refrain.

"Don't answer it. Come sit down with your brother."

"Why not?" she asked. "Isn't it Brittany?"

But it wasn't Brittany. It was Victor. The lights wouldn't be flickering otherwise.

"Mom? Why can't we open the door?"

"Mom? Can we turn off the lights?"

I was bone-cold, shivering maniacally in my little black dress. "Stay here," I said. "It must be some strange electrical surge. I'm sure it will stop in a moment."

There was one last round of knocking, followed by a long silence. Not long after, the lights returned to normal.

"Mom?"

"Yes?" I said, still utterly distracted. "What?"

"Why didn't you let Brittany in? Why did we have to hide?"

"It wasn't Brittany."

"How do you know? You didn't even look through the peephole. You always tell *us* to look through the peephole."

I said something confusing and hypocritical. I was telling them, yes, they should use the peephole, when the knocking returned.

Knock, knock, knock.

I looked at the children's lamp and realized it was emitting steady light.

I'm at your place, Brittany texted. *Are you here?*

I ran for the door. "Sorry. I was in the shower."

Brittany looked uncertainly at my dry hair.

"I don't suppose you passed anyone in the hallway?" I said.

Brittany bent down and opened her arms to Cat. "Just some guy."

"In a dark suit?"

"Maybe."

"Maybe, as in yes?"

She tugged down her crop top. "I think so."

"You missed the disco!" Cat told Brittany. "The lights were blinking like crazy."

"Yes. The building's having some electrical problems. There are flashlights under the sink. I doubt you'll need them. Listen, was the man in the suit with anyone?"

I pulled back the curtain. I was picturing Victor waiting for me on the street with Bahram investigators and half of the NYPD. But I didn't see any marked vehicles.

"Are you expecting someone?" Brittany asked with an overly polite tone that told me I'd begun to creep her out.

"Never mind. I'm just being a nosy neighbor. It's nothing."

The Viceroy's bar was chockablock with venture capitalists and wealth managers, with a few shiny young women sprinkled in. The space was so crowded, I could only stand in place, people-watching. Every smiley person there looked as though they were about to shag. That, or like they'd just finished the task. I had underwear sets older than most of them.

A voice came from behind me: "Grace."

I turned and looked for signs of the husband I remembered, but the past ten years had changed him in shocking ways. It wasn't just that things had sagged and moved about. It was more that the exuberance that once flowed throughout all of him—like those times he'd run for a train whilst smoking and carrying two rucksacks—had concentrated in his eyes, giving him an intense gaze that was unsettling.

"Oz."

He kissed both my cheeks. His scent was tobacco, hair product, and something else—a whiff of anise.

"Look at you, with your witchy hair. Just like Varanasi. Remember that night we used that henna? My more excitable parts were black for weeks." He was wearing tightly tailored trousers and speaking too loudly.

"I remember."

"But then, you're pretending to be Italian now, aren't you? Beautiful alias. You know the difference between the Italian flag and the Irish one?" He paused for effect: "Don't worry, no one else does either."

I didn't even pretend to laugh.

"And your accent. American! It's as good as your father's. Better even. He'd be proud."

I murmured something about learning from the best.

"Fancy a cocktail?" he asked. "They put jalapenos in everything here. You'll love it. I find myself wondering if I ordered a martini or gazpacho."

"I'll have a martini." There was a time when I'd have wondered how many sips before I fell into a lorazepam coma or got myself chucked into the East River. But I'd looked up the article Francis had mentioned and, subsequently, quit being afraid.

"So," I said, after we'd sat opposite each other at a small, metallic table. "What's the latest with Albina?"

"Albina?" He leaned back on his black pleather ottoman. "Wow, I haven't thought about that name in years."

I relished the way he squirmed and rubbed the back of his neck in fake shock. "Oh really? She left Dubai for France last month and got extradited to Britain. Didn't you hear?"

"Albina? No! Wasn't she a marchioness? I didn't realize you'd kept in contact with her. Albina, huh. You're taking me back. As I remember, her idea of 'criminal' was lemon in a gin and tonic. What on earth did a posh whippet like her do?"

"Among other things, she played a role in the Turkish scheme. *Your* Turkish scheme."

He made a weak gesture—*What? Mine?*—then dropped the act and skulled what remained of his drink. "Look," he said with a cheeky smile, as if I'd just caught him stealing a barman's cash tips. "It was business. She brought in brilliant clients."

"It's all about the bottom line, then."

"We were protecting you. You got to keep your hands clean."

"Ha!"

He made a good effort to soften his voice. "I wanted to tell you, Erin. But she swore me to secrecy. It was difficult for her after your dad died. She needed cash."

"She needed cash after my dad died," I repeated, slow and deliberate.

"Yes," he said, sipping a glass that was all ice.

Even after so many years, I looked at Oz's room with a hotel housekeeper's eye. From the looks of things, he'd had the Do Not Disturb sign on the door for days. I could barely see the bedside table through the empty crisp packets and bottles of liquor. The carpet was cluttered with financial newspapers. On the bed, a copy of *New York* magazine lay open to an article about "Fifty New York City Start-Ups You Need to Know About."

I looked around for signs of my father.

It finally made sense, the reason why my father had been so keen to have me visit Clacherdon all those years ago. In over their heads with the marks they'd made of Albina's posh friends, they must have needed a third-party witness when they staged my father's death. Otherwise, Albina herself might have been a murder suspect.

Only, when Dad discovered I went to Ireland, he must have known instantly that he'd lost me as an ally. So he'd recruited Oz instead, paying him off with money, promising to cut him in when he and Albina established a new con in London.

"So, let's get to it, shall we?"

He did something suggestive with his mouth, suggesting "old times."

"Your proposal," I clarified. "Tell me what you have in mind."

"Oh, that. Yes, let's. I'm spoken for anyway. Russian girl. Vera. Very good with investors. Not as good as you. But then, it's a different skill set. *Set* being the operative word."

I rolled my eyes.

"At any rate, you always said the Internet was the way to win at business. Your dad thought it lacked intimacy, remember that?"

Now, more than ever, I couldn't stomach Oz talking about my dad. "I have a babysitter waiting."

"You want the fast version?"

"Yes. Please."

"Major web start-ups are coming out of New York City these days. WayUp, A Plus, SeatGeek, Vibe. All the enthusiasm of Palo Alto but with fewer players. There are more early-stage start-ups than you can shake a fist at. We've been investing for this stuff for months, ever since we started diversifying."

My eyes narrowed at the mention of the word "we."

"So, what? You've big plans to fake a start-up and get yourself funded?"

He gave me a flash of his old, know-it-all smile. "One better. We've got it down. Vera—that's my Russian doll—and I go in and present ourselves as venture capitalists. We dress the part. We let the tech babies wow us with their presentations. I say, 'Eh, I don't know.' Vera is all compliments. 'Yes, it's genius.' Et cetera. She loves it and wants to invest a large sum. And we watch them piss themselves, right? So excited. Kids, most of them. Better, they're computer kids. So they've never been within two feet of a real-life woman."

Computer kids. It was like it had never crossed his mind that he was asking me to turn against my own kind. "Then what?"

"Then I get my man to work on the 'legals.' We have a meeting, present them with a fraudulent cashier's check, and open an expensive bubbly while they sign the contracts. They bring the check to the bank, it clears, the funds appear in their account, until weeks later when their bank discovers it's fraudulent."

"But why do you want to own Internet start-ups?"

"I don't. When they realize the scam, I demand money to cancel the contract."

"So it's extortion."

He tutted. "Grace. You always had to give names to things like this. Why?"

But I was in no mood for his what's-in-a-name speech. "Sounds like you've got it sorted. What do you want me for?"

"The challenge has been transparency. Or, at least, publicity. We need many webpages to make the venture capital firm look legitimate. Also, we need a trade blog. It excites the children about the deal, seeing it reported. 'Venture Capital Firm Pumps Two Million Pounds into a Log-Analytics Cloud Company.' "

"Won't that incriminate you as well? Leaving behind a trail of evidence online?"

"Well, the name of the VC firm will change all the time."

I should have guessed as much. "So you want me to be a full-time fake tech journalist. Surely you can pay someone else to do that."

"But remember when I said it might fall on you someday to give *me* a reference? Someone else couldn't give a glowing testimonial in a pinch. Tell the cyberkids just how much my company helped your start-up. You're the only one who brings both sorts of script to the table. I need the actress *and* the computer nerd."

"And what makes you think I have time for all this?"

"You're looking for work anyway, right? Now that you're giving up teaching? You *are* giving up teaching, yes?"

I flinched.

"Your Henry Upton made it sound like there was some doubt. I'd hate to think you were lying to me."

When he first got out of prison, I'd thought serving hard time had changed him. But it wasn't jail that hardened him. It was studying with my dad.

He brought his hand to his waist, flashing his designer belt.

"How long have you been coming to New York, Oz?"

"Four years. No, five?"

Gears were turning in my head. "Four or five years ago, you

were meant to be in Britain serving a prison sentence. I sent you letters."

"Correction. Seema sent me letters. I got an early release. I might have told you, but then, you're hardly the portrait of honesty. You left Britain without telling *me*."

"And what makes you so certain?"

"I have friends, Grace. People in the council estate. You didn't think they'd tell me when your lesbian computer friend moved in?"

"You know full well her name is Seema."

"When I heard that, I had someone at the company call in some favors in immigration. I couldn't believe you didn't bother with new passports. Fitzpatrick was still Fitz. You entered the country as 'Grace.' "

Back when I'd moved to America, I hadn't been able to bear changing Fitz's name. We'd named him Fitzpatrick because it had such a noble Irish lineage and because Oz liked the Fitzpatrick motto *Fortis sub Forte Fatiscet*, which meant "strong will yield to strong."

It was time for strength.

"If I do your scheme—and I'm not agreeing yet, by the way—but if I do, it will be on three conditions. One, you are never to contact any of my employers again."

He just watched me with a look of friendly competition. He knew better than to agree to anything straight out of the gate.

"Two, you're not garnishing my wages. Not now. Not ever. Lastly, you work in close conjunction with me. You proofread every file, and you sign off on every word before each post goes up."

"That's it? Deal."

"There's more. Number three: I do all the work on one of your computers, not mine. And I don't want a stolen laptop either. I want a legit one with a serial number that can be traced to back to you. That's my insurance policy."

"Good on you. You can have this one if you think it's sufficient."

He brought me the midrange Windows laptop that had been sitting on the desk.

"So, do we have a deal?"

"Deal."

He shook my hand with a glimmer of the old chumminess. And for a second, I pitied him. Yes, he'd chosen my father over me, but who could say if he would have made the same decision if I'd found the courage to tell him all that my father had done in my youth.

As we were saying goodbye, my phone buzzed. Victor had emailed Bahram:

I'd like to speak more about your theory that my wife communicated with her killer on a burner phone. Will you take a DNA sample on the same day you do Randy's polygraph?

CHAPTER THIRTY-TWO

I was already up to my neck in it, what with Oz headhunting me and Victor ominously visiting the flat, plus the sinking knowledge that, somewhere in Florida, Randy was a human potato radio, with polygraph wires coming out of his fingers.

But the next day was an even more personalized corner of hell. Because Francis had planned a screen-free weekend.

He was determined for us to have a life outside of our fifty-three-hour workweek, and banning electronic devices on Saturdays ensured we would have at least one day when we weren't responding to parent emails and filling out online grade books.

When he proposed the idea, it sounded lovely. Contemplative, even. I pictured the children playing their favorite card games while Francis rewrote his novel in feverish longhand. I told myself I could pass the time cooking an elaborate brunch and listening to *Weekend Edition* on WNYC.

But twenty minutes in, the smoke detector was bleating. The children were in a wrestling lock over a crazy-eights dispute, and I couldn't Google the rules of the game any more than I could look up "how to fix a broken hollandaise sauce."

After a full hour, I was having heart palpitations and a creeping sense of despair. If I heard another NPR tosser say the word "privilege" in dull monotone, I was going to put the radio in the oven in place of sticky buns.

Breakfast had barely finished before I was in bed, faking a migraine.

"Mom!" Cat called. "*Mo-om!* We're leaving!"

Francis opened the door to the darkened bedroom. "Mari?" he whispered. "Mari, are you all right?" He was a P-shaped silhouette, a basketball under one arm.

I clutched my "throbbing" head, and made a timorous apology. "It's my own fault. I've had too much coffee. I replaced Internet addiction with caffeine."

He came closer. "Don't be sorry. I'm going to take the kids up to the Great Lawn. We'll probably grab lunch uptown too."

"Brunch was a disaster. Hockey pucks. The dough needed longer to rise. I feel terrible—"

He drummed the ball with two fingers. "Don't. Take some aspirin. Rest. I think the way you operate is catching up with you."

"The 'way I operate'?"

"The workload. What did you think I meant?"

We studied each other's faces in the dim.

"I don't know," I said. "It's difficult to think. It feels like my brain's dribbling blood. I really ought to be out there with the kids."

"Constant stress and tension will break anyone down. Listen, don't worry about the kids. We have lots more time to bond as a family. We have the Singapore trip, for instance. Vic's invited us to chaperone. I forgot to tell you last night."

"I know. Vic told me when he and Henry stopped by the theater."

"You sound like you don't want to go."

"No, it's not that. The trip sounds great. I just worry about the expense."

Francis gave me a perplexed look. "But it's all-expenses-paid. Courtesy of Vic."

I sank deeper into my pillow. "I just want to give it some thought. Can we wait until after *Modern Tragedies* to decide?"

"OK. I'll hold the dogs off for a week. Henry will understand.

He knows the play is the priority. So do I. You need your strength for it. So try to rest, OK?"

"I will."

They were barely gone five minutes before I cracked open an eyelid and went for my laptop.

The video chat rang twice, and I began to worry that I'd phoned Seema during scuba-diving club, which was the one hour a week when she and Gwen didn't have their faces pressed to a monitor. But the next moment, my screen filled with her half-frame glasses. There were her rounded shoulders and the asymmetrical bob haircut she'd got the day she moved out of her parents' flat.

"Grace." She smiled. She'd begun doing that more in recent years. It still seemed out of character.

Behind her, the council flat looked better than ever. There was a vintage fairground sign, reading QUALITY PRIZES. I spotted a restaurant-grade juicer on the counter. It was good luck that most of the neighbors lived there illegally as well, otherwise they might have seen Seema's pink-pound home design and reported her for tenancy fraud.

"Is that Grace?" Gwen called. She shouldered her way into the chat screen. "How are you getting on?" She was wearing a studded jean waistcoat and sipping tea from a mug with a crocheted sleeve.

"Do you remember that laptop you wiped clean for me five years ago?"

"Uh-huh," Gwen said. "Why? You want it back?"

"You kept it?"

Gwen folded her arms, depositing her palms inside her armpits. "It seemed like a waste to chuck it away. It was a brand-new machine. We needed a Mac to develop for iOS and OSX."

"You see what I'm dealing with?" Seema said. "Hoarding, that's what it is. I keep threatening to box it all up while she's asleep." But of course she didn't mean it.

"No, it's fine. It's been safer with you than it would have been in some London skip. Listen, I don't suppose you read any of the owner's old emails as you were deleting them?"

Seema twiddled her earring—the one in an upper reach of cartilage. "Maybe a few?"

"Was Randy mentioned anywhere?"

"Not that I remember. I'd have told you if he was."

Then, what did Vic expect to find in Melanie's old emails? Had Bahram decided Randy was in on the extension scam? Had they promised him immunity if he lured me to them?

Gwen sipped her tea and smirked, "Ha! They were plenty randy, remember? Although they made no mention of yours."

Seema reddened.

"Oh, don't pretend like you don't remember. What was it she used to say all the time? 'Close your eyes and dream about it.' For a while, it was something of a catchphrase around here. Terrible to say, but we quite enjoyed reading them."

"Yes. Mel kept it saucy," I said, remembering her cheeky smile as she jaunted off in a wet bikini to video chat with Vic.

Gwen threw an arm over Seema's shoulder. "Well, they *were* saucy until they took a pathetic turn: 'I'm *begging* you. You're the only man I want. Tell me to walk away, and I'll give up everything for you.' I don't have much experience with men. But even I know they run a mile when a bird says she's leaving her husband for them."

"Wait. Mel was having an affair?"

I didn't believe it. Not with the way she was always banging on like she and Victor were the world's perfect couple. They "made time for each other." They'd had that "off-the-hook" wedding.

"No," I said. "No, that isn't possible. Melanie told me everything. If she was cheating on Victor, I would have been the first to know."

Or would I? What was it she'd said?

I can't even look at you now. There's no way we can be friends after this.

What if she hadn't told me because I'd called Vanessa "cheap"? Because I'd played up the way Randy's affair had broken my trust?

Seema leaned forward. "Grace? Are you all right?"

When Seema's family disowned her, her ideas about lawfulness changed. If homophobia was the "moral" way, then she was happy to take the sinful approach from that point on. She lived in my illegal sublet. She designed the Flash and navigation for my fake boarding school sites. She hadn't entertained a single thought about phoning the police when I told her I'd drowned a mark.

"I overreacted . . . the night she died."

They stared at me somberly.

"She said her husband had been phoning solicitors," I said. "I just assumed she was going to take me to court over the extension. Do you think she meant divorce lawyers?"

"Possibly?" Seema said.

Gwen nudged her. "*Probably*, more like. Don't you remember that message where he went on about how she had to live with the choices she'd made?" She edged over to take up more of the screen. "It was bitter stuff. He said he wouldn't leave her with a pot to piss in. If you ask me, he was dead set on taking the daughter as well—"

"Divorce brings out the worst in people," I said. "Why didn't you say anything at the time?"

"We thought you knew," Gwen said. "You play your marks like fiddles."

"If Mel's case is reopened as murder," I said, "he needn't feel sorry for driving her to suicide. That's why he needs her emails."

"Why don't they just get a search warrant for her lover's hard drive?" Seema said. "That would accomplish the same thing."

"Oh my God," I said. "They don't know who he is. That's what Melanie told me, 'I haven't named names.' But why would she keep it secret?"

Both women shook their heads, stumped.

"I imagine she was embarrassed," Gwen said. "She'd told her

side piece that her marriage was well and truly over, and he said outright, 'It's been fun. But I'll never leave my wife.'"

"Bahram said they think she communicated with her killer by burner phone. You don't suppose they think this lover killed her?"

"Maybe."

"They might think Randy was her lover," Seema said suddenly.

"No," Gwen said. "They think *Randy* was shagging Melanie?"

Seema wore the same patient look I remembered from the time she taught me Sting/Array algorithms. "They might do, if they're working backward from the crime. After all, you and Melanie died at the same time. At least, according to the death certificates—"

"Which they know now are fake," Gwen said.

"Plus, they already suspect Randy of insurance fraud. They know he lied about collecting Grace's remains."

"That does look dodgy."

They were now talking exclusively to each other in a way that would have almost passed for romantic—two best friends lost to the world—were it not for the grim subject matter.

"Maybe they think Randy killed you so he could be with Melanie," Seema said, remembering me. "And when she found out, she changed her mind about being with him. Plus, if she was sleeping with her best friend's husband, she might be too ashamed to tell anybody his name."

I reached for the aspirin bottle Francis had left on my bedside table. My head had begun legitimately throbbing. Not only had I killed Melanie, I had buggered up Randy's life as well. He was a pisshead and a cheat, yes. He was terrible with money. But that didn't necessarily mean he deserved a lifelong prison stint for murder.

I stared intently at Seema. "Do you think you could recover Melanie's files?"

Gwen squinted at me, disbelieving. "Seema wiped the whole drive."

"That's true. I did," Seema said. "But it's not like pressing Erase. If I deleted everything, police would notice. So instead, I hid her old files inside new ones. I don't know if I could recover *all* of them. Some, maybe."

"Enough for it to look like no one's tampered with it?"

Gwen still looked agitated. "I can't believe my ears. Gracie, you asked her to scrub that thing so clean even the best analyst could eat off of it. She used *steganography*."

"Yeah, but doesn't the illegal file get hidden within an ordinary file?" As I understood it, it was a lot like the way high-risk mortgages got bundled with AA-rated ones during the bubble.

Seema cleaned her glasses lenses with one tail of her flannel shirt. "Essentially, I still have the steg application, the passcode, and most of the carrier files where I hid the payload—that's your friend's secret files. I'm not making any promises. But it's not difficult."

"And her emails?"

"They ought to be there."

"Could you fake emails from her account? Give them old time stamps?"

"Yeah. What do you have in mind?"

"Just the beginnings of an idea. I need to check the details. If we can manage it, the scheme would help both Randy *and* Vic."

"Will it clear you as well?" Seema asked with a look of concern.

"Yes," I said. "I suppose it might."

Later that screen-free evening, Francis proposed family game night and the children selected bloody Operation, of all things. I couldn't look at the miniature bucket for "Water on the Knee" without thinking of Melanie. Worse, every time the tweezers hit the silver edges of "Cavity Sam," the buzzer's loud, grating noise made me think of the swinging needle on Randy's polygraph.

When did your wife first suspect you were having an affair? Bahram, thinking of Melanie, would ask him.

It was too easy to imagine Randy's blanket denial: *I—I didn't cheat on Grace.*

Buzzzzzzzz.

You and Grace hadn't been getting along for some time, isn't that right? Money problems. Disappointing sex life. Listen, no one blames you for looking for fulfillment elsewhere. But we need to talk about how you got Grace and the kids out of the picture after you decided to make this side relationship a regular thing. We need to talk about the bodies and the insurance payout.

Buzzzzzzzzzzzzzz.

Randy had been drinking so heavily when we left, he might not remember his whereabouts or have an alibi.

"Aha! I've got the spare rib!" Francis said. Then, he looked at his extraction more closely: "Wait. This isn't a spare rib. It's a—it's a potato chip! Who was eating the last time they played this? Was it you, Gio?"

"No!"

Cat was laughing like mad. "Yes, you did!"

"Whoever denied it supplied it!" Francis said, pretending to nip them both with the tweezers. "You two are looking at a malpractice lawsuit right there."

"Sorry, what?" I said.

The children were wriggling around on the floor laughing.

"I was joking about malpractice," Francis said.

How's the lawsuit coming on?

Good. We won. With a despondent look.

"Oh, of course," I said. "Hilarious. Just excuse me one moment."

"You're not checking your email, are you?" Cat asked with a provocative smile.

"Just making a quick visit to the bathroom, if you *must* know. Sheesh, nosy."

The next moment, I was in the loo with the door locked, bent over my smartphone in that illicit way that Randy used to snuffle coke off toilets.

An Internet search for "Education Lawyer + Hudson Valley, NY" retrieved only two hits, and one, Elizabeth Edward, was female. I clicked on the other—a man named Elliot Loeb, who was employed at the firm of Basch, Lefkowitz & Loeb.

Scrolling, I read:

Our firm's attorneys have practiced in all the state and federal court systems . . . They have extensive experience in all aspects of school and municipal governments . . .

Elliot Loeb's lawyer profile revealed the kind of man I always avoided when I was selecting my marks. Voluminous hair. Small, stingy eyes. *I might have warned her . . .* I thought. If only Melanie had confided in me. I might have told her that men like Elliot dream of happy endings, but then they also work out every possible permutation and pitfall. They take their treats where they can, and play it safe.

I switched back to the search engine and asked Google if it was illegal for a lawyer to sleep with his client. My reading told me Elliot could be suspended from law for up to three years for sleeping with Melanie. It was no wonder he had given her a burner phone—the same one she'd returned when he'd said he would never leave his wife.

"Marianna," Francis called.

When I went for the bathroom door, I found him and Cat.

"Sorry to bother you."

"It's an *emergency*," my daughter said, adding something about a group of people outside.

In the entryway, I was confronted with a man in a grease-stained Jets sweatshirt and a couple I wasn't certain I had ever seen before. The woman held a small child in footed pajamas and wore an expression like an actress in a disaster movie. I half expected to see a twister behind her.

"These are our downstairs neighbors," Francis said. "And the plumber. One of our pipes has burst and flooded their living room."

"Oh dear," I said, too British. "Oh no. What a disaster."

Francis continued to interpret as though there were a language barrier: "We'll have to vacate the apartment while they try to find the source of the blockage."

The strangers nodded. Their faces looked accusatory—almost as though we'd deluged their flat on purpose.

"Oh, OK. So we'll go to a hotel?"

"Can we go to Trump SoHo?" Cat asked. "Every time Nora's mom and dad have a fight, she gets to stay at Trump SoHo."

Francis smiled. "I'll see if there's a room at the Holiday Inn on Sixth Avenue."

I looked over at Gio. He was sunk deep in the corner beanbag, gripping his knees and staring into space.

After the neighbors were gone, Francis and I dragged our suitcases out from under the beds, and asked the children to get packing.

But when I went to check their progress, their room looked like a bomb site.

Cat was stretched out on the bottom bunk, painting her fingernails, the suitcase at her feet filled entirely with stuffed animals and Alice bands.

"Cat. Hello? You need to bring more than that. Your school uniform, for example."

"Why?"

"Because we might not be home for a week. They need rain boots downstairs. They're wearing the ceiling around their necks."

She still didn't move.

"Come on, Cat. I need your cooperation. It's the least you can do, given this flood is your doing."

"I didn't explode the pipes."

"No, it was a natural disaster. Explain to me, then, how your dolls get in the drain?"

"I don't know."

While she took a minimalist approach to packing, Gio had gone in the opposite direction, flinging too many books and clothes into a duffel bag, then dumping them out when the zipper failed to close.

"You needn't bring everything, darling. Just a few changes of clothes."

"I can't make it Fitz!" he said, bursting into tears.

"You mean you can't make it *fit*?"

"That's what I said!"

His helpless frustration brought me deeper into my own. I was powerless to prevent him saying the very thing that put us in danger. How do you stop a child from saying their own name? You can't. Not without the ongoing threat of violence.

That's when it returned to me: the image of my father pointing that shotgun at me at Clacherdon. Only, for the first time, it dragged along phantom others as well—memories I *still* wasn't entirely ready to see clearly. I had a blinding flash of Dad in what might have been that Peel hotel, holding the old-fashioned rotary phone in one hand, like he meant to throw it at me. Another visceral sensation of him holding my hand tight enough to make me yelp out in pain.

I was breathless with horror, staring at Gio in a way that only further freaked him out. In retrospect, I wish I'd stepped over the untidy heap on the floor and given him the hug he needed. But at the moment, it didn't even occur to me. I was frozen.

Francis poked his head in. "How's the packing coming?"

I gestured wordlessly, pointing to the shambles on the floor, unable or unwilling to make up an excuse.

"Good for you," he told Gio. "I can tell you're being thorough. I like that. I do the same thing. Why don't I help you with this, while your mom goes and packs up the rest of her things?"

On my way out the door, I heard Francis tell Cat to bring her bathing suit. "The hotel has a pool."

"I don't want to," she said. "I can't swim anyway."

Nearly eight and she'd never had a swimming lesson.

. . .

After check-in, I tried to leave Cat, Gio, and Francis in the hotel gym so I could run the errands I needed to carry off my plan.

Only Gio, still acting out of sorts, was glued to my side.

"Can I come?" he asked.

"Fair warning: it's going to be boring. Wouldn't you rather stay and swim in the pool?"

"I can teach you how to cannonball," Francis said, luring him.

But Gio just shook his head.

"What's that?" Gio asked me at the UPS Store, where I was express shipping the laptop Oz gave me.

"It's a computer."

"Where are you sending it?"

"To a friend—my oldest friend—back in Britain. She's something of a computer whiz, and she's going to reprogram it for me. That's what I used to do for fun when I wasn't much older than you."

"*Really?*"

"Uh-huh. If you're interested in computer science, maybe she can give you some lessons in coding."

He thought about that whilst I filled in the customs form and prayed to Jesus the parcel wouldn't get lost in the post.

"Yeah," he finally said. "OK."

"But Gio?"

"Yeah?"

"Before you learn to code, you should pick a goal. Whether it's websites, games, or phone apps, and study accordingly."

"OK." He paused. "Is it hard?"

"Coding?"

"Yeah. But it's all down to effort. Not talent. In coding, there's no failure. Only learning from one's mistakes. We keep trying. That's all we can do."

As we waited for the light, he threaded his arm through mine, drawing on me for warmth in a way he hadn't done in years.

. . .

Our next stop was Boulevard, because Upton had given me the green light to begin hanging *Modern Tragedies* posters, and because I needed a quiet place, away from Francis, to make the phone call that was the linchpin of my plan.

I told Gio I was going to step outside for a minute. "Would you mind waiting here? Maybe you can help me untangle this box of cabling? Wrap it over and under your arm the way I've showed you, OK?"

He agreed, and the next moment, I was out in the hallway beside a Jiao Xingtao bust made entirely out of Wrigley's gum wrappers, dialing the cell number I found listed on RandallMueller Realty.com. It rang too many times, then went to voicemail. I suspected Randy was screening. Perhaps I had freaked him out with my New York phone number. He might have even thought I was Bahram calling to schedule a repeat polygraph.

I was redialing when I heard someone say: "Marianna."

When I looked up, Vic was striding toward me.

"Victor. Hi. This is a surprise," I said, scrolling through my phone. While I was dialing Randy, I'd missed the text that had been set off by Vic's location—the one alerting me that he was in the building.

"I saw you on the live feed," he said, looking urgent and formal.

"You saw me in the auditorium? Just now? With Gio?"

"Yes, well, I was in the neighborhood. And Henry has been trying out the motion-operated function on the cameras. Whenever someone is in the room, they turn on."

"You came here specifically to see *me*?"

Intellectually, I knew Bahram suspected Randy, not me. But I still wasn't keen to be alone with Vic.

"I went to your apartment the other night. I was worried I pressed too hard about Singapore. You know, obviously, why I want you to go."

I smiled noncommittally.

"I mean"—he stepped toward me, close enough to make my hands and feet numb with fear—"we've been dancing around it for a while."

"Yes," I said, feeling my mind and body separate. I glanced past him to the Wrigley's chewing gum statue, where the pattern of red arrows had begun to leap out.

"But I know you feel it too. I see how shy you are with me. You're not like that with the other parents. And then you followed me online. I know it's wrong, believe me. I've been on the receiving end of this kind of thing. I know what it's going to do to Francis and Camille. It feels like lying to her, feeling all these things for you—"

I turned away from the sculpture just in time to see his face crash into mine. My mouth slung itself open in surprise, giving him the necessary leverage for a full-on kiss. I wriggled away from his hand as it slid across my waist.

"And the way you are with Gabby. The way you favor her. Camille is even colder to my daughter than she is to me." He was still holding me tightly, wall at my back. "Our marriage is beginning to feel like a debt I took on in ignorance. And here I am, paying it off for the rest of my life—"

"You're a good father, Victor. You're really there for your girl." I put a distancing hand on his chest.

"Oh." The moment's awkwardness widened with every inch I put between us. "I just want things to be easier for her. When she lost Melanie—" His eyes were reddening.

"I'm so sorry, Victor. I really am. That must have been terribly lonely for you."

He pulled a handkerchief from his pocket, nodding. "I still miss her, Melanie. I really thought Camille was a second chance. I was going to be more attentive this time around. More forgiving—"

"I'm sorry," I said again, hit by a wave of real remorse. "I wish I could do something to make it better. Something aside from this, that is. I can't do *this*. I'm really trying to build an honest life with Francis."

"I'm so embarrassed," he said, blinking and befuddled. "You have no idea." He said something about what a creep I must think he is. What a stalker.

"I've taken an unhealthy amount of interest in you too. Believe me," I said. "But I'm taking steps to stop."

After Vic left, I blocked my outbound caller ID and redialed.

"Hello. Randolph Mueller." The feverish slur was gone from his voice. There was no infernal racket in the background.

"Randy?"

"Who is this?"

"I—"

"I said, 'Who is this?'!"

"Randy, I know this is difficult—"

"Grace? Fucking Grace?!"

"Yes."

"What do you want?! Where are you?"

I began to say New York, but he cut me off.

"Fuck you. It doesn't even matter. Tell it to the police."

"And what do you expect them to do?" I said, making an effort to sound unemotional. Pragmatic.

"Trace your phone number. Take you to jail for kidnapping."

"Just give me a chance—"

"You faked our children's deaths! That's some evil shit, Grace! It's criminal!"

As I was explaining that it wasn't, actually, because the Internet laws hadn't caught up, he hung up.

But I phoned back a moment later, and was relieved he answered.

"I don't see this conversation going anywhere, Grace. Mainly because I don't trust a damn word you say. You never loved me. You don't take accountability. It's not just me either. When we met, you had no family. No friends. It's not natural or healthy—"

"Just shut up, all right? You're in trouble."

"Wow, Grace. Thanks for calling, after five fucking years, with that update."

"I know you've been meeting with investigators."

"So you're stalking me too?"

"Did you have a solicitor with you?"

"Oh no. You don't get to interrogate me. You lost that right when you blew off with my kid—"

"Answer the question."

"No. I don't have an attorney yet. All right?"

The idiot. "Why on earth not?"

"I can't afford the expense right now."

"What happened to the cash from the insurance payout?"

"It went into my business."

"*All* of it?" How much did it cost to start a real estate firm?

"I had to pay off some debts."

"How responsible. Couldn't be bothered to reverse the foreclosure, though."

He made the disgusted sound I remembered. The one he always used to rebuke my inquiries about the cases of wine that arrived by mail or whether he'd driven himself home from the Berkshires drunk.

"Randy, look. I've made a royal mess."

"Yes, Grace. You did."

"I did. I'm putting my hands up. I've fucked up badly. I had no right to leave with the children the way I did. But I'm willing to renegotiate our custody agreement—"

"*Renegotiate?* You make it sound like we drew up papers or something! You just took them! Oh, right, because we *couldn't* get a divorce, could we? Seeing as we were never actually married! Wanna know how I figured that one out?"

"It hardly matters—"

"It matters to *me* when it makes me look like a *liar.* I told the detective, 'No, I wasn't sleeping with that woman. I was married.' And he told me, 'That's a lie, Mr. Mueller! There's no record of your marriage anywhere!' "

"Don't go imagining some moral high ground for yourself, Randy. You didn't sleep with Melanie. But there was Vanessa."

"I'm hanging up now."

"Listen, I have zero interest in rehashing our marriage. I only phoned you because I can get you out of the trouble you're in. And I can give you a relationship with Gio and Cat."

"Who the fuck are Gio and Cat?"

"Kit. I mean Kitty and Fitz."

"You changed their names? God, Grace! What kind of mother are you?"

"I'm a good mother. Most of the time. But for my ID issues."

" 'ID issues.' That's one way to put it."

"Come see me in New York," I said again. "I can help you."

"You don't give a shit about me, Gracie. You're the most selfish woman I've ever met. You only want me in New York so I can help *you*."

"Fair play, but if we work together, we both stand to benefit. We can help each other. The way we should have helped each other all those years we were married. Did you tell the investigators you thought I killed Melanie?"

"Did you? Did you kill her, I mean."

"Answer the question."

"I *wish*. I'd love nothing more than to help you go down for murder. But I couldn't."

"Not without admitting you cheated MetLife out of half a million dollars. Didn't you ever think to sell the business and give the money back?"

"I told you . . . it didn't all go into the firm."

"So where *is* it?"

There was a shifty pause.

"Just tell me, Randy. It's not like we're married. What do I care how you spent the money? I only care that you're not tried for murder."

"I owed a dealer, OK?"

"How much?"

Another long silence elapsed.

"Randy? I said, how much did you owe?"

He cleared his throat. "Twenty-five."

"Grand?! Jesus! Twenty-five thousand dollars' worth of coke?! How have you not had a heart attack?"

"Oh no you don't. You don't get to judge me. Not you. Besides, it wasn't all mine. I had this thing going after the foreclosure, when money got tight. I'd buy an eight-ball for the weekend, split it up into grams, and sell it on to the junior agents at a markup."

"Very enterprising."

"It helped pay the bills. For a time."

"Meaning what?"

"Look, Grace. It's complicated." He waited for a moment. "I had twenty-five grand I was going to put toward the next month's kilo. But it was opening weekend for college football, and I decided to put it on Florida State."

"You made a bad bet."

"It wasn't bad. I had it on good confidence they'd win. And I thought we could use the money to buy a new condo, all cash. That way we wouldn't have to worry about our credit. Ole Miss pulled it out in the last minutes. It wasn't just me. *No one* saw that coming. Plus, I still had a million-dollar sale in the works."

He went on to tell me how he borrowed a kilo from his dealer on credit, thinking he'd repay him after the seller closed on the house.

"We were doing the final walk-through when the buyer pulled out and the deal fell through."

"You always said, 'Never count your closings before they hatch.'"

"The deal had been smooth sailing. It was an all-cash offer. It was supposed to be a sure thing."

"So you took the insurance payout to clear the debt," I said, keeping my voice calm and devoid of judgment.

"I was thirty grand in the hole. My dealer was charging me a grand a day in interest."

"Have you consulted a lawyer about that at least?"

"Yeah."

"What did he say?"

"He said I should admit nothing and accept that I'm a human being who makes mistakes. That, or I should confess to insurance fraud and serve my time in jail."

"What if there's a third option?"

"I'm not going to take you back, Grace."

"You think I've phoned to *reconcile*? Look, you need proof you didn't kill me, and I'm you're walking, talking acquittal. What's more, I want you to be part of the children's lives."

"Ha! You sure don't act like it."

"You share biology with them. Kit, at least. And you and Gio have history. You deserve a place at the table."

"How do I know you're not setting me up?"

"Jesus, just come to New York, Randy. I'll buy your ticket."

When I turned around, I saw Gio in the theater doorway, large-eyed and clenching his fists.

CHAPTER THIRTY-THREE

"*Why* is Randy coming to New York?" Gio demanded.

I began to explain, but he kept saying the same things in an endless loop, actively enraged, talking to himself every bit as much as he was speaking to me.

"I don't want Randy to come here," he said. "He can't come."

"Can't we just have a short visit and see how it goes? There's a chance he could be one more loving person in your life."

"Mom! No!"

"It's just one afternoon at most. He'd really like to see you."

He sat down on the floor in defiance, crisscross applesauce, exactly the way I instructed the kindergarteners to do. "This is why I wanted Oz to come back!"

"*Oz*?" I reached for his elbow and hauled him up from the floor. "You think Oz is a better man than Francis or Randy? He isn't, love. Believe me. He's a criminal. Lord knows, I don't always do the right thing. But Oz traffics in fear. He bullies people."

Gio turned and walked away from me. His sneakers squealed against the polished concrete. "That's exactly why he *should* be here! To protect us from Randy!"

I jogged behind, dumbstruck, reaching for him. "What? Turn around. Randy never hurt us."

He quickened his pace. "He hurt you!"

I eyed the high ceilings, worried there might be an IP camera within range. "With words, yes. Not physically."

He stopped suddenly, and when he turned there was a pale, drawn look on his face. "You're just lying for him. I *saw* it. I was little. And it was dark. I heard shouting—"

My vision tunneled. All those years, I had been changing our names and histories, ducking and weaving around even the smallest reminders of Woodstock. And all the while, my son had spent the past five years dragging it around like a hopeless bucket of congealed shite—all the fear and shame that I couldn't bring myself to look at.

"Why didn't you ever mention this before now?"

His dark eyes ran over with tears. "I've tried! But you get this look on your face! 'Oh,' you'll say. Like a robot. 'Oh!' Like it's not you. Like someone's invaded your body. So I stopped. I don't talk about him."

I took his hands—his long brown fingers. "Listen, you're right. I didn't always stand up for myself when we were living with Randy. There were times I let him shout at me or call me names. It wasn't right. Especially because I've always tried to teach you to stand up for yourself. But you didn't see what you thought you saw in the water that night."

He rubbed his face. "He tried to drown you. I should have helped. I could have got the raft. Or called the police."

"You've been wanting to talk about this for some time, haven't you? Is that why you've been putting things down the sink? I thought it was Cat."

"No," he said. Then, with less certainty: "I didn't do that because I wanted to talk about it. It's my secret. Just something I have to do to feel better. You wouldn't understand."

I thought for a moment about how I felt when I met a fantastic mark or chanced upon a useful identity. "Your heart beats faster, right?"

He nodded.

"And you feel terrified, but excited too."

He gave a slow blink of his eyes.

"And for a while afterward, you feel numb. In a good way. You feel separate from the things that hurt and scared you."

A tear rolled down his cheek.

"Oh, my sweet boy, come here to me. I know just what you mean. I do."

The week leading up to the play was the happiest of my life. I felt oddly light, entirely myself. During the day, I watched my pupils run their lines in heeled boots and pointed headdresses. And at night, I curled up beside Francis in our vast hotel bed, feeling knackered but useful.

My heart was in my throat every time I watched one of the children I'd coached find their mark. It was a joy to see them living truthfully under the imaginary circumstances of the play.

No, with more feeling. It was bloody near *inspirational*: the way they approached every scene with a plan of action, but also welcomed the unexpected. When the time came for me to negotiate with Randy, Oz, Vic, and the investigators from Bahram, I could only hope I would be as firm but flexible, as adept at sorting out my actions from my reactions. In the end, it occurred to me that's all drama was: chaos. Acting it out, we returned things to their proper places and names. Terror to terror. Joy to joy. As I called cues and coordinated light and sound, there were times when I had to remind myself that this was no homecoming, that I was readying to implode my life.

I was in constant contact with Seema and Gwen by email. In addition to planting evidence on the laptop Oz gave me, Seema was also building early drafts of the tech blog he and my father required. The mock-ups she sent him from my email account were in attachment form, so he would forward them to my dad, along with the incriminating documents that were encrypted inside. While she was busy with that, Gwen rebuilt Melanie's laptop, restoring all my late friend's files (minus the emails from Elliot) and writing new ones that cast Oz as Mel's romantic lead.

I kept my laptop open during my free periods at school, and we hashed out the details in email chat:

Gwen: *How do Oz and Mel meet?*

Marianna: *Fake an email from Tracey Bueller, introducing Oz as a colleague from her architecture firm.*

Gwen: *Is it a cut-and-paste job from there?*

Marianna: *Mostly. Replace any mentions of the lawsuit with chat about the extension.*

Gwen: *She and Elliot talked a lot about her kids. Should I cut those bits out?*

Marianna: *They did?*

As the wavy-line icon showed—"Gwen is typing"—I tried to wrap my mind around the idea of Mel chatting about motherhood in between fielding photos of Elliot's bell end.

Gwen: *Ya. Her daughter was the chat-up line. "How is Gabby holding up?" And "Don't you worry, we're going to get that big, bad school. They can't do that to our girl and get away with it."*

Marianna: *Retch.*

Gwen: *Ya. Total knob.*

Gwen: *Alright. Then what?*

Me: *Oz fills her time and builds her confidence. She feels less lonely and rejected than when Vic first went away. He's a bit of naughty fun until it gets out of hand.*

Gwen: *And she's gutted when Oz won't leave his wife?*

Me: *Girlfriend. Vera.*

Me: *No. Wait. On second thought, rewrite it so Melanie's the one who backs out.*

It wasn't in my power to bring Melanie back, but at the very least I could change the way Vic remembered her. I could use my powers toward the simple, actable goal of telling Vic, by way of these emails, all the things I cheated Melanie out of the chance to say.

Gwen: *I'm out of practice dumping someone.*

Me: *Let's keep it that way, yeah?*

Gwen: *Please. Seema and I aren't breaking up. We just bought a new Samsung monitor together.*

Me: *????*

Gwen: *It cost twelve hundred pounds. It's like we've adopted a baby. Trust. What should Mel tell Oz?*

Me: *Have her say the affair only showed her how much she appreciates her marriage. Mel realizes she wasn't just unfaithful to Vic. She sees she cheated herself as well. She robbed herself of the chance to sit back, in later life, and admire what she and Vic have grown together. Oh, and make certain Mel tells Oz she can't work with him or Tracey anymore. She's going to hire a new architect for the project.*

Gwen: *Will do.*

Me: *How soon can you finish and send both computers to me?*

Gwen: *We'll post them tomorrow by global express. It's apt to cost more than two-round trip tickets to France. But we'll get them to you.*

Me: *Thank you. France is on me. Take Seema, my treat, when this whole thing is over.*

For two working days, I tracked the parcel's slow journey across the Atlantic, praying the private shipping company Gwen used was more reliable than the US Postal Service, which had a special knack for only attempting to deliver packages at the exact moment I left for the post office to collect them.

The laptops weren't just props. They were the entire stage play. I couldn't possibly carry my plan off without them.

Thankfully, the main office texted during my planning period to say I had a package to sign for in the office.

"Looks like someone's been Internet shopping," Henry Upton said, rounding the corner as I juggled the massive brown box.

"Last-minute props," I said sheepishly.

"The play's right around the corner now."

"Yes. Opening night's almost here." I looked at my watch. Randy had just boarded his flight to JFK. "But we're ready."

"I know you are. In fact, I've been meaning to call a meeting with you. Do you have time to step into my office right now?"

I nodded agreeably, pretending I had a choice in the matter.

He called to his assistant. "Constance?"

"Yes, sir?"

"Do I have a few minutes before that interview with the *Wall Street Journal*?"

"The call's scheduled for eleven."

"Excellent. Marianna, shall we? You can leave your package here with Connie."

. . .

Inside his office, he pushed aside the massive stack of press mentions on the desk. There was the newest issue of *Education World*. Beside it, clippings from a number of international newspapers. There were headlines in Russian and Portuguese.

"Sorry," Henry said. "Let me move that. The PR machine is working overtime at the moment. Just between you and me, we're going public soon. There's all this press leading up to the announcement."

"Public?" I didn't have the first idea what he was talking about. "As in, part of the New York City system?"

He laughed, genuinely tickled. "Wouldn't that be something? No, Wall Street public. Publicly traded."

"Wow. I had no idea."

"It will really help revenue. No more tuition hikes, which satisfies the PAC to no end. Anyway, you're not here to talk about that. We're here to talk about your position."

"'Acting music and drama teacher.' Yes."

"It probably comes as no surprise to you that you've become one of our most popular teachers. Ainsley and Darius just scheduled a meeting to discuss a large donation to the Theatre Department, to be used at your full discretion. Hardly a day goes by when Victor Ashworth's not in here singing your praises."

I stifled a flashback of Victor touching me up. "Yes. Mr. Ashworth has been very supportive."

"When I look at your live stream, I see someone who is taking the same small steps she's teaching the students."

I said I was pleased to hear it. "We've learned the building process together. A bigger goal doesn't mean bigger steps, just more of the same steady, manageable ones."

He smoothed the diagonal stripes of his Charvet tie. "So let's extend your contract, shall we? I'd like to take out the 'Acting' and make you our *permanent* music and drama teacher."

"I'm flattered. Quite honestly. My time at Boulevard has been transformative."

He frowned. "That sounds very much like you're turning me down."

"Can I take a week to consider? You might change your mind after *Modern Tragedies*."

"I very much doubt that. I was impressed by your rehearsal the other day."

"Oh dear. There's an old theatre superstition: a bad dress rehearsal foretells a good opening night."

He smiled. "In that case, it was terrible."

"I'm so pleased for the offer. I really am, but I ought to talk it over with Francis."

"I'm prepared to double your salary. So if this is about money . . . If your old headmaster is still sniffing around, offering you more—"

"That's not it. I'll never work for him again."

"Whew. I wasn't looking forward to a bidding war with that guy."

"Awful man."

He gave me a look of surprise.

"I don't mean to sound ungrateful. He's a passionate educator. He truly believes in his approach. But I've come to disagree with his methods. I have it on good authority he'll be retiring soon."

"Yes, he's due for it," Upton added. "He must be, what—pushing eighty?"

"Eighty?" Unable to hide my puzzlement.

"Sorry. Seventy? Premature aging is one of the side effects of our job."

And then it dawned on me: Oz hadn't Skyped Upton. My father had.

I swore it was the last honking lie I'd ever tell Francis: saying I was going with Ainsley Doyle to see *Twelfth Night* on Broadway when I was actually off to see Oz at Tamarind Tribeca.

"Is she sending a car for you?" he asked, watching me step out of the bedroom in low heels and the gown I'd bought specifically for *Modern Tragedies* but was wearing in advance. It was a literal dress rehearsal.

"Oh, no. I'm just meeting her at the theater."

"Aren't you running late? The Internet says the show starts at seven."

"Ainsley wants to go after the house lights are down and there's no one to gawk or ask for autographs. Celebrity, it's terribly inconvenient."

"Right, well, have fun."

"I will," I answered honestly.

"Cheers," Oz said, lifting his glass. We were surrounded by gold columns of light. The smell of lobster masala was in the air.

"Cheers."

"Here's to lucrative new business opportunities. My partner and I were very impressed with the mock-ups you sent through."

"So you didn't have any trouble with the attachments? You both managed to open them?"

I had asked him to meet me at the absolute best Indian restaurant in New York because it was safer than meeting at the Viceroy. At the hotel, with my father in an adjoining room, I might have found myself looking down the barrel of a firearm again. Or with another pillow over my face.

"No technical trouble. As always, you do flawless work."

"Brilliant."

"So let's talk about the next stage."

"Yes," I said. "Let's."

"I want to stage a meeting with the founders of an app we want to acquire. You'll pretend to have your own Internet start-up. Tell them how far our venture capital has taken you—"

I shook my head, then thanked the waiter who was setting down my bhel puri.

"No."

Oz gave a poor impression of a laugh for the server's benefit. The instant we were alone, he gave me the predatory stare he'd acquired in prison. "Saying no is a privilege you can't afford right now. You already agreed to this, Grace."

"I lied." Taking fork and knife to my crispy noodles.

There was some cognitive dissonance on his face. His dark brows were hitched in surprise, but his jaw was hard. He gripped the table's corner. "Your intention counts for shit, love. You hold up your end of the arrangement. You *meet* these people. Otherwise, there are consequences. Serious ones. Worse than me going to your headmaster."

I brought my napkin to the corner of my mouth and gave him a look that was withering and amused.

"I'm not the one you ought to be afraid of, love," he said. "It's my colleagues."

"You mean my *father*?"

I savored his split second of shock. But the next moment, he was playing it exasperated, as though I'd been harping on this betrayal for years.

He rolled his eyes. "So what? What do you want me to say?"

"Other than 'I'm a selfish arse? Ditching you for your last remaining family? Letting you believe you had a hand in killing him and then swearing by a false situation'?"

"It was to your benefit at the start. We needed money. And he and Albina needed help. They were in an impossible situation up in Scotland. And he knew you wouldn't lift a finger. Some kind of daughter you were, always dodging his phone calls. Letting his emails go unanswered."

I didn't have the time or the inclination to undo two decades of indoctrination at the hands of a master manipulator. Besides, part of owning my history meant deciding whom to share it with. And

Oz didn't deserve to hear the truth about my mother. He'd only ever find some way to spin it to his advantage.

"Listen, what's done is done. You were the middleman. And you're good in that role, which is precisely why you're going to play it again now."

"It's very amusing. This new affectation. You playing like you can tell me what to do."

"I'm not acting."

"I make the plans. You execute them. It's always been this way."

"Not this time."

"You—you're the ornamentation. You show up in your pretty frocks and distract everyone with your hair and your laugh. You make your little websites the way other women arrange flowers."

"That's what this is about. My little arrangements."

He narrowed his eyes, deciding how serious I was.

"The laptop you gave me?" I said. "I've already brought it to a private investigative firm by the name of Bahram—"

"You think you're the first person to report us for venture capital fraud? It's not an unlikely scenario in our business. We make contingency plans."

"Oz. Listen, please. This particular laptop, and another, are loaded with evidence that pertains to a murder investigation. A woman named Melanie Ashworth, from Woodstock. She drowned suspiciously five years ago."

He looked almost invigorated. Oz loved an adversary.

"You're framing me for murder? That's very ambitious, Erin. But you're out of luck, I'm afraid. I was in the UK five years ago. Prison, remember?"

"No, you weren't. You got early release. You were here in the States."

"You sound awfully certain about that."

"Yes. I ought to be. It was confirmed by the HM Prison Service. And the visa department at the US embassy. Normally, they don't release that kind of personal information. But I'm your wife.

Remember?" I tossed my "ornamental" hair over one shoulder and laughed.

"Fuck you," he said. "Your father was right about you."

"Well, I learned from the best. As did you."

He stood, trying and failing to hide the fear that was overtaking his face. "I'm leaving."

"I'm afraid not." I signaled to the waiter. "Another round of drinks, please? Relax. Sit down, Oz. Seriously, *sit down*."

"Do you know what the sentence is for murder? I'm not doing that much time."

"Did I *say* that was the plan? No. I said you're playing the middleman."

"And why would I ever agree to that?"

"Because if you don't, I'll ensure you *will* go down for murder. There's more than enough hard evidence to prove it on the laptops I turned over. Your fingerprints are all over the one you gave me, and both that computer and Melanie's are loaded with digital proof that you had an affair with her, followed by an explosive row on the day she died."

He took a bite of aloo tikkiyas with renewed hunger, like a man who worried he might never again see food that didn't come on a plastic tray. "So what do you want?"

"When Bahram investigators come looking for you, and they *will*, I want you to say that you, me, and my father engaged Melanie in the kind of real estate scam we used to run back in London. Only this time, we were working on a sham extension."

He smiled and put down his fork. "You've not thought this through. You've left yourself exposed. In order to frame your dad and me for this one, you'll have to admit you were part of our Turkish scheme. The British government will make you do your time, same as me."

"The period of limitations is six years." I looked at my phone. "You're wasting my time, and I need to be home to the children soon."

"*My* child."

"You say that like you want to see him now. After all this time."

He looked minorly conflicted. Like he was unclear whether he really wanted to see Gio or whether he just wanted to make demands of me as well.

"Do as I say and we can arrange some sort of supervised visitation."

"You mean that?"

"Why not? A boy can never have too many cautionary tales."

"Do I get a cut of the money from the fake extension?"

"No. You get to live a life of relative freedom."

"I won't if I have to serve time in an American prison for fraud."

"Your role as an informant will probably exonerate you."

"*Probably?*"

"The case hinges on your eyewitness testimony."

The curry had brought beads of sweat to his brow. "What did I see?"

"Melanie fired us from the extension when she broke off your affair. My father wasn't happy about that. He wanted the contract. So you went together, to her house at Byrdcliffe Drive, and tried to talk her back into the deal. When it didn't work, my father pushed her into the water from a great height. You wanted to save her, but he wouldn't let you."

Oz shook his head. "You'll need hard evidence to prove it."

"All the mock-ups you sent to my father? They were encrypted with the extension contracts. So the evidence is on Dad's computer as well."

"Like a computer virus?"

"That's the basic idea."

"What about DNA?"

"The crime took place outside. Water and wind washed and blew most of it away. Worse comes to worst, Gio's forensic matter was in the cottage. You're closely related. His DNA will be so close to my father's and yours that it will be difficult to rule out the prospect that you were there."

He shook his head vigorously. "Impossible. Investigators won't be able to find your father. He has so many passports these days. He goes by dozens of names."

"It won't be a problem. Because you're going to bring my dad to them."

"Your father would never set foot in a police station."

"You won't be bringing him to a precinct. You'll bring him to my school play."

"Your *school play*? Ha! Erin, you sound like a little girl when you say it that way. Why would he want to go to that?"

"That's my concern, not yours. Just give him this. He'll come. Believe me."

I brought my handbag to my lap and took out the *Modern Tragedies* flyer I'd printed especially for him. You could even say it was an engraved invitation, featuring a dented white skull against a high-gloss red background. Above it, an avalanche of sugar poured down from a bowl painted with clovers.

"Macabre. All right. I'll give it to him. We'll see if he shares your interest in children's theatre."

"I'm staging a story that he knows well. Make certain you tell him that."

CHAPTER THIRTY-FOUR

I had educated Francis and the children in all the opening-night superstitions. Visitors were meant to enter the dressing room with their right foot. Say "Break a leg" as opposed to "Good luck." Give flowers after the performance, *never* before. Actually, after a play closed, it was the traditional thing for actors to give the director flowers they had stolen from a graveyard—symbolizing the death of the show, laying it to rest.

But then, this play itself was my way of saying goodbye. By the time the house lights came up and the theater emptied, I'd be finished with all of it, not least of all my working relationship with Oz and the daily damage control I'd had to run ever since Gabby enrolled in Boulevard.

One day earlier, I had walked into Bahram with both laptops under my arm and a confession that my "colleagues" and I had defrauded Melanie Ashworth by pretending we could design an extension for her house.

They spoke to me for hours.

"How do you know about this investigation?" they asked.

"You interviewed my ex, Randall Mueller."

"Why didn't you come forward five years ago?"

"Isn't it obvious? I'm an illegal immigrant. Plus, I wasn't keen to get convicted of fraud. And I didn't know for certain that Melanie had been murdered. It was only recently Oz told me what he saw that night."

"How did you come by these laptops?"

"I took them from his temporary office at the Viceroy."

"Why?"

"Because he was extorting me into working for him again. I'm not up for it."

"I don't suppose there's someone else who can confirm this story? The one about you working with this outfit in London?"

"I'll give you a list of our marks. You can contact them yourself. I'd recommend speaking with the Crown Prosecution Service as well."

"You've been teaching at the school Gabby Ashworth attends?"

"Yes. That was another reason to come forward. I really care for the Ashworths, as a family. They deserve closure."

Maybe I should have felt guilty for framing these formative men in my life, but using them to spare Randy felt like a fair trade. And besides, I wasn't accusing them of a crime they hadn't done. My father was a murderer. And Oz played the middleman for twenty years. He was the one who'd schooled me in the Chomsky-Foucault debate.

The investigators gave me overlong stares. Finally, one tapped the laptop and said, "Sit tight while we find someone to take a look at this, and get in touch with Mr. Jabbur."

Backstage, Janet and I adjusted costumes and reassured the children, who were stricken with stage fright.

"It's a wonderful thing, those butterflies in your stomach," I said. "It means you take pride in what you're doing. It means you really care." But I myself was weathering a flurry of second thoughts.

With thirty minutes to curtain, I dashed to the toilet in the teachers' lounge and chundered at the prospect that Oz and my father might never show up. After I'd finished, I ran cold water on my wrists and tried to remember what Francis had said earlier in the week, when I'd cryptically asked if he'd look after Gio and Cat in the event that something ever happened to me.

Of course, he'd told me. *You know, it's such a surreal thing. There are days I feel so proud of them, but then I don't feel I deserve to be. I feel really protective of them, but then I never want to overstep my bounds either. But I really think of your children as mine. What we have here, it's a family.*

I was dabbing a wet hand towel against my neck when I heard the door. I immediately left the bathroom, expecting Randy, who had arrived in the city late last night. But instead, I found Francis.

"Hi," I said, hoarsely. "I was worried you were a mother, here to pressure me into casting her daughter as Dorothy in the spring musical."

Francis kept swallowing as though trying to hold back tears.

"What is it?" I said, bridging the distance between us.

"I know this is probably the worst time to come to you, demanding big answers."

I felt the wind go out of me. Makeup stung my eyes. I was already bleary with mascara and tears. "No. I owe you big answers. There's a lot to account for—"

"I was just really disturbed by what you said yesterday, asking me if I was prepared to look after the kids."

"I'm just trying to prepare for the future. Small, manageable steps. Like you say." I wiped away a tear with the back of my hand. "Before you, I never really planned or thought beyond the near-future. Which is a ridiculous thing for a mother. But I think I was rather stuck in the past."

He looked quite pale. "I don't want a future without you."

"I don't want that either. But there's a chance, a rather likely one, that after tonight—"

"Can we get married?"

I mopped my wet cheeks again, and realized he was down on one knee, with a blue velvet box in his hand.

"I know it's bad luck, giving you this before the show. But"—he stood to face me squarely—"I never expected any of this. I've been on my own for a long time. So long, in fact, that it stopped bothering me. And then—you, Gio, Cat. There's no home like the one I've found in you. I need to know you're not going anywhere."

He was tearing up as well. I kissed him and felt his damp lashes brush my face.

"I love you," I said, feeling a torque in my chest. "There's not one thing you haven't changed. I see everything from an entirely different perspective than I did last year."

"You've buried the lede, right?" he said, squeezing me. "Please tell me there's a 'yes' coming."

"I think you should ask me again, another night. After these tragedies play out."

Delusional, maybe, but all week long, I'd been telling myself there was a chance—a small and only slightly ludicrous chance—that Francis would be able to see I'd been on the sort of hero's journey he teaches in class. That each role I'd adopted played a part in bringing the truth to light.

The bell chimed, signaling the parents to take their seats.

"Ugh, Mari. You're always saved by the bell. This conversation isn't over."

"Good. I really don't want it to be over."

"Randy?" I whispered. I'd found him outside the stage door, chewing gum, his eyes glazed with fear.

He jumped when I touched his arm. "Gracie? Fuck. I didn't recognize you. Shit. I would have walked right past you on the street."

"You look different yourself."

It was true. In sobriety, he was less splotchy in the face. He was also as slender and well-groomed as he'd been back when we first met.

"Is your hotel all right? You got checked in without issue?"

"Yeah, it's fine." He hunched over, hands on his knees, but when I patted his back in reassurance, he shook me off.

"What?"

"I just don't know if I'm being stupid."

"In what way?"

"Oh . . . being here. Trusting you. You said you were going to clear my name. But now I see that investigator who practically held me captive last week—"

"You're scared. I understand. Randy, look at me. This isn't a trick, OK? Everything's going to plan. Listen, we need each other."

"Remind me what you need from *me*? Because from the looks of it, you're doing just fine with your new hair and your private school. Neil Patrick Harris is out there, did you know that? And Tom Brady. Did you see Jay-Z?"

"Yes. And yes. I need you here to confirm my identity to Bahram. And I need you here because you're Cat's dad."

The bell chimed again, and I heard the sound of Henry Upton asking parents to take their seats.

"Just come watch the show from backstage. Come along and trust me. Jesus, Randy. Let's go. Everyone's waiting. You'll be the death of me."

Backstage, I peered through the curtains, scanning the crowd in search of Oz and my dad. There were rows of balding men and women in heavy jewelry and tight, tailored dresses. Ainsley Doyle spotted me and waved. So did Lily of the PAC. But the worst-case scenario looked like the most likely one. I didn't see Oz anywhere.

Gio tapped me. "Mom?"

"Yes, darling. Are you ready for your first scene? Are you nervous?"

"Is that *Randy*?"

He used his mask to point to the director's desk, where Randy was biting a thumbnail and staring existentially at a spot of electric tape on the floor.

"Yes. I'm so sorry. I shouldn't have brought him back here. I wasn't thinking. I'll ask him to wait outside."

"It's OK."

"Are you sure?"

"Uh-huh. As long as I don't have to say hi."

"Of course. You don't have to do anything you don't want to. It's new for all of us, having the whole family together in one place. We'll take it as it comes."

I took one last opportunity to gather the cast together for an opening-night speech.

"I'm so proud of each and every one of you," I said, surveying all their little faces, some in white face paint, others in grotesque masks. "I'm going to remember you always, as the class that made me. You taught me to be in charge of my own learning, to put in effort and create my own success. Nothing ever happens unless you make it happen. Life's a lot like acting that way. Emotion's an important part of it. Memories and feelings, they're unavoidable. They come up. How could they not? But in the end, it all comes down to action."

Gabby pulled off her mask to better see me.

I gave her a smile.

"I don't want you to take yourselves too seriously tonight. I want you to remember acting is just a big, fat trick we play on the audience. You've already done the hard work in rehearsals. You've figured out what your characters want, and now you just need to act in ways that look like you're making it up as you go along. You're feeling nervous right now, but that's OK. Just because you're really scared doesn't mean you're not also really ready."

I told them all to break a leg, and then Henry Upton was upon us.

"Well," he said. "Shall we get this show started?"

I felt a flood of adrenaline I hadn't felt since Guildhall—a feeling like I could lift a car with my bare hands. "Yes. Let's."

I stepped out onto the stage, and took one last look at the crowd before the house lights went down. There was Vic, smiling with anticipation at Camille's side. Ainsley and Darius. There were Francis and Cat flashing me twin thumbs-up. Bahram investigators stood near the exits, glancing with interest at the last stragglers to come in. Everyone was accounted for, with two exceptions. There was no Oz. No Dad.

"The children and I want to begin by telling you more about your role tonight, as our audience," I began.

Behind me, the Boulevard logo dissolved into the first of our video backdrops. It began with one of the Petras, spinning in eerie slow motion on the playground's modern merry-go-round, wearing a lavish robe and a tragedy mask.

"Mom!" she called from the screen. She lifted her mask: "Mom!"

There was a camera on the theater floor and it panned, Academy Awards–style, to Petra's mom, projecting her live onto the same screen the pre-recording of her daughter had just filled. The woman looked comedically put on the spot, clutching her temples and laughing. She gave a self-conscious wave.

Same thing with Gabby, whom I'd shot on the playground swings. "Dad! Dad!"

The real-time Vic hammed it up for the camera, shrugging and shouting, "What's wrong, honey?"

I gave him an appreciative smile.

"As perhaps you've noticed, your participation is a central part of our experience here tonight. You've probably heard the phrase 'breaking the fourth wall' to describe when actors acknowledge the audience. A lot of modern productions don't do that. We call them 'illusion-preserving.' But tonight, here, we are. So we use the term 'illusion-breaking.' So please don't be surprised if the actors speak to you directly. Nothing's wrong. It's all part of the show. Also, as you've probably noticed, our third graders are wearing traditional Greek masks. They have microphones to amplify their voices."

I looked to the stage wing and called forth the line of students in traditional orange robes.

"With that, I'd like to introduce you to our reactionary Greek chorus, who will provide a bridge between you and our actors. They're really the voice of the community, commentating on the action you'll be seeing onstage."

The chorus filed forward quite professionally, in lifelike masks with expressions that ranged from awe to shock.

They descended to orchestra-level. I was about to cue the hired flutists when I noticed two shadows coming down the center aisle. I might have been wrong, but one seemed to have Oz's long limbs and puppetlike gait.

I decided to ad-lib. "Might I ask the Greek chorus to please repeat after me? 'An ill-timed promise makes for a lie.' "

The children hesitated but rolled with the change of script. "*An ill-timed promise makes for a lie!*"

" 'And a well-timed lie can speak the truth.' "

In singsong, the children repeated the line.

"Can I please get some spotlight and camera on our latecomers?"

After a moment's hesitation—we had never rehearsed this—harsh white light beamed down on the center aisle and widened to better ring both men. There he was: white-haired, with pronounced ears and jowls. He was wearing sunglasses indoors as though he had celebrity status or was playing the role of his own bodyguard.

He was just an old man, nothing at all like the monster in my memory, but the sight of him still pierced me with terror. For a moment, *I* felt exposed. Even though he was the one the camera held close up and projected on-screen.

All his life lessons came back to me at once.

It's not just me who left your mam. You did too.

When people find out, they'll be disgusted by you. They'll hate you for it.

But the next moment, another voice—my own—reared up just as strong.

But he *was wrong,* I thought. *It wasn't my crime. It was his.*

Raising the microphone to my lips, I said: "Ladies and gentlemen, I'd like to introduce Ronan Aelish."

Everything that followed unfolded in slow motion. The Bahram investigators rushed toward him: their suit jackets fanning open and their ties swinging like pendulums. The NYPD entered through the emergency exits: young men in safety glasses with gun-shaped hands on their holsters, ready to fire if necessary. The stage provided a good view. I saw the flurry of movement and confusion in panorama. Fabric rippled as the children fled to the wings. Diamonds twinkled as the audience ducked self-protectively or angled for a better view.

Oz put up his hands and moved to the side as police brought my father to the floor.

I watched the kneeling mass of men. The arresting officer barked commands like: "Facedown!" "Stay down!" "Give me your hands!"

There was a raised baton. I heard the small, sharp sounds of closing handcuffs.

"Who is that?" I heard parents say. "Do you recognize him?" "I don't know." "I can't see."

"Is this a gun?" an officer asked, withdrawing a pistol from Dad's waistband holster. The audience screamed. "Is this registered, sir?! Are you familiar with New York City gun laws?"

"You're in a *school*!" a woman in the crowd called out, to a swell of applause.

Dad's Miranda rights were drowned out by the sound of Upton taking the microphone and apologizing for the disruption. "Please! Keep your seats! Please, parents, give me your attention! The children are secure in the school cafeteria. After this—Yes, ma'am. Yes, the school counselor is with the students as we speak. In light of this unexpected disruption, we're going to take an early intermission, fifteen minutes, then return to the performance they've worked so hard for."

There was a standing ovation as the officers formed a procession up the aisle. My father's horrible mirrored sunglasses were kicked aside in the wake of large black boots.

And through it all, I held my chin high. I didn't move from my mark. I anchored myself to the black X of electrical tape under my shoes. I thought maybe, just maybe, if I stayed very still, there'd be no end to the places I'd go.

ERIN AELISH

Emerson said, *Do you love me?* means *Do you see the same truth?* Or at least, "Do you *care about* the same truth?"

—C. S. Lewis, *The Four Loves*

EPILOGUE

You may not care where I am, but I'm going to tell you anyway. Because that's what I do now. Leave a trail. Communicate. Let people know where I am, and where I've been, and how to find me in future.

Truthfully, there are days when "future" still feels like a foreign concept. Funny, isn't it? That for all my acting, as in "performing," I'm only just learning how to *act*—that is, "produce long-term effects on my life."

It goes back to childhood, of course. As a girl, I was always trying in subtle ways to alter my circumstances. But we were always in motion, moving from Ireland to the Isle and beyond, and answering to as many names as Northerners have for bread rolls. The cumulative effect was like trying to pop a balloon in midair: impossible. No matter how hard I tried, I couldn't stop us moving. I couldn't make my father a normal human being or thwart his crimes. I grew into a woman who hurt people accidentally—the men I love included—because experience taught me nothing I did could affect them.

Just so you know: I don't bring up childhood to play on your sympathy. Having disclosed all my old trade secrets to you, I don't expect to be able to use them again. And I don't want to. I've no desire to use my traumas the way my father used his bar tricks. They're not a ploy. Or a crutch. Or a way to make myself too pitiable to turn down. I just want to be clear about my history. Because if it's true what they say—if lying is both a failure of understanding and the unwillingness to be understood—I want to eliminate the second possibility.

I want you to understand where I've been so, should you ever decide you want to live with me again, you're not surprised when a flashback pops up like an insulin shock. That's what the past is to me: incurable.

Not that the "poor me" act ever worked on you anyway. Believing the best in me (believing the best in everyone, really), you're apt to poke holes in my theory. You'd say that my children, my marriages, and even my grifts are proof that I've never been entirely stuck in survival mode. I've always shown a certain motivation that's true to where I've come from—an ambition that's very Irish in its way.

Even after all the ways I've betrayed you, I know you'd cling to your "growth mind-set" and tell me the characters I've dreamt up and acted out ("Marianna," "Gracie," "Tracey") are proof that my imaginative powers run deep and I can draw on them to manifest what I want for my life.

I'm trying, Francis. I really am. I have a job. Two, actually.

From nine to five, I work as skip tracer for the Bahram Intelligence Agency, which sponsored my green card. My official title is "web specialist," which is code for "reputation manager." I don't "find" missing people so much as I help them erase the incriminating parts of their digital pasts. I have "reactive" clients who want whitewashing—people like Wall Street bankers who hire Bahram to remove their bonuses and pending litigation from the general public record. And then I have "proactive" clients—pop stars and actresses who want to take hurtful gossip and unflattering photos offline. I spent most of last year expunging photos from Beyoncé's Super Bowl halftime show.

I suppose I can break confidentiality to tell you that Ainsley Doyle is a client. I strike paparazzi photos of her daughter from the Internet free of charge. If it weren't for her and Darius, I might have had to make do with my public defender when I had to answer for faking my teaching credentials. Not only did Ainsley show up on my doorstep with a high-priced criminal defense lawyer, she got half the parents at Boulevard to write affidavits on my behalf. When my day in court came, I had over fifty letters, detailing the ways I fed the children's curiosity. I'd given the children permission to be brave and wild, they said. I'd convinced them they were more than the meaningless, impractical, or trivial image that's ascribed to the jeunesse dorée. I'd had to look up "jeunesse dorée," of course. But my point is: having access to wealth (or at least friends with it), I got off easier. I was better equipped to navigate the criminal justice system, which exonerated Oz but sent my father down for nineteen years.

But wait, it gets worse. In my spare time, I moonlight as an online security consultant for the US government, which cleared Randy and me of our charges (kidnapping, child endangerment, and insurance fraud) in exchange for my showing them precisely how I faked our deaths and helping them close the massive online loophole.

But what could I do? Faced with prison or hypocrisy, I chose the latter.

I'd like to think that I did it for the good of the children. But when I look out my bedroom window onto Central Park every morning, the truth is: I just don't know. I've done a lot of horrid things for "the children's benefit" when, really, I was just trying to protect the child I used to be from the horrors she had already lived through.

I'm safe.

So are the children. They're growing up before my eyes, lighting up Central Park South with their happiness and presence. I regret it, of course, all that time I spent worrying about giving them posh holidays and schools. Turns out all I really needed to do in order to improve their lives was be the man I always wanted to marry.

Their legal names are Fitzpatrick and Katherine Mueller again, but they prefer to be called Gio and Cat. It's messy, I know. And names are only one way my actions have complicated their personal histories.

But at least so far, by some miracle, they haven't inherited my imposter syndrome. For them, sugar is sugar, not a metaphor for history repeating. They don't appear to have lost any more hope, sense of control, or self-value than any other children of divorce. Cat's lies have subsided. Gio no longer fills Manhattan's sewers with dismembered toys. After we left your flat, they were teary and irritable. And during the trial, our life was riddled with sleep troubles and separation anxiety; at a certain point, I just gave up and let them sleep with me in bed.

The shine of having an honest identity still hasn't worn off. It's still astonishing to me that I can walk into a medical office, fill in my Social Security number, and receive help.

It's a large part of the reason I work—so I'll have health insurance. But my jobs have also given me a real visa and helped keep me out of jail.

As for the money? I'm ashamed to say I don't need it. I bought a three-bedroom condominium in the Plaza when the Bitcoin hit $600, meaning the ฿30,000 I have left over from 2009 (I'd nearly forgotten about them, these pennies in my digital couch), are now worth roughly $20 million. I also put some cash toward a condo in Miami Beach, where I take the children to visit Randy on school holidays.

They've suffered intangible losses, and my main focus, for the moment, is giving them balance, peace, calm, and security. Once we're all on steadier ground, I'm going to give up work and go back to university. I've realized school is my home, the truest one I had after I left Ireland. And I'm so homesick it hurts. I need to live and work in a place where there's intellect to balance out my natural emotion. A place where the learning's never finished and there are no absurd questions.

I understand that you're on the defense. I lied to you. I lied when I "ran into you" that day at the museum. I put up false fronts about who I was. I claimed rightful ownership of things I didn't earn: the job, and your heart, included. How could I have known I would find so much truth here?

It was very generous, that thing you said in your penultimate letter last year about how it's "impossible to impersonate a teacher" because if you've taught someone something, you're a teacher, period. Boulevard's stock may have collapsed in the most dramatic way possible, but there's no market cap on the way you teach humanity.

But I also understand your cynicism. I heard every word you said about the sleepless nights you've spent trying to sort out which parts, if any, of our relationship were real—worrying about this or that confession, looking for hidden motives behind every promise or kiss. I get that your biggest concern, beyond my lies, was that I had made a liar of you. I was floored by what you said. I had no idea that you'd put an ultimatum to Henry, nor that the two of you conned the board on my behalf, knowing full well that my qualifications were thin.

I don't know which part of your letter was harder to bear. The way you let me down so gently or the way you closed the door so firmly behind you.

I've thought of a number of schemes to get you back. I e-stalked you to Beijing's Dulwich College, and even though I didn't act on it, I allowed myself a day or two's scheming about how I might get a job there. By the time I worked up the nerve to phone you—not as a "headhunter," or a "parent," or a "colleague from a sister school," just as myself—the head office told me you'd left to pursue a career outside of education.

I saw the single, untagged photo you posted of your houseboat on a nameless river or lake (#amwriting) and wondered if it was Lake Austen or Tomahawk Island. I'm ashamed to say I even spent a few days scheming: *What if I posed as a publisher and mailed you a six-figure advance? Maybe I could location track you based on your Wi-Fi access point and approach you in person.* So you see, I'm not a changed woman. But I am slowly stripping away my training and mastering the forces that once mastered me.

Absurd question: could you love me? Is that the reason you put so much physical distance between us? To eliminate the possibility of taking me back?

You're a brilliant writer, Francis. And if you wrote a love story, it would be understated and matter-of-fact. There'd be no exes. No murder. No ambiguity. No darkness—or at least, not the sort that clings to you for decades and makes you delude or evade the very people whose inner brightness might combat it.

You remind me of Cleary in that way, always encouraging me to drive for the light, to love more than the sad songs, the tragic ending, the fatal flaw. And I will. I'm learning to make allowances for hopeful endings, especially within the context of this relationship. That is, if you're ever willing to embrace tangential irony and the possibility that love—sometimes the better love, the *truer* love—isn't the most straightforward.

I've put all this on paper for my own benefit, but you've been my muse and my mentor. You're the one who inspired me to be a fuller person—not just a pick 'n' mix of national identities and the worst events in my life. I think often of what you used to tell your students: "We are not what we were, but rather what we long to become."

To be clear: my name is Erin Aelish. I'm an Irish-born only child, gifted with my father's way with words and my mother's easy devotion. At the start, I was affectionate and curious, quick to forgive, and slow to run away from things that were new or unusual or difficult. When my father killed my mother, I watched and I didn't. I left my body. I disconnected from my source of strength, my intuition, my heart, everything. Like someone who has stayed in cold water too long.

My mother's death was the great disruption of my life. Later the fact that I'd blocked it out only seemed like further proof that I was every bit as unfeeling as the man who stole my soul and dragged the rest of me around Britain for years. Knowing fuck-all about the central nervous system, I just assumed forgetting proved I was a stone-cold sociopath, and my patterns of freezing or fleeing got worse. I'd go long periods feeling stuck, working hard to blend in to places I didn't want to be, then plunge headfirst into crime, or work, or perfectionism, or relationships with people who seemed to offer salvation.

One day, I even killed one of those people by failing to rescue her. I deserted her in her hour of need. History taught me to associate a dying woman with my own coming annihilation. I fled my feelings. I ditched my awareness and humanity. I ran a mile from Melanie and what I knew, deep down, was right. And the worst part: it was easy. Instinctual, even.

I'm not blameless. Not even close. And I understand if your values preclude associating with anyone who could do what I've done.

I let Melanie die. Am I a murderer?

Some days, I think so. Others, I think I'm someone who got brainwashed into believing I *am* the roles I tried on in an attempt to survive my early life. I'm not a "seducer," pursuing passing conquests, or an "actor," compressing the lives of hundreds into a single career, or a "hacker," exploiting vulnerabilities in the system. I'm not a "waif" or a "conqueror" or a "political rebel" or, even, an "artist." I'm Erin Aelish, and I love you.

The thing is: I just can't forget you. None of my old defense mechanisms are working. I've tried to lose myself in work. I've tried imagining I have some moral or intellectual high ground in this split. I've catered to the children in the hope that their feelings and desires might drown out the way I miss you. But none of it works. Because you're not a trauma, Francis. You're not a threat to my survival. The reason that I can't outrun you is: you've cut straight through to the heart of my identity.

Now, I don't mean that in a fearful, dependent sense, like I've grafted my sense of self onto yours. I just mean that the people we love become ingrained in our synapses, in the same pathways where memories are created and stored. The connection we had grew out of my travels and experiences, my triumphs and missteps, my wounds, memories, values, and dreams—all these things together—and now that I'm more individualized, my love for you is inextricable. I can't disown it any better than I can deny who I am. I'm Erin Aelish. I believe in human resilience. I value education. I love you.

I'd love to do my lifelong learning by your side. But I don't expect instant reciprocity. (Want it, yes. Expect it, no.) It's only right that I ought to begin at zero with you, slowly rebuilding all the trust, routine, and closeness we had. Both of us would have to agree to begin again like children starting a new school year, feeling excitement about what could be and melancholy for what was. We'd have to begin with the understanding that mistakes go hand in hand with learning and agree to ask each other questions when we struggle.

Even in the best of times, you like to work slowly and methodically, considering things from all angles and reading the fine print. Take your time. My love isn't going anywhere. You're under zero obligation to answer to my struggle, if you ever do. And obviously, you're free to think whatever you like about it. You trust your own intuition and wisdom. And I trust you.

That said, I'm hopeful. At least, some days I am. Sometimes I imagine you're "holding the space" for me, in Woodstock-parlance, even though we're living like strangers. Maybe, as my kindly shrink suggests, you're taking time to heal and remove your own emotional blocks so you can one day come back to me with a clear, trusting heart.

Still, I could swear you love me, Francis. On occasion, when it doesn't hurt too much, I look back on the social media accounts you still use to connect with students and colleagues. And there at least, it seems like you're still working shoulder to shoulder with me, sharing interests and ambitions the same way you used to when we'd talk together over dinner, our elbows on the table and that thoughtful look on your face while you steeple your fingers in front of your lips. You've written: "#teachingtip: Good teaching is one-fifth preparation and four-fifths theatre." And: "#advicetograduates: New technologies make great scene partners; just don't let them upstage you." There are days I could swear I feel your love for me like moisture in the air.

God knows, I've hunted down a lot of wisdom about the "truth" over the years. And honesty? I want to run screaming from most of it.

"Truth hurts," people say.

No it doesn't, not if it helps you say goodbye to outdated ways of thinking. Then it heals.

"The truth will set you free."

Bollocks. Only you can do that.

"A liar is not believed even when he tells the truth."

But doesn't my truth deserve even *more* credence, given how hard and long I worked to suppress it?

There *is* objective truth in this world, I believe that. If we struggle to pin it down, that's only because it keeps expanding and increasing in complexity the longer you study it. It's like a wallpaper pattern that way. Or a research paper topic. Or the universe.

The truth is like that solar system video you and Gio love. The one where graphics begin on Planet Earth, then pull back through the moon's orbit, through the solar system and all the Zodiac constellations, showing the sun's "true" brightness in dim comparison to other stars. And then the truth keeps going, past the extent of all human radio signals and the Milky Way galaxy, 100,000 light-years away, then 100 million light-years away, then 5 billion light-years away, expanding beyond all the galaxies scientists know, out past the blank spots they've yet to map, and the quasars, the farthest objects they can see.

For the moment, you are out there, beyond radio contact. You and everything you hold true are 100 million light-years from me. But our truths revolve around a common truth—I believe that.

And there's even more beyond it—uncharted truths that we can only hope to know one day, if we are committed to learning.

I'm here to say, I see your true brightness.

And I have the faith, courage, and curiosity to go out far past what I know about "you" or "me" or "the world"—to learn, even if it means discovering I'm dead wrong about something I've believed with absolute certainty.

Like I've said, education is the greatest, truest love of my life.

But it's not the only one.

I send this to you hoping it's true what they say: when the student is ready, the teacher arrives. Come back soon. I swear, I'll teach you things too.

ACKNOWLEDGMENTS

I am forever grateful to Amanda Urban, who directed me to the place where sociopathy meets sympathy, inspiring the voice that became Erin Aelish. Likewise, I never would have embarked on this journey without Molly Stern and her persistent encouragements to think bigger and bigger. Alexis Washam, Sarah Bedingfield, and Jillian Buckley were immersed in this story for years, and their clarity and wisdom brought it to far greater depths, as did the passion of Sarah Breivogel and the compassion of everyone at Crown. Kathleen Caproni helped me move on to the next chapter, in every sense. Joan and David Lehmann are love embodied, and they have taught me close to everything that I haven't divined from a classroom or book. Jonathan Eaton taught me teaching, in addition to growth mind-set and radical courage. Josie Freeman helped Erin bring her modern tragedy to a larger stage. David Gates accepted who I am as a writer and encouraged me to do the same. To paraphrase Edith Wharton, there is one friend in the life of each of us who seems like an expansion of one's soul; in Claire McMillan and Yvonne Georgina Puig, I found two.

I could not have written this novel without the additional inspiration, insight, support, and/or friendship of: The American Program Bureau, Heather Artner, Elizabeth Bailey, Devon Banks, Christy Bennett, Stephanie Gould Bensley, Megan Mayhew

Bergman, Sven Birkerts, Kelly Braffet, Angela Braselmann, Dave Burgess, Raven Casey, Bert Darga, Amy Federico, Jordonna Grace, Frances Morgan Greathead, Eamon Hamilton, Sarah C. Harwell, Amy Hempel, Sarah Hendrick, Keith Hughes, Corvette Hunt, everyone at International Creative Management (particularly Molly Atlas and Rebecca Czochor), Tom and Jackie Jackson, Mary Karr, Aisling Keogh, Jeff Klingman, Christie LaFranchi, Amy Lyons, Meghan Maike, Rebecka McDougall, Brooke McEwen, Stuart Nadler, Beth O'Neil, Rena O'Connor, Tess Page, Patricia Pin, Irene Goldman-Price, Keith Robinson, Acadia Wallace Roessner, Gina Lee Ronhovde, the Sachs family (Caroline, Duane, Dylan, and Katherine), Patrick Sheeley, Nina Shengold, my friends at the Stone Ridge Public Library (Barbara, Jude, Tim, and in loving memory of Sandi Zinaman), Lynne Sharon Schwartz, Kyanna Sutton, Milana Tepermayster, Piper Ticknor, Shalini Trehan, Anamyn Turowski, Abbie Wilson, Susan Wissler, and Mark Wunderlich. Additional gratitude goes out to the Bennington College MFA Writing Program, Edith Wharton's historic home The Mount in Lenox, Massachusetts, and Postmark Books in Rosendale, New York. Last, but not least, I'd like to thank my children, who teach me authenticity by example and remain the best family anyone could ask for.

ABOUT THE AUTHOR

KOREN ZAILCKAS is the internationally bestselling author of the memoirs *Smashed* and *Fury* and the novel *Mother, Mother,* as well as a journalist and creative writing instructor. She currently lives in New York's Hudson Valley.